Fall From Grace

Kitty Neale was brought up in Battersea, a child born during World War II. She wrote gritty sagas for many years, drawing on her experiences of growing up in London. Her daughter, Sam, now carries on the Kitty Neale legacy. She lives in Spain.

Fall From Grace

Kitty Neale

First published in Great Britain in 2026 by Orion Fiction,
an imprint of The Orion Publishing Group Ltd.
Carmelite House, 50 Victoria Embankment
London EC4Y 0DZ

The authorised representative in the EEA is Hachette Ireland,
8 Castlecourt Centre, Castleknock Road, Castleknock, Dublin 15, D15 XTP3,
Republic of Ireland (email: info@hbgi.ie)

An Hachette UK Company

1 3 5 7 9 10 8 6 4 2

All the characters in this book are fictitious, and any resemblance
to actual persons, living or dead, is purely coincidental.

A CIP catalogue record for this book is
available from the British Library.

ISBN (Mass Market Paperback) 978 1 3987 1375 8
ISBN (eBook) 978 1 3987 1376 5
ISBN (Audio) 978 1 3987 1377 2

Typeset at The Spartan Press Ltd,
Lymington, Hants

Printed and bound in Great Britain by Clays Ltd,
Elcograf S.p.A.

www.orionbooks.co.uk

For Simon, my wonderful husband.
Thank you for your never-ending support,
your patience and your love.
My quiet hero xxx

1

Clapham
October 1916

'He's dead. Your father has been killed.'

Louisa Best studied her mother's face for any sign of emotion, but the woman's expression remained stony. 'Dead?' Louisa parroted. 'Father has been killed?' she mumbled, shocked.

'Yes, Louisa, that is what this form states. Killed in action. And no doubt, the next form I receive in the post will be to notify me of his burial in French soil. Form B104-82 has left me a widow. A fine way for a wife to learn of her husband's passing.'

Louisa sank onto the sumptuous, green velvet sofa, her mind reeling. *Father … dead …* She supposed it shouldn't have come as such a horrific surprise. After all, thousands of men were being killed in this Great War that had raged for the past two years, the first of its kind worldwide. Yet Louisa had never contemplated the notion that her adored and loving father wouldn't return home. Now, along with countless other families of the fallen, they wouldn't even receive a body to bury. As her shoulders slumped, and tears pricked her eyes, her mother's tart tone snapped her from her melancholy thoughts.

'Louisa! Don't just sit there with your mouth gaping, it's quite unbecoming! And dry your eyes, girl. There's much to do, starting with finding you a respectable husband.'

A knot of grief caught in Louisa's throat. She swallowed hard as her mother's words spun around her head. *A husband … find a husband*. At seventeen years old, Louisa didn't feel ready to be a wife. Anyway, what man would want to marry her? After all, she hadn't been blessed with beauty or grace.

From under her lashes, she discreetly gazed at her mother, who was pacing back and forth in front of the tall sash window. As she paced, her long skirts swished around her ankles. Women's dresses had become shorter of late, exposing the merest glimpse of the calf. But Myrtle Best still wore her skirts almost to the floor.

She turned to face Louisa, who quickly lowered her eyes to look at her hands resting on her lap. She was careful not to fidget; her mother often scolded her for nervously wringing her hands.

Myrtle, her tone cold, eyed Louisa with disdain. 'Unfortunately, you resemble your father, which means your choice of husband will be limited.'

The harsh words stabbed at Louisa. She wished she had the same deep blue eyes and coal-black, thick hair as her mother. Instead, Louisa's eyes were a dull grey and didn't sit straight. For years, she'd been forced to wear an eye patch in a failed attempt to straighten her eyes. Still, her right eye drifted outwards. And her thin, brown hair was impossible to manage, wisps of straggly strands always falling from the pins holding her bun in place. Her mother's delicate features were in stark contrast to her own – a bulbous nose, like her father's, and teeth that seemed too large for her mouth. She had her father's build, too. Thickset, short legs and broad shoulders. Her father had always joked that she would have made a good navvy. Oh, how she missed the dear man.

Feeling a tear slip from her eye, Louisa quickly dashed it away as her mother's stark voice addressed her again.

'Louisa, you are to present yourself impeccably on Sunday afternoon. I shall invite Mr Mullen for afternoon tea. It has been a year since Mrs Mullen passed away. The man must be ready for a new wife now. And he always asks after you.'

Louisa's head shot up, her eyes widening. 'No, Mother, surely not Mr Mullen!' she blurted. 'He's older than Father!'

Myrtle glared angrily at Louisa. 'Do not question my judgement! Mr Mullen is a wealthy, well-respected man and a union between our families will give us the financial security we require.'

Shaking her head, tears flowing, Louisa begged, 'Please, Mother, please don't force me to marry Mr Mullen!'

'You seem to think we have other options available to us, but we don't, Louisa. You're clearly unhappy with my decision, but the blame lies with your father. His gambling debts have left us ruined! We won't have a roof over our heads soon. Is that what you want? Would you see us homeless? Begging?'

Louisa sighed heavily. Their beautiful home and everything inside had been leased, and the lease was due to expire in four months. And then what? 'I could find work,' Louisa suggested. 'With so many men away fighting the Germans, many women have taken their jobs.'

Myrtle looked down her nose. 'Don't be ridiculous,' she scoffed scathingly. 'What work could you possibly do? You're unskilled, Louisa. You do not have the capacity to earn nearly enough to maintain this house. Forget any frivolous ideas. You *will* marry Mr Mullen, and that's an end to it.'

Louisa knew it would be futile to argue with her mother. The woman was quite a force to be reckoned with. On the verge of bawling hysterically, she fled the room, grabbed her hat and cloak, and hurried out through the front door. As the autumn sun was close to setting, and dark clouds gathering, she felt a chill in the damp air. Shivering, she pulled on her cloak, tied it under her chin, and placed her wide-brimmed hat on her head. She looked every bit the respectable young woman, but she knew they were paupers. *Why, Father, why?* she cried inwardly. *Why did you leave us in this awful mess? I can't marry Mr Mullen . . . I won't!*

Yet, no matter how much she protested, in reality Louisa knew her destiny lay with the wealthy, rotund, old man – her mother would make sure of that!

2

Dickie Newman stood on the pavement and looked up at his substantial new house. 'Yep, this will do me very nicely,' he grinned, proud of his latest investment.

'Beg your pardon, sir, where do you want these crates?'

'Can't you read?' Dickie spat to the removal's lad. 'Every crate is clearly labelled. Get a bloody move on. I want that van emptied by sunset.'

The removal's lad tugged his flat cap, dipping his head. 'Yes, sir, sorry, sir.'

Dickie rolled his eyes. He had no time for incompetence and no patience for stupidity. He looked up and down the affluent Clapham street, thinking that his life had changed beyond recognition from the slums of Battersea where he'd grown up. Now, as he was about to turn thirty, he would have happily patted himself on his broad back, proud of his achievements.

As the removal's lad passed him, Dickie announced, 'Hard work. This is what hard work gets you. Take it from me, boy – if you want something, work hard for it. You'll get nothing in life by sitting on your laurels.'

The removal's lad half-smiled awkwardly at Dickie. He looked scared, and Dickie liked that. People's fear of him had earned him his money, and Dickie had earned a great deal of it.

Striding towards the steps that led up to the front door of his grand house, grinning proudly as he admired the *posh* entrance, he was taken by surprise when he felt someone bump into him.

'S-sorry,' a young woman with tearful eyes muttered as she hurried past.

'Oi, what's the rush?' Dickie called after her.

The woman glanced over her shoulder but carried on trotting away.

'Wait, you've dropped this,' Dickie said, bending down to pick up her handkerchief.

When the woman ignored him and carried on her way, Dickie studied the handkerchief before shoving it into his coat pocket. *LB*. The initials on the handkerchief. *LB*. He wondered what the young woman's name was and what had upset her.

'We're, erm, we're all finished here, sir.'

The removal's lad stood clutching his flat cap tensely.

'Right you are. If anything's broken, I'll be docking your pay.'

'Yes, sir, but you'll find everything to your satisfaction.'

'It had better be,' Dickie growled.

Marching up the eight steps, he wandered into his house, admiring the extraordinarily high ceilings and wood-panelled walls. Four rooms downstairs, plus a kitchen and pantry. And four bedrooms upstairs. It was a big house for him to rattle around in alone, but he relished the prestige that owning a house on this street would bring him. And he'd purchased the property for a fraction of what it was worth. *Another good investment*, he praised himself.

Dickie stood at the window and drew in a long breath. Trees lined the elegant avenue. Each house was adorned with heavy drapes at the windows. Yes indeed, this was an *upmarket* area, but Dickie wasn't concerned about feeling out of place. *Money talks*, he thought, and Dickie had plenty to talk for him!

As he went to turn away from the window, he spotted the young woman who'd bumped into him. She was standing on the corner of the street, looking somewhat lost. It was clear from her attire that she came from wealth and Dickie wondered if she was one of his neighbours. Well, he thought, now was as good a time as any to acquaint himself with the residents of Clapham Old Town.

Stepping outside, he swaggered confidently towards the young woman.

'I believe this belongs to you,' he said, proffering the handkerchief she'd dropped.

The woman appeared startled and at a loss for words.

'You dropped it, when you ran into me earlier,' Dickie explained.

'Oh, thank you,' she answered.

Dickie hid a smile as he noticed her wonky eye. He'd known a boy at school whose eyes had been the same, and he remembered how he'd teased him. *One eye has gone for the fish, and the other for the chips*, he'd laughed.

'I'm new to the area. That house over there is mine,' Dickie explained, pointing. 'Do you live on this street?'

The woman nodded.

'Dickie's me name, Dickie Newman.'

'Louisa Best,' the woman replied shyly.

Louisa Best! Dickie couldn't believe his own ears. He knew her father, Herbert Best. The sly bastard had gone off to war, leaving an unpaid loan behind. Dickie had lent the man a sizeable amount of money, but Herbert Best had avoided him thus far and hadn't paid back a penny. He'd agreed to the loan in good faith, believing him to be a man of means. And Dickie had hoped that by lending Herbert the money, he would have had the opportunity to get in with Herbert Best's classy crowd. Granted, Dickie was a reasonably rich man, but he lacked the class he yearned for. He wanted to be accepted by the bankers, politicians and even the aristocracy. Unfortunately, Best had failed to open those doors for Dickie, but at least now, running into the man's daughter, he had the chance to recoup some of his cash.

'Pleased to make your acquaintance, Miss Best. Excuse me for talking bluntly, but you seem a bit out of sorts. Is everything all right?'

Louisa twiddled the handkerchief through her fingers. She was obviously distraught about something.

'Everything is fine, Mr Newman, thank you.'

'If you say so.' Dickie shrugged. ''Ere, I reckon I know your dad,' Dickie continued. 'Herbert Best.'

Lowering her head, Louisa said weakly, 'My father is dead. Killed in action.'

Dickie tried not to snarl with anger. But, he reasoned, it would make no difference to him that Herbert Best was dead. He'd get his money back, one way or another.

Trying to sound sincere, Dickie spoke softly. 'I'm sorry to

hear that, Miss Best. Tell me, is your mother at home? I'd like to offer my condolences.'

'She is, Mr Newman, though I'm not sure that she is receiving visitors.'

'I reckon she'll be very pleased to see me once she knows who I am,' Dickie lied. 'Come on, let's get you home. It's dark now and you know the streetlights are dipped 'cos of this war. You shouldn't be out alone, should you?'

'No, I don't suppose I should. But … but I can't face going home to my mother.'

'Why on earth not?'

'I, erm, I … It doesn't matter.'

'Come on, then,' Dickie urged, offering his arm to Louisa to hold. 'Which house is yours?'

Dickie's mind turned as Louisa showed him the way. When she stopped outside the biggest house on the street, he gawped, and the interest on Herbert Best's unpaid loan instantly tripled.

'Please, come in,' Louisa offered. 'Wait in here,' she instructed, gesturing her hand towards an open door. 'I'll fetch my mother.'

Dickie's eyes wandered around the large room, which was used as a library. Books rested neatly on in-built shelves that stretched from the floor to the high ceiling, and two comfortable looking armchairs sat each side of the empty hearth. The fire wasn't lit, but a large, gilded lamp bathed the room in a warm glow. The magnificent house stunk of opulence, which pleased Dickie. There was no doubt in Dickie's mind that Best's loan would soon be cleared, and with a tidy profit, too.

The door opened and a slim, elegant woman glided in. 'Mr Newman,' she said, her smile not reaching her eyes.

It struck Dickie that the woman was quite a looker, unlike her daughter. Removing his stiff, black hat, and trying to sound earnest, he said, 'Mrs Best. Please accept my deepest condolences.'

'I understand from Louisa that you knew my husband. Is that correct?'

'Yes, Mrs Best, I knew Herbert well.'

'How?'

'Well, that's the thing, see. I gave your late husband a loan,' Dickie explained. 'A big loan an' all, it was.' Then, leaning forward, his face closer to hers, Dickie sneered, 'And I want paying back.'

Mrs Best, looking alarmed, stepped back. Her face had already been pale, but now she looked deathly white. 'That's out of the question,' she replied, her voice shaky. 'What proof do you have that my husband owes you money?'

'Don't you worry about proof, Mrs Best. I've got proof, a written contract signed by the man. I can show you all the proof you need, but what I wanna know is, when and how am I gonna get me money?'

Her back ramrod straight and her hands clasped in front of her, Mrs Best's lips were set in a grim line. 'You won't be seeing any money from my husband's estate. Mr Best left us penniless and in a great deal of debt. I'm afraid, Mr Newman, that you are just another in a long list of debtors.'

'We'll see about that,' Dickie barked. 'I'll have me money, you'll see. What about this house, eh? It's worth more than a few bob.'

'The house is leased, with only four months remaining.'

'The furniture,' Dickie suggested. 'You've got stuff in here that could get good money.'

'None of it belongs to me. The house came furnished. There's nothing, Mr Newman, nothing.'

Dickie couldn't abide to lose money, and he hated feeling ripped-off. Rage ripped through his bulky body as he swept his hand along the mantelpiece. Silver candlestick holders and an ornate clock smashed to the floor as Dickie growled menacingly, 'I want my money, Mrs Best, and so help me God, I'll have it. Whatever it takes, you *will* repay your husband's debt to me.'

3

Myrtle Best bit the inside of her cheek, her body trembling as she lowered herself to sit stiffly on an armchair. She was grateful that Mr Newman had stormed out of the house, slamming doors closed behind him, but she had a feeling she hadn't seen the last of the dreadful man. *Oh, Herbert*, she thought, shaking her head in despair. She wondered what sort of company her husband had been keeping, and if any more unscrupulous debtors would emerge like woodlice from the woodwork.

The door creaked as it opened, and Myrtle watched contemptuously as her daughter walked uncomfortably into the room.

'Do *not* invite strangers into my home again, is that clear, Louisa?' she snapped, trying her utmost to sound composed.

'Yes, sorry, Mother. I thought he was a friend of Father's. Why … why did he leave so angrily?'

'That man claims to have given your father a loan and I've no reason to doubt him. I'm sure once word has spread about your father's death, there will be others looking to be reimbursed. This unexpected situation only reinforces the urgency for you to marry, and I see no other option than Mr Mullen.'

Myrtle did feel a semblance of sympathy for her daughter. She could understand Louisa's obvious repulsion at the idea of being married to a stout, balding man of at least three and a half times her age. Had they had another viable option open to them, then Myrtle would have taken it. But they didn't. The bank account was empty. Even her store credit accounts at Harrods, Selfridges and Fortnum and Mason were up to the limits and payments were overdue. In fact, with the maids and the cook long since gone, what provisions remained in the kitchen would have to last, as there was no money to buy even the basics.

'Mr Mullen will make a good husband, Louisa. He is kind, and generous, and he isn't a gambler!'

'But I don't love him … and … and I don't think I can share his bed.'

Myrtle drew in a long breath through her small, pinched nose and sucked in her cheeks. She didn't have time for this sort of nonsense. 'Your father has left us destitute, which means you do not have the luxury of choosing a husband whom you love. *Love* will not put a roof over our heads. Neither will *love* feed and clothe us. Forget any childish and silly notions you have regarding romance. You must be practical, Louisa, and you *will* marry Mr Mullen.'

Myrtle noticed her daughter gulp, and she could see that Louisa was fighting to hold back tears. The girl had her father's traits – she was too soft and a dreamer. Herbert's gentle temperament had first attracted Myrtle to him, yet she'd soon become infuriated by his unattainable dreams and irritated by his empathy for those less fortunate. Ironically, she herself was one of those less fortunate people now, thanks to Herbert!

Softening her harsh tone, Myrtle forced a smile. 'Sweetest daughter,' she soothed, 'you need not fear sharing Mr Mullen's bed. The man is old, and I believe that the *desire* lessens with age. It is your duty as a wife to tolerate your husband's wants and needs; *love* does not play a part. It is not something for you to enjoy, rather it is an act for you to endure. And a comfortable lifestyle free of financial burden will be your compensation for your endurance. Do you understand?'

Louisa, though appearing downcast, nodded.

Myrtle sighed with relief, pleased her daughter wasn't offering further resistance to marrying Mr Mullen. Now, she just had to gently persuade Mr Mullen to take Louisa to be his wife. Her daughter hadn't been blessed with beauty, but she had youth, and Myrtle felt sure that Mr Mullen would be more than satisfied with a young bride to care for him in his dotage. Best of all, the man had no heirs to his wealth. One day, hopefully sooner rather than later, *Mrs Louisa Mullen* would be a very rich widow.

4

Three days later, Louisa glanced in the mirror on her dressing table and pinched her cheeks to add some colour to her pallid skin. Mr Mullen would be arriving shortly for afternoon tea, and she'd promised her mother that she'd make a good impression. As the hands of the clock slowly ticked, Louisa wanted to run from the house, to flee through the streets of London and escape her fate. The thought of marrying Mr Mullen left her feeling sick in the pit of her stomach. But as her mother had pointed out on many occasions – she had no choice. Either she married Mr Mullen, or they would find themselves starving and on the streets, possibly in the workhouse. Even Louisa had admitted to herself that a life as Mrs Mullen must be more palatable than struggling to live in poverty. She gazed up at the high ceiling, her mind wandering as she imagined a large Zeppelin airship floating in the sky above their house. Perhaps a German pilot would drop a bomb on their house and put her out of her misery. It wasn't an unrealistic dream. Only last month, a Zeppelin air raid over Streatham had caused much damage to the railway line, and a bomb exploding in a school garden had killed four passengers on a nearby tramcar. Louisa shuddered with fear. She couldn't abide the thought of marrying Mr Mullen, but she didn't want to die, either.

Her mother's voice reached her ears from the bottom of the stairs. 'Louisa ... Louisa, are you ready?'

Louisa straightened herself and smoothed down the front of her best dress. In pale blue, with heavy, dark blue velvet trimmings, the dress had been her father's favourite. She recalled the smile on his face when she'd waltzed into the drawing room on his birthday, and he'd told her she was the fairest maid in all of London. Of course, Louisa had known she wasn't pretty, and she hadn't *waltzed* into the drawing room, either. It had been more of a clumsy fall, first tripping over the rug, and then stumbling towards the table. She grimaced at the memory, and her mother frowning, saying she had the grace of a seal on land. Today would be different. Louisa would carry herself like a swan, or later face her mother's fierce wrath.

Downstairs, her mother seemed perplexed.

'Is everything all right?' Louisa dared to ask. She hoped against all hope that Mr Mullen had cancelled the arrangements for today.

'Yes, Louisa, of course everything is fine. Sit up straight, girl. And keep your hands still.'

Louisa knew how important today was for her mother. After all, their future depended on it. It was little wonder she seemed even more highly strung than usual, and to make matters more fraught, they no longer had a maid to serve the tea. Louisa pondered how her mother would explain the lack of staff. Surely she wouldn't admit their dire situation to Mr Mullen?

'That will be him,' Myrtle announced, eyes wide, when the doorbell rang.

After a few moments, Louisa prompted, 'Are you going to let him in?'

Myrtle sniffed. 'Yes, yes of course. Stand up, Louisa. And smile.'

When Mr Mullen entered the lounge, Louisa's heart plummeted. He looked even fatter than she'd remembered, and with his hat in one hand, he used the other to brush over thin, grey strands of hair across his shining, bald scalp. Beads of sweat glistened on his forehead, and his plump cheeks glowed red.

'I'm not good with stairs,' Mr Mullen panted.

'Please, do sit down,' Myrtle offered, gesturing towards the sofa.

'Don't mind if I do.' As Mr Mullen threw himself down onto the sofa, his eyes roamed up and down Louisa. She could feel herself cringing under his gaze and she lowered her eyes. Horrific thoughts of living with this man bombarded her mind. Her stomach twisted and bile burned the back of her throat as she pictured his hands, with their sausage-like fingers, touching her body.

Her mother, seemingly oblivious to Louisa's torment, busied herself pouring tea and making nervous chit-chat with Mr Mullen. All the while, his eyes continued to rake Louisa.

Leaping to her feet, nausea washing over her, Louisa held her hand to her mouth, sure that she was about to vomit. 'Sorry ... I can't do this,' she mumbled through gritted teeth as she ran from the room.

Her mother's voice followed her. 'Louisa! Louisa! How dare you!'

As Louisa hurried towards the front door, she could hear her mother apologising to Mr Mullen for her unacceptable behaviour. 'I really don't know what has come over Louisa. The girl must be quite overwhelmed. You do understand, Mr Mullen, Louisa is *innocent* and not experienced in keeping company with a man. Though I'm confident that with a little patience, she will make a gentleman like yourself a very fine wife indeed.'

Louisa had heard enough and flung open the front door. Granted, poverty was hanging over them like a dark, foreboding cloud, following them wherever they went, but Louisa couldn't bear the notion of being Mr Mullen's wife!

Fleeing along the street, tears streaking her cheeks, her heart dropped even further when she saw Dickie Newman emerging from his house. She was about to turn on her heel and run in the opposite direction, but the man had caught her eye and was beckoning her to him as he marched towards her. Louisa stopped running, her shoulders heaving as she stood on the street and drew in a long, juddering breath.

'Every time I see you, you're crying. What is it, girl? What's so bad, eh?'

Louisa should have been terrified of the man. The last encounter she'd had with Dickie Newman ended with a smashed clock on the library floor, as he'd stormed out, banging doors and snarling obscenities. But when she looked up into his dark brown eyes, she saw only warmth. And when he placed a sympathetic hand on her arm, Louisa flung herself at him, sobbing into his chest.

'Come on, sweetheart, what's this all about, eh? Is it your dad? Are you missing him?' Dickie asked, as he gently wrapped his arms around her.

Louisa sniffed, suddenly realising her behaviour was very inappropriate. Pulling away from Mr Newman, she could feel her cheeks burning with embarrassment as she reached into her pocket for her handkerchief.

'I, erm, please forgive me, Mr Newman,' she said, trying to compose herself.

'Dickie. Call me Dickie. After all, we're neighbours, ain't we?'

'Yes, I suppose we are.'

'Now then, are you gonna tell me why you're crying enough tears to flood the Thames and burst its banks? Has someone upset you? Do I need to go and sort them out for you?'

Louisa's eyes shot up to look at Dickie, and she was relieved to see he was gently smiling.

'Don't look so worried,' he reassured her. 'I'm just kidding. But if someone does need a word in their ear, I'd be more than happy to oblige.'

'No. No, thank you, Mr New— I mean, Dickie. No one has upset me.'

'If you say so.'

'I do. Thank you, Dickie.'

'So, what's the problem?' he pushed.

Louisa desperately wanted to talk to someone about her terrible predicament, but she knew better than to discuss her family business with relative strangers. Her mother would have a fit if she had even an inkling that Louisa was sharing her problems with Dickie Newman, of all people! Myrtle had made her thoughts about the man more than clear. *Ruffian, lowlife, rogue* and many other unpleasant words had been bandied around to describe him. Yet Louisa felt strangely drawn to him.

'My mother wants me to marry Mr Mullen,' she finally admitted.

'What? Mullen who owns that big insurance firm?'

Louisa nodded and Dickie grimaced.

'I take it you don't want to marry the old timer?'

'No, of course I don't!'

'I can't say I blame you. But he must be worth a few bob.'

'Which is exactly the reason my mother is insisting I marry him.'

'I see. She's skint, so she expects you to marry a rich bloke.'

Again, Louisa nodded and could feel tears welling in her eyes.

'Don't start bawling again,' Dickie chuckled. 'Worse things happen at sea.'

Louisa frowned, annoyed that he wasn't taking her seriously, and she spat indignantly, 'What could be worse than marrying Mr Mullen?'

'Not much,' Dickie sighed. 'Have you got to do what your mother tells you?'

'I don't think I have a choice,' Louisa shrugged. 'And I don't think I'm overreacting when I say it's Mr Mullen or the workhouse.'

'Christ, girl, marrying Mullen will be a walk in the park compared to the workhouse. You don't want to end up in one of those places. Evil, they are, pure, rotten evil.'

'It seems my fate is sealed.'

There were a few moments of silence, and then, eyes glinting with mischief, Dickie asked, 'Would you rather marry me?'

Louisa stared up at him, blinking hard. Had she heard correctly, or was he just teasing her? 'I beg your pardon?' she said slowly.

'You could marry me instead of that Mullen bloke. I'm rich, I'm easy on the eye and I'm half the age of Mullen. What do you reckon, eh? Do you think your old dear would be agreeable?'

Dickie was right, he was easy on the eye. With a thick mop of greased-back dark hair, long lashes framing his brown eyes and a muscular build, Louisa thought him very attractive. But she didn't feel ready for marriage and dreamed of falling in love. As her mind turned, she found her mouth opening and closing, yet no words were coming out.

Dickie grinned. 'You ain't said no, so I'll take your goldfish impression as a yes, then,' he said. 'Come on, let's go and tell your mum the good news.'

5

Dickie Newman led the way into Louisa's house, swaggering confidently into the lounge. The expression on Myrtle Best's face was a picture! The woman's jaw dropped, and she looked as though her eyes had just fallen upon the monster in Shelley's *Frankenstein*.

Louisa cowered behind him as Mrs Best sprang to her feet.

'You have the audacity to come into my home unannounced and uninvited! I must insist that you leave at once, Mr Newman.'

Dickie ignored Mrs Best and glowered at the old man. 'You, out,' he ordered, pointing his thumb over his shoulder towards the door.

Rising to his feet, Mr Mullen appeared flustered as he puffed out his chest, asking, 'I say, who the Devil are you?'

'I, Mr Mullen, am Mrs Best's future son-in-law, so your services are no longer required. Go on, clear orf!'

Dickie glanced round at Louisa, giving the worried-looking girl a reassuring wink.

Mr Mullen bustled towards the door. 'This is preposterous!' Stopping briefly for a moment, he glared at Mrs Best. 'You, madam, are no longer in my favour. Never have I kept such rude company.'

Mrs Best dashed after him. 'Wait … Mr Mullen, please, wait. Let me explain … I have no idea what this appalling man is talking about!'

Then, striding back into the room, she addressed Dickie. 'You need to leave this instant, or I shall have the police onto you.'

Dickie smirked as he made himself comfortable in an armchair. Taking out a cigar, he lit it and blew out the smoke, watching as it formed swirling patterns in the weak sunlight streaming through the tall window. With Mr Mullen gone, he had Mrs Best over a barrel. 'Shut your mouth and sit your arse down,' he hissed.

Mrs Best audibly gulped, but she was a little firecracker, and defiantly threw her nose in the air. 'I won't be spoken to in that tone in my own house. And I shan't ask you again – leave. At once!'

Louder now, Dickie shouted, 'I said, shut up and sit down!' He pointed to the armchair adjacent to him. Then, turning to Louisa, he instructed, 'Be a sweetheart and pour me and your mother a cuppa.'

Louisa scuttled towards the table and the fancy teapot set on a silver tray.

As Mrs Best settled on the edge of the armchair, Dickie flicked the ash from the end of his cigar onto the floor, relishing the reproachful look that Mrs Best threw him. 'Right, Mrs Best, let's get down to business, shall we?' he said. 'You ain't got a pot to piss in, and me, well, I'm a very rich man. So, I'm going to marry your daughter, and you are going to be eternally grateful.'

'Why, Mr Newman? Why would you want to marry Louisa?'

'I can see she ain't no oil painting, but she's a nice girl.'

Mrs Best pursed her lips. 'And how will I be expected to show my gratitude?'

'You'll stop nagging for a start. And then you'll introduce me to all your top-notch friends. You'll tell them what a bloody brilliant son-in-law I am. How wealthy I am. Clever, too. We'll go to the best places in London and you, Mrs Best, will convince your aristocrat circle that the bleedin' sun shines out of my backside.'

'Aristocrats?!' Mrs Best scoffed. 'I don't have aristocrat friends.'

'You must know plenty of toffee-nosed folk. I want introductions, and you're gonna do it.'

'Huh. I see. So, you want to marry my daughter as you believe it will offer you higher standing in society. I can lie and say the most wonderful things about you, Mr Newman, but you'll *never* be accepted by those with class.'

Dickie could feel his anger rising at Mrs Best's condescending manner. 'Yeah, well, we'll see about that. You just do as you're told and leave the rest to me.' Heading towards the door, he continued. 'Have her ready to wed me as soon as possible. There won't be no big fancy do. A registry office. And once we're married, she'll be moving in with me.'

'And me, Mr Newman? What will become of me?'

Dickie looked around the luxurious room as if there was a bad smell under his nose. 'You can keep your fancy house, Mrs Best, and I'll make sure you don't go short. Your husband's debt will be written off, too. But you stick to your end of the bargain … or else. You think you're in a bad situation now. Mess with me and you won't know what's hit ya.'

Outside, Dickie smiled to himself, pleased with his latest deal. He'd be lumbered with a young lady who didn't stir his groin, but he could still visit his other woman. Pippa was always pleased to see him. *Cor, Pippa*, he thought, remembering how her huge, bouncy breasts almost smothered him. Pippa wasn't the sort of woman to take as a wife, but she knew how to pleasure him like no other woman ever had. He wondered if he should tell her about marrying Louisa or keep it a secret from her. He liked Pippa a lot, but she was prone to sulking to get her own way. And she'd already dropped several hints about wanting his ring on her finger. Desire burned in him as he thought about her voluptuous curves. He needed to be in her bed tonight. Though he decided it was probably for the best to keep quiet about Louisa.

6

Three months later
16th January 1917

Myrtle Best sat in the passenger seat of her son-in-law's car, staring blankly out of the side window as they passed by some of London's finest buildings made with Portland Stone. Today wouldn't be the first introduction she had made for Dickie, but it was the one she was most dreading.

Pamela Babcock had been a close friend of Myrtle's for many years. In fact, Myrtle had been a bridesmaid at Pamela's wedding to Ernest Babcock, a wealthy private banker. The friendship had drifted after Louisa had been born, but Myrtle and Pamela had reconnected a few years ago when both had attended a grand event in Harrods' restaurant. Pamela had discovered her husband's love affair with a French dancer and had been heartbroken. She'd needed a friend to confide in and had shared her distress with Myrtle, questioning if she should remain with her unfaithful husband. Myrtle had given her friend sound advice, for which Pamela was grateful, and though the married couple now had separate bedrooms, the affair with the French dancer had come to an end and Pamela lived in the style only the wealthiest in London could afford.

But with Pamela's riches came a snootiness, and Myrtle felt sure that Dickie would embarrass her.

Her chest felt tight. Though Dickie often made faux pas, he was proving he could acquaint himself well with classes far above his own. But the Babcocks were a different kettle of fish: old money, and Pamela was second cousin once removed to the King. That was the reason for the invitation today. Pamela was keen to show her house renovations to Myrtle and had mentioned several times that the interiors had been designed by Charles Allom, decorator to the Royal Family. It worried Myrtle what the Babcocks would think of Dickie's crudeness.

Arriving outside the eleven-bedroom house, Dickie walked around and opened the car door for Myrtle, offering his hand to assist her out, which she quickly dismissed.

'Suit yourself,' he sniffed.

'Try not to be vulgar today. Pamela Babcock has a great deal of influence within London society. I do not wish for my name and reputation to be tarnished by your unsolicited conversation.'

Feigning a look of hurt, Dickie said, 'I don't know what you mean, Myrtle.'

'Yes, you do. Suggesting that any woman can sing soprano in an opera if you pinch them hard enough, and asking what the point is of a conductor of an orchestra, as after all, and I quote, "*He just waves a stick about.*" But to have said that in front of Adelina Patti's nephew was astonishingly rude! Miss Patti is the greatest opera singer of our time. Verdi described her as a stupendous artist, and King George said of her last performance for the Red Cross that she sang wonderfully.

Yet you dare to belittle such accomplishments, when actually, Dickie, it's only yourself you are making look ridiculous.'

'I speak as I find, and your lot can take me as they find me. Let's face it, Myrtle, none of your posh friends have thrown me out, have they? No, they ain't. And do you know why? It's 'cos I've got money and I'm throwing it in their direction. Half of your lot live in big, swanky houses, and they talk with their hoity-toity accents, but they ain't got two ha'pennies to rub together. It's all for show. Then along comes someone like me, being flash with me cash, and they can't get enough of me because they want my money. And they love a bit of cheekiness, especially the women. I make them laugh, Myrtle. You should try it one day, though it might crack your sour face.'

'I'd laugh if I found you funny. Which I do not. And neither will the Babcocks. Mr and Mrs Babcock don't need your money, Dickie. I really do not understand the reason for you coming here today. What could Ernest Babcock possibly do for you, and what do you have to offer him?'

Dickie tapped the side of his nose. 'You'll see,' he said.

Myrtle pursed her lips as she pulled her fur stole over her shoulders and marched towards the impressive entrance to the Babcock residence. A servant dressed in a black suit and white shirt opened the door and showed them through to the drawing room.

Pamela beamed with delight as she rushed across the large room to greet Myrtle warmly.

'Good afternoon, my dear friend. I'm so glad you accepted my invitation. I can't wait to give you the tour. What do you think?' Pamela asked, slowly waving her upturned hand to indicate the freshly decorated room.

Myrtle admired the gold-leaf finishes around the light fittings, and the subtle gold flowers in the thick wall coverings. The huge rug on the Italian marble floor had flecks of gold running through it, too, which matched the gold-coloured legs of the large, cream sofas.

'Quite stunning,' Myrtle praised, trying to hide her jealousy.

'Look at me running away with myself. I'm so excited to show you the work that Mr Allom has completed. Did I tell you that Charles Allom is the decorator for the Royal Family? Yes, I'm sure I did. But I must apologise for my terrible manners. Sorry, you must be Mr Newman. Myrtle has told me much about you.'

'Oh, I bet she has. I hope everything she's told you is bad, 'cos if Myrtle has said anything good about me, she'd be telling fibs,' Dickie grinned. 'Pleased to meet you, Mrs Babcock. And I can't say I blame you for being excited to show Myrtle your renovations. You have exquisite taste. This room, if you don't mind me saying so bluntly, it's bloody lovely.'

Pamela threw Myrtle a bemused look before giggling slightly awkwardly and then saying to Dickie, 'Yes, you're quite right. It is *bloody lovely*!'

Mr Babcock entered the room, asking, 'What's so bloody lovely?'

'Our drawing room, Ernest.'

'Oh, that, right, yes. To be perfectly honest, I'm tired of admiring the house, as bloody lovely as it is,' he chuckled. 'You must be young Louisa's husband. Pleased to meet you.'

'Likewise,' Dickie said, shaking the man's hand.

'Drink?'

'Brandy,' Dickie answered.

'Shall we have a sherry, Myrtle, or would you prefer a cup of tea?' Pamela asked.

'Oh, I think a sherry.'

As a maid poured the drinks, Myrtle studied Dickie's face. She thought he was looking smug about something, which gave her an uneasy feeling.

Ernest raised his glass to Dickie, and asked, 'So, young man, how are you finding married life?'

'It has its benefits,' Dickie smiled.

Pamela was beaming. 'I can't possibly wait for another second. Come, Myrtle, bring your glass with you, I'll show you around.'

As Myrtle left the room, she looked over her shoulder at Dickie, her eyes narrowing as she gave him a look of warning. The idea of leaving him alone with Ernest made her cringe inside, and she hoped the tour of the house would be quick.

'I must say, Myrtle,' Pamela whispered, as they walked towards the ballroom. 'Mr Newman isn't what I was expecting.'

'No, he wasn't who I would have chosen for Louisa, but the girl is smitten with him. I tried to keep her away from him, but one cannot help whom one falls in love with. I feared losing her if I didn't agree to the marriage. And now, well, to be frank, Dickie has rather grown on me.'

'I can see the attraction for Louisa; he is quite a dish in a roguish sort of way. She isn't the first young lady to marry below her class, and I'm sure she won't be the last. Times are changing, Myrtle, and I fear that if we aren't more open-minded, then we will be left behind. I mean, there are women working now, and Meriel Talbot is in the process of establishing the Women's Land Army. We still don't have the right to vote, but at least women can now go unaccompanied to many places where they couldn't before the war.'

'I find change difficult, Pamela. I don't think anything has ever been the same since Queen Victoria passed away.'

'Oh, Myrtle, don't be such a fuddy-duddy. You're old before your time. Let me take you shopping tomorrow and perhaps I can persuade you to dress more fashionably.'

Myrtle eyed Pamela up and down. She thought the woman's clothes were bordering on risqué, showing far too much ankle, and her once tight-fitting dress and under corset that shaped her body had been lost to a loose-fitting dress with oversized pockets. Pamela's long, auburn hair had been cut short and curled to chin length, which Myrtle thought looked boyish.

'I'll pass, if you don't mind,' Myrtle said, hoping she hadn't offended her friend.

'I suppose you can stay a fuddy-duddy,' Pamela teased. 'After all, you might be a grandmother soon.'

God forbid! Myrtle thought, forcing a smile. The notion of Dickie Newman breeding and creating a smaller version of himself turned her stomach, though she supposed it was inevitable.

After half an hour of saying all the correct things at the correct times, Myrtle was pleased to be returning to the drawing room. It came as a great relief to find the atmosphere felt light.

'Myrtle approves of the decorating, Ernest.'

'I should hope so. We could have bought a place in Switzerland for the cost of the renovations here, not to mention the months of disruption with the decorators.'

'Do stop complaining, dearest, you know you like it really.'

'If you say so. Do you see, chap, it's easier for a husband to agree with his wife. It pertains to a quieter life.'

'What have you two been discussing in our absence?' Myrtle asked.

'Cars,' Ernest replied. 'I was admiring Mr Newman's Crossley. Quite a dependable vehicle, I believe.'

'It gets me from A to B. I don't like to be reliant on a driver.'

'It must be useful in your line of work. I understand you're in property?'

'Yeah, that's right. I own a significant amount of property in Battersea, which gives me a good return in rental incomes.'

Ernest twiddled the end of his upturned moustache. 'Hmm, maybe there could be a collaboration here. High returns require reliable investments. Money makes money, chap, and I know the best places to position your money for the least risks and highest yields.'

'Oh, Ernest, please, let's not talk business before lunch,' Pamela moaned. 'Perhaps after we've eaten, you might like to take Mr Newman to the library for a cigar, and then you can talk about investments and returns until the cows come home.'

Myrtle was pleased to see that Ernest was in a cheerier mood than usual. She suspected he'd consumed several glasses of alcohol. The man was known to be quite a misery when sober. And, so far, Dickie hadn't embarrassed her.

'I'm keen to discuss investments and returns with you, Mr Babcock, if the ladies don't mind?' Dickie asked, directing his question towards Myrtle.

'I think Pamela would prefer that the conversation is deferred until after lunch,' Myrtle answered, though she was curious to hear what Dickie had to say.

Pamela waved her hand in front of her face as though there was a bad smell in the room. 'Go ahead,' she said with a roll of her large, hazel eyes. 'Us ladies shall sit here quietly and be astonished at the world of business, which we know nothing about and have no desire to understand.'

'Right you are, chap,' Ernest said with enthusiasm and clapped his hands together. 'What size of investment are we talking here? I'm sure you appreciate that I only deal in sizeable amounts of no less than one thousand pounds. And of course, we must discuss government bonds. It's our duty to help with the war effort. A war loan is crucial, let's say for five hundred pounds?'

Dickie cleared his throat and sipped his brandy. 'See, the thing is, Mr Babcock, I'm not a gambler. I'm reluctant to give you my hard earned without a guarantee of a good return. I'm talking at least double.'

'There's no guarantee, but I'm very successful and experienced. You won't lose money, Mr Newman.'

Dickie placed his glass on a side table and stepped closer to Ernest. Myrtle noticed that Dickie's painted-on, affable smile had changed to a sneer.

'I know you can give me a guarantee, and I know how you do it. I also know that there's two *chaps* who have cleverly swindled the government and the good British public, and one of them chaps is you, Mr Babcock. So how about we cut the crap and *really* get down to business.'

Myrtle closed her eyes as she felt her face redden. Dickie had dropped the friendly façade, and the menacing side of his unsavoury character was showing its ugly self.

Ernest frowned and demanded, 'Explain yourself.'

'Let's start with Saddleworth Electronics.'

Ernest shifted his feet uncomfortably and gulped down his brandy.

'You see, Mr Babcock, I had a good drink with a certain Member of Parliament last week. You'd be surprised what some of these politicians blab about when they're three sheets to the wind. The Right Honourable Sir William Hestor was celebrating because he'd just made a killing on an investment, brokered through you. Ring any bells now?'

'Nonsense!'

'It ain't nonsense though, is it, Mr Babcock? From what I understand, the Chancellor of the Exchequer was about to sign off on a big contract with Saddleworth Electronics. I'm talking about a contract worth hundreds of thousands of pounds. A contract like that, well, it would send the company shares sky-high. So, if the information about the impending contract was to leak out, and the shares were bought cheap before the public announcement was made, well, that would be a stroke of luck for the shareholder who bought the shares cheap before the prices increased, eh? And that's what happened, Mr Babcock. You and your politician friend made a lot of money. Three times what you invested. Some might say it was fraudulent. If the newspapers got a hold of this information, it would be a scandal. I reckon you'd go broke, and it might even bring down the government. But me … I don't see nothing wrong with it. And I want a piece of it. A big piece.'

Pamela leapt to her feet, looking flustered. 'You're very much mistaken if you believe my husband to be dishonest, Mr Newman. I think this conversation should stop right now.'

'I ain't calling your husband dishonest, Mrs Babcock. Please forgive me, I never meant to offend. But I think your husband understands what I'm saying, don't you, Mr Babcock?'

'It was a one-off,' Ernest replied.

'Now, now, now, Mr Babcock, that's not true. Please don't tell fibs in front of the ladies. We both know that there's military and government contracts being given out hand over fist. You've invested in two other companies and on both occasions, you've made more money than any frontline soldier makes in a lifetime. I know you've got an insider in the government, and I know you pay him for the information. That insider is your good wife's young nephew. The only reason Sir William Heston profited from your scheme is because he asked too many awkward questions, so you had to cut him in the deal, too.'

His head hung low, Ernest asked, 'How much?'

'We can talk about the finer details after lunch. Let's not bore the ladies any longer.'

Myrtle, though ashamed to call Dickie her son-in-law, had to admit to herself that she'd been somewhat impressed with him. She didn't agree with his tactics but, somehow, he'd exposed a weakness in Ernest, and he intended to use it. Her mind turned. She thought back over the past couple of months, trying to recall any introductions she'd made that could have led Dickie to Sir William Heston. *The Liberal Party Fundraiser.* Dickie had accompanied her, but she hadn't seen Sir William there. She assumed that one politician had led to another, and her wily son-in-law had managed to wangle his way into the company of Sir William, probably at the man's exclusive club, where cigars were smoked and business deals discussed behind closed and guarded doors. Dickie was hateful. Vile. Disgusting and savage. But he was also clever and sly, a frightful combination that sent a cold shiver of fear down her spine. Myrtle had underestimated Dickie, and realised he would stop at nothing and stoop as low as he needed to make money. She knew that the more money he had, the more he believed he'd be accepted in her upper-class world.

The following day, Dickie pulled up the collar of his expensive, long wool coat in a bid to keep out the cold wind that funnelled through the narrow street of rundown terraced houses. He'd grown up in this part of Battersea, born in a two-up, two-down around the corner, and the house had been shared with another family. His mother had borne five boys in that small, cold room, Dickie being the last born and the only child to have survived. His brothers had all died before reaching their tenth birthdays, and his mother and father had passed away years ago, too. The filth of poverty had killed them. Hunger and disease had taken the lives of many destitute Londoners. But being poor had given Dickie ambition, and he'd clawed his way out of the slums, now owning most of them. And now he was mixing with the rich people of London. Life was on the up again.

Turning into *his* road, Dickie admired his three-storey buildings, though the houses were overcrowded with thieves, prostitutes and general labourers who couldn't afford to keep their families. But Dickie didn't care about how many people were crammed into his houses. As far as he was concerned, more folk meant more rent to line his deep pockets.

'Let's get this done as quick as possible,' he said to Ernie. 'It's too bloody cold to be out.'

'Right you are, Boss,' Ernie replied. He walked beside

Dickie, his long arms swinging and his huge, ungloved hands clenched into fists. An ex-boxer, Ernie's cauliflower ears glowed pink in the biting wind, and a dewdrop of snot hung on the end of his crooked nose. The man wasn't as tall as Dickie, but he was twice as wide. He reminded Dickie of a gorilla, and just like the huge beast, Ernie's knuckles nearly scraped the ground. Dickie reckoned Ernie had the same level of intelligence as a gorilla too, but he was loyal and had worked for him for years.

'Right, Ernie, you know what to do,' he said, nodding his head towards a scruffy, wooden door.

Dickie stood back and surveyed his property as Ernie rapped on the door. A sackcloth over a broken windowpane moved and Dickie saw a pair of doe-like, terrified eyes peeping down at him. Little Millicent Marchwood bit her bottom lip, and Dickie offered her a smile. He could see the girl's hair was matted and her face looked dark with ingrained dirt. He wrinkled his nose, hoping he wouldn't have to barge into the house to collect his rent money. The last time he'd stepped inside, the stench had been overwhelming. But with only a cold tap and no money for coal, bathing was low down on the family's list of priorities.

Bob Marchwood opened the front door, still bearing the remnants of a black eye and swollen nose from the beating Dickie had given him two weeks earlier. He really didn't want to have to give Bob another pasting, especially with Millicent in the house. The girl had already witnessed her father getting a kick in the head.

'I hope you can pay up today, Bob,' Dickie said menacingly.

'Yes, Mr Newman. I've got your money,' Bob replied fearfully, and handed several coins to Ernie.

'Good man. See you in a fortnight.'

'Erm … Mr Newman … the window upstairs … it's broken. It was no fault of ours. The wood's rotten, and the glass just fell out.'

'Best you get it fixed then, man. It'll be freezing in that room.'

'It is, Mr Newman, and the old sack don't keep the wind out. But, with respect, sir, you're the landlord. Ain't it down to you to repair it?'

Dickie rolled his eyes. *Here we go again*, he thought. These lazy, dirty bastards want everything for nothing. Always moaning. Always expecting more. 'You pay me a mere pittance for two rooms upstairs, which doesn't include putting in new windows. Get it fixed, Bob, or your rent will be going up to cover the cost of repair. Is that clear?'

'Yes, Mr Newman, of course, Mr Newman.'

'Good. And by the way, there's a new family moving in downstairs. Get your Dot to clear out your stuff, and thank your lucky stars that I ain't charged you extra rent for those rooms.'

'Yes, Mr Newman, thank you.'

As Dickie turned to walk to the next house, he tutted, saying to Ernie, 'Eight of them living in those two rooms upstairs. And Dot's in the family way again. Bob needs to tie a bleedin' knot in it. He can't afford for his missus to keep churning out babies.'

Ernie knocked on the door of the next house, and as expected, no one answered. It wasn't unusual for his tenants to hide on the day the rent was due. If no one came to the door, Dickie would give instructions for Ernie to kick it in. Then they'd inevitably find the tenant, pretending to be asleep or, if the tenant was fortunate enough to have a wardrobe, squirrelling themselves away in it.

'Betty's at it again,' Ernie sighed. 'Shall I give the door a boot?'

'Not yet. Give her a chance. Warn her first.'

Ernie drew in a deep breath before yelling, 'BETTY! Open up or I'm coming in.'

The door slowly opened, and Betty sashayed onto the step. The top buttons of her dress were undone, revealing a sizeable cleavage, and she'd swept a colour across her full lips. Dickie knew what was coming. Betty wasn't the first penniless wife to offer to pay the rent in exchange for *services.*

'Has your old man been spending the rent money over the bar of The Woodman, eh?'

'My George is a waste of space, Mr Newman. Do you want to come inside? It's cold out there and, well, it's lovely and warm inside. Come and have a feel, Mr Newman. I think you'll enjoy it.'

'Leave it out, Betty. I ain't being funny, love, but I ain't dipping my wick in anything that George Bastin has been in.'

'You don't know what you're missing,' Betty purred.

'Can you pay your rent, Betty?'

Betty pulled a sulky face and dipped her hand into her pocket. 'Yes, I can pay,' she said, sounding narked. 'But I was hoping to get some money off.'

'Nice try, sweetheart. Give George my regards.'

''Ere, before you go, what are you gonna do about those fourteen fellas living upstairs? I can't get no peace with the racket they make at night. They're always boozing and the language, well, it ain't good for my three girls to hear it.'

'Button your moaning, Betty. You and me both know that

business is booming for you with them lot upstairs. You don't have to walk the streets no more looking for customers, do you?'

'All right, but that ain't the point.'

'I don't have time for this, Betty. If you don't like it, then find somewhere else to live.'

'I would if I could. Do you think I want to live in this shithole? But with my George guzzling his wages, I can't afford anywhere decent!'

'Not my problem, Betty.'

'You're a mean bastard, Dickie Newman. You're making money out of our misery. And tell me something else . . . How come you ain't fighting in the war? Why ain't you been conscripted? Don't tell me you got turned down on medical grounds, 'cos I know you ain't malnourished like most of the blokes on this street.'

'Mind your own, Betty,' Dickie snapped, walking away.

His business was no concern of Betty Bastin's. And his conscience was clear. It wasn't his fault if his tenants couldn't manage to pay for a reasonable place to rent. Dickie believed he was providing a good service for them. After all, they had a roof over their heads. And as for being conscripted, again, he felt no shame. Why should he risk his life for King and country? King George had never done anything for him! Dickie was grateful for the falsified exemption papers that he'd paid well for. Keeping him off the battlefields had been worth every penny.

By the time Dickie had reached the end of the street, Ernie had pockets full of cash and they'd only had to rough up two tenants who couldn't pay. Dickie had bruised his knuckles on Mick Gilbert's jaw, but overall, it had been a good day's work.

'We'll collect the interest on the loans tomorrow, Ernie. And find more borrowers. Target the mothers. The ones whose husbands are always in the pub. They'll be desperate for a few bob.'

'Will do, Boss.'

Sitting behind the wheel of his Crossley, he was looking forward to getting home. He couldn't say he was keen to see his wife, but he wanted to relish the warmth of the hearth and enjoy a hot meal. Louisa irritated him and aways looked so sullen, but the woman was a good cook, and she kept the house clean. It had been a bit hit and miss at first. His wife had come from a privileged background and had never lifted a duster before or fried eggs and bacon. But after a few weeks of scolding her, Louisa had been a fast learner and had fallen into her stride with the household duties. Having a wife wasn't so bad. It had saved him a small fortune on staff.

Louisa tensed when she heard the front door open. It meant Dickie was home, and she hoped he wouldn't be disappointed with her efforts today. She'd laundered and ironed seven of his shirts, one for each day of the week. Swept the house from top to bottom and had the coal fire roaring. A beef stew was simmering on the stove, and she was ready to serve it dressed in her best attire. Yet Dickie was never happy. She hadn't blamed him at first. Her incompetence at running a home had clearly irked him. But with practice, she'd soon become a reasonable cook and now took pride in her cleaning. Though, no matter how hard she tried, it never seemed good enough for her husband. He rarely spoke and was often out until late, coming home smelling of expensive perfume and bleary-eyed from swigging brandy. Granted, he kept her well enough. He'd adorned her with fashionable dresses made by the best seamstresses in the area. She could shop in any store in London if she wanted. But Louisa wasn't concerned with clothes and shopping. She yearned for company and wanted nothing more than affection.

Running to the door, Louisa helped Dickie off with his coat and took his hat. 'Hello,' she welcomed him, forcing a smile, hoping she'd at least receive a smile in return.

Dickie grunted, barely acknowledging her. She noticed his knuckles were swollen and guessed he'd inflicted violence on one of his unpaying tenants. It wasn't something Louisa would dwell on. She knew he owned properties and collected rents, and sometimes there were altercations with his renters, but Dickie hadn't spoken much about his work. In fact, he'd barely spoken to her about anything.

'Are you hungry?' she asked.

'Yes. I'll have my dinner at my desk.'

Louisa's heart sank. That meant she'd be eating alone again this evening.

'Can I draw you a bath after you've eaten?'

'No, I'll be going out.'

'Must you?' Louisa blurted.

Dickie frowned, glaring at her with disapproval. 'I've got work to do. If I didn't work, you wouldn't have your fancy dresses, and your mother wouldn't be flouncing about in her big house.'

Louisa regretted her outburst and tried to explain. 'I'm sorry, Dickie. I realise how hard you work. It's just … well … I'm so bored and lonely.'

'Haven't you got any friends you can spend time with?'

'No, not really. There's Emily, my best friend from boarding school, but she lives in Suffolk.'

'Your mother? Go and sit with her for the evening.'

'I'd rather not. Mother's such a cold fish, and I always feel I'm in her way. Anyway, she's usually busy with her bridge club or charity events. She never has time for me.'

As far back as Louisa could remember, she'd felt she was an inconvenience to her mother. The woman had never shown her any love. Louisa had only known love from her father. He'd openly displayed his affection, cuddling her, tickling her ribs and planting big kisses on her forehead. Oh, how she missed him. She tried to quell her emotions, but they felt so painfully raw, and a tear slipped from her eye.

'Christ, not this again!' Dickie moaned. 'You're always bleedin' crying. A man shouldn't have to come home to this every night. I've had enough, forget my dinner. I'm going out.'

Dickie stormed past her, grabbing his hat and coat before charging out of the front door, leaving it wide open in his wake.

Louisa ran after him, calling, 'I'm sorry, Dickie ... Really, I am.'

But Dickie was out of earshot and her words were lost to the wind.

She watched him drive away at speed. Then, closing the door and shutting out the freezing temperatures, Louisa slumped to the marble-tiled floor. An eruption of grief spurted from the depths of her stomach as she threw her head back and wailed. 'Father ...' she cried, 'I miss you so much.'

As she sobbed, a sudden loud boom blasted, rattling the windows and making the front door shake. Louisa gasped and held her breath, staring towards the ceiling. Was there a silent German airship passing overhead? Had it dropped a bomb? Terrified, her body trembling, she picked herself up from the floor. Fear gripped her, making her legs feel as though they would give way. Stumbling, she managed to run to the cupboard under the stairs. Opening the door, she threw herself into the darkness. Sitting on the floor with her knees huddled to her chest, Louisa silently prayed. 'Please, Lord, keep me safe. Don't let me die in this dismal cupboard.'

She thought about how ridiculous her pitiful life was – a married woman with a successful husband, her mother living on the same street, yet Louisa was still a virgin and had never felt so alone.

Dickie let himself into Pippa's house. He felt he had every right just to walk in. After all, he owned the property, and Pippa was living in the comfortable house rent-free. She was a kept woman and that's how Dickie liked it, beholden to him.

It had been over a week since he'd last seen Pippa, and he was eager to get the woman into bed. Throwing open the lounge door, he saw her stretched out on the sofa. Her flame-red hair, piled high, shimmering in the light of the coal fire. Dickie licked his lips, but the flames of his passion were quickly extinguished when he saw a hateful look in Pippa's green eyes.

'I wondered when you'd show your face,' she hissed.

'Yeah, sorry, sweetheart, I've been busy.'

'I've heard ... *busy* getting married! *Busy* taking a wife! You've got some nerve, you. Was you ever going to tell me?'

Dickie drew in a long breath and could feel his jaw tighten. So, she'd heard about Louisa through the Battersea gossip.

Word spread in this area quicker than a wildfire. He could have kicked himself. If he'd been upfront with Pippa and explained his motives for marrying Louisa, she might have been understanding. But he hadn't, and now he had an infuriated woman to deal with. Sloping over to the drinks cabinet, Dickie poured himself a large brandy and downed it in a few gulps. Then he poured himself another before turning to look at Pippa.

She was sitting upright now, glaring at him through narrowed eyes and sucking hard on a cigarette. 'How could you, Dickie? How could you do this to me? I've wasted nine years of my life on you. Nine years! And for what, eh? For a kick in the teeth, that's what!'

Dickie knocked back the brandy in his glass and quickly poured another as he tried to calm Pippa and explain. 'It's not what you think, darling. It's a marriage of convenience, that's all. A business arrangement. We haven't even, you know, done the deed to make the marriage legal. You should see her, Pip, she ain't even my cup of tea.'

'I couldn't give two hoots if she was a glamorous film star or a swamp monster. You married another woman, Dickie, which means I'll never be your wife, and I'll never have your children!'

Dickie drank the brandy and crouched in front of Pippa. Taking her hand, he spoke softly. 'But we're all right as we are, ain't we? Nothing needs to change. Me and you, we're good together.'

Pippa snatched her hand away, her face twisting with rage. 'The other women, I could tolerate. I knew you'd always come crawling back to me. But marriage! No, Dickie, I won't stand for it. You know how much I want a family. Babies,

Dickie, *your* babies. Either you divorce her and marry me, or we're finished.'

Dickie shook his head. He couldn't divorce Louisa now, not when he was on the verge of gaining membership to one of London's most elite gentlemen's clubs. He hoped to have a senior policeman in his pocket next, and the local Member of Parliament. Myrtle Best's introductions were already starting to pay dividends, and this was just the tip of the iceberg. Divorce was out of the question. 'Please, Pip, try to understand. I can't divorce her.'

'Then we're done. Get out, and don't bother coming back. Ever!'

'I think you're forgetting something, *my lovely*,' Dickie snarled, as he poured himself another brandy. 'This is *my* house, and all the fine furniture in it belongs to me. You can't throw me out of me own house.'

'Fine. I'll leave. I don't need you, Dickie Newman! In fact, I wish that bomb I heard explode earlier had dropped on your rotten head!'

Pippa dashed out of the room and up the stairs. Dickie could hear drawers opening and slamming shut. He guessed she was packing her clothes. As he tossed back another drink, her heels click-clacked down the stairs and towards the front door.

'You're nothing without me,' he yelled. 'Do you hear me, Pippa? Nothing!'

Pippa paused for a moment, placed her suitcase on the floor, and threw a bold look over her shoulder, her eyes filled with unshed tears. 'Goodbye, Dickie, and good bloody riddance! You've just lost the best thing that ever happened to you, and you're too stupid to see it. You're pathetic. A jumped-up landlord and unscrupulous money lender who reckons he's something that he ain't. I'm best off without you. You were *never* good enough for me.'

Dickie gripped the steering wheel and squinted, trying to focus on the road ahead, but he was seeing double of everything. The orange glow of a large blaze was in the distance, on the other side of the Thames. If that was the cause of the thunderous blast he'd felt and heard earlier, then he thought it must have been an incredible bomb that the Germans had dropped on the docks.

Finally reaching home, he staggered up the steps, losing his footing twice. 'Ungrateful bitch,' he slurred, thinking of Pippa. 'Fucking cheek, walking out on me after all I've done for her.' Pippa having the nerve to leave him had affected Dickie more than he cared to admit.

Inside, the house was in darkness. Dickie bounced off the walls as he made his way along the wide passageway towards the kitchen. His stomach growled with hunger, and he remembered the stew that Louisa had cooked. As he passed the cupboard under the stairs, a quiet whimpering sound caught his attention. Pulling open the door, Dickie peered inside.

'Louisa … What the bleedin' 'ell are you doing in there?'

Louisa sprang to her feet and launched herself at Dickie, almost knocking him off his unsteady feet. Throwing her arms around him, she cried, 'Oh, Dickie, I'm so glad you're home. I've been so scared.'

'Why? What's the matter? Who scared ya?'

'That blast, Dickie … The Germans … It sounded very close. I thought I was going to die.'

Dickie peeled her arms away from him. *The silly cow*, he

thought. Crying again, over nothing. 'If it was an air raid, then it was over the East End. You ain't got nothing to worry about, so pull yourself together.'

'Thank goodness, but my heart breaks for the poor souls affected.'

'Yeah, yeah, yeah,' Dickie sighed, exasperated. 'Get me some food. That stew. And a drink. Brandy.'

'Don't you think you've had enough brandy?'

Fury instantly ripped through Dickie. 'I'm pissed off with you bleedin' women telling me what to do. Who the hell are you to tell me when I've had enough, eh? And that other tart, walking out on me. I must be going soft in the head. It's about time that you bitches remember who you're dealing with.'

Grabbing Louisa by the hair, he dragged her through to the kitchen, rage rendering him oblivious to her screams. Pippa leaving him in the way she had, and her parting words, had left him feeling humiliated. 'I'll show you who's the boss around here,' he shrieked, as he slung Louisa towards the stove. Slumping onto a seat at the table, he demanded, 'Warm me some food!'

As Louisa lit the gas under the pot, her hand shaking, Dickie grimaced, thoughts of Pippa running through his mind. Picking up a vase of almost-wilted flowers, he lobbed it angrily in Louisa's direction. 'I'll fuckin' ruin her,' he hissed, 'I'll destroy her fuckin' life!'

7

Louisa lay awake in bed, unmoving, hardly daring to breathe, whilst Dickie snored loudly beside her. As the morning sun began to rise, she slipped out from under the blankets, hoping her husband wouldn't stir.

Pulling on her clothes, Louisa felt sore down below and fought to hold back tears. She'd always known it would be her duty to accommodate Dickie's needs, but she hadn't expected him to be so cold. There'd been no kisses, no cuddles, no affection. Just a drunken fumble as he'd taken her virginity whilst mumbling another woman's name. It had been a relief when he'd finally finished and rolled off, leaving her crying silently in the darkness.

Padding quietly down the stairs, she raked out the embers from the hearth and got the coals burning before preparing Dickie's breakfast. Her body stiffened when she heard the floorboards above creaking. Would he mention anything about last night? The smashed vase, the uncaring lovemaking. He was so drunk; she wondered if he'd even remember. It was something she'd *never* forget, and she hoped it wouldn't happen often.

Dickie came into the kitchen and stood at the sink splashing cold water on his face.

Louisa stood nervously over the stove, stirring thick porridge. She peeked sideways at her husband, her stomach twisting into tight knots, though his rage from the night before seemed to have subsided.

'Get me coffee,' he demanded.

Louisa hurried to do his bidding, saying, 'Your breakfast is ready.'

Dickie glanced at the pot on the stove and pulled a disgusted face. 'I'm not eating that muck. Get me some bread and eggs.'

Finally, once Dickie had filled his belly, he left the house and Louisa felt she could breathe again. Abandoning the dirty pots and plate in the sink, she grabbed her coat and hat before fleeing to her mother's house.

A light frost covered the pavement, glistening and sparkling in the sunlight. Louisa trod carefully up the steps to her mother's door and tapped lightly.

'Louisa,' Myrtle exclaimed, appearing surprised to see her daughter. 'It's very early.'

'Is it?' Louisa asked. 'I didn't realise. Sorry, may I come in?'

Myrtle sighed and pulled the door open wider. 'You look tired,' she remarked. 'You must be finding married life demanding.'

Sitting on the sofa, Louisa bit on her bottom lip, struggling to conceal her sadness.

Myrtle bristled. She had never been comfortable discussing anything to do with emotions. But Louisa needed to talk to somebody. She couldn't keep her feelings bottled up any longer, and her tears spilled out.

Her mother handed her a cup of tea. 'I hope you're not expecting sympathy from me. You chose to marry Dickie over Mr Mullen. Now you must tolerate the dreadful man, just as I must.'

'You seem to get on better with him than I do!'

'No, Louisa, that is not a true statement, though I clearly tolerate him better than you.'

'But you don't know what he's like.'

'I'm sure I don't. May I remind you that you're not the only one who's unhappy with this situation. I've been forced to tell some remarkable lies to convince my friends that you fell in love with his *rough* charms. I refuse to have the likes of Mrs Bellamy and Lady Beardsley believe we were poor enough that I had to stoop so low as to find you *that* man as a husband to support us. It's been simply awful, Louisa. I can barely keep up with my fibs.'

'It must be truly horrid for you,' Louisa said sarcastically.

'It is! I'm not sure everyone believes me, and though my friends find Dickie somewhat of a laughing stock, his generous *gifts* are gaining him acceptance.'

'Good for him,' Louisa scoffed.

'Come now, Louisa, there's no need for that tone. As I said, *you* chose him over Mr Mullen. I tried to tell you it was an unwise choice, but you wouldn't listen. Now you must grin and bear it.'

Lowering her head, the memories of Dickie's outburst in the kitchen last night were still fresh in her mind, and the gash on the back of her neck was a testament to the enormous force he'd used when hurling the vase. Had it hit her on the head, it surely would have killed her! And then afterwards... the sting as he'd heartlessly consummated their marriage.

Myrtle breezed across the room and gazed out of the window. 'It isn't so bad, Louisa. You live in a sumptuous property, have the finest wardrobe, you eat well and want for nothing. I don't like to discuss such matters, but I'm sure you find your husband far more bearable in the marital bed than you would have Mr Mullen. Count your blessings.'

'Oh, Mother,' Louisa cried. 'You have no idea ...'

'And I do not wish to know! What occurs between a husband and wife is a private affair.'

'But ... Mother ... He doesn't show me—'

'Enough!' Myrtle interrupted abruptly. 'Dry your eyes and pull yourself together, Louisa. I suggest you go home and think about how fortunate you are. I always said that your father was spoiling you, and now I can see how right I was!'

Louisa should have known better than to have expected a listening ear from her mother. As she mooched back to the emptiness of Dickie's house, she questioned her untenable situation. She could leave Dickie. She could run away and start a new life. It was a selfish notion, which would result in her mother ending up destitute. But why should she care about the woman? Then horrifying images of her mother being thrown out of her precious home and onto the streets flitted through Louisa's mind. Traipsing up the steps to the front door, Louisa knew she would have to remain married to Dickie, if only for the sake of her mother.

It had been a long and bitterly cold night for twenty-four-year-old Pippa. With no money, she'd slept fretfully in a shop doorway. She had no friends to turn to for help, Dickie had made sure of that. He'd liked to keep her to himself and had discouraged any contact with friends and family. Though

Pippa had often seen her sister, Joanne, and her two nieces. But Joanne lived in Silvertown, the other side of London, and Pippa didn't have the funds to travel there.

Tired, chilly and hungry, Pippa heaved up her heavy suitcase and trekked to the second-hand jewellery shop in Clapham Junction. The biting wind stung her cheeks and made her eyes water. When her hat blew off and tumbled along the street, Pippa didn't have the energy to chase after it. Soon, she hoped to have some much-needed cash in her purse. She couldn't face another night outside. If the freezing temperatures didn't kill her, then she felt sure a robber would. She'd stuffed an expensive pair of earrings and matching necklace into her bloomers for safekeeping. If a thief stole her suitcase, at least her jewellery would be protected. The set had been a birthday gift from Dickie. Now all she had to do was sell it. The sale would give her enough money for a room for a few weeks, and in the meantime, Pippa intended to look for work. *Gawd knows what I'll do*, she thought, dismayed at her lack of experience and skills in anything. *Nine flippin' years wasted*, she thought. She'd met Dickie when she'd been fifteen years old. He was all she'd ever known and she'd loved him deeply.

Turning a corner, she baulked when she saw his car driving towards her. There were so few motor vehicles on the streets of Battersea, she was sure it had to be him. Darting back around the corner, Pippa pushed her back against the wall and breathed in, hoping that Dickie hadn't seen her and would drive past. She wasn't afraid of him, but she knew him well enough to know he wouldn't have taken their break-up well. The man was prone to dark moods and a short temper. She'd once seen Dickie lose his rag, and it wasn't something she wanted to witness again. He'd flown into a blind rage when a bloke had tried to pick-pocket him. Dickie had rained down blow after blow until Pippa felt sure he was going to kill the thief! She'd do all she could to avoid seeing that fury again.

Her toes were numb from the cold when Pippa eventually arrived at the jewellers, and her shoes had rubbed her heels, giving her painful blisters. Discreetly fishing the jewellery from her undergarments, she gazed at the emerald and diamond set. She wouldn't be sorry to see them sold and soon, so she could sit in the warmth of the tearooms and buy herself a hot drink.

When she walked into the shop, the middle-aged man behind the counter studied her suspiciously over the top of his spectacles. Smartly dressed in a three-piece suit with a pocket watch on a gold chain, Pippa realised she must look a mess in contrast. Her clothes were creased and grubby, her hair tangled. She hoped it wasn't too obvious that she'd spent the night on the streets.

'Can I help you?' the man asked curtly.

'Yes,' Pippa said, placing the earrings and necklace on the glass-topped counter. 'I'd like to sell these.'

The jeweller removed the spectacles balancing on the end of his nose and regarded Pippa with annoyance. 'I do not purchase stolen goods,' he stated firmly, his hands spread flat on the counter.

Pippa protested. 'They're not stolen! The earrings and necklace were a gift for my birthday.'

'I've had your sort in here before and there's always a tale to tell. I wasn't born yesterday, young lady. Take your stolen items and your thieving self from my shop … or I shall send for the police.'

'Please, you don't understand. I promise, the jewellery is mine. I'm not a thief. My, erm, circumstances have changed, and I've found myself fallen on hard times. This jewellery is all I have, and I really need to sell it. Look,' Pippa said desperately, picking up one of the earrings and shoving it towards the man's face. 'Look, emeralds and diamonds. It must be worth a good price.'

'The stones are coloured glass. Your *jewellery* is worthless.'

'No … No, you're wrong. Take a closer look, please. They're real diamonds.'

'I've been looking at real diamonds since I was a lad. I can assure you I don't need to take a closer look to tell you that the stones are fake. And not very good fakes, either.'

Pippa didn't believe him. She thought he was denying their worth so he could buy them cheaply. 'How much would you give me for the set?' she asked, anxious.

'Nothing. I only buy and sell *real* stones.'

'Please, they must be worth something!'

'Not to me.'

Before Pippa could plead further, the door swung open, and a couple entered the shop. Pippa noticed that the man looked remarkably similar to the jeweller. The woman appeared harassed, and her puffy eyes suggested she'd been crying.

The jeweller looked past Pippa and addressed the couple. 'Isaac, Sara, what are you doing here? Is everything well?'

'No, Saul, everything is not well, my brother. Far from well. We've lost our house, the business, the lot! I didn't know what to do, so —'

'So you came here,' the jeweller said, 'and you did the right thing.'

The woman began to cry quietly. 'Oh, Saul, you couldn't imagine the horrors we've seen. So many dead. Children blown apart. Blood, smoke, flames. Homes destroyed. I ... I think I may faint again.'

Saul rushed out from behind the counter with a chair and urged Sara to sit down.

'Was it an airship dropping bombs?' he asked Isaac.

'We don't know. We thought it was at first, but there are rumours that a fire caused an explosion in Brunner Mond, the TNT refinery. All of Silvertown is destroyed, Saul. And the gasometer at Greenwich went up, too. A huge fireball filled the sky above it. Didn't you see it?'

'No, but I heard the explosion. There must have been a lot of TNT in the factory for me to have heard a blast in the East End docks here! And I saw the orange glow in the sky, but I didn't realise you were caught up in it.'

'I can't tell you how bad it is. The fires were still burning when we left. Hundreds and thousands of homes gone or damaged, and I dread to think how many dead. There were tugboats ferrying folk to the hospital, but some of the injuries I saw were beyond belief. I'm sorry to ask, Saul, but can we stay with you for a while?'

'You don't need to ask,' Saul assured him.

Pippa's mind was reeling. Her sister lived near Silvertown with her two children. 'My family,' she mumbled. Then looking at Isaac, she blurted in panic, 'Do you know what has become of the residents of Albert Road? My sister lives on Albert Road. Joanne. Mrs Joanne Hudson, and her two girls. Do you know them? Are they safe?'

Isaac had a look of pity in his dark eyes. 'I'm sorry, I

couldn't say. But to be honest with you, Albert Road would have taken the brunt of the blast.'

Pippa's mouth was so dry, she could barely swallow. Her sister and her two nieces were the only family she had, and Joanne was her best friend. 'I must find them … how – how can I get there? I don't have any money.'

'You can't get into the area,' Isaac explained. 'The police won't let you through. I don't know what to suggest. Maybe check the hospitals. Here,' he said, and pulled several coins from a small leather pouch. 'This will cover your fare.'

'I – I don't know what to say,' Pippa said, blinking back tears. 'Thank you. Thank you very much.'

As she went to leave the shop, forgetting her worthless jewellery on the counter, Saul called to her.

'Wait.' The jeweller opened his cash register and handed Pippa some coins. 'I'll pray for your sister,' he said softly.

The kindness of strangers astounded Pippa, but the overwhelming feeling of fear for the safety of her family swamped her. Her heart was pounding fast and hard. She had to know if her sister was alive. Hurrying to the door, she called over her shoulder, 'Thank you. You're both so kind. I'll be praying for her, too.'

8

Three months later – April 1917
Canning Town, East London

It had taken Pippa over a week to learn that her sister and the girls had been killed in the explosion at Silvertown. Speculation still hung in the air that it was something to do with German sabotage. No one really knew the truth about what had caused the blast. Reports stated that seventy-three people had lost their lives, but after seeing the devastation first hand, Pippa suspected the death toll was probably higher.

She'd spent weeks wandering the unfamiliar area, a lost soul, not knowing what to do with herself. Begging, even singing for her supper, sleeping rough or finding warmth and refuge in the bed of a dock worker. Losing her sister had sent Pippa into a downward spiral of misery. Her life felt hopeless, cheap beer being her only solace and her new best friend.

Wandering aimlessly through the slum area of Canning Town, Pippa smacked her lips together, desperate for a drink.

A man passed her, and she held out her grubby hand. 'Spare a ha'penny, sir?' she begged.

'Get lost,' he replied, eyeing her with revulsion.

Pippa's filthy dress was ripped and frayed around the hem, and dark patches of days- or even weeks-old vomit encrusted the front. Catching her reflection in a shop window, Pippa peered at herself. She was unrecognisable from the smartly dressed woman who'd walked out on Dickie and left her hometown of Battersea. Her hair tangled and thick with muck, her face grimy and her clothes in rags, Pippa shrugged. Her suitcase had been stolen. She had nothing, and she needed a drink. The beer helped her to forget. It blocked out the pain of her grief. It stopped her from dwelling on the life she'd lost with Dickie, and it numbed the longing for a baby of her own to hold.

Slipping into the shop, the shopkeeper rushed out from behind his counter.

'Out,' he yelled, shooing her towards the door. 'I won't have the likes of you in here.'

Pippa had hoped to pinch something from the convenience store, something she could sell to make a few pennies to buy some beer. But the eagle-eyed shopkeeper had scuppered her plans.

'All right, get your hands off me,' she moaned, flailing her arms.

'Get out and stay out!'

'I will. I'll take my money elsewhere!'

'Money, huh! Who are you trying to kid? Just clear off.'

A while later, Pippa found herself standing outside the Liverpool Arms, a huge pub on the corner of Barking Road. When the doors opened, she breathed in deeply, inhaling the smell of beer wafting from inside.

She saw two men in flat caps and heavy donkey-jackets heading towards the pub, their heads down and their shoulders hunched. As they walked to the door, Pippa stood in front of them, blocking their way.

'Can I pleasure you for the cost of a beer?'

The shorter of the men turned his face away. 'You stink, love. You won't get no trade smelling like that.'

'Please, just one beer. I'll do anything you like …'

The taller man nudged the shorter one, and they both shook their heads before walking around Pippa and into the pub.

Pippa didn't care that she stunk, she just wanted a drink. But she knew she'd have to freshen up if she were to have any hope of finding a man to pay her for sex. Heading towards the River Lee, she wasn't enthused about the idea of bathing in its cold waters, though she was thankful that at least the sun was shining, offering some light warmth.

Pushing through the reeds, Pippa held her breath as she waded into the river. *Flippin' 'eck*, she thought, gasping as the icy-feeling water reached the top of her thighs. As she went to dunk herself deeper, a painful cramp gripped her womb. Bending forwards and holding her lower stomach, Pippa groaned in agony. She saw blood rising to the surface of the water. Her blood. It was coming from between her legs. Another unbearable cramp clenched, and Pippa felt the urge to bear down. 'Oh, God, help me,' she cried, as the terrible truth dawned on her. Sobbing, she wailed, 'Not again … Please, not again. I can't lose another child … I can't.'

Pippa was pregnant, but amongst the reeds of the River Lee, in the cold water, she lost Dickie's unborn child, and her heart broke.

9

Six months later – October 1917
Sunday

'Push, Mrs Newman, push. That's it, I can see the head.'

Louisa gritted her teeth, writhing in agony as another contraction ripped through her body and sweat dripped down the back of her neck. Her dignity was gone; Louisa was in too much pain to be concerned about the doctor's face between her legs.

The doctor moved from the end of the bed to stand beside her, and placed a strange, funnel-like contraption on her hugely swollen stomach. Lowering his head, he put his ear to the top of the contraption and smiled. 'A good, strong heartbeat.'

'Arghhh,' Louisa screeched.

'You're nearly there now, Mrs Newman. Nice quick breaths. Quite right. Terrible business in Camberwell last week, wouldn't you agree?'

Louisa didn't know what the doctor was talking about, and didn't care. If he was trying to take her mind from the pain, then he was failing dismally.

'Several were killed in the night raid. The Zeppelins are atrocious. Silent and deadly. Though the daytime air raids by the fleets of Gotha aircraft are equally as fearsome. Have you seen the planes in the sky, Mrs Newman? It's quite a sight!'

Another contraction gripped Louisa and she felt the overwhelming urge to push.

'There we are,' the doctor soothed, 'welcome to the world, Miss Newman.'

Louisa strained her neck, trying to get a first glimpse of her newborn baby. A nurse swaddled the child in a blanket and smiled warmly as she handed the bundle to Louisa.

'A girl, you say?' Louisa asked, elated but disappointed at the same time.

'Yes, a bonny lass,' the nurse replied.

Dickie had hoped for a boy. A son. Louisa's heart raced as she wondered how her husband would react to discovering he had a daughter instead.

As the infant girl stretched her lungs and let out an almighty cry, the bedroom door was flung open wide. Louisa turned her head to see Dickie filling the frame.

'Well?' he asked.

Louisa swallowed hard and tilted the bundle so that Dickie could see the beautiful face of his daughter. 'A girl,' she said anxiously. 'We have a beautiful baby girl.'

Dickie's expression of anticipation changed to a contorted look of contempt. 'A snivelling, useless girl. Christ, woman, can't you do anything right?'

'But ... but ... but she's beautiful, Dickie,' Louisa protested.

Dickie couldn't have heard her. He'd already stormed off, making his displeasure more than clear by slamming the front door closed.

The nurse smiled awkwardly. 'Don't worry, dear, he'll come round to the idea of having a daughter. They always do.'

Louisa nodded her head, but she knew Dickie would never be interested in his daughter. His heart had been set on a boy. 'It's all right, little one. You'll be adored. I have enough love for you.'

'Does she have a name?' the nurse asked.

Louisa peered dotingly at her daughter. 'Grace,' she whispered, 'her name is Grace Newman.'

Dickie's jaw was taut as his booted feet thudded along the street, his arms swinging. 'Keep up, Ernie,' he barked over his shoulder.

'You all right, Boss?'

'No. I flamin' well ain't!'

Catching him up, Ernie was obviously waiting for an explanation for Dickie's foul mood.

'She had a girl,' he enlightened the man.

'Oh, right. Judging by your reaction, I'm guessing congratulations ain't in order.'

'No. I tell you, Ernie, I hope no one fucks me about today, 'cos I'm ready to kick the shit out of anyone who crosses me.'

Fortunately for the health of his tenants, everyone paid the due rents without a problem. Until they knocked on the door of the third house from the end of the street. No one answered.

'Who lives in this place?' Dickie asked impatiently.

Ernie glanced at the rent book. 'That Irish family have one ground room, and Mrs Love the other. They're both paid up to date. Fred Rippon is on the middle floor. His missus paid in advance. But Wally Kingston on the top floor is in arrears. A month now. I've been looking for the slippery bastard, but no one's seen hide nor hair of him.'

'Right, he's out. Bang on the window.'

Mrs Love pulled back the ragged curtain, frowning when she saw Dickie. Opening the front door, she folded her frail arms across her flat chest. 'My rent isn't due,' she said, her voice gravelly.

Dickie thought that the old woman had lost a lot of weight and didn't look well. He hoped she wasn't about to croak it. Mrs Love had lived in the property for years and had never fallen behind with her rent. She was one of his best tenants.

'Have you seen Wally Kingston?' Ernie asked. 'Has he been home lately?'

'Yeah. He's upstairs, him and a woman.'

Ernie looked behind to Dickie, smirking, then gently pushed past Mrs Love.

'Don't be too hard on him,' Mrs Love said, as Dickie followed in behind Ernie.

Dickie didn't answer the old woman and took the rickety stairs two at a time. When he reached the top landing, Ernie had already given Wally's door a kick. The rotten wood easily splintered, and the door flew open.

Ernie stood to one side to allow Dickie to charge in first. The room was in darkness, pallet wood nailed to the windows.

'What's going on?' a woman yelled.

Dickie recognised the voice. His eyes searched the gloomy room until they fell upon a single bed. And then he saw her. Pippa. She was sitting up in the bed, her red hair dishevelled, holding the covers to her naked chest to hide her modesty. Dickie was taken aback to see the woman who'd boldly walked out on him nine months earlier. He'd tried to track her down, searching Battersea for her, determined to make her life hell. And now, here she was, in Wally Kingston's bed.

Dickie didn't need to ruin her life. The woman had done a good enough job of that herself.

'Where is he?' Ernie growled.

'He's not here,' Pippa replied, her eyes on Dickie.

Ernie stomped towards the bed and grabbed the thin blankets.

'What do you think you're doing?' Pippa screeched, trying to bat Ernie away.

He yanked the blankets off the bed, revealing Pippa's nude body and Wally Kingston attempting to hide between her legs.

Wally jumped up, his eyes wide with fear, and clumsily ran towards the door. As he attempted to escape, Dickie pulled back his arm and landed a heavy punch square on Wally's nose.

Wally's feet lifted from the floor as he fell backwards, landing on his back with a thump.

Pippa screamed. 'Don't hurt him … Please, Dickie, don't hurt him!' she begged.

'Get dressed,' he snarled at her.

As Pippa scrambled for her clothes, Ernie towered over Wally.

'You owe a month's rent. Time to pay up,' he said threateningly.

'I will pay ya … I promise, I will … I'll get the money. Tomorrow. I'll have the money tomorrow.'

Dickie picked up the man's trousers from the floor and searched his pockets. Empty. Then he saw Wally's jacket and searched it. A few pennies but not nearly enough to cover the debt.

'Consider yourself evicted,' he said, and then nodded to Ernie.

Ernie stood astride Wally and threw down punch after punch.

Pippa had quickly pulled on her dress and went to yank at Ernie, but Dickie grabbed her from behind, his strong arms wrapped around her waist, tugging her back.

As he held her firmly in his grip, she begged for mercy for Wally. 'Please, stop! Christ, you're going to kill him! Stop, Ernie, he's had enough!'

Dickie growled in her ear. 'He's had enough when I say he's had enough.'

'You bastard,' Pippa screamed. 'Stop him, Dickie, stop him!'

Dickie waited a few more moments, holding Pippa firmly as she wriggled to free herself.

'All right, Ernie,' he said at last.

Ernie finally stopped punishing Wally and stood upright, looking down at the bloodied mess on the floor. 'He ain't so good looking now.' Then he turned to Dickie. 'What about her? What you gonna do with her?'

Dickie could think of several things that he wanted to do with Pippa. He would have liked to slap some sense into her for a start. Wally Kingston. Pippa had lowered herself to be with Wally Kingston! The man was known for putting women to work on the streets as prostitutes. He wondered if that's what Wally had done with Pippa and his stomach turned. Dickie couldn't abide the thought of another man touching her.

He grabbed Pippa's arms, gripping them tightly. Shaking her, he demanded, 'Are you his whore? Is that what you're doing with him? Is he pimping you out?'

Pippa glared rebelliously at him. 'No, I'm not his whore,' she spat. 'And even if I was, it's none of your business!'

Spinning her around, he grabbed a handful of hair at the back of her head and wrenched her towards Wally. Shoving her face down, he forced her to look at the man's pummelled face. 'See that ... Take a good look. That is what will happen to any man I find you with,' he warned through gritted teeth.

Pippa began to cry. 'I hate you, Dickie Newman,' she sobbed.

Dickie glanced at Ernie, and ordered, 'You can piss off now, and take him with you.'

'See you later, Boss,' Ernie said, as he sloped out of the room, dragging the unconscious body of Wally with him.

Pippa held her head high and sucked in her tear-streaked cheeks. 'Am I free to leave, too?' she asked.

Dickie drew in a long breath as he thought about what to do with her. She still aroused feelings in him that no other woman ever had. He remembered her humour, and how he used to laugh with her. Real, proper belly laughing. He'd been so happy with her. And she'd blown his mind between the sheets. Christ, he wished things could go back to how they'd been before he'd married Louisa. But they couldn't. Not ever. Pippa had been with Wally Kingston and gawd knows who else. Dickie could never lie with her again, and he'd lost all respect for the woman. Yet he couldn't let her go, either. His mind was in turmoil.

'Well,' Pippa pressed. 'Can I go?'

Dickie shoved her away from him, glaring at her with revulsion. 'Yeah, go on, fuck off. But I'm warning you, Pippa ... I ain't finished with you yet.'

'What's that supposed to mean?'

'The day you walked out on me, I told you I'd ruin you. And believe you me, I will.'

'Huh, do your worst, Dickie. You can't do anything to me that could be half as bad as what I've been through recently.'

Pippa grabbed her coat and a small bag from the end of the bed and headed towards the door. Before walking out, she glanced at Dickie, holding his gaze.

'I miss you … I miss us … Goodbye, Dickie.'

He wanted to call after her, to take her in his arms and kiss her full lips. But he looked down at the worn floorboards and saw Wally's blood. *She's vile*, he thought, reminded of where he'd found her. *Disgusting and vile. I won't have her, and I'll make sure no one else has her, either.*

10

Pippa sat on a wooden bench in the graveyard and stared aimlessly at folk leaving the church in their Sunday best. The reverend stood on the steps, shaking hands with the wealthier men of his congregation, ignoring those dressed in tatters. She'd never stepped inside a church, not even for the funerals of her sister and two nieces. But she had prayed. She'd prayed the day she'd miscarried in the River Lee, pleading with God to keep her three unborn children safe until she could be with them. She'd asked God for strength to help her overcome her demons. Pippa couldn't be sure if her prayers had been answered, but after climbing out of the River Lee, beer had never touched her lips again.

Losing the baby had been a wake-up call. Pippa had known she couldn't continue living that way, and she'd managed to find a job in domestic service as a scullery maid. At the time, she'd been grateful for the opportunity, especially as she believed she'd looked unemployable. But a kind housekeeper had given her a chance, so Pippa had cleaned herself up and worked hard. Unfortunately, the job hadn't lasted. She had walked out when one of the butlers had accosted her.

But she'd managed to save a few shillings from her meagre wages and had made her way back to Battersea, where she'd walked into a job cleaning train carriages, work once done exclusively by men before the war.

A familiar figure broke away from the congregation and walked towards her. Pippa smiled weakly at Lillian Blackshaw, a woman she worked with who'd become a close friend.

Lillian sat beside Pippa on the bench. 'Hello, Pip. Was you contemplating coming to church this morning?' she asked.

Pippa shook her head. 'No, I'm not religious.'

'What are you doing sat here, then? You look ever so downcast.'

'I dunno. Thinking.'

'Penny for your thoughts.'

Pippa sighed. 'I was thinking about my sister.'

'You must miss her. That explosion in Silvertown was such a tragedy.'

'I think about her and the girls every day. I hope they didn't suffer.'

Lillian reached out and placed her gloved hand over Pippa's, giving it a gentle squeeze. 'I thought you were seeing Wally today?' she asked.

Pippa shuddered and closed her eyes, trying to block out the horrendous sight of Wally's battered face. She was silent for a moment before saying, 'I'm not with Wally anymore.'

'I thought you really liked him.'

'I did, but let's face it, Lillian, Wally was never going to amount to anything. The man didn't have a job. I could never have married him and had a family.'

'No, and I know it's not my place to say, but I never liked him. I've heard things about him, bad things.'

'I always pick the wrong men. All I want is a good husband and lots of children. I yearn for children, Lillian, but it looks like I'm destined to become an old spinster.'

'We'll see about that. I'm about to head home. There's a Victoria sponge waiting for me. Won't you join me?'

Pippa shrugged. She didn't think she'd be good company, but didn't want to be alone. 'If you're sure?'

'Yes, of course. Mother always enjoys me bringing friends home for her to meet. She's housebound.'

'Why? Is she poorly?'

'Not that you can see. Her mind is sick. She's terrified of leaving the house. She won't even walk out onto the front step. Come on, see for yourself. You'll like Mother.'

Pippa walked along the street, feeling rather scruffy compared to Lillian. Her friend, just two years older, had immaculately groomed blonde hair, pinned in small curls under her hat. Her boots were polished, and the white collar of her dress was neatly starched.

They chatted easily, mostly about the weather and the Suffragette movement. Lillian didn't believe women would ever receive the right to vote, and Pippa thought it was an outrage they were doing the jobs of men, yet earning a fraction of the wages.

'What are you two nattering and moaning about?' Mrs Blackshaw asked, beckoning the young women inside.

'Women's rights,' Lillian answered. 'Mother, this is Pippa. You remember I told you about Pip. We work together.'

'Yes, yes you did. Such a pleasure to meet you. Please, make yourself comfortable. I'll fetch some tea.'

Pippa's nose twitched at the homely aroma wafting through the house. Freshly baked bread, lavender and a faint whiff of carbolic soap. The smell brought back memories of her childhood and the loving home she'd shared with her sister.

Mrs Blackshaw bustled back into the room. 'I like the colour of your hair, Pippa. I had a cat with that same colour hair. Sooty, we called him.'

'Wouldn't the name Sooty have suited a black cat better?' Pippa asked, bemused.

'When he was alive, we called him Carrot, on account of him being orange. Carrot died when a dog got hold of him. My husband burned Carrot's body in an oil drum in the back yard. And that's when his name changed to Sooty. See. It all makes sense.'

Pippa exchanged a glance with Lillian and they both chuckled.

'What's so funny?' Mrs Blackshaw asked, her eyes flitting between the two women.

'You, Mother. You're so funny.'

'Oh, I don't know about that. Pack it in, the pair of you, and eat your cake. It's a Victoria sponge. I met the Queen, you know, on the Isle of Wight.'

'You met Queen Victoria?' Pippa asked, intrigued.

'Yes, I did. It was late in the last century. My husband took me on a steam-ferry across the Solent to the Isle of Wight. I thought it would be such an adventure, but it was awful. The contents of my stomach ended up feeding the fish. Anyways, I was in a little rowing boat, minding me own business with my husband on the oars, and I looks over, and I sees this head bobbing about in the water. *Look, Fin*, I shouts, Fin being my husband, *there's someone drowning in the water.* Then Fin points out the bathing machine in the sea just off the shoreline, and explains to me that the person's head I can see in the waves is none other than the Queen herself, and the wooden shed-like contraption on wheels that's on the beach were what the Queen used to change into her bathing costume. It were private for her, and Fin said the bathing machine would be rolled out into the sea, and when the Queen had finished swimming, she'd climb back inside and be winched back to the sands. All very modest. We were just off the private beach of Osborne House, see.'

'So, Mother didn't actually *meet* the Queen,' Lillian pointed out. 'But she did see her head, from a distance. Quite a long distance.'

Pippa chuckled again. It felt good to laugh, though the traumatic encounter with Dickie Newman and the state of poor Wally were still at the forefront of her mind.

Mrs Blackshaw continued. 'That were a Sunday when I saw the Queen, so every Sunday since that day, I bakes a Victoria sponge in her honour.'

'It's delicious, Mrs Blackshaw, thank you.'

'You're more than welcome, pet.'

'Where's our Billy?' Lillian asked, and threw Pippa a cheeky grin.

'Here I am.'

Pippa looked towards the door where the deep voice had come from and saw a tall, blond man standing there with his hands shoved into his trouser pockets.

'This is Pippa, my friend from work,' Lillian announced to her brother. 'She's just been hearing about Mother's encounter with Queen Victoria.'

Billy smiled and looked at Pippa, extending his arm to shake her hand. 'Nice to meet you,' he said, gazing into her eyes.

Pippa's stomach flipped, and she could feel her cheeks flushing pink. Lillian had mentioned that her brother was home on ten days' leave after being away on the frontline in France for fifteen months, but she'd failed to say how handsome Billy was!

'Sit down, pet, and join us. I expect you've missed my cakes,' Mrs Blackshaw said, looking proudly at her son.

'Cor, I have, Mother. I don't know how you're going to bake your cakes when the government introduces compulsory rationing. Sugar will be rationed soon, you mark my words.'

'I hope not, son.'

'David Lloyd George won't have a choice. The voluntary schemes are failing. If the prime minister doesn't bring in rationing soon, the nation will starve.'

Pippa wasn't knowledgeable on current affairs. It wasn't something she took much of an interest in. But she was impressed with Billy's well-informed conversation. And when he turned to look at her again, she felt her pulse race.

Lillian leaned into Pippa, whispering in her ear. 'I knew you'd like him.'

She did, she really did! *Stop it*, Pippa chastised herself, reminding herself that Wally was lying in an alley somewhere, bruised and sore. And it had only been a few hours ago when Dickie had warned her about what would happen to any man she became involved with. Blinking hard, she tried to get the image of Wally's blood out of her mind. She didn't want to be responsible for Billy meeting the same fate as Wally. After all, Dickie Newman was a man of his word.

11

'Isn't she the cutest thing you've ever seen?' Louisa gushed to her mother, proudly showing off Grace.

Myrtle sat beside the bed, only throwing the child the merest of glimpses. 'At least she takes after her father and not you. Her eyes appear straight, and she has Dickie's more delicate, though striking, features. But babies change. She's only one day old. I do hope the resemblance to her father remains. God help the girl if she ends up looking like you.'

Louisa wasn't hurt by her mother's cruel words. In fact, she agreed with the woman and had thought the same.

'Don't look at me like that, Louisa, I'm only being honest.'

'And rightly so,' Louisa said. 'Do you think Dickie will ever love her? He's not been in to see her yet and was so upset when he learned I'd birthed a girl.'

'I don't know, dear. Dickie is an enigma. He can be so charming, as I've seen with many of my friends and acquaintances, yet he seems to have a swinging brick for a heart.'

'I know. But how could he not fall in love with Grace?'

'I've been closely observing Dickie of late, and I believe I know what makes him tick. Dickie is drawn to powerful men.

He respects strength. You rarely listen to my advice, Louisa, but trust me – do not spoil your daughter as your father did you. Raise her to be a strong woman. In that way, Dickie may come to love her.'

Louisa's eyebrows raised, believing her mother was making a good point. 'But how? How do I raise Grace to be strong?'

'Admonish her when she cries. Do not pander to her when she falls and grazes herself. Do not mollycoddle her when she's poorly. Be firm. Be strict. Do not do everything for her. Teach her to be independent. Imagine that Grace is a boy. Wouldn't you treat a son differently? Yes, of course you would. Raise Grace as if she were a boy.'

'Oh, I see. I'm not sure I can do that.'

'If you want your child to have her father's respect and to be held in his affections, then you must put your nurturing instincts aside, and be tough with her. Otherwise, I'm afraid Dickie will show Grace the same derision he shows you.'

Louisa peered at Grace sleeping peacefully in her arms. Her mother's words spun around in her head. *Be tough with her.* She could see it made good sense. She wanted Dickie to love their daughter, and if that meant being harsh with the girl, then so be it.

Dickie tried to concentrate but he couldn't shake thoughts of Pippa. He wondered where she was living, what she was doing.

'As it stands, Mr Newman, the properties you're referring to are on the plans for slum clearance.'

Dickie exhaled the smoke from his cigar and swirled the brandy in his glass. Sitting in the luxury of the elite gentlemen's club in Mayfair, he smiled at the man who could sway the council's and the local government's decision. Sir John Staples happened to be the most influential peer in the borough of Wandsworth and sat in the House of Lords.

'That would be a shame, that, Sir John. If my properties are pulled down to make way for better housing, I can guarantee you that Battersea will find itself with a homeless crisis. I've got hundreds living in conditions that ain't fit for a pig, but they've got cover. Four walls and a roof, and that's important. They're robbers, tarts and heavy drinkers. At least ninety percent of them will end up dying on the borough's streets, 'cos when I say they won't afford the rents of this so-called *better* housing, I ain't telling untruths.'

'Of course, Mr Newman, the rents will be levelled at an affordable cost, probably below market value.'

'With respect, Sir John, you don't know these people like I do. Any price above what they are paying now won't be doable for them. And even if they could afford to pay, they won't respect the properties. Give it six months, and all that nice, new, comfortable housing will be in a shit state.'

'The plans are already drawn.'

'Yeah, I understand, but surely it would be better to bypass the two streets I'm referring to, save the council a load of money and headaches, and reinvest somewhere more *worthy*. What do you say, Sir John, am I talking sense?'

'It's really not my decision to make, Mr Newman.'

'I know, but you can change their minds. And by the way, whilst I think of it, I happen to know it's Lady Staples' birthday next week. I hope you don't mind, but I've taken the liberty of treating your good wife.'

Dickie took an envelope stuffed with cash from the inside pocket of his jacket and placed it on the highly polished, dark wood table. Sliding it across to Sir John, he smiled. 'You know your wife better than me. Perhaps you'd like to buy her a gift with this.'

Sir John glanced around uncomfortably, checking that no one was witnessing the exchange, before quickly picking up the envelope and stuffing it in his pocket. 'I'm sure Lady Staples will be most grateful,' he said, with a nod of his head. Rising to his feet, he added, 'Rest assured, Mr Newman. Your properties will remain as they are.'

Dickie felt smug as Sir John made a hasty exit. Just as he'd always believed, money talked with the rich and he was realising how much he could buy. All it took was a generous handshake and a word in the right ear.

'Anything else, sir?' the waiter asked.

'Has Chief Constable Crawford been in?'

'Yes, sir, earlier today. He left an hour ago.'

Dickie scowled, disappointed that he'd missed the man, though he was satisfied with the rapport they were building. He felt confident that it wouldn't be long before he had the coppers eating out of his hand, too. *This wealthy and fancy set are more bleedin' corrupt than the rest of us*, he thought, glad they were easily bought. Myrtle's introductions were paying dividends, and though he'd been lumbered with a wife and now a daughter for whom he had no time, he had no regrets about marrying Louisa – except for Pippa. The thought of her left a gnarled knot in his stomach. He hated her, or did he love her? He couldn't be sure. But he'd make certain that no man ever touched her again.

12

Two weeks had passed, and Pippa had managed to avoid seeing Billy again, though Lillian had tried to arrange for her brother to meet Pippa on many occasions. She'd found her thoughts often drifting to the handsome Billy, but the memory of what had happened to Wally haunted her dreams. And deep down, although Dickie was an evil bastard, she still loved the man and dreamed of a life with him and their children.

After finishing work, Pippa strolled down St John's Hill with Lillian by her side. A woman passed, pushing a cumbersome perambulator. Pippa gazed yearningly inside, her heart aching for a child.

'You and my brother would make beautiful babies,' Lillian teased.

Pippa shook her head, sighing.

'Won't you write to him, Pip? I know Billy would be overjoyed to hear from you.'

'Oh, Lillian, I wish I could, but you don't understand.'

'No, I don't. Billy knocks spots off that Wally fella that you were with. Why won't you get to know Billy better? He's a good man, Pip, and even though I'm his sister, I can say he's very good looking.'

'I know. But it's ... It's complicated. Tell me, have you heard from Eddie?'

Lillian sighed. 'Changing the subject again. All right, I get it. You don't want to talk about Billy, and you won't tell me what's so complicated. Fine. But I know how much you want a family, Pip, and Billy would be a great father. And best of all, you'd be my sister-in law!'

'I'd love that, Lillian, truly I would. But unfortunately, it can't ever happen.'

'Sometimes I feel like I'm banging my head against a brick wall.'

'I'm sorry. Anyway, you were going to tell me about Eddie.'

Lillian beamed, and Pippa instantly knew she had received a letter from her fella. 'Tell me,' she encouraged, giving her friend a gentle nudge in the ribs.

'I've been dying to tell you ... I haven't said anything to Mother yet ... Oh, Pip, I think I might burst with excitement ... Eddie has said we should marry when he's next on leave!'

Pippa smiled, delighted to see her friend so happy. Throwing her arms around Lillian, she gushed, 'Congratulations!'

'Thank you. I'm going to be Mrs Redditch, and I can't wait!'

'That's lovely news, Lillian, and I'm sure your mother will be thrilled, too.'

'I hope so. She likes Eddie, which is good, because we shall have to live at Mother's. I can't leave her, Pip. She needs me.'

Another woman passed them, holding the hand of a small girl. Pippa met the girl's eyes, wishing she could scoop the child into her arms and hold her as her own.

Lillian's voice broke her thoughts. 'So, do you?'

'Sorry, pardon?'

'That man, do you know him?'

Lillian discreetly nodded her head to the other side of the road, and Pippa saw Ernie glaring across at her.

'Oh, him. Yes. Don't look his way. Just keep on walking. Hurry.'

'Who is he? He doesn't look very friendly!'

'Please, Lillian, just hurry!'

Pippa looped her arm through Lillian's and almost dragged her along the street.

'You're scaring me. Who is he, Pip?'

'Trust me, Lillian, he's not a nice man and the less you know, the better.'

Pippa looked across the street, but she couldn't see Ernie. Then her breath caught in her throat when she felt a harsh tap on her shoulder. Spinning around, her heart pounding, she came face to face with him.

'Dickie sends his regards,' he sneered. 'He's none too pleased about your job on the railways.'

Pippa stood speechless as fear flooded her. With clammy hands, and as her heart hammered and blood rushed through her veins, she began to feel light-headed.

Ernie's menacing eyes fell on Lillian. 'And he's not happy about the company you're keeping, Pippa,' he warned. 'I'll be seeing you, so best you watch your back, *sweetheart*,' he added, before stomping away.

'Who was that?' Lillian demanded to know, her voice shaky.

Pippa still couldn't speak. Her mind raced. She'd have to leave her job and find somewhere else to live, away from Battersea. The chances were, if Dickie knew where she was working, then he'd also know where she was living. Her eyes shot to Lillian. The woman looked petrified.

'I'm sorry, I can't be your friend,' Pippa blurted. 'It's not safe for you to know me. Stay away, Lillian. Please, stay away from me and never speak to me again!'

Lillian's face screwed up in consternation as Pippa fled. She ran and ran until her lungs ached for air. Gasping for breath, Pippa leaned against a garden wall, tears pricking her eyes. *I hate you, Dickie Newman. Hate, hate, hate you!*

Pippa didn't own much. It wouldn't take her long to pack her clothes. Though reluctant to run away from Dickie, she knew she had no choice. He'd told her he would ruin her, and now he was sticking to his words. She'd have to start again. A new town. A new job. New friends. It wouldn't be easy, but it was better than staying put and having her world destroyed.

Pippa raced home and packed her belongings, but soon realised it was too late to travel. Knowing that she'd have to spend another night in Battersea made her heart race with fear. Sitting on the edge of her single bed, Pippa nervously chewed on her thumbnail, straining her ears to listen for any sounds outside her door. *This is going to be a long night*, she thought.

The sun had set, and with the thin curtains pulled across the window, Pippa sat in darkness. She dared not light the oil lamp. Every noise sent her heart thudding.

Creeping to the window, she moved the curtain just a tad and peeked out onto the street, praying she wouldn't see anyone hiding in the shadows. The fine hair on the back of her neck prickled. She felt sure she was being watched.

Back on her bed, Pippa decided to sleep in her clothes. She wanted to be prepared in case she had to run for her life. With her shoes still on her feet, she climbed under the covers and lay on her back, staring at the ceiling. The cry of a baby reached her ears. Pippa felt her insides tug and, placing a hand on her stomach, a tear slipped from her eye. *Oh, Dickie*, she whispered. *It could have been so different. All I ever wanted was you by my side and lots of our children.* The single tear turned into a sob as Pippa bawled for her unborn babies.

Although she tried to stay awake, she eventually cried herself to sleep and images of the babies she'd lost haunted her dreams. Pippa woke with a start, and gasped. Lying deathly still, she held her breath and watched the door, convinced that Dickie was about to burst in. Had she dreamt she'd heard his voice, threatening her, telling her he was going to kill her, or was it real? In the depths of the dark night, Pippa wasn't sure of anything anymore and didn't trust her own senses.

The minutes passed slowly, the hours even slower. Pippa tried to push her fears away, but paranoia had crept in, and she'd never felt so afraid. When the sun began to rise, she was glad of the light, but it didn't calm her nerves. Clammy, her pulse racing, her breaths fast and shallow, she knew it would take every ounce of strength she could muster to force herself out of the door. She had to get away, but that meant navigating the streets of Battersea, and Dickie could pounce at any time.

Still on her back, with the blankets up to her chin, Pippa's mind turned. Then she heard the crying baby again. 'It's all right, my love, I'm coming,' she called.

Throwing back the blankets, Pippa heaved her weary body from the bed and began searching the room. Calmly at first, but when she couldn't find the baby, she became frantic.

'Where are you, my love, where are you?'

The sound of the crying grew louder.

'It's all right, sweetie, Mummy's here,' she soothed.

Under the bed, under the wooden chair, in the wardrobe, Pippa looked everywhere and began throwing the blankets around. 'I'm here, my love, Mummy's here. Where are you hiding?'

The baby stopped crying. Pippa, her eyes wild and staring, spun from left to right. 'Don't die ... please don't die ... I can't lose another child ...'

The silence was deafening.

'Mummy's here, little one. Everything is going to be fine. Mummy and Daddy love you very much, sweetie. Mummy and Daddy ...'

Mummy and Daddy. Pippa shook her head as she remembered that Daddy wanted to ruin Mummy. 'Oh, dear God,' she said, throwing her hands over her mouth. 'What's happening to me?'

Marching back and forth along the length of the small room, Pippa tried to summon the courage to leave. The thought of opening the door and stepping outside left her feeling faint. *I've got to do this*, she told herself. *If I don't, I'll end up in a lunatic asylum!* Back and forth she paced, encouraging herself to leave.

Checking through the window again, Pippa thought she saw a man lurking behind a lamp-post. He wasn't tall enough to be Dickie, but was it Ernie? She squinted her eyes and peered harder, but there was no one there. She'd been sure she'd seen someone. Had she imagined it?

Drawing in a long and deep breath to steady her nerves, Pippa picked up her packed bag and stared hard at the door. *I can't do it, but I can't stay here, either.*

As the day passed, she began to drift into a realm between real life and fantasy. From believing she was a mother and wanting to hold her child, to convincing herself that Dickie was lying in wait on the other side of the door, ready to plunge a knife into her heart and take their child away from her. It was almost sunset before she finally opened the door. And once she did, her resolve was strong. Though beaten, Pippa had one final defiant thought: *I won't go without a parting gift for you, Dickie bleedin' Newman!* She knew he lived in a grand house somewhere in Clapham. If she could find his car, then she would find his house. *I'll burn it down*, she thought. *I won't allow my fear to win.*

Louisa couldn't settle Grace. It was late evening, and she worried that Grace's bawling would irritate Dickie. Her husband wasn't home yet, but Louisa knew he wouldn't want to walk in to hear the baby screaming.

Tucking her into a pram, Louisa cooed at the infant before carefully bonking the pram down the front steps. The motion of a gentle walk usually settled Grace. Though this evening, the girl was more fractious than normal.

Heading across Clapham Common, Grace finally began to quieten, and Louisa hoped it wouldn't be long until her daughter fell asleep. She sat on a bench, pushing the pram back and forth. 'There's a good girl,' Louisa whispered. 'Sleep now, my little one.'

A red-haired woman ambled along the path towards them. Louisa smiled politely, noticing she was carrying a large, cloth bag that looked stuffed to bursting. The woman didn't return Louisa's smile; instead, she peered at Grace's peaceful face.

'Beautiful,' the woman said admiringly, her gaze on Grace. 'Boy or a girl?'

'Girl. This is Grace,' Louisa answered proudly. 'She's only been in the world for a little over two weeks.'

Grace pulled her legs up to her chest and her tiny fists made balls as she let out a high-pitched wail.

'Oh dear,' Louisa said, jumping to her feet. 'I'm having trouble settling her this evening.'

As she reached into the pram to take Grace into her arms, the woman leaned forward.

'Please, may I? I'm good with babies.'

Louisa nodded. 'Be my guest,' she said, and stood back to allow her to pick up Grace.

The woman held Grace close to her chest, gently swaying as she patted the baby's back. 'There, there, there. What's all this noise about?' she soothed softly.

Almost instantly, Grace stopped crying and quietly began to gurgle.

'See,' the woman said. 'I told you I'm good with babies.'

Louisa smiled. 'That's amazing. I wish I could take you home with me and hire you as a nanny!'

'I'm looking for work,' the woman blurted.

Louisa suddenly felt awkward. She'd made the comment light-heartedly, though she would have appreciated a nanny to help care for Grace. The baby woke several times a night, leaving Louisa feeling exhausted. But Dickie would never agree to having any staff. He was a wealthy man, but tight with his money.

The woman continued, 'You can see I'm good with kids. I'm hard-working and trustworthy. I'd care for this one as if she were my own.'

'Oh, erm, I'm sorry, but I'm not in a position to offer you work,' Louisa explained. 'If I could, I would hire you in a second. I do apologise for the misunderstanding.'

Grace stirred, and the woman patted her back again.

'You are very good with her,' Louisa praised. 'What's your secret?'

'Keep calm. They can sense when you're uptight.'

'That's good advice, thank you.'

Louisa held her arms out towards the woman, expecting her to place Grace in them. 'I'm Mrs Newman. Louisa Newman. It's been a pleasure to meet you. Do you come to the common often?'

The woman frowned, and stepped back from Louisa, holding Grace tighter.

Louisa moved closer, saying, 'Please, I think Grace needs to lay down in the pram now.'

The woman turned her back, and Louisa could hear her mumbling.

'Grace Newman. You should have been *my* baby … Oh, my beautiful girl … Oh, my darling child, my love, I've missed you so much.'

Panic surged through Louisa. 'Excuse me, please … hand my child to me.'

The woman's head turned to look over her shoulder, and she spat, 'She's not your child! She's mine!'

She's a lunatic! Louisa thought, her body trembling. She struggled to keep her voice steady and firm. 'You are mistaken. Grace is my baby, and I need you to give her to me.'

'No! Don't touch me! Don't try and take my child from me. I won't lose another one, I won't!'

'Give me Grace,' Louisa insisted, 'please, I'm begging you.'

Louisa waited with bated breath. She didn't want to antagonise the woman, but she was desperate for her to hand over Grace. 'Please,' she pleaded, 'please give my daughter back to me.'

To Louisa's horror, the woman suddenly took off, running along the path, clutching Grace to her.

Louisa gave chase, afraid of what the stranger might do. 'Wait ... don't hurt her. Don't harm my child!'

The red-haired woman, holding Grace tightly to her, didn't look back and carried on running.

Louisa was struggling to keep up with the stranger, her eyes searching the common as she ran. 'Stop that woman,' she yelled. 'Stop her, she's stolen my baby!'

The common was unusually quiet. Louisa couldn't see anyone, yet still she shouted for help. 'Stop her! Stop that woman!'

The daylight had diminished as the woman reached the edge of the common.

Louisa wasn't far behind and continued to scream. 'Stop her! Stop her! She's stolen my baby!'

Racing across the road, the woman glanced back, her eyes wide when she saw how close Louisa was.

'WAIT!' Louisa screeched, as she ran into the road.

Excruciating pain struck and Louisa was knocked to the ground. The side of her face walloped the road. Dizzy and weak, she managed to lift her head to see a man on the ground too, a bicycle by his side. She hadn't seen the bicycle coming and realised she must have run out in front of it.

'Grace,' she murmured helplessly, as she saw the woman disappearing. 'Bring back my baby ...'

13

Word had reached Dickie that his daughter had been stolen. He raced home, screeching to a halt at the kerbside. He saw a policeman standing at the front door.

Running up the eight steps, he asked urgently, 'Have you found her?'

The policeman shook his head.

Dickie barged past the man, his mind turning. He knew the sort of depravity that was on the streets of London. Sick, evil bastards, capable of the unimaginable. Granted, he hadn't been bothered about Grace, but the notion of her being harmed turned his stomach.

He found Louisa sitting on the sofa, Myrtle beside her, and a policeman in the room, standing in front of the hearth.

'What happened?' he asked his wife.

Louisa, her eyes full of sorrow and her face grazed and swollen, cried into her handkerchief.

Myrtle answered instead. 'A woman befriended Louisa on the common and then ran off with Grace. Louisa did all she could to catch her, but was knocked to the ground by a bicycle. The police are searching for her. There haven't been any confirmed sightings of her yet.'

'Who was she?' Dickie growled. 'Who was the woman who stole my girl?'

'Louisa doesn't know. As I explained, she met her on the common, just in passing. Grace was fretful and the woman managed to calm her.'

'Didn't you get her name?'

Louisa shook her head, still quietly sobbing into her handkerchief.

Dickie ran his hand through his hair. 'Let me get this straight,' he said angrily. 'You allowed a complete stranger to pick up my girl? Someone you've never met before, obviously a deranged fuckin' nutter, you let her hold Grace and run off. Is that right?'

As Louisa cried harder, Myrtle spoke curtly. 'Louisa wasn't to know the woman was deranged. And she wasn't to know the woman would steal Grace. Please, Dickie, your language.'

'I'll speak how I see fit in my own house, Myrtle. If you don't like it, then fuck off!'

Dickie stomped to the window and pulled back the nets to look out onto the dark street. His fists clenched as abhorrent thoughts raced through his mind – anything could be happening to his daughter. Squeezing his eyes shut to try to block out the unsettling thoughts, he turned and shouted at Louisa.

'What sort of mother are you, eh? How could you let this happen? Useless, flamin' useless!' Then he spun to face the policeman. 'And what are your lot doing? Why are you in here? You should be out there searching for my girl!'

The policeman cleared his throat before replying. 'I can

assure you, Mr Newman, all our available officers are out there looking for your daughter. We won't leave a stone unturned, not until we find her and bring her home safe and sound.' He looked down at his polished boots, and added awkwardly, 'But we haven't got a lot to go on. All we know is we're looking for a red-haired woman in her twenties.'

Dickie sucked in a sharp breath. *A red-haired woman.* It was Pippa. It had to be her. The mad bitch had stolen his daughter, and Dickie muttered seethingly, 'I'll kill her. I'll fuckin' kill her!'

14

It had been hours since Pippa had run through Clapham Common with little Grace. Her arms were heavy, aching from holding the baby as she whispered, 'I'll never let you go, my sweetie, never. You're with me now. Mummy will look after you.'

The baby howled, and Pippa knew she needed feeding. 'Not long now, my sweetie, not long,' she soothed.

Pippa had managed to get back to Battersea unchallenged. She planned on returning to her room, just for the night, because she knew she had to keep the baby warm. As she turned onto her street, she baulked when she saw Ernie standing outside the front door. *Christ, what shall I do now?* she wondered. Then a thought struck her. Lillian. Her friend would help, and Pippa felt sure that Mrs Blackshaw wouldn't turn away a woman with a baby.

Darting through the labyrinth of streets, careful to be unseen, Pippa arrived at Lillian's house and tapped lightly on the door.

The house was in darkness. Pippa knocked harder.

When the door finally opened, Mrs Blackshaw looked confused.

'Pippa, is that you, pet? What are you doing here at this time of the night? And why have you got a baby?'

'Please, Mrs Blackshaw, I can explain. Can I come in?'

The woman pulled the door open wider. 'Yes, yes, of course, pet.'

In the front room, Pippa sat on the sofa, relieved to take the weight off her feet, and told Mrs Blackshaw, 'She needs feeding.'

'I'll get some Carnation milk. But I want to know what's going on.'

Pippa nodded. As Mrs Blackshaw went to the kitchen, Lillian came into the room, rubbing her eyes.

'Pippa, what are you doing here? Whose child is that?'

'As I told your mother, I can explain everything. Please, let me feed her first.'

Mrs Blackshaw returned with a tin of milk. 'You'll have to spoon it into her mouth,' she said.

Lillian gawped at the child. 'She's so tiny. Where's her mother?'

Pippa's eyes shot up to look at Lillian, and she stated adamantly, 'I'm her mother.'

She saw Lillian and Mrs Blackshaw exchange a concerned look. Gulping, she asked, 'Can we stay for the night? We'll be gone at first light.'

'Yes, pet, you're always welcome here,' Mrs Blackshaw assured her.

As Pippa tried to spoon the sweet milk into the baby's mouth, she noticed Mrs Blackshaw catch Lillian's eye and nod towards the door.

The women slipped out of the room, leaving Pippa struggling to get the baby to accept the milk. But at least Grace was quiet now. She placed the girl on the sofa, and tiptoed to the door, straining her ears to listen to the whispered conversation in the hallway.

'I reckon she's lost her marbles,' Mrs Blackshaw said quietly.

'I don't know what's happened, Mother, but that baby isn't Pippa's.'

'You're right. Let's see if we can get some sense out of her. If not, you'll have to get the police. I'm worried though, Lillian. Poor Pippa could end up in an asylum.'

Darting back to the sofa, Pippa gathered up the baby. As she went to walk out of the room, Mrs Blackshaw and Lillian came in.

'I'm sorry to have disturbed you, but I must leave,' Pippa said, her heart racing.

Mrs Blackshaw gestured to the sofa. 'Don't be daft, it's the middle of the night. Sit down, pet.'

'No, no, I really must leave.'

'I won't have you and that child wandering the streets in the dark. Sit down, Pippa, and tell me what this is all about.'

'Come on,' Lillian coaxed, gently ushering Pippa towards the sofa. 'There's nothing that can't be sorted between the three of us.'

The baby began to cry again, and Pippa swayed from side to side. 'It's all right, my love. Mummy's here.'

Lillian spoke softly, placing her hand on Pippa's arm. 'But you're not her mummy, are you, Pip?'

'Yes, yes I am! She's my baby, my baby girl.'

'I've been with you almost every day, Pippa. You've not shown any signs of being in the family way.'

'I was. I was pregnant. She's my girl. Why won't you believe me?'

'Who is her father? Wally?'

'No, don't be absurd. This little beauty is baby Newman.'

Mrs Blackshaw gasped. 'Dickie Newman? Dickie Newman is her father?'

'Yes. Isn't she adorable, Mrs Blackshaw, and she has a good set of lungs on her. Do you think you could help me to feed her? I can't seem to get her to take the milk.'

Mrs Blackshaw looked aghast, though Pippa wasn't surprised. Everyone knew Dickie, or at least had heard of him, and it was common knowledge the man had a reputation for violence.

Shaking her head in disbelief, Mrs Blackshaw outstretched her arms. 'Give her here, pet,' the woman offered kindly.

'No. No, I'll hold her, and you see if you can get the milk in her.'

'It will be much easier if you let me hold her,' Mrs Blackshaw pressed.

Pippa gazed at the girl in her arms. Her child needed nourishment, but she was reluctant to hand her to Mrs Blackshaw. 'Please try whilst I keep hold of her.'

Mrs Blackshaw sighed heavily. 'All right, if you insist. But if she won't take the milk, you'll have to give her to me.'

Pippa nodded in agreement. 'Come on, sweetie,' she encouraged the baby, 'be a good girl for Mummy and take your milk.'

A sudden and loud pounding on the front door startled Pippa. 'Don't answer it,' she hissed. 'Please, don't answer the door.'

Mrs Blackshaw tutted. 'I don't know what sort of trouble

you've got yourself in, but that baby needs to be with her mother.'

'I'm her mother,' Pippa insisted. 'Don't let them take her from me, please, Mrs Blackshaw, I'm begging you!'

'Oh, pet, think of the girl's *real* mother. She'll be going out of her mind with worry.'

Dickie's voice boomed outside. 'Open the door, or I'll kick it in!'

Pippa leapt to her feet, grasping Grace to her chest. 'He's not taking my baby,' she cried, and ran out of the door towards the kitchen. As she scrambled to open the back door, she glanced behind and saw Dickie standing in the kitchen doorway.

She could see the fury in his eyes and feared for her life. Spotting a breadknife on the table, she made a grab for it, and held the knife in front of her, her hand trembling.

'Don't come any closer,' she warned.

Dickie stepped forward, saying firmly, 'Put the knife down, Pippa.'

'You're not taking my baby.'

'She's not your baby.'

'She is, Dickie. She's *our* girl.'

Dickie came closer. 'Give her to me.'

Pippa turned the knife, holding it to her own throat. Grace cried louder. 'If you try and take her from me, I'll slit my throat, Dickie, I will.'

'Fill your boots, Pip. You'll be doing us all a favour.'

Tears fell from Pippa's eyes.

Mrs Blackshaw came to stand behind Dickie. 'Now, pet, there's no need for all this malarkey.' Then, walking around Dickie, and smiling sympathetically, she held out her arms. 'Ignore that big brute,' she said, nodding her head towards

Dickie. 'Give the baby to me, pet, and let's all sit down and have a nice cup of tea. Come on, pet, it'll all come out in the wash.'

Pippa shook her head. 'He'll take her. He'll take my baby away from me.'

'No, pet, he won't. I won't let him. Look at her, Pippa. Look at your baby. She needs a good feed and a clean bum. All this upset isn't doing her any good, is it? And you look exhausted. Being a mother is hard work. Let me help you. Give me the baby, and I'll take the very best care of her, I promise.'

Grace's screams were filling the small room. Pippa knew the child was frantic for food. 'I must do what's best for my daughter,' she sniffed. 'You will feed her, won't you, Mrs Blackshaw? She's so hungry.'

'Yes, pet, I will. Give her here, she'll be fine.'

As Pippa dropped the knife and slowly stretched her arms towards Mrs Blackshaw, Dickie lunged forward. Pippa quickly retracted her arms, and she saw Mrs Blackshaw punch Dickie's arm.

'Get out of here,' Mrs Blackshaw snapped at Dickie. 'You're only making matters worse.'

Dickie gave the woman a reproachful look before stamping out of the room.

'There you go, pet. He's gone. It's just you and me now. Right, pull out a chair at the table for me. I'll sit down to feed your baby.'

Pippa did as instructed, but she still wasn't sure about handing over her daughter.

'Give her here, then,' Mrs Blackshaw encouraged. 'She won't be quiet until she's been fed. And I don't know about you, but the racket she's making is giving me a headache, bless her. The poor little love must be ravenous.'

'She is, Mrs Blackshaw. She has a good appetite.'

'Well, she looks healthy enough, so you must have been taking very good care of your daughter. Here, let me hold her.'

Pippa's mind was screaming at her. *You can't trust Mrs Blackshaw. You can't trust anyone.* But Grace's cries drowned out the noise in Pippa's head.

'Take her, quickly, before I change my mind. She's desperate for food.'

Mrs Blackshaw smiled as Pippa placed the screaming baby in her arms.

'Go and get the milk from the other room. Don't worry about Mr Newman, and he won't worry about you.'

Pippa edged towards the kitchen door, her eyes on her baby. She passed Dickie, not daring to meet his eyes, though she felt sure he was glaring at her. In the front room, Pippa picked up the can of milk and hurried back towards the kitchen. She heard the front door open and looked behind to see Lillian rushing in, followed by three policemen.

'That's her,' Lillian told the policemen, pointing.

Pippa froze on the spot, her heart thumping. They had betrayed her. Lillian had fetched the police, and now her baby would be taken from her.

As the policemen came towards her, Pippa felt Dickie's strong hands grab her arms. He stood behind her, growling in her ear, 'You're a dead woman walking.'

Pippa wasn't afraid anymore. The pain of losing another child overwhelmed her. 'I'd rather be dead,' she muttered. 'Kill me, Dickie. I truly hope you kill me.'

*

Dickie watched the police take Pippa away. She offered no protest, though she did ask for her baby. Dickie couldn't fathom what had made her lose her mind. And he didn't care, either. As far as he was concerned, Pippa had had a lucky escape. Fortunately for her, Lillian Blackshaw had brought the police. If she hadn't, Dickie would have throttled Pippa and happily watched the life drain out of her eyes. On reflection, he thought that a lengthy prison sentence was the best outcome. After all, he'd always know exactly where she was, and no men would be touching her. A quiet word and a backhander to the relevant judge would guarantee that Pippa would be sent down for many, many years.

Mrs Blackshaw approached Dickie.

'Your daughter, I believe,' the woman said, placing Grace into his arms.

Dickie held her uneasily and looked down at the baby. 'What do I do with her?' he asked. 'She's crying.'

'Take her back to her mother.'

'But she won't stop bawling.'

'She's hungry, Mr Newman. That's why she's crying.'

Dickie grimaced at the child. He knew he couldn't put up with her crying all the way back to Clapham. 'How can I shut her up?' he asked.

'Try bobbing her up and down, gently mind, and pop the tip of your little finger in her mouth.'

'Eh?'

'Just try it.'

Dickie swallowed hard. He'd never held a baby before and was uncomfortable. But something in him stirred. He realised how vulnerable she was, and he felt the need to protect her.

Softly offering the tip of his finger to Grace's rosebud lips, he was taken aback when she latched on. Immediately, the girl stopped crying and sucked hard on his finger.

Dickie grinned. 'Well, I'll be buggered, will you look at that!' he said, astounded.

Mrs Blackshaw winked at him. 'I think she might grow up to be a daddy's girl.'

Dickie gazed at Grace, taking in her tiny features as his heart filled with love. 'I reckon you might be right, Mrs Blackshaw,' he answered proudly.

Overcome with pride, from that moment on, Dickie was smitten with his daughter.

15

Five years later
Thursday, 30th March 1922

Louisa held her head low against the sleet and hail that had been battering the south of England since the early hours of the morning. She hadn't realised how strong the winds were until she'd stepped outside and had seen fallen tree branches littering the street.

'I don't like it, Mummy,' Grace whimpered.

'No, it isn't ideal. I think you'll have to miss school today. Mummy has some errands to run, so I'll drop you with Grandma.'

Knocking urgently on her mother's front door, Louisa pulled Grace closer to protect her from the stinging hailstones.

'What on earth are you doing out in this abysmal weather?' Myrtle asked, as she ushered them inside.

'I didn't realise it was quite as bad until I stepped outside.'

'Look at that child, she's shivering.'

'Do you mind if I leave her here for an hour, while I get some groceries?' Louisa asked. Her mother had never watched over Grace before, and Louisa could tell by the repulsed expression on her face that she wasn't keen on the idea. 'Please,' Louisa pushed. 'I'll be as quick as I can. Grace won't be any bother. Just sit her down with some paper and a pencil.'

'Yes, I'm sure I can manage, but what is so important that it demands you go out in this storm?'

'Just shopping, Mother. If I don't buy some food, then Dickie won't have any dinner this evening.'

'Can't you make do with what you have in your larder?'

'It's empty. I promise I won't be long.'

'Go, but do be careful, Louisa. The wind is dreadful.'

'Thank you.'

Louisa could have kicked herself for allowing her cupboards to become so bare, but she'd been busy the past few days with laundering sheets. Grace had wet the bed in her sleep for four days running. The girl had been chastised with a slap across the back of the legs and a good telling off, but Louisa had a niggly feeling that Grace was wetting the bed deliberately to provoke her. She was often naughty, yet always an angel for her father.

The wind tore around the corner of the street, whipping Louisa's hat off as the hailstones stung her cheeks and made her eyes water. Thankfully, there was a convenience store locally, though it wasn't a shop Louisa normally frequented. She'd heard the prices were inflated and she preferred to buy her goods from the larger shops on the high street.

Inside Pope's convenience store, Louisa pushed the door closed and sighed with relief to be out of the cold.

'Good morning. You did well to brave the storm!'

Louisa turned to see an odd-looking man behind the counter. A few years older than her, with thin, wispy brown hair that barely covered his head, his face had fallen on one side, and he appeared to be very thin.

'There are trees down,' Louisa said, as she approached the counter.

'You look cold and wet. I have a pot of hot tea in the back room and a fire on. Perhaps you'd like to warm yourself through. I don't think you should be venturing back outside just yet. The storm may pass soon. You're more than welcome to shelter in the back.'

'Oh, thank you, that's very kind of you, but I've left my daughter with my mother and must return to them as soon as possible.'

'I'm sure ten minutes or so won't hurt. Look at it out there. It's getting worse and it's not safe outside.'

Louisa glanced through the storefront window as the ferocious wind carried debris flying past. 'Hmm, you might be right.'

'I am. Please, come through.'

Sitting on a lumpy armchair, Louisa was grateful for the warmth in the small room and for the cup of strong tea.

As they made their introductions and Louisa learned that the thoughtful man was named Jack Pope, she noticed he had the kindest eyes she'd ever seen. Like herself, he hadn't been blessed with beauty, but she found there was something about him that was quite magnetising. Sipping the hot tea, she chatted easily with Mr Pope and surprised herself when she talked about her loveless marriage. Mr Pope proved himself to be a good listener. He was amusing too, entertaining her with silly stories that made her smile. As Louisa stood to leave, she realised she'd been sat with him for almost an hour; the time had flown by so quickly.

'Goodness, I really must get going,' she said.

'It's been such a pleasure,' Jack smiled, albeit lopsidedly.

'It really has,' Louisa agreed. She could have quite happily sat with him all day.

'I hope you'll call in again.'

'Yes, I shall.'

Outside, her basket full and heavy, the wind had eased somewhat, though sleet was still falling. Louisa didn't mind the atrocious weather now. She felt warm inside, a peculiar feeling that she hadn't experienced before. Recalling the caring look in Mr Pope's eyes brought a smile to her face. She had a new friend. A secret friend. A special friend who made her pulse quicken. Although Louisa hadn't done anything wrong, she knew that come what may, Dickie must never find out about her time spent with Jack Pope. And though their relationship was innocent, Louisa was aware that she was already harbouring feelings for him. She hoped she could keep those feelings under control!

Dickie looked at the governor of the women's prison square in the eyes, asking, 'Has she had any visitors?'

'No, Mr Newman. Only your annual visit,' the man answered.

'Good. You are to inform me of any visits. Is that clear?'

'Yes, Mr Newman, of course. I've arranged a discreet room for your visit today. I hope you'll find it more comfortable than the public meeting place. I'll have one of my wardens escort you.'

Dickie sat at a flimsy table on an uncomfortable wooden seat and waited for Pippa to be brought in. He noticed the bars on the small window that was positioned too high to afford a view. Women's cries and hollers echoed through the cold building. Misery seemed to bounce off every wall. The prison was a dismal place, filled with broken women, living in nightmarish conditions. Yet Dickie felt no sorrow for Pippa, though he longed to hold her in his arms.

The door clanged open, and a woman warden roughly pushed Pippa into the room.

'Keep your bleedin' hands off her!' Dickie barked.

Pippa stood ramrod straight, her head held high, and Dickie could see that five years of imprisonment hadn't dampened her fiery spirit.

'Happy birthday, sweetheart,' he said, pushing a small, wrapped box across the table as he held her gaze. 'Sit down. Open your gift,' he instructed.

Pippa's eyes held love in them, yet her expression was hard and her body language defiant.

'Go on, Pip, sit down. How are you?'

'What do you care?' she spat.

'You know I care. I don't like seeing you in this shithole.'

'Don't you? I reckon you love it. You said you'd ruin me, and you did!'

'Let's not go over this again, eh? Every year it's the same conversation. You kidnapped my Grace, Pip. I ain't got any control over the law. I didn't sentence you, a judge did. Just open your gift.'

Pippa scraped back the seat and sat opposite him, unshed tears in her eyes. Dickie wanted to reach across the table and take her hands in his, to gently kiss her pale, soft cheeks, to run his hands over her full breasts and whisper sweet words in her ears. She looked so vulnerable, and he could see she'd lost weight.

'How are you?' he asked.

Pippa shrugged.

'Are they treating you all right?'

'I suppose so.'

'If you get any problems with any of the guards, you're to let me know.'

'I just want to get out of here, Dickie. How many more birthdays have I got to spend behind bars? I was sick when I took Grace, but I'm better now. Why can't they see that? Why won't they let me out?'

'You've done five years, Pip. You're halfway through your sentence. Hang in there.'

'Five more years in here feels like a lifetime.'

'I'm sure it does, but you could have got a lot longer. Are you gonna open your birthday present or not?'

Pippa dashed away a tear and reached for the box before carefully and slowly unwrapping it.

'Just rip the paper off,' Dickie chuckled.

Looking deeply into his eyes, Pippa replied, 'No. It's the only gift I receive, and I want to savour every moment of it.'

As Pippa lifted the lid and her eyes lit up with delight, Dickie smiled. He enjoyed seeing the pleasure he'd brought her.

'Thank you, Dickie,' she said softly. 'You know my favourites.'

He had meticulously packed three Fry's chocolate cream bars and a Cadbury Flake, which had only been introduced two years earlier, so Pippa would never have seen one before. Five packets of cigarettes, a bar of rose petal soap, a set of linen handkerchiefs, a soft pink lipstick, a small bottle of Chanel Number Five, a jar of Pond's cold cream, and a dried, red rose. He felt rather proud of his choices.

'Tell me what's been happening in the world outside of these prison walls.'

'I dunno, let me think ... Erm, fashions are changing, and hems are rising. Jazz music is all the rage now. Women are out dancing. Some are still trying to get the age to vote down from thirty years old. Ernest Shackleton died. The flu has been wiping people out. Princess Mary got married to some Viscount bloke. An explosion at a factory in Tipton killed a load of young girls who were dismantling explosive cartridges. There's a new football stadium being built at Wembley. I can't think of anything else off the top of my head.'

'Oh, what I wouldn't give to dance! I hate being in here, Dickie, and I'm not sure I want you to come and see me again.'

'You like my birthday gifts, don't you?'

'Yes, but seeing you every year is just a cruel reminder of what I'm missing on the outside. And then to think of you going to your comfortable home with your wife and daughter. What have I got? Nothing, Dickie. No family of my own. No husband or children, and nothing to look forward to. I can't stand it, Dickie, it's just too tragic.'

'You'll make a life for yourself when you get out of here.'

'Will I, Dickie? Will you allow me to find a husband? Will you ever let me be happy?'

Dickie clasped his hands behind his head as his mind turned. 'Is that what you want, Pip? You want a husband?'

'I don't know ... Maybe, one day. And why shouldn't I? You'll never marry me, so I've every right to find a man of my own.'

Rage simmered in the pit of his gut. Fury heated his veins. Jumping from his seat, Dickie swept his hand across the table, sending the box of small gifts hurtling through the air. 'You can't help yourself. Banged up in here, but you're still thinking about blokes. You're a fucking whore, Pip, and you turn my stomach. I hope you rot in fuckin' hell,' he growled.

Marching to the door, Dickie banged hard. 'I'm done with her,' he told the female warden. 'But if I find out that any of you have laid a finger on her, there'll be trouble. Got it?'

'Yes, sir.'

As Dickie drove away from the prison, his head was a mess. Seeing Pippa always evoked a deep passion, and the thought of her wanting to start a new life with a man had sent him into a jealous rage. At least with her locked away, his mind could rest knowing that no men could touch her. But in five years, maybe sooner, she'd be a free woman. Dickie would never accept a man in her life. Never.

16

Five years later
Friday, 15th April 1927

Louisa could feel her cheeks reddening as she pushed open the door of Pope's convenience store, and blushed even deeper when she tripped inside. It was the third time this week she'd found an excuse to call in to the corner shop. Butter this time, she needed butter. Though in truth, Louisa had ample at home.

'Good morning, Mrs Newman, it's always a pleasure to see you,' the shopkeeper greeted her.

'Good morning to you, Mr Pope,' Louisa smiled, her pulse racing.

Jack Pope rushed out from behind his counter, limping and walking with the aid of a cane. 'Here. Let me help you with your basket,' he offered, taking it from Louisa.

The man, his face lopsided, appeared flustered. Louisa wasn't sure if he was always so fidgety, or if he was only on edge around her. But it was a funny sort of fluster, a nervous energy, and he could never do enough for her. Their friendship had blossomed over the years, yet they still remained formal with each other, though there had been many long gazes and the odd brush of hands.

Placing her basket on the counter, Mr Pope smoothed down his very fine, light brown hair, and offered Louisa a skewed smile. 'What can I get for you today?' he asked.

'Butter, please, Mr Pope. Half a pound.'

'I trust you're keeping well?' he enquired.

'Yes, rather well, thank you. And yourself?'

'Yes, fine. I was just about to pour myself a cup of tea. Would you care to join me, if you're not too busy, of course?'

'A cup of tea would be most acceptable,' Louisa replied. She'd hoped he'd offer her tea again, as he often did.

Sitting in the back of the shop, on a lumpy and uncomfortable armchair, Louisa had come to enjoy Mr Pope's company and always looked forward to sharing a pot of tea with him. He was only a few years older than her, and they had much in common. A good friend, Mr Pope had no idea how Louisa felt about him. He was clueless to the fact that she thought about him almost every minute of every day. And he didn't know that she often dreamed about him, too.

'Have you seen the designs for the new Electric House opening later this year on Lavender Hill?'

'No, Mr Pope, I can't say that I have.'

'It's impressive! I've noticed that they are covering the frontage with Portland Stone. I believe the showroom will be a welcome addition to Battersea.'

Louisa nodded. 'I heard the council are hoping the showroom will encourage the residents to uptake electricity supply to their homes.'

'Yes, Mrs Newman, I heard the same. I must admit that I was unsure about electricity at first, yet now I can't envisage my life without it.'

'Can you imagine going back to using oil lamps?' Louisa said, rolling her eyes.

Mr Pope handed Louisa a cup of tea. She could hear the cup clattering in the saucer as his hand shook.

'Thank you, Mr Pope, I'm quite parched.'

'Please, call me Jack. We've been friends for many years now.'

'Yes, *Jack*, we have. And it's probably time you called me Louisa. Though I think in public, it may be better to remain proper.'

Sipping on the hot, sweet tea, Louisa looked over the top of her cup at Jack, and when he looked back at her, she felt butterflies in her stomach. The man wasn't nearly as handsome as her husband. In fact, Louisa thought Jack was a bit of an oddball, much like herself. But his warm personality compensated for his irregular looks.

'And Grace, is she well?' Jack asked.

'Oh, Jack, I'm beside myself with the girl. Would you believe I found a dead mouse in her pocket! I've no idea where she got it from, and yesterday, when I collected her from school, her knees were grazed, her shoes scuffed, and she was absolutely filthy! My daughter takes after her father and is like a bull in a china shop.'

'She's lively, that's for sure,' Jack chuckled.

'I'm pleased at her fearless nature, but I wish the child would take more notice of what I say. Really, Jack, I believe she dislikes me.'

'I doubt that, Louisa. You're her mother, and I'm sure Grace loves you very much.'

Louisa sighed. 'I don't think so. I've only myself to blame. I raised her to be strong and independent, but I fear I may have been too aloof with the girl. And it doesn't help that Dickie shows me little respect. Grace picks up on things. She's beginning to talk to me in a similar tone to the one her father uses. It's upsetting.'

Jack reached over and rubbed his hand up and down Louisa's arm. 'You're an amazing woman, Louisa, and a wonderful mother.'

'Thank you. You have no idea how much our cups of tea and little chats mean to me.'

Jack peered into his cup, and without lifting his eyes, he said clearly, 'I'll always be here for you, Louisa. I'm in love with you.'

Louisa gasped. She'd longed to hear those words from him, but feared the consequences.

Quickly rising to his feet and leaning heavily on his cane, Jack apologised. 'I'm sorry ... I shouldn't have said that. Please, Louisa, forget my words. I wouldn't want to spoil our friendship.'

Louisa could feel her heart pounding so hard, she wondered if it would thump out of her chest! 'I ... I ... I feel the same, Jack,' she said quietly, lowering her eyes to look at the threadbare rug on the floor. 'But I'm a married woman, Jack. And my husband is a very dangerous man.'

'I know all there is to know about Dickie Newman. He's a loan-shark and a rotten landlord who likes to rough people up. He doesn't deserve you, Louisa, but you're too sweet and kind to see it.'

'We shouldn't be speaking like this. Honestly, Jack, if Dickie knew, I'm confident he'd have you badly beaten, or worse! This ... us ... it's bad for your health and I'm scared. I'm afraid for you, and I can't abide the idea of losing your friendship.

You're the only person in the world I can talk to. And the only person who makes me smile.'

Louisa began to weep, and Jack rushed over to where she was sitting. Placing his hand on her shoulder, he soothed, 'Please don't cry, Louisa. Don't shed tears over losing our friendship, because that's never going to happen. I'll always be here for you. I can't imagine my life without you.'

Louisa looked up at Jack and placed her hand over his. 'No matter our feelings, we can never be more than friends.'

'I know. Fate has been kind to me. It brought me home from the frontline with just a leg injury, which could have been a whole lot worse. It has given me this shop, inherited from my parents, and a nice home upstairs. And fate brought you to me. I would have been a lonely man without you, Louisa. I'm happy with us being friends.'

Louisa smiled weakly. She wanted Jack to sweep her up in his scrawny arms, to smother her with kisses and, if he had, she knew she wouldn't have offered any resistance. But she also knew she would have been putting Jack's life at risk, and Louisa wasn't prepared to do that. Pushing her wants and desires aside, Louisa would have to be satisfied with just being Jack's friend. She could justify having a friend. It was innocent, and she wasn't committing adultery. Though Louisa wasn't convinced that Dickie would see it like that.

'I must go,' she said. 'Will I see you on Sunday as usual?'

'Of course,' Jack replied. 'I'll bring some stale bread for the ducks.'

Dickie shook the prison governor's hand. 'Nice work, Mr Byrne,' he said, satisfied with the man's cooperation.

'As I've said before, Mr Newman, it's always a pleasure

doing business with you. If there's anything else I can do, don't hesitate to contact me.'

'Thanks, but I reckon all's well for now. You did a fine job of getting that bitch's sentence extended.'

'Miss Pippa Lampton shouldn't have attempted to abscond. We take prison breaks very seriously here, which was reflected in the woman's extended sentence. Let it be an example to any other women who are contemplating breaking free.'

Dickie chuckled. 'You stitched her up good and proper. Who's gonna believe her word over yours, eh? No one. Well, if Pippa was ever thinking about trying to escape, she'll think twice about it now. Thanks again, Mr Byrne. Your fabricated story has kept the streets a safer place from loonies like Pippa Lampton. I'll tell you something though – the woman is quite a looker and I've seen you now have a few men working here. I hope they're keeping their hands to themselves.'

'Miss Lampton, a looker? I reckon you're mistaken, Mr Newman. You haven't seen her for some time. Maybe your recollections are unreliable.'

'I doubt it. I'll never forget that woman – she stole my daughter.'

'Come with me,' the governor instructed.

Mr Byrne led Dickie through many corridors until they came to a central area of the prison. 'The prison officers can see all along the wings from this standpoint. Look, down there. That's Lampton.'

Dickie's eyes followed the governor's pointing finger, sure that he was indicating the wrong woman. 'Nah, that ain't her,' he said, and sniffed. Dickie was excited at the thought of seeing Pippa, especially as she had refused his visits for the past five years.

'That's her, Mr Newman. That is most definitely Pippa Lampton. She's not quite the looker you remember, is she?'

Dickie's jaw hung wide as he slowly shook his head. He couldn't believe that the grey-haired woman with a lumpy, purple scar across her face, whose prison-issue clothes hung from her skinny and frail frame, was the same Pippa Lampton who'd once been a voluptuous and striking redhead. 'That's never her,' he mumbled.

'I can assure you, Mr Newman, that is Lampton.'

Dickie felt sorry for the woman. She was skin and bone and, by the way she carried herself, he could tell she was deeply downhearted. 'How did she get that scar?' he asked.

'A disagreement with another inmate. There's always brawls in here, Mr Newman. I sometimes think the women prisoners are more difficult to manage than the men.'

'See to it that Miss Lampton isn't injured again. Do you understand?'

'Er, yes, Mr Newman, if that's your wish.'

'It is. And I want her to have a comfortable cell, with good food. Can you arrange that?'

'I can, but there will be a cost involved.'

'Do it. You'll get a good drink from me.'

Dickie left the prison, shocked at what he'd seen. Maybe it was time for him to allow the woman to walk free. It was too late to change anything now, as Pippa's sentence had already been lengthened, thanks to him. But he believed she wouldn't last much longer behind bars. As he started the car engine, Dickie felt bad. He'd wanted to take Pippa in his arms and tell her he was sorry. *Pack it in*, he scolded himself. *You're going soft, you stupid bugger.* Even looking as she did, Pippa still evoked feelings in Dickie that he couldn't get his head around and couldn't shake off, either.

17

On Saturday morning, Dickie had a spring in his step and was in good spirits. He'd bought Grace a big chocolate Easter egg and he couldn't wait to see the look of delight on her face tomorrow. But first there was work to do, and he greeted Ernie cheerily.

'I've already made a start, Boss,' Ernie announced. 'They're all paid up,' he said, pointing to the first dozen houses on the street.

'Good work, Ernie. What about Mrs Moss? She's three weeks behind.'

'I was waiting for you before I went knocking. I weren't sure what you'd want me to do if she still can't pay. I know you ain't keen on me slapping the women about, and she's got that nipper, Gordon. Do you want me to sling 'em out?'

'Hold your horses, Ernie. Let's see if she can pay first.'

As they approached the rundown house, Dickie noticed a bundle of rags on the doorstep. Getting closer, he saw a pair of bare, dirty feet and skinny, almost blue legs sticking out from a thin, grey blanket. 'Christ, is that Gordon? Is the boy alive?'

Ernie leaned forward, gave the blanket a firm jab with his finger, and a young lad popped his head out.

'What the bloomin' 'eck are you doing out 'ere, lad?' Ernie asked.

Gordon, his yellow teeth chattering, replied, 'I couldn't get indoors. Me muvver's done a midnight flit and left me behind. I dunno where she's gawn.'

Dickie rolled his eyes. Undernourished and impoverished, little Gordon was about the same age as his Grace, but their lives couldn't have been more different. Looking into the scared mite's sunken brown eyes, Gordon's plight tugged on his heartstrings.

'You can't stay there,' Ernie said. 'Move on, lad.'

'Where shall I go, mister?'

'I dunno, but you ain't got no right to sit on Mr Newman's step. Are you sure you don't know where your mum is?'

'Yeah, I'm sure. If I did know, do you fink I'd be sat here freezing me knackers off! Cor, if only I had a brain as big as yours.'

Ernie glanced at Dickie, saying, 'He's a cheeky one.'

Dickie smiled. He liked the boy's spirit. There were few folk in Battersea who would give Ernie any lip.

''Ere, mister, I know who you are,' Gordon said, addressing Dickie. 'You're loaded and you're the guv'nor round this place.'

'That's right, I am,' Dickie agreed.

The boy rose to his feet, and the blanket dropped to the ground, revealing his ragged shorts and holey jumper. 'I've got a proposition for you, mister, and you, being a good businessman, you'll know a good thing when you see it. It ain't for me to say, but you'd be a fool to turn me down.'

'Go on then, let's hear your proposition.'

'I'll come and work for you. You can pay me a wage and I'll live in me old room and I'll pay you to live there. That way, you ain't losing no money.' He spat on his grubby hand and held it towards Dickie to shake. 'Do we have a deal?'

Dickie chuckled, and asked, 'Tell me, Gordon, what work could you do for me, eh?'

'I can dip for ya.'

'I'm not in the pickpocketing game.'

'I'm good at pinching stuff from shops. I nicked me mum two loaves of bread once, and a jar of pickles. You name it, I'll steal it. Then you can sell it on.'

'I don't make my money from thieving.'

'How about I clean your car ... and ... and ...' the boy chewed his dirty thumbnail as he thought.

'You're a nice kid, Gordon. I'll give you a break. But you only get one chance with me. Mess up, and you're out on your ear. Do you understand?'

'Yes, sir, I do. Fanks, mister, I won't let you down, I promise.'

'All right. Get in the car. First things first, you need a bloody good bath.'

Gordon raced to the car, as Ernie asked, 'Where are you taking him?'

'Home.'

Ernie looked astounded. 'Are you sure about this, Boss? He's a little urchin.'

'He is, but the boy's got more character and street smarts than anyone I know. I like him. And I reckon the look on my mother-in-law's face will be bleedin' priceless when she meets Gordon. That alone will be worth any hassle the lad gives me.'

Ernie shrugged. 'It's your lookout, Boss. Good luck.'

*

Louisa was surprised to see Dickie's car pull up so early, and she was even more surprised when she saw a young boy climb out. The child had the appearance of a vagrant, like one of the children she'd seen begging on the streets. She wondered why he was in her husband's car and hoped Dickie wasn't bringing him inside.

When the front door opened, Dickie urged the lad through, and announced, 'This is Gordon. He'll be living with us from now on. He can sleep in the basement.'

Louisa was taken aback. 'Oh, erm, I see. Does the boy have any clean clothes?' she asked, concerned about fleas infesting their home.

'No. Buy him what he needs. And get him in the bath.'

'Yes, Dickie, I think a bath is a very good idea. But what shall I dress him in for now?'

'I don't know, woman, use your imagination.'

Louisa eyed the dirty child and thought he must be a similar age to Grace. Concerned for her daughter's welfare, she frowned, and whispered to Dickie, 'Are you sure Grace will be safe with him in the house? And he could be a bad influence on the girl. I'm not sure this is a good idea.'

'My house, my rules. Just do as you're told, woman.'

'But, Dickie, do you know anything about the boy? Where are his parents?'

'Stop asking so many bloody questions and see to him!'

'I'm worried, Dickie. I'm worried for Grace.'

'Shut it and do as you're told!'

Louisa swallowed hard. She realised Dickie was losing his temper, and she also saw the pitiful look in the young boy's eyes. Drawing in a deep breath, she crouched in front of Gordon and introduced herself.

'Hello. I'm Mrs Newman, but if you're to be living here, then you can call me Louisa. And once you're bathed, I shall introduce you to my daughter, Grace. How old are you, Gordon?'

'I'm ten, I fink, or eleven. I might be twelve. Me mum said she lost count after me fifth birthday.'

'I see, and when is your birthday?'

'Gawd knows. Mum never bothered telling me, but I reckon it might be on the same day that Jesus was born.'

'Oh, and why do you think that?'

''Cos me muvver said I was a flippin' miracle and she told me that the storks wot brought me were angels, and that me dad weren't really me dad. See, just like baby Jesus.'

'And where is your mother?' Louisa asked.

'No one knows. She's legged it 'cos she couldn't pay your old man the rent.'

Dickie spoke. 'Right, that's enough chatter. Get him bathed.'

Louisa showed Gordon to the bathroom and watched as he ran into the room, looking around in awe.

'You've got a crapper indoors! And a bath, a real, proper bath with taps an' all! Cor blimey, I ain't never seen nothing like it! Does the water come out hot?'

'Yes, Gordon, very hot, so be careful,' Louisa said, turning on the taps. 'Leave your clothes outside the door. Here's a fresh towel and be sure to use plenty of soap. I want to see your face gleaming and no dirt under your fingernails.'

'Yes, missus, fanks, missus.'

As the room filled with steam, Louisa closed the door

behind her and hurried to find Dickie, many questions racing through her mind.

In the substantial garden at the rear of the house, she found her husband pushing Grace on a swing he'd made and hung from a strong oak branch.

Dickie saw her coming, and she was stunned when he smiled at her. She couldn't remember the last time her husband had looked at her with consideration.

'I've just been telling Grace about Gordon,' he said.

'I've promised Papa I'll be kind to Gordon.'

Louisa nodded. 'I know you will, Grace. You're always kind.' Then she asked, 'Dickie, may I have a word?'

'Put the kettle on,' Dickie said, and walked towards the house.

In the kitchen, Louisa placed water on the stove to heat and turned to her husband, asking, 'What am I expected to do with Gordon?'

'Care for him like you would Grace. If he gives you any bother, tell me and I'll sort him out.'

'I shall have to burn his clothes.'

'Yeah, I should think so.'

'Should I enrol him at school? Or does he already attend one?'

'No, don't bother. He'll be coming with me most of the time.'

'But we could be in trouble with the authorities if we fail to send him to school?'

'I don't suppose the authorities know that he exists. So long as he can read, write and add up, he'll learn more from working with me than he would at any poxy school.'

'I'm still not sure about this arrangement, Dickie. Have you thought it through? What if he harms Grace?'

'He won't. He's a little urchin, but he's harmless.'

Louisa swallowed hard before nervously asking, 'Is – Is he your son, Dickie?'

'No. He's just a kid who needs a home.'

Gordon called down from upstairs. 'I'm clean, Mrs Newman. Where's me clobber?'

'Perhaps I can encourage him to speak better,' Louisa said, as she walked out of the kitchen.

'There's nothing wrong with how he talks,' Dickie called after her.

Hmm, we'll see about that, she thought, trotting up the stairs. She wasn't comfortable with him living under the same roof as Grace, and Dickie's reassurances hadn't quelled her concerns, but she knew she'd have to accept the child. Once her husband's mind was made up, he never changed it, and she didn't want to anger him by keeping on.

Gordon was standing in the bathroom doorway, wrapped in a towel, almost unrecognisable from the grimy child she'd first met. His greasy, lank hair that Louisa had thought was brown now shone light blond, and his cheeks were flushed pink from the heat.

'That's better,' she smiled. 'You wait there, and I'll fetch you something of Mr Newman's to wear for now.'

'Fanks, missus. That's the first time I've been in a bath. It was bloody lovely!'

'Good, but please refrain from using bad language.'

'Yeah, sorry 'bout that. Me muvver used to tell me off for that an' all.'

As Louisa went to find some clothes for Gordon, she

pitied the poor boy. He must be missing his mother, but she wondered what sort of woman would run off without her child. He seemed a cheerful lad, but Louisa still wasn't sure it was a good idea to open their home to him. And she felt sure that her mother would have much to say on the subject, and would no doubt take an instant dislike to him.

18

On Easter Sunday, Myrtle Best sat bolt upright on the edge of her daughter's sofa, sipping tea whilst waiting for lunch to be served. Dickie was home, which wasn't unusual nowadays. The man had a soft spot for his daughter and liked to spend time with her. As Dickie pretended to steal the end of Grace's nose, Myrtle looked on with disapproval. In her opinion, he was spoiling the girl, just as Herbert had spoiled Louisa.

Over Grace's raucous laughter, Myrtle said, 'Little girls should be seen and not heard.'

'Behave yourself,' Dickie answered. 'We ain't living in the Victorian days no more.'

'I know, Dickie, you don't have to remind me of that fact, thank you. You've only to look at the disgracefully short lengths of women's skirts to know that society no longer embraces Victorian values.'

'Grandma's an old stuffed shirt,' Dickie chortled, holding his hand aloft for Grace to punch. Then glancing at Myrtle, he said, 'I don't mind the short skirts.'

'No, well, you wouldn't. I'm sure most men are thrilled at seeing a woman's calf. Call me old-fashioned, but I do not agree with skirts and dresses falling to only slightly below the knee.'

'Harder,' Dickie ordered Grace.

Grace pulled back her arm and punched his palm as hard as she could.

Dickie smiled proudly and ruffled the top of his daughter's dark and glossy hair. 'Good girl, Grace. I reckon you could knock Ernie clean off his feet with a punch like that.'

'And another thing, Dickie,' Myrtle continued. 'Teaching Grace to fight is not appropriate and most unbecoming for a girl.'

'She enjoys it, don't you, darling?'

'I do,' Grace beamed. 'And I'm good at it, Grandma. Last week, in school, I punched Timmy Holder in the mouth and made him bleed.'

Myrtle couldn't hide her discontent; the expression on her face said it all. 'Really, Grace, that's appalling behaviour.'

'No, Grandma, he asked for it. He said girls are stupid and weaklings, so I showed him that I wasn't!'

Dickie chuckled again. 'She's her father's daughter, all right. 'Ere, Grace, I've got something for you. Have a look behind the curtain.'

Grace ran to the window and whipped back the drapes. Gasping with glee, she picked up the biggest chocolate Easter egg Myrtle had ever seen.

'Oh, Papa, is this really for me?' Grace asked.

'Yes, darling, all yours. But I think you oughta share it with Gordon.'

'Wow! Happy fuckin' Easter,' she yelled.

Myrtle shrieked, 'Grace!'

'That's my girl,' Dickie laughed.

Louisa had walked into the room. 'Goodness, Grace, you mustn't ever use that language!'

'Disgraceful!' Myrtle snapped, horrified. 'Absolutely disgraceful! Really, Grace, you should be ashamed of yourself!'

Grace's bottom lip began to quiver. 'But … but Papa says it all the time,' she cried.

Dickie rushed over and picked up his daughter. Sitting down on the opposite end of the sofa from Myrtle, he wrapped his arms around the girl and bobbed her up and down on his knee. 'Don't you worry, my darling. You ain't in trouble.'

'You'll ruin that girl,' Myrtle spat. 'She should be spanked.'

'No one spanks my girl,' Dickie growled. 'No one, man or woman, will ever lay a finger on her.'

'A child needs discipline, Dickie. *Spare the rod—*'

'Don't quote the bible to me,' Dickie cut in. 'And don't you dare tell me how to raise my girl. Let's face it, Myrtle, you didn't do a great job with her,' he said, flicking his head towards Louisa. 'She's got the spine of a jellyfish and the personality of dishwater. Not my Grace. My Grace is strong, and she's got spirit. She takes after her old dad, don't you, my girl?'

Myrtle had heard and seen enough. She wasn't close to her granddaughter and found it difficult to love the child. As Grace grew, and the years passed, it was apparent that she was becoming more and more like her father – a man Myrtle detested. 'I'll see you next week,' Myrtle addressed her daughter as she rose to her feet to leave.

'What about lunch? I thought you were staying for lunch?'

'No, thank you, Louisa. Good afternoon.'

Dickie's voice followed her, grating as ever. 'Cheerio then, mother-in-law. Have a nice day, you old bag.'

At the front door, Louisa whispered, 'I'm sorry, Mother, but you know what he's like. Couldn't you just let it go over the top of your head?'

'I can't, Louisa. The man is a thug, and I can not sit back and watch him turn Grace into the same. Fortunately, you have separate bedrooms, so there hasn't been and never will be any more children. I'm afraid Grace is beyond hope. She will *never* be a lady.'

Louisa glared accusingly at her mother. 'But it was you who told me to raise my daughter to be tough. You advised me to make her strong and independent.'

'Yes, Louisa, I did. But I never told you to let her become a copy of her father. I can't stand it, Louisa, I simply can not stand to be around the girl. And by the way, who is Gordon? Dickie told Grace she should share her egg with him.'

'Ah,' Louisa answered, pursing her lips. 'I was going to tell you about Gordon. He's a boy in need of a home and has come to live with us.'

'I hope he has come from a good family. Where is he?'

'In the basement, which I think is disgraceful, but Dickie won't have him staying in any of the bedrooms upstairs. I've had to keep him out of the way today, as he doesn't have any suitable clothes until I go shopping tomorrow.'

'What do you mean, how can the boy be without clothes?'

'He came here with nothing but filthy rags, Mother.'

Myrtle had a dreadful feeling that her daughter had picked up a ragamuffin from the streets. It wouldn't surprise her; Louisa was much like her father, too kind-hearted for her own good. 'You have a waif and stray in your house?'

'Yes, Mother, though he's no longer a waif and stray.'

'You are impossible and quite mad! Have you considered Grace? How old is the child?'

'A few years older than Grace.'

'This will end in trouble, Louisa. I hope you are fully aware of the problems this will bring.'

'I am, and I'm not happy about the situation, but it was Dickie's decision, and he won't listen to my concerns. I'm sure everything will be fine, or at least, I hope it will be.'

'It's nothing to do with me and I refuse to get involved. On your head be it.'

Myrtle held her head high as she marched away. She was sure that *Gordon* would corrupt Grace. She was a beautiful girl, but she spent far too much time around Dickie. That hateful man even took her to work with him on some days. Myrtle shuddered to think about what Grace had been exposed to and what sort of people she'd met. And now she had a homeless, probably moral-less boy to contend with, too.

Opening her front door, the grandeur of her house lifted her spirits. For all of Dickie's faults, at least Myrtle had her fine home to be grateful for. The walls, the roof and everything inside her elegant house meant the world to her. Myrtle's place oozed opulence and wealth. Within the confines of her refined world, she could forget about Louisa's unhappiness and Grace's inappropriate upbringing. She was at her most content when surrounded by expensive art and precious ornaments, dressed in lavish fabrics and dining in exclusive restaurants. Dickie funded her lifestyle, so Myrtle would have to tread carefully. But, she thought, perhaps it was time to try to find a way to stand on her own two feet.

*

After lunch, Louisa cleared the table and allowed Grace to indulge in the chocolate Easter egg that Dickie had bought her.

'Don't make yourself sick,' Dickie warned his daughter. 'I've got work to do. I won't be home until past your bedtime. I'll see you tomorrow.' Then, as a throwaway comment, he said to Louisa, 'You can tell your mother that she's moving in with us. The lease on her gaff ends next month and I ain't renewing it.'

'Oh dear, Mother will be disappointed.'

'Yeah, well, she'll have to lump it. I ain't forking out for her to live in that posh house no more. There's room here for her.'

Louisa sighed with relief when her husband closed the front door behind him. She always felt as though she was walking on eggshells around him and much preferred it when he wasn't at home. And now she'd have to contend with her mother, too. She was dreading breaking the news to her.

'That's enough now, Grace,' Louisa uttered. Her daughter had chocolate all around her mouth. 'You heard what your father said. You're not to make yourself sick. And you should share it with Gordon.'

As Louisa went to take the chocolate from Grace, the girl snatched it away.

'Grace, I said *enough*. Give it to me.'

'No!'

'You will do as you are told, young lady.'

'You can't tell me what to do. Only Papa can.'

'I *can* tell you what to do, and if you don't do as you're told, I'll spank you!'

'If you spank me, I'll tell Papa, and he'll beat you up.'

Louisa gasped, shocked at Grace's threat. 'Your father would never beat me up; do not ever talk like that again. Give me that egg, and go and wash your face, or I shall tell Papa what a naughty girl you are!'

Grace pouted as she handed Louisa the chocolate and stamped out of the room. Louisa closed her eyes and breathed deeply, trying to calm her jangled nerves. Her mother was right, Grace was becoming too much like her father, and it unnerved Louisa. *I need to talk to Jack*, she thought, grabbing her coat and instructing Grace to do the same.

'Why? Where are we going?' Grace asked.

'For a walk on the common.'

'I don't want to go for a walk,' Grace moaned.

'I don't care. I do. Come on.'

Calling down the stairs to Gordon, he came to stand at the bottom. Louisa thought he looked quite comical in Dickie's shirt, which hung on the boy like a dress. 'I'm taking Grace for a walk on the common. We won't be long. Stay here, you can't come out dressed like that. See you soon.'

Strolling through Clapham Common, Louisa thought about the implications of having her mother living under the same roof. She was a critical woman, often putting Louisa down and complaining about Grace. It wasn't going to be a harmonious situation, and Louisa's heart dropped. But when she saw Jack Pope waving at her, her mood lightened, and she felt the familiar butterflies in her stomach.

'Good afternoon, Louisa,' he smiled crookedly. 'And hello, young Grace. Look what I have,' he said, holding out a paper bag stuffed with bread. 'Shall we feed the ducks?'

Grace grabbed the bag, squealing, 'Yes, please, Mr Pope.'

Louisa wanted privacy with Jack and told her daughter, 'You run ahead, Grace, we'll catch you up.'

As Grace sprinted towards the pond, Jack asked, concerned, 'Is everything all right, Louisa?'

'No, Jack, not really. Dickie has said that my mother is to move in with us.'

'Ah, and you're not happy about that, and rightly so! From what you've told me about her, I can imagine you think she'll make your life a misery.'

'Yes, more so than it already is.'

'I always believe you should make the best of any situation. Think on it this way – one, you'll have some company. Two, your mother can help with Grace and the chores. And three, it might be an opportunity for you and your mother to build a closer relationship. It doesn't have to be all bad, you know.'

'Oh, Jack, I appreciate your optimism, you always make me feel better. Though on this occasion, I'm not convinced you're right.'

'Think positive. You might be pleasantly surprised.'

Louisa walked with Jack, and he roared with laughter when she told him about Grace swearing earlier.

'It's not funny,' she chided, with a chuckle.

'I know, I shouldn't laugh. But Grace is such a pretty little girl. I can just see the look of horror on your mother's face.'

'And on mine!'

When she told him about Gordon Moss, Jack was surprised to hear that Dickie had shown compassion to anyone.

'I know, I was surprised, too! I've never known my husband to do anything kind for anyone, not unless there was something in it for him.'

'How does Grace get on with the boy?'

'So far, so good. I think she likes the idea of having a brother. But I'm really unhappy about the boy living with us. I feel sorry for him, you understand, but Grace must be my priority, and I worry that he may harm her in some way.'

The hours passed too quickly, and soon the sun was dipping. 'I don't want to go home,' Louisa said, sighing.

'I wish you didn't have to. I've been giving an outrageous idea a lot of thought. Don't say anything. Let me explain first ... We could run away together, you, me and Grace, Gordon too if you want. I could sell my shop and my house, and we could start a new life together, somewhere miles away from here, where your husband would never find us. What do you think, Louisa?'

Louisa stared wide eyed at Jack's hopeful face, her thoughts spinning.

'Say yes,' Jack urged. 'Say you'll do it. Please, Louisa, think about how happy we could be.'

Louisa's every sinew wanted to say yes. Her heart soared at the notion of being with Jack and free of Dickie. But her head warned her of the reality of Jack's madcap idea. 'He'd find us, and then he'd kill you. I could never take Grace away from him, because Dickie would hunt me down to the ends of the earth to get his daughter back. I can't, Jack, as much as I'd like to, I simply can't.'

'Leave Grace with him. Maybe he wouldn't search as hard for you if you didn't take his daughter away.'

'No, Jack, I couldn't leave Grace! She's difficult but she's my daughter. I love her, Jack, I love her more than anything or anyone in the world. I could never, never leave her.'

Jack's shoulders slumped and he looked sorely disappointed. 'I'm sorry, that was a stupid thing to suggest. Of course you couldn't leave Grace behind. I'm willing to risk everything to be with you, Louisa; even the risk of losing my life doesn't put me off. We could do it. We could move to Scotland. Scotland is as far away from here as you can imagine. Yes, Dickie would look for us, but he might not find us. Isn't it worth a chance?'

Louisa thought it would be like a dream come true, yet it could also turn into her worst nightmare. 'I love you too much to do it, Jack. I couldn't live with myself if anything bad were to happen to you. And we'd spend the rest of our lives looking over our shoulders, living in fear of Dickie finding us. It just isn't a feasible idea. I'm so sorry.' A tear slipped from her eye as she called to Grace. 'Come on, time to go home.'

'Maybe we shouldn't see each other anymore,' she whispered to Jack. 'I feel I'm holding you back from living your life and finding happiness with a woman who could be with you properly. I'm sorry, Jack, but I can't do this anymore.'

Grabbing Grace's hand, Louisa hurried away, trying not to cry in front of her daughter. Almost running, she knew Jack wouldn't be able to keep up with her, not with his gammy leg and cane.

His voice carried on the breeze. 'Wait, Louisa, please, let me talk to you …'

Louisa didn't look back. If she had, her emotions would have caved, and she might have run into his arms. She had to be strong and walk away from her only friend, and the love of her life. For his sake. Jack needed to be free to find a wife. It broke Louisa's heart, and as she battled to hold in her sadness, she knew she'd be crying into her pillow tonight.

19

The following day, Louisa splashed cold water on her eyes to try to take down the swelling. She'd spent most of the night silently sobbing, yearning for Jack to hold her. Her mind had swayed several times, and she'd considered running away with him. But she always came to the same conclusion – Dickie would end up killing Jack. She had to put Jack in the past and move on with her everyday life. And she could never allow anyone to see her broken heart. *Oh, Jack, I love you so much*, she thought, her mind once again swaying to the idea of running away with him. It was an impossible dream, yet one she yearned for more than anything. Maybe they could do it. Maybe they could be happy. Shaking her head, she knew it could never happen.

She spent the next few hours in Clapham Junction, shopping in Arding and Hobbs department store for clothes for Gordon. Buying boy's wear was a new concept for Louisa and she'd found it challenging, but it had taken her mind off Jack for a short while.

Now, home and rested, she glanced out of the window and saw Dickie's car pull up. He was home early, which meant he'd come to pick up Grace. It was becoming a regular routine, Dickie taking Grace with him after the girl had finished school. Louisa wasn't happy about her daughter seeing Dickie's world, but she didn't have the courage to speak up to him. When it came to her husband, she felt she had no voice at all.

Grace rushed down the stairs, Gordon following, and she leapt into Dickie's arms, excited to see her father. 'Am I coming to work with you again, Papa?' she asked.

'Yep, and I'm taking you and Gordon out for dinner this evening. How about that, eh?'

'Shall I wear my best dress?'

'No, you look beautiful as you are. And it's nice to see you properly dressed too, Gordon. Come on, get your coats and let's go.'

'What about Mother? I want Mother to come out with us, too.'

Louisa met his eyes, and crossed her fingers behind her back, silently wishing he'd say no. There had been a time, years ago, when she'd craved Dickie's attention and hoped for his affection. That time had long passed, and now she didn't like to be around him. Thankfully, her wish was granted, and Dickie shook his head.

'Nope, not today. It's just you, me and Gordon for dinner this evening, in a nice fancy restaurant on Park Lane. We'll go to where all the Bright Young Things go. I know you like to look at the Flappers' dresses and beads.'

'Look, Papa, I can do the Charleston.'

Dickie grinned as Grace jigged around, and Louisa was impressed with her daughter's footwork.

'Very good, darling,' Dickie praised.

‘Oh, Papa, I do like to look at the dresses, but can’t we have fish and chips again?’

Dickie chuckled. ‘Cor blimey, Grace, you really are a girl after my own heart. All right, fish and chips it is.’

Grace and Gordon ran down the steps to his car, and as Dickie left, he turned to Louisa. ‘Have you told your mother about moving in here?’ he asked.

‘No, not yet. I’ll see her tomorrow.’

‘Make sure you do. And if the old cow kicks up a stink, you tell her that if she don’t like it, then she’s free to make her own arrangements, but I won’t be funding her.’

Louisa nodded. Of course her mother was going to kick up a stink, and being penniless, she couldn’t possibly make her own arrangements. *She’ll be even more impossible than usual*, Louisa thought, shrinking from having to tell her. The notion of running away with Jack was becoming more and more appealing! Louisa would have peace in her life with a man she adored and who cherished her, too. Escaping from Dickie and taking Grace away from her father was a terrifying thought, but the pain of Jack being out of her life was ripping her heart apart. She wanted to be with the man she loved, and she was slowly coming around to the idea of fleeing to Scotland with Jack and Grace.

‘Take him round the back,’ Dickie told Ernie. ‘I’ve got Grace in the car. I don’t want her to see Frank getting his head kicked in.’

As Ernie began to drag Frank away, the man pleaded, ‘Wait, Mr Newman, please, I’ve got kids. Five girls to feed.’

‘You should have thought about your girls before you

defaulted on your repayments to me,' Dickie replied, without sympathy.

Frank struggled against Ernie's strong grip. 'I need to work. I need to feed me kids. I'll pay, I will, I promise.'

Ernie looked at Dickie, but Dickie refused Frank any mercy. 'You've taken the piss out of me. You knew the score when you borrowed the money.' Then he told Ernie, 'Get him out of my sight.'

Walking back to his car, with Gordon swaggering beside him, Grace was peering out the window, her eyes wide.

'What is Ernie doing with that man?' she asked.

'Listen, darling. In this world, there are people who will take liberties if you let them. I gave that man a loan. He had a lot of money from me, which he must pay back. His debt to me should be his priority, but blokes like him will spend their wages in the pub before paying me. So, Ernie is going to tell him off.'

'Is Ernie going to spank the man?'

'Yes, darling, he is.'

'And then the man won't be naughty again, will he, Papa?'

'I hope not, 'cos if he's naughty again, Ernie will have to give him another spank.'

Gordon piped up, 'Ernie's giving Frank more than a spanking. He's gonna smash his flippin' head in!'

Dickie glared sharply at Gordon and warned, 'We don't discuss business in front of the fair ladies.'

Gordon, who always seemed so keen to please, was quick to apologise. 'Sorry, Mr Newman, I won't do it again.'

Grace sounded worried as she asked, 'Is he, Papa? Is Ernie going to smash that man's head in?'

'Don't concern yourself with blokes like Frank, Grace. Right, who's hungry?'

'We are,' Grace and Gordon answered in unison.

In the fish and chip shop, Dickie sat beside Gordon and opposite his daughter, watching as she soaked her chips in vinegar. 'Your chips will be swimming on your plate,' he chuckled.

'Papa, you never eat the bread and butter. Can I have it, please?' Grace asked.

'You've got all that fish to eat.'

'I know. I don't want to eat the bread, I want to save it for the ducks.'

'What ducks?' Dickie questioned.

'The ducks on the pond at the common. Mr Pope sometimes brings bread for them.'

'Who is Mr Pope?'

'Mother's friend.'

Dickie felt rage burning through his veins. 'When does Mother see Mr Pope?' he asked, trying to keep his voice calm.

'All the time. Sometimes we go to his shop and sometimes we meet him on the common.'

'What shop, darling?'

'The corner shop.'

Pope's Convenience Store. Dickie had driven past it many times. 'Eat up,' he said, losing his appetite. 'Time to go home.'

The moment Dickie came home, Louisa's stomach knotted with nerves. She knew her husband was in a dark mood – he looked angry, and his footsteps were heavy.

After bidding goodnight to Gordon, and then settling Grace into bed, Louisa crept down the stairs and into the kitchen, hoping to avoid Dickie. She warmed herself a cup of milk, and slipped out of the kitchen, heading for her bedroom. Quietly passing Dickie's office, she saw him from the corner of her eye. He was sitting in his studded leather armchair, a glass of brandy in one hand, his leg jigging up and down. Something had obviously infuriated him. Hurrying away, Louisa cringed when he shouted to her.

'Oi, woman, get in here!'

Standing still for a second, she closed her eyes and tried to calm her jangled nerves.

'Louisa!'

Louisa jolted. She could hear the venom in his voice. Pushing the door wider, she cautiously walked into the dimly lit room.

'Let me make something very clear,' Dickie said. 'You're *my* wife, which means you're out of bounds to other men.'

Louisa nodded with urgency. 'I know, Dickie.'

'Do you? Are you sure about that?'

'Yes, Dickie.'

'So, who the bleedin' 'ell is Mr Pope, eh?'

Louisa felt her blood run cold, like ice freezing in her veins. Her mouth was dry and warm milk spilt over the edge of the cup as her hand trembled.

'The cat got your tongue?' Dickie asked sarcastically.

'No, Dickie. Sorry, I think you have the wrong idea about Mr Pope. He owns the store where I shop. I've known him for many years, but I can assure you that Mr Pope has never behaved inappropriately.'

'Is that right? You don't think that meeting him on Clapham Common is *inappropriate*?'

Louisa swallowed hard, her heart racing. 'I've bumped into

him on the common a few times. All quite innocent,' she fibbed, trying to force a smile.

'How do you think that looks, eh? My wife, walking on the common with another man. Are you deliberately trying to make me look like a mug?'

'No, Dickie, I wouldn't do that! I can't help bumping into him, and it would be rude to ignore him.'

'All you have to do is say hello, you tell him you're very well, and then you say goodbye.' Jumping to his feet, Dickie slammed the glass of brandy down hard onto his desk, and shouted, 'You don't go and feed the fucking ducks with him!'

Louisa flinched and searched her mind for something to say. 'But … but Grace likes to feed the ducks,' she blurted.

'Very cosy. My wife, my daughter and Mr fuckin' Pope. Does he know who you're married to?'

Louisa stared at her husband, her breaths rapid, fear dazzling her.

'Does he?' Dickie's voice boomed.

She flinched and nodded.

'Perhaps he needs reminding of who I am.'

Dickie turned to his desk and threw the brandy down his neck, then marched across the room, shoving Louisa out of his way.

She stumbled, falling against a low table, and saw Dickie grab his coat. Regaining her footing, Louisa chased after her husband. 'Dickie, please, where are you going?' she asked.

He didn't answer, and pulled open the front door. Louisa took hold of his arm and tried to wrench Dickie back.

'Please, Dickie, Jack hasn't done anything wrong.'

'*Jack … Jack …* On first name terms, are ya?'

Shaking her loose, Dickie gripped her arm and dragged her

up the stairs. Louisa tried to pull back, afraid of what he was going to do, and fearing he might lock her in her bedroom.

Reaching the top landing, she complained, 'You're hurting me. Please, Dickie, don't do this.'

But instead of hauling her towards her bedroom, Dickie pulled her towards Grace's room. He gave the door a powerful kick and it flew open, flooding the room with light. Grace sat up in her bed, rubbing her eyes as she looked towards the door.

Dickie pushed Louisa in with so much force that she nearly fell forwards to the floor. Then, clumping in behind her, he grabbed the hair on the back of her head.

'You see this woman?' Dickie shouted towards Grace. 'Your mother … She's a slut! Your mother is a dirty, filthy whore!'

Tears streaked down Louisa's face as she peered regretfully at her daughter. The poor girl had looked confused, but now she looked terrified and had begun to cry, too. 'It's all right,' Louisa mouthed silently, hoping to alleviate Grace's fears. The girl rarely cried, as Louisa had brought her up to think crying was a sign of weakness. It was a shock to see tears from her daughter's eyes.

Dickie finally released Louisa, and marched away. She ran to the bed and wrapped her arms around Grace. 'It's all right,' she soothed, stroking the girl's silky hair. 'He's gone now.'

'Why was Papa so angry and why did he say those bad words about you?'

'Don't worry, Grace. Your Papa didn't mean to upset you.'

'Where's Papa gone?' Grace asked.

'I don't know,' Louisa answered, as a wave of nausea washed over her. She had a good idea where Dickie was going and knew she had to stop him. But how? The police wouldn't help her, as they danced to Dickie's drum. And Louisa couldn't leave Grace alone and distressed. Granted, Gordon was in the basement, but they hardly knew him, and Louisa assumed the boy was probably terrified, too. He must have heard the commotion.

Holding her daughter and gently rocking, Louisa's mind raced with images of Jack's battered face. *Oh, Jack*, she cried in her head. *I can't stop him. I'm so sorry.*

Grace finally calmed and drifted back to a fretful sleep. Gently closing her bedroom door, Louisa went into her own and threw herself onto her bed. Curling into a ball, she allowed her tears to come and sobbed uncontrollably for the man she loved. *It's not fair*, she thought. Jack hadn't done anything wrong except for loving her. And stupidly, she'd allowed it. Now Jack would be paying the price. It hurt Louisa to think of Jack in pain. She hoped Dickie hadn't been too hard on him and prayed her husband had just given Jack a stern warning, but having witnessed the man's rage, she feared Jack had received a vicious beating.

The sound of bells rang through the air outside. Louisa lifted her head, listening, and realised it was the fire brigade. Rushing to the window, she pulled back the curtains, horrified to see an orange glow in the night sky and dark smoke rising over the rooftops. She couldn't be sure, but the fire appeared to be in the direction of Jack's shop!

Racing down the stairs, Louisa ran along the street and around the corner towards Pope's Convenience Store. She'd left Grace alone in the house with Gordon and hoped they'd both stay asleep, but her immediate concern was for Jack.

Breathless, her shoeless feet sore from pounding the

pavement and her knitted stockings ripped at the heels, she turned another corner and saw the shocking sight of Jack's shop engulfed in flames. The fierce fire had ravaged the building, and as firemen fought to bring the blaze under control, Louisa fell to her knees, howling to the sky.

'Jack… Oh, Jack!' she cried.

The roof timbers crashed to the ground in flames. Jack's home, his livelihood and his life were gone. Burned to a cinder. Louisa couldn't bear to watch the firemen battle to contain the ferocious blaze. In a blur of disbelief, she stood up and staggered back towards home. Jack was gone, murdered at the hands of her evil husband. Grief consumed her heart, sticking in her throat, tightening around her chest. The pain was unbearable, and she knew that death would be the only escape from it. She wanted to die. To make the agony stop. But Louisa would have to live with the torturous truth of knowing that the man she loved had been killed because of her. It was her fault that Jack was dead. A beautiful, innocent man's life had been cruelly snuffed out because she'd fallen in love with him. She'd never forget Jack for as long as she lived, and neither would she ever forgive herself. As much as she wanted to throw herself into the Thames River or under the wheels of a moving steam train, Louisa had to endure a miserable, painful existence. She had to survive for the sake of her daughter.

20

Seven years later
May 1934

Louisa rolled over in her large, empty bed. The sun had long since risen, yet she remained under the covers, blocking out the world. She heard the door open, and peeked from under the blankets to see her mother come in, carrying a cup of tea, which she placed on the table beside the bed. She'd hoped it would be Grace. Her daughter came in every morning, always greeting her with a beautiful smile. Grace was the only good thing in her life, and she felt guilty for letting the girl down. They never went on shopping trips together or enjoyed lunches out. Louisa never had the energy. But she did relish their little chats and tried her best to show an interest.

Myrtle huffed, tutting at Louisa. 'Do you intend to stay in bed all day again, or will you get up and get dressed?'

Louisa didn't answer, hoping her mother would leave her be.

'You need to bathe, Louisa, and your sheets require washing.'

Louisa didn't care.

'This really won't do,' Myrtle snapped. 'I know you're not sick. There is no reason for you to lay in bed all day.

You're a married woman, Louisa, and a mother, you have responsibilities!'

'Leave me alone,' Louisa moaned, muffled by the bedclothes.

'I've left you alone for seven years, and nothing has changed. If you're not isolating yourself up here, then you're walking around the house in a state of uncaring indifference. Enough is enough, Louisa.'

Quite right, Louisa thought, *nothing has changed.* She was still married to a vile man. A killer. A murderer. *Oh, Jack, I miss you.*

Myrtle's heeled boots click-clacked across the floorboards, snapping Louisa from her thoughts. 'Disgraceful,' the woman muttered, as she left the bedroom.

Louisa threw the covers back and reached for the cup of tea. Had it really been seven years since Dickie had burned Pope's Convenience Store to the ground? Seven years since she'd last seen Jack Pope. It still felt like yesterday when they'd fed the ducks, and she'd said goodbye to him on Clapham Common. Louisa suspected her husband had killed Jack, though she hoped the man had fled in fear for his life. She imagined him living happily in Scotland, and she greatly regretted declining his offer to run away with him.

Climbing out of bed, Louisa pulled a chamber pot from underneath and relieved herself. Then, covering the urine-filled pot with a towel, she pushed it back under the bed. *I'll empty it later*, she thought, then, feeling drained and exhausted, she got back under the covers. Closing her eyes, her mind wandered to Jack again. His crooked smile that always warmed her heart. His silly jokes that used to make her giggle. The kind-hearted man hadn't deserved his fate. It had been her fault. If she had nipped their friendship in the bud when it had first begun, then Jack Pope would still be trading in his shop. But she'd allowed herself to fall in love with him, and now, instead of him leading a normal life, his store was a pile of ashes, and no one had ever heard from the man again. *I'm so sorry*, she wept.

Stuck in a rut of deep melancholy, the same sorrowful thoughts about Jack Pope went around and around in her head. And then she'd think about Dickie, hating the man, yet even the power of her hatred didn't energise Louisa. *Seven years*, she pondered. *I've been crying for seven years.*

She heard a light tap on the door and was pleased to see Grace come bounding in.

'Good morning, Mother. Grandma tells me you're under the weather again.'

'I'm tired, Grace. Come, sit here,' she said, patting the side of the bed.

'How can you be so tired all the time? You never do much to wear you out.'

'I don't know. I wish I had more energy.'

'I wish you did, too. I want you to come and see my shop.'

'I will, one day, I promise,' Louisa said sadly, forcing a smile. 'I'm so proud of you being a working woman. Will you promise me something, Grace?'

'I'll try. What would you like me to promise?'

Louisa took hold of her daughter's hand and looked her deeply in the eyes. 'Promise me that you will never be reliant on a man to support you financially. Work hard and make your own money, and only ever marry for love. True love.'

'I think I can promise you that, Mother. My shop isn't yet making a fortune, but I hope it will in the future. And I don't have any intentions of marrying anyone yet. It won't be easy to get Papa's approval, you know how he is with me.'

'Just remember that you are not your father's property and you are entitled to marry a man who makes you happy, regardless of what your father thinks.'

Grace nodded. 'I must dash. I'm late opening the shop. Are you coming downstairs for breakfast?'

'Not today, Grace. Maybe later.'

The door closed and Louisa pulled the covers under her chin. She hoped her daughter would heed her advice, but Dickie had a firm grip on the girl's affairs and was a big influence in her life. At least Grace seemed happy for now and that was the most that Louisa could hope for.

Myrtle rinsed the breakfast plates before sitting at the table with a cup of tea. She'd been living under Dickie's roof for seven years, yet it still didn't feel like home and never would. She had to get out. She was fed up with the household chores, cleaning up after Dickie and cooking for the man. She had Grace to help, and at least she didn't have to launder his clothes, as the dirty washing was sent out to a woman whose daughter collected and returned it twice a week. Myrtle tutted. It was Louisa's job to look after her husband, but Myrtle had seen her daughter slip further and further into a state of depression. At least Myrtle's work in the house had stopped Dickie from having Louisa committed to an asylum, though she was beginning to reason that maybe it was time for her hopeless daughter to go into a mental hospital. But Myrtle could never condemn her daughter to a place of such misery. The dark mood that shrouded the house had become unbearable and Myrtle's patience had reached breaking point.

To make matters worse, she couldn't abide Gordon. He was just as rough and just as common as Dickie. If she continued to live in Dickie's house, she thought she might end up in the same sorry state as her daughter. Her stomach flipped when she thought about the audacious plan she'd concocted. A plan that would be coming to fruition later today. Dickie Newman was finally going to get his comeuppance, and Myrtle would reap the benefits. Her only regret – she wished she'd had the nerve to do it years ago!

Seventeen-year-old Grace Newman flipped the sign on her hat boutique door from open to closed. Glancing over her shoulder at the array of colourful and stylish hats, she smiled. Today had been the first day in the six months since opening that she'd turned a profit, and she couldn't wait to tell her papa. He'd bought her the shop and stocked it too, though they had battled over the location. Her father had wanted the shop to be in Chelsea, where a 'better' class of people resided, but Grace had insisted on Battersea. As usual, Grace had won her own way.

Locking the door behind her, she walked proudly along Falcon Road, enjoying seeing heads turning to look at her. She hoped they were admiring her shallow crown hat, worn at a deep angle to one side and almost covering one of her eyes. The black and white spotted fabric matched her scarf, and Grace felt like a fashion icon. She thought she was a good advert for her millinery shop.

Rushing to her father's properties, she knew she'd find him somewhere in the area, as it was rent collection day. They'd arranged to meet in Clapham Junction at Lyons tea shop, but Grace was eager to share her news about how much money the shop had taken. She knew he didn't like her being around his properties, because he said she drew too much attention in her fancy clothes and hats. Though Grace was sure that when her father saw her, she'd soon be forgiven. After all, as her grandma often said, she had her papa wrapped around her little finger. Grace smiled to herself. She adored her father and their close relationship. At least she had one parent she could rely on. Her mother … well, Grace tried not to think about the pitiful woman who spent her days wallowing in woe, and when she wasn't in her bed, walked around in a fog, like a dead person living. She loved her mother, but the woman seemed so helpless. Grace wouldn't give up on her, though. One day, she hoped to persuade her mother to visit the hat boutique. It would be a big step for her and Grace would keep on pushing. Anything to get her out of the house and to enjoy living again.

Popping into the baker's shop, she thought it would be nice to treat her papa, Gordon and Ernie to a cake. She stood in the queue behind a ragged woman carrying a baby in her arms and with three children beside her. The woman wore a grimy scarf covering her hair, and Grace noticed the children were in tatters, too. A little girl with bright, blue eyes turned and gazed at Grace. She smiled warmly at the child, thinking how pretty she was, and such a shame that her golden locks were matted and her pretty eyes sunken.

The baker, his voice stern, told the woman, 'I don't give store credit. If I did, I'd never make any money, because you wouldn't pay your credit off.'

'Please, sir, if you won't give me credit, won't you grant me a few scraps of stale bread? Me kids are hungry, their bellies empty. Just a stale loaf, that's all I'm asking for.'

Grace's heart went out to the woman and her children. Stepping forward, she approached the counter. 'Excuse me, sorry to interrupt. Wrap two of your freshest loaves for this woman, and I'll take a rock cake for each of the children. Thank you.'

Turning to the woman and smiling, Grace expected gratitude for her good deed. Instead, she found herself meeting the eyes of someone who looked as though she wanted to slap her around the face.

'I'm sorry, I hope you don't mind me buying you the bread and the cakes for the children?'

'You've got some nerve,' the woman spat bitterly. 'I suppose buying me some bread eases your conscience. I don't know how you and your family sleep at night! Evil, rotten bastards, the lot of ya!'

'I beg your pardon?' Grace replied, disturbed.

'You ain't little Miss Innocent, so don't pretend that you don't know what your dad and his heavies get up to. I've seen you on our street with them, dressed up to the nines, flaunting your fancy hats. And all the while, there's babes starving and mother's pulling their hair out in despair 'cos they can't feed their kids.'

Grace hadn't meant to cause offence, but she clearly had. And it wasn't her fault that poorer families struggled to pay for housing and put food on the table. Her papa said they were lazy, or drunks, and he was providing a service with his cheap rents.

'You don't care. You couldn't care less if we all rotted in our own filth. Just so long as your dad and the rest of you get paid. You get rich, and my kids go hungry.'

'I'm not to blame, and neither is my father. If he didn't offer cheap accommodation, you'd be homeless.'

The woman's eyes narrowed. 'We live in one room and share a privy in the back yard with several other families. We ain't got running water indoors, just a standpipe next to the privy. The whole house is infested with bugs and vermin. The windows are nailed shut, so in the summer it's hot and stuffy, but I can't afford to pay your dad to have the nails out. There's no heating, so in the winter, we have ice on the inside of the windows. Am I supposed to be grateful to you and your family?'

Grace swallowed hard, unsure of what to say.

'My eldest nearly died. The doctor saved him, but it cost money. I'd put that money aside to pay the rent, and when I couldn't pay 'cos I had to pay the doc instead, your dad had my husband battered. He was beaten so badly that he couldn't do his labouring job for four days. I begged your dad for a little leeway. He knew my boy had been sick. That man is wicked to his core, and I reckon the apple ain't fallen far from the tree.'

Handing the baby to the biggest of the children, the feisty woman snatched the bread and cakes from the counter, before marching out.

Grace stood, her mind reeling. Was her father *really* so uncharitable? She didn't need to search far for answers. She recollected a scene she'd witnessed as a child. A man being dragged away by Ernie to receive a *spanking.* She remembered Mrs Love, an old woman who spent her days in a creaky rocking chair. She'd died in that chair, and Grace had heard Gordon say that the old biddy had frozen to death. Yes, she supposed there were times when her father had treated people atrociously, but her father had explained that folk only got smacked if they had taken liberties. And Mrs Love had been old. Though the words of the woman with the starving children were still ringing in her ears. Had Grace been ignoring what had been under her nose for all her life? Was her father such a monster? She didn't want to believe so, but maybe it was time to delve into his business a little deeper. If she found anything untoward, she'd insist on making changes. Her papa *always* listened to her because she was his favourite, after all, and could do no wrong in his eyes.

Gordon strutted alongside Dickie, with Ernie walking a few steps behind.

'I'm meeting Grace up the junction,' Dickie said. 'You can either come with me or bugger off down the pub with Ernie.'

'If you're going to that poncy tea and cake place again, then I think I'll go with Ernie.'

Dickie chuckled. 'Can't say I blame you, son.'

Gordon liked it when Dickie called him son. The man had become like a father to him. The same couldn't be said for Louisa Newman being like a mother. Gordon felt he hardly knew her, because she rarely left her bedroom and when she did, she pretty much ignored him. And as for Mrs Myrtle Best, it was no secret that she didn't like him, and the feelings were mutual. *She's an old battleaxe*, he thought, and he knew his opinion was vindicated, because Dickie couldn't stand her, either. In fact, though Gordon was grateful to Dickie for taking him in when he'd been abandoned by his mother, there were many unpleasant memories of growing up in the Newman household that often popped into his head. He'd always tried so hard to be accepted, but Mrs Best had made her disdain for him more than apparent. And he'd hoped that Louisa would have given him the mother's love he'd been deprived of, but the woman walked around in almost a trance-like state and had never made him feel wanted.

Gordon thought back to many of his birthdays spent with the family, though no one knew his *real* date of birth. The celebrations had been limited. He'd receive a small gift from Dickie, usually a few coins slipped into his pocket. No thought had gone into it. There had been no birthday cake. Unlike Grace's birthdays. Over the years, he'd stood in the corner of the room watching with envy as she excitedly opened her pile of expensive gifts and blown out the candles on her cake. Even Louisa would smile and cheer. Christmas was the same. Grace's stocking would be stuffed with toys and games, whilst he'd receive a few coins and a piece of fruit. It wasn't just the differences in the birthdays that upset Gordon. It was also the lack of affection he'd receive from Dickie. When the man scooped Grace into his arms, or played with her, Gordon had yearned for the same attention. Instead, Dickie had shown him how to fight, forcing him to hit boys a lot older and bigger than himself, and warning him that if he didn't do it, he'd receive Dickie's belt across his backside. Gordon had been scared, but he'd done what Dickie had told him and faced the bigger boys rather than Dickie's belt. It had been tough, and he had always been jealous of the gifts and affection lavished on Grace. That's why he'd never liked her, though he hid his resentment well.

'Don't be coming home drunk,' Dickie warned. 'We've got an early start tomorrow.'

'You know me, I can't hold me beer. Just a few halves is my limit.'

'Yeah, you say that, but Ernie had to carry you home last week.'

'Cor, I didn't 'alf feel rough the next day. That was Ernie's fault. He got me on the whisky. I ain't drinking like that again, ever.'

'We've all said that before, son. But I mean it, stick to beer, no spirits. Grace wasn't happy about you throwing up all over the stairs and the bathroom.'

'I know, she's still bending my ear about it. Cor, that woman can nag! I pity any bloke who marries her.'

'She ain't getting married,' Dickie growled. 'Not without my say so. And I ain't met a bloke yet who's good enough for my Grace. Is she seeing anyone? She'd tell you if she was.'

Gordon shook his head. 'Nah, Dickie, she wouldn't tell me if she had a fella.'

'You two are close.'

'Yeah, but you brought me up to protect her with me own life, Dickie. Grace knows that any fella who wanted to step out with her would have to get my approval first. He'd have to be something bloody special for me to be agreeable.'

'Good man, Gordon. She's your little sister. You make sure you always look out for her.'

'I will, Dickie, you can count on me,' Gordon assured him. He'd do and say anything to keep Dickie happy, but in truth, he resented Grace. He thought she was spoiled, and he was still jealous of the attention Dickie gave her. Grace had everything handed to her on a plate, even her posh hat shop, whereas Gordon had to work for a living, and he'd worked since he'd been knee-high to a grasshopper. Dickie had introduced him to his violent world from a young age, and Gordon had seen things that no tender-aged lad should have seen. It had shaped him into a callous, hard young man who feared no one – exactly how Dickie had wanted him to be. The man had said it several times. *You're like the son I never had.* Those words pleased Gordon, and he treasured them more than anything.

'When are we gonna meet your new lady friend?' Dickie asked.

'Soon. She already knows Grace from when they were kids, but I don't want you lot to scare her off,' Gordon laughed.

'We'll be as good as gold. Is it getting serious with her?'

Gordon grinned. He couldn't help beaming when he thought of Anna. 'Yeah, Dickie, I reckon it is.'

'Good for you, son. But I want an introduction before you go putting a ring on her finger. Right, I'll see you later. Don't do anything I wouldn't do,' Dickie joked, as he climbed into his car.

As Dickie sped off, Ernie tugged his flat cap. 'See ya, Boss.'

''Ere, Ernie, I'll race you to the pub,' Gordon challenged.

'I'll meet you there,' Ernie replied. 'I don't run unless I'm chasing someone for money.'

'How long have you worked for Dickie?'

'Too bleedin' long,' Ernie snorted.

'Has he ever killed anyone? I mean, we rough 'em up a bit, and all that, but has he ever put anyone six feet under?'

'That ain't my business to talk about, and you shouldn't be asking those sorts of questions.'

Gordon stayed quiet for the rest of the walk to the pub, his thoughts racing. Ernie hadn't denied anything. The man's response suggested that Dickie was a murderer. He thought about Mrs Newman and recalled first meeting her. She'd been welcoming, but shortly after, there had been a kerfuffle,

Dickie calling his wife a slut. The woman had spent a lot of time in her room since that night and never smiled. Gordon had often sneaked around the house and had heard her nightmares. Night after night, she cried in her sleep, and he'd listened with his ear to the door when she'd called for *Jack*. Gordon didn't know who Jack was, but from what he'd heard of Mrs Newman's almost incoherent mumblings, he'd concluded that Jack was dead, and Dickie had killed him. *Blimey*, he thought, smiling again as he pictured his girlfriend, Anna. *She'd be mortified if she knew what sort of family she was getting involved with.*

Grace walked with purpose, hurrying to reach her father and excited to tell him about making a profit today. She turned a corner, pleased when she saw his car at the end of the street. He was driving towards her, but as Grace went to wave him down, a small group of men jumped in front of the vehicle.

Grace watched in horror as the masked men forced her father to stop the car, and then they yanked open the door before pulling her father out. Dragging him to the ground, she saw them kicking his body, his face and his head.

'Stop!' she screamed, racing towards them. 'Get off him!'

As she drew closer, her heart pounding, she screamed again. 'Stop! Leave him alone!'

One of the gang members, who'd been standing by watching, glanced around at her, and she saw his mask slip. Their eyes met momentarily, but then a glint caught Grace's eyes, and she shrieked in panic. Another of the men had a knife, which he plunged into her father.

Grace ran faster, and the attackers fled. When she reached the car, her father was on the ground, lying in his own blood, barely conscious. She noticed the imprint of a boot on his cheek, his white shirt soaked red.

'Oh, Papa ... Papa,' Grace whimpered, falling to her knees and scooping his head into her arms.

'I'm all right,' he groaned, his voice only just audible, and his eyes half closed.

Grace looked around; the street was empty. 'Help!' she shouted. 'Somebody help us!'

She placed her hands over the stab wound in her father's stomach, pushing down to try to stem the bleeding. Blood oozed between her fingers and her father groaned in pain. 'Stay with me, Papa ... Please ... Don't die.'

21

Six days later, on Sunday morning, Grace was pouring a cup of tea to take upstairs to her father, and one for her mother who was sitting in the lounge, when her grandmother walked into the kitchen, dressed in her fur-trimmed coat and wearing a hat from Grace's boutique.

'You look very smart. The hat suits you. Where are you going?' Grace asked.

'Out,' her grandmother answered abruptly. 'I assume your father is still alive?'

'Yes, and I think he might be out of bed soon. The doctor said the puncture wound wasn't very deep and Papa won't suffer any long-term damage.'

'More's the pity,' Myrtle sniffed coldly.

'Grandma!'

Myrtle showed no remorse for her comment and turned to leave. Grace shook her head. There had always been animosity between her father and grandmother, but she hadn't realised how bitterly her grandmother felt. Anger burned inside, and she chased after the woman.

As Myrtle pulled open the front door, Grace hissed, 'You

should show a bit more gratitude. I'm not stupid, Grandma, I know you're reliant on my father for everything. If it wasn't for Papa, you'd have nothing.'

'*Gratitude! Gratitude!* I'll show gratitude when that man is dead, and my daughter is a wealthy woman.'

Grace stood speechless, and as her grandmother flounced down the steps to the street, she saw Gordon approaching with a young and pretty woman on his arm. She immediately knew the petite woman with blonde, curly hair was Anna. After all, Anna was all Gordon spoke about lately. And as they drew closer, Grace's face broke into a wide grin. She couldn't believe that Gordon's girlfriend was the same Anna who Grace had been friends with in the Brownies and then the Girl Guides.

Her grandmother passed the couple without acknowledging them, merely glancing down her uppity nose.

'Where's she off to?' Gordon asked, flicking his head at Myrtle.

'I don't know, and I don't care. She's a frightful woman.' Then, warmly greeting the lady on Gordon's arm, she gushed, 'I can't believe it's you! It's so lovely to see you again, Anna.'

'And you, Grace,' Anna replied, smiling. 'You're looking great, and Gordon tells me you have a shop now.'

'Yes, I do. Come in. I've just made tea and we can have a good catch up.'

Grace had always liked Anna and was pleased to see her friend. They hadn't kept in touch since Grace had left the Girl Guides, which she regretted now, but she'd been so busy that friendships hadn't seemed a priority.

In the kitchen, Gordon asked, 'How is he?'

'Papa? He's great! He looks worse than he feels. He's sitting up and itching to get back to work, but I've insisted he rests for at least another day or two. Any news on who attacked him?'

'Nah, nothing. Everyone's keeping tight-lipped, but I'll find out, and when I do, I'll kill 'em, I swear I'll skin 'em alive.'

Grace noticed Anna baulk and could see she felt uncomfortable with Gordon's threatening talk. Quickly changing the subject, she said, 'You must call in to my boutique. I have a gorgeous hat that will match your blue eyes and would look wonderful on you.'

'I'd like that,' Anna replied. 'Perhaps Gordon will treat me to it.'

'*I'll* treat you to it,' Grace offered. 'And we could have a look at the latest dresses in Arding and Hobbs, then have tea in Lyons,' she suggested, keen to rekindle their friendship.

Gordon sighed, and said with a smile, 'I can see this is gonna cost me a pretty packet.'

'And Papa, too. I'll have to ask him for some money. I've not opened the shop since he was attacked, so my purse is empty.'

'You've not left his bedside, Grace. Me and Anna are here now. Why don't you go out and get some fresh air? It's a lovely morning and you're looking a bit peaky.'

Grace nodded in agreement. 'I could do with getting out for a while, but do you think it's safe?'

Gordon placed his strong arm over her shoulder and gave her a quick and gentle squeeze. 'Seeing Dickie attacked like you did is bound to have left you feeling unsettled, but you ain't got nothing to worry about. The blokes who set on him were out to rob him. They must have known he had a lot of money on him. I reckon they'd been watching him for a while, and knew it was rent collection day. They weren't after you, Grace. Get your coat and bugger off. We'll look after Dickie until you get back.'

'Are you sure?'

Anna placed her hand on Grace's arm. 'Yes, we're sure. I work as an auxiliary in the Bolingbroke hospital and I'm going to train to be a nurse. Your dad will be in good hands.'

'Thank you. That puts my mind at rest. I always knew you'd go into nursing, Anna. Will you check on my mother, too? She came down for breakfast and is sitting in the lounge, but she'll retire back to her room soon. I worry about her. She never leaves the house and is always very tired.'

'Of course,' Anna assured her. 'Has the doctor seen your mother?'

'Yes, several times, but he insists there's nothing wrong with her physically. He said she is suffering from melancholia. He suggested electric shock therapy but my grandma won't allow it.'

'Oh, I'm sorry to hear that. Don't worry. Go and relax for a few hours. Take a stroll on the common. We'll be fine here, and I'll still be here when you get back.'

'You're very kind. I won't stay out long.'

Grace pulled open the front door and looked nervously up and down the street. She felt foolish for being unsure about stepping outside. Nothing had ever scared Grace before, and she knew she was tougher than most women. But witnessing her father being stomped on and stabbed had left her nerves jangled. *Stop being silly*, she told herself, mustering her courage. *You're a Newman. You're Dickie Newman's daughter and you're not scared of anything!*

★

At the bandstand on Clapham Common, Myrtle Best tapped her foot impatiently. She'd been waiting for over half an hour, yet there was still no sign of John Dander. They'd prearranged a meeting for today, and Myrtle was eager to get her hands on some cash.

'Don't let me down,' she muttered under her breath.

She sighed with relief when she saw the rogue making his way towards her. Dander had the benefit of youth on his side, and she noticed the man was light on his feet, especially considering his bulk. His shoulders were broad and his arms thick with muscle from lugging heavy sacks of coal. With the sun on his tanned face highlighting his chiselled features, Myrtle thought he looked quite handsome, let down by his scruffy clothes that showed he was a commoner. Dander was the coalman's lackey, and she'd first met him when he'd hauled sacks into the coal-store at the back of the house. It hadn't taken Myrtle long to persuade Dander to carry out her wishes; he'd been easily manipulated.

'You're late,' she snapped.

John Dander removed his flat cap. 'Yeah, sorry 'bout that, Mrs Best.'

'Well, where's my money?' she demanded.

The man shoved his large hand into his trouser pocket and pulled out a leather pouch. 'There's not much in it,' he said sheepishly.

Myrtle snatched the pouch and looked inside. 'Where is the rest of the money?' she asked shortly.

'The others ... they wouldn't give me any more for you. They've kept it for themselves.'

Myrtle's lips pursed. 'We had an agreement.'

'I know, but there's nothing I can do.'

'I knew I should never have trusted you! You are useless, Dander, and you didn't even do the job properly. Mr Newman is alive and well. You were supposed to have killed him.'

'He looked 'alf dead when we left him on the road.'

'Well, he wasn't, which means there will be no inheritance, so you and your gang can sing for the rest of the payment we agreed.'

'Suits me, Mrs Best. It ain't worth swinging for. I'm glad Mr Newman is alive. I wouldn't want my neck to be in a noose 'cos of him. I never wanted to do the job in the first place.'

'Get out of my sight, Dander, and *never* speak to me again. Is that clear?'

John Dander placed his flat cap back on his head and walked away without saying a word, leaving Myrtle seething. She'd taken a great risk in setting up the robbery and Dickie's murder, though she'd thought the risk had been worth it to be free of the man and have access to his money. Yet Myrtle was in exactly the same position as she'd always been, thanks to Dander's incompetence. If she wanted rid of Dickie, she'd have to get blood on her hands and do it herself. Myrtle shuddered. Arranging the man's death had been easy, but carrying out the act was something beyond her capabilities, and Myrtle knew she'd be trapped under his rule for a long time to come.

Grace could feel herself shaking, stunned at what she'd seen. When she'd first spotted the man on the common, she'd instantly recognised him as one of the gang members, whose scarf had slipped when he'd been watching her father being attacked. Keeping her distance, Grace had followed him to the bandstand. When she'd seen him approaching her grandmother, she'd almost screamed out a warning to the woman, and had been about to run over to protect her from the evil man. But then she'd seen him remove his cap, and it was clear that her grandmother knew him. In fact, it looked like Myrtle had been waiting for him. Grace had hidden behind a tree and watched from a distance. She couldn't hear their exchange of words, but she'd seen the man take something from his pocket and hand it to her grandmother.

As realisation dawned on Grace, she felt as though she'd been punched in the stomach. Her grandmother, her own flesh and blood, was in cahoots with one of the men who'd robbed and tried to kill her father. It was clear Myrtle was behind the attack. *How could she?* Grace wondered in disbelief. She didn't want to believe that her grandmother could do something so extraordinarily awful, but it was the only explanation. The woman was wicked beyond anything Grace could have imagined, and she feared what else her grandmother might have planned, and what the woman was capable of.

As Grace hurried through the common, her legs felt like jelly, and she wasn't sure that they'd carry her home without giving way. Her mind raced, questions bombarding her, questions for which she had no answers. Should she confront her grandmother? Myrtle would only deny any accusations. Should she tell her father? She worried what that might lead to. Maybe confide in Gordon? There would be dreadful repercussions. Grace didn't know what to do with the information, but one thing she did know – she'd sleep uneasily tonight, and with her bedroom door locked.

22

The next day, Dickie grimaced uncomfortably as he threw his legs over the edge of the bed. Gordon stepped forward to help him to his feet. Dickie batted him away, saying, 'Get off, I can do it myself.'

'Are you sure you're well enough for this?' Gordon asked, his voice dripping with concern. 'Me and Ernie can manage without you.'

Dickie was in pain, but he was determined to show his face in Battersea. 'I ain't letting them robbing bastards think they've got one over on me. I need to know who had the bloody nerve to have a go at me, and I won't find out by laying in me bed.'

'Me and Ernie have been asking around, but no one's talking.'

'It's time to put the pressure on. And when I find out who it was, they're gonna wish they'd never been born. Pass me my shirt.'

Gordon handed him the shirt with a soppy grin, and Dickie knew the lad was going to talk about his girlfriend.

'What did you think of Anna?' Gordon asked. 'She's a looker, and she's a good girl, Dickie.'

'Yeah, nice. Grace thinks a lot of her. They were good friends when they were kids.'

'Yeah, they were. I never met Anna back then 'cos Grace never brought her friends home.'

'I reckon she was ashamed of her mother. The woman is a waste of good air. Take my advice, son, don't get yourself lumbered with a weak woman.'

'Actually, I was thinking of asking Anna to marry me.'

'Bloody hell, son, you've only known her a few weeks. What's the rush, eh? Have you got her in the family way?'

'No, Dickie, nothing like that. I told you, Anna's a good girl. She wouldn't do, you know, the other, not until we're married.'

Dickie smirked. 'So that's why you want to get wed so quickly, you dirty sod.'

'She's the one, Dickie, I know she is.'

'I'm sure she is, but if you want my advice, then I reckon you should slow down a bit, son. Get to know her better. And if you're serious about marrying her, then keep it in your trousers. Stop letting the likes of Mary Hatch pay the rent in kindness, and then I won't have to keep docking your pay. You're gonna need your wages to fork out for a wedding.'

'Yeah, you're probably right, but Mary's an hard woman to say no to.'

'And what about what's-her-name at number eighty-nine? Is she hard to say no to an' all, eh? And that little Irish one on the next street.'

'It's a good job you pay me well, Dickie,' Gordon sniggered.

'If Anna finds out, don't come crying to me about it. You've been warned.'

*

Grace spent a tense day in the boutique, her mind going over and over what she'd witnessed on Clapham Common. She'd tried to convince herself that she'd misunderstood the situation between her grandmother and the man who'd attacked her father, yet time after time, she had to admit to herself that her grandmother was guilty of arranging her father's demise. A knot twisted in her stomach, and her hands felt clammy. Grace knew she had to do something with the information she'd gleaned, but she couldn't decide what. The burden of holding the secret weighed heavy on her taut shoulders, and she had a thumping headache.

She glanced out the window onto the busy street. It was almost closing time, and Grace regretted arranging to meet Anna. As she saw the pretty woman walking towards the shop, she tried to hide her turmoil behind a plastered-on smile.

'Hello, Grace,' Anna greeted her, her eyes roaming the boutique. 'Wow, this is wonderful! You have so many lovely hats in here.'

'And this is the one I was talking about,' Grace said, taking a blue velvet slouched cloche hat from its stand. 'Here, try this on. It's great for everyday wear, and I have another that will look smashing on you for special occasions.'

As the women tried on hats and checked their reflections in a tall mirror, Grace found herself enjoying Anna's company, and her gloomy mood brightening. It felt wonderful to reconnect. She didn't really have any other friends, only Gordon, and he was more like a brother.

Anna giggled, laughing at an oversized hat on her head, and Grace's mind wandered back to her grandmother. She wanted to confide in Anna. They'd told each other everything when they'd been friends as children. But could she trust her to keep a secret from Gordon? Grace wasn't sure, though she hoped so, and blurted, 'I know who arranged for my father to be attacked.' Her heart was pounding hard, her mouth dry, but it was a relief to confess.

Anna immediately stopped giggling and removed the hat as she turned to look at Grace with wide eyes, her mouth open.

'Can I trust you, Anna? Will you tell anyone?'

'I won't if you don't want me to.'

'Not even Gordon. Gordon's the last person who should know what I know. Christ, Anna, I think if Gordon was to find out, he'd do something that would end him in gaol or swinging from the gallows. Please, Anna, please don't say anything to Gordon.'

'I won't, Grace, I promise. You don't have to tell me anything, but I think you need to unburden yourself. I realise we haven't seen one another in a while, but I know you, Grace, and I can see that something is deeply troubling you.'

Grace slumped into a chair. 'Oh, Anna, it is. I've not slept; I can't eat. My stomach is churning, and I feel like I can't breathe sometimes.'

Anna rushed towards the chair and crouched in front of it. Taking Grace's hands in hers, and peering deeply into Grace's eyes, she urged, 'You can trust me, Grace. We've been friends for years. Tell me what it is that's troubling you.'

Grace hoped she wouldn't regret telling Anna, and breathed in a long breath before saying, 'My grandmother arranged the attack.'

'Your grandmother ... Are you sure?'

'Yes, sadly, I am. When Papa was being beaten, I saw the face of one of the men when his scarf slipped. And yesterday,

I saw that same man on Clapham Common. He met with my grandmother, they exchanged something, presumably money, and then they went their separate ways. Anna, you must understand, my grandmother doesn't associate with men like those who robbed my father. She would *never* speak to a man like that, not even to say hello. It proves to me that she's behind it.'

Anna rose to her feet and clasped her hands in front of her face.

'What are you thinking?' Grace asked.

'I don't know. I think we should tell Gordon.'

'No, Anna, no, we really shouldn't! Do you have any idea what Gordon is capable of?'

Anna's head dropped and she looked at the floor. 'Yes, I think I do. Perhaps you're right. Maybe telling Gordon isn't a good idea.'

'You see my dilemma? I don't know what to do. I'm sorry, I shouldn't have said anything. I never should have involved you.'

Anna shook her head vigorously. 'No, Grace, I'm glad you told me. You and your father are the closest thing that Gordon has to family, and when we're married, that will make us like sisters. We should help each other. That's what sisters do.'

'Has Gordon proposed?' Grace asked, surprised.

'Not yet,' Anna answered coyly, 'but he walked me past a jewellery store and asked me which ring I liked.' Then, after a short pause, she added, 'Don't worry about your grandma, Grace. Together, we'll work out what to do for the best.'

Sitting on a bench, Gordon stuffed the last chip into his mouth and screwed up the greasy newspaper that his chips had been in. 'I suppose I should think about walking you home,' he said to Anna. 'It's getting late, and I don't want your dad giving me an hard time.'

Anna said nothing as she gazed up at the full moon. She'd been quiet all evening and Gordon wondered what was bothering her.

'Have I done something wrong?' he quizzed her.

'Eh?'

'I said, have I done something to upset you?'

'No,' Anna replied. 'Of course you haven't.'

'Only, you ain't said more than two words tonight. I feel like I'm in the doghouse, but I don't know why.'

Anna looked down at her shoes. 'Sorry, Gordon. I've got things on my mind, that's all. Nothing for you to worry about.'

'What things?' he pressed.

'Just stuff.'

'Tell me. If someone's upset you, I'll have a word with them.'

'No one's upset me.'

'What's wrong, then? You ain't yourself.'

'I told you, just things on my mind, and I'd rather not talk about it.'

'Fine, don't tell me,' Gordon huffed, and leapt to his feet. 'Come on, I'm taking you home,' he said moodily, and stomped away.

Anna caught up with him and tugged on his arm. 'Please, Gordon, don't be like this.'

He spun around and glared at her. 'I want to marry you, Anna. I want you to be my wife. You shouldn't have *stuff* on your mind that you can't tell me about.'

'You want to marry me?' Anna checked, smiling.

'Yeah, I do. But I won't ask you to be my wife if you can't even talk to me.'

'I can talk to you, Gordon, just not about this.'

Gordon stomped away again, angry and feeling rejected.

'Stop sulking,' Anna called, and fell into step beside him.

'I ain't a kid, Anna, I don't sulk,' he spat.

'Yeah, you are. You're throwing your toys out of the pram.'

'You shouldn't keep secrets from me.'

'I'm not. I just don't want to talk about what's on my mind.'

'Then you're keeping a bloomin' secret, Anna, and it ain't on. You've had a face like a smacked arse all evening. I know when something ain't right, so stop lying to me. I won't be lied to, Anna, and I won't be made a fool of. Tell me what's bothering you, or I'll say goodnight to you at your front door and you'll never see me again.'

'Oh, Gordon, please don't make me tell you. It's not even my secret to divulge.'

'It's your choice, Anna.'

'Would you really walk out on us over this?'

Gordon nodded. He didn't want to end his relationship with Anna, but the woman had to know who was boss. He couldn't have her keeping things from him.

'All right. But when I tell you, you have to promise me that you're not going to do anything stupid. Promise me that you'll think before you act.'

'Just spit it out.'

'Promise me,' Anna demanded.

'Yeah, yeah, all right, I promise. Now, tell me.'

'I want to tell you, Gordon. I've wanted to tell you all evening, but I'm scared of how you're going to take it.'

Gordon was losing his patience. 'For Christ's sake, Anna,' he said, his voice rising. 'I ain't gonna ask you again. Just bloody tell me!'

'All right, calm down! See, this is exactly what I'm talking about. You're already in a bad mood, and I'm worried that what I'm going to tell you will send you flying off the handle!'

'I've had enough of this,' Gordon ground out. 'Don't tell me, and don't expect to see me again.'

Picking up his pace, Gordon shoved his hands in his pockets and raced ahead.

'Wait,' Anna yelled. 'I know who arranged for Mr Newman to be attacked.'

Gordon instantly stopped and spun to look back at Anna. 'Who?' he demanded.

Anna had stopped walking, too. She stood, staring back at him with imploring eyes.

'Who?' he barked. 'Who arranged for Dickie's beating?' Then, marching towards her, he grabbed her shoulders and shook her. 'Who was it?' he shouted.

Anna began to cry. 'Please, Gordon, you're scaring me,' she sobbed.

His face in hers, his mouth twisted, he shouted, 'Tell me who it was!'

'Grace's grandmother,' Anna finally wailed. 'It was Mrs Best,' she wept.

Gordon let go of Anna and staggered a few steps backwards. It couldn't be true. He didn't like the old hag, but she couldn't have arranged for Dickie's attack ... could she? 'How do you know?' he asked.

The woman's shoulders jerked up and down as she cried.

'Grace told me. I promised her that I wouldn't say anything. Please, Gordon, don't tell her I told you.'

'Grace … Grace said it was Mrs Best?'

'Yes. She saw her on the common yesterday with one of the blokes that beat Dickie. She doesn't know what to do and she's worried about you knowing the truth.'

'Yeah, I bet she is,' Gordon hissed.

'What are you going to do?'

Gordon's thoughts were tumbling one after the other. He didn't know what he was going to do, but one thing he did know for sure – Mrs Best wasn't going to get away with it!

23

Dickie rested his head back and closed his eyes, listening to the record playing on his gramophone. Roy Fox sang with his backing orchestra, *Thanks for the Memory*, and as the melodic tones swathed Dickie, he found himself listening to the words of the song and reminiscing about Pippa. She wasn't the vibrant woman she'd once been, but Dickie had always been fond of her. He recalled the good times they'd shared and the precious moments that were indelibly inked onto his mind. He missed her, and felt the urge to hold her close, to smell her sweet perfume and stroke her soft skin. As the record came to an end, he gulped down a large glass of brandy and tried to convince himself that Pippa hadn't been the love of his life.

Dickie didn't hear the front door open, but he heard Gordon shrieking his name.

'Dickie! Dickie!'

'In here, son,' he called back.

His office door flew open with a crash, and Gordon stood in the doorway, his eyes glaring and his face ashen.

Dickie jumped to his feet, alarmed. 'What's happened?' he asked cautiously.

Gordon clenched his fists and scowled. 'That fuckin' old bag was behind you getting robbed,' he announced. 'I'll kill her, Dickie, I'll rip her stuck-up bleedin' head off, the scheming bitch!'

'Whoa, hold your horses, what are you talking about?'

'Mrs Best! That's what I'm talking about! It was her, Dickie, she arranged for you to get attacked.'

Dickie almost laughed. 'Don't be ridiculous,' he scoffed.

'I'm telling you, Dickie, it's true and I'll prove it to you!'

Gordon turned and poked his head through the door, shouting for Grace.

'Grace! Grace! Get down here, NOW!'

'Oi,' Dickie warned. 'Mind how you talk to Grace. She ain't answerable to you.'

'Yeah, Dickie, but Grace knows that it was her bloody grandmother who did it.'

Dickie poured himself another brandy and lifted the arm of the gramophone from the record, his mind turning. *Surely Myrtle had nothing to do with the robbery? And if she did, why hadn't Grace said anything?*

Grace entered the room, tying the cord of her dressing gown tightly around her slim waist. Looking from Dickie to Gordon, confused, she asked, 'Where's the fire? What's going on?'

'Tell him,' Gordon spat accusingly. 'Tell him what your grandmother did!'

Dickie saw the colour drain from his daughter's face.

'Tell him!' Gordon shouted, making Grace flinch.

'That's enough!' Dickie barked. 'Don't talk to Grace in that tone, do you 'ear me, Gordon?'

Gordon sucked in a long, slow, steadying breath. Then, lowering his voice, he said, 'Grace, will you please confirm to your father that your grandmother arranged for him to be attacked.'

Dickie didn't need Grace to verbally confirm anything. He could tell by her mortified expression that it was true. 'If you knew, why didn't you tell me?' he asked, feeling betrayed.

'I only found out the truth yesterday, Papa. I wanted to tell you, but I was afraid of the consequences.'

'All right, fair enough. But Grace, don't *ever* keep something like this from me again.'

'I won't, and I'm sorry. What are you going to do?'

Dickie knew exactly what he wanted to do, but killing the woman wasn't a viable option. Yes, he had the police in his pocket and the force turned a blind eye to most of his dodgy dealings, but that didn't mean he could get away with murder. And as much as he'd like to batter Myrtle and knock her through to next year, he couldn't hit an old woman. Dickie sneered. He knew what motivated Myrtle more than anything. Status. Class. Wealth. 'I'll bring the old witch down,' he growled.

'You won't hurt her, Papa, will you?'

Dickie frowned at his daughter. 'What sort of a man do you think I am, Grace?'

Grace dropped her head and looked at the floor.

'Christ, girl, I'm a lot of things, and I've done some wicked deeds, but you don't really believe that I'd hurt your grandma, do you?'

'No, I hope not.'

Gordon stepped between them and faced Grace. 'Where is she?' he snapped. 'Dickie might be too soft to kick her head in, but I ain't!'

Grace ran to the door and slammed it shut, her back against it. 'You'll have to get past me to get to my grandma,' she threatened. 'And I'll scratch your eyes out!'

Dickie grabbed Gordon by the back of his neck, pinching his fingers into the man's muscles. 'Listen to me, son, and listen well. I realise you're pissed off and you hate that witch for what she did to me, but you ain't laying a finger on her. Got it?'

'But you could have been killed because of her!'

'I raised you better than that, boy. No good will come out of hitting an old woman. Think smart. Use your noddle. I want to hurt Myrtle and I will, but I'm gonna hurt her where it will cause her the most pain. The woman is going to be cut off from what she loves the most – my money.'

Letting go of Gordon, Dickie looked over to Grace. 'Fetch your grandmother downstairs.'

Grace, though appearing scared, nodded and slipped out of the room.

'Remember what I said, Gordon. No violence. Just leave the old witch to me.'

Grace walked up the stairs, feeling let down by Anna for divulging her secret, but relieved that it was finally out in the open. She'd feared for her grandmother's life, and the consequences the woman's death might have for her father and Gordon. But surprisingly, her father seemed remarkably calm and had even quietened down Gordon. Grace understood they'd want revenge, and rightly so. She detested what her grandmother had done. It had almost cost her father his life. Whatever the woman had coming to her was her own fault. Myrtle had brought it on herself, and Grace had no sympathy for her.

She didn't tap on her grandmother's bedroom door; instead, she threw it open and glared angrily at her. 'You're wanted downstairs,' she said gravely.

Myrtle lifted her eyes from the book she was reading and looked stunned. Propped up in her bed with luxurious pillows plumped behind her, she said, 'Where are your manners, girl? Knock and wait to be invited in.'

Grace wasn't apologetic. 'Get up and come downstairs.'

'I'll do no such thing, and I don't take orders from you!'

'You will if you know what's good for you,' Grace snarled.

'Who do you think you are talking to? Have you lost your mind?'

'I'm talking to the woman who had my father beaten half to death.'

Myrtle breathed in sharply, and Grace saw fear etched on her face.

'I have no idea what you are talking about,' Myrtle said, her voice shaking.

'Save your breath. You can explain yourself to Papa. I'll see you downstairs in two minutes.'

Grace left the door open and rejoined her father and Gordon, saying, 'She'll be down shortly.'

Gordon sidled up to Grace. 'I'm sorry about the way I spoke to you.'

'It's fine, you're angry, and so am I.'

All heads turned towards the door when they saw Myrtle pass and head towards the kitchen at the back of the house.

Grace followed her grandmother, with her father and Gordon close behind.

Myrtle didn't look at any of them as she poured herself a cup of lukewarm tea from the teapot.

Grace stepped to one side, allowing her father to move forward.

'Have you got anything to say for yourself?' he asked.

Myrtle spun quickly and glared at him with accusing eyes. 'You've wrecked my daughter and made her life a living hell. You've ruined Grace and turned her into anything but a lady. And you brought that vile creature into our home,' she said, waving a gnarled finger towards Gordon. 'I'm not sorry. My only regret is that you're still breathing.'

Gordon rushed towards Myrtle, almost foaming at the mouth as he screamed, 'You wicked bitch! I'll fuckin' kill you!'

Grace saw him pull his arm back, ready to punch her grandmother, and hollered, 'NO!'

Luckily, her father grabbed him and yanked Gordon back before he could do any damage.

Myrtle, though pale and visibly trembling, spat, 'Thugs, you're all low-life bottom feeders. Savages, and he has just proved it!'

Dickie stepped nearer to the woman, his face close to hers. His stance intimidating, he ground out, 'I knew you'd never like me, and I never liked you. I've kept you in the lifestyle you wanted, and I didn't want or expect any thanks. But that's it, Myrtle. You won't get another ha'penny, tanner or shilling out of me. Pack your bags and get out of my house.'

Grace watched her grandmother's face drop, and then she saw defiance in the old woman.

'Where do you expect me to go at this time of night and with no money?'

Dickie shrugged, nonchalant. 'Not my problem, old woman.'

Myrtle raised her voice. 'I've cooked and cleaned for you for seven years! I demand payment for my work!'

Dickie threw his head back and roared with ironic laughter. Then his tone turned sinister. 'Get out, you mad old bat!' he shouted. Towering over her, intimidating her by pushing his torso against hers, he stretched his arm, pointed to the door, and bellowed, 'OUT!'

Grace felt a pang of sorrow for her grandmother. She looked so small, and old, and terrified. But then she reminded herself of what the woman had done, and shouted, 'Go on, *Grandma*, you heard him. Get out. You ain't welcome in this house no more. And don't come back!'

Louisa threw back the bed covers, padded across the bedroom floor and opened the door a tad. Straining her ears, she tried to listen to the angry voices drifting up the stairs. Dickie was shouting, and so was Grace, and Louisa was sure she heard her mother, too.

It sounded like a very heated argument, and she thought she heard Dickie threatening to throw her mother out. Pulling on her dressing gown, Louisa sped down the stairs and into the kitchen. Gawping eyes fell on her, and she looked around, confused.

'Go back to bed, Mother,' Grace urged. 'This has nothing to do with you.'

Louisa looked past Grace and noticed that Dickie seemed to be bullying her mother, who appeared very distressed.

'What's going on?' Louisa asked, pushing past Gordon and Grace.

'They're throwing me out! What am I supposed to do? Sleep on a bench? I'm an old woman, this is outrageous!'

Louisa turned to face her daughter, shocked and horrified. 'Is it true?' she asked.

'Grandma arranged for Papa to be attacked. So, yes, it's true.'

Louisa gasped, her head shooting round to look at her mother. 'You didn't? Did you?'

'Yes, I did, but regretfully, your husband wasn't killed!'

Louisa was staggered. 'Why, Mother, why would you do something so wicked?'

'I did it for you, Louisa. You would have been a wealthy widow, and I hoped you might have smiled for once.'

'She didn't do it for you,' Dickie scoffed. 'Myrtle only cares about herself.'

'Even so, you can't throw her out, Dickie. At least give her some time to make arrangements,' Louisa begged.

'We know all about the sorts of arrangements she makes,' Gordon uttered viciously. 'Dickie nearly died 'cos of you,' he snarled. 'I wanna smash your fuckin' head through the window.'

As Gordon scrambled towards her mother, Louisa instinctively grabbed hold of his arm, trying to pull him back. Gordon wrenched his arm free and jerked it backwards, his elbow whacking Louisa on the nose. The force of the blow dazed her and almost knocked her off her unsteady legs. The room was spinning, and her vision became blurred. Stumbling sideways, Louisa could feel the world slipping away, and she fainted with a heavy thump.

★

A stunned silence hung in the air as Gordon peered down at Louisa, blood seeping from her head and spreading across the tiled floor. Her body was still, her eyes unblinking and staring into nothingness.

Grace broke the silence. 'Is – Is my mother dead?'

'I'd say so,' Dickie said, sighing.

Panic surged through Gordon as he lifted his eyes from Louisa and glanced around the room. Mrs Best held her hands to her mouth and stifled a sob. Grace had turned grey and was biting her nails. Dickie ran his hand through his greased-back hair. They were all staring at the dead woman, horrified.

'I didn't kill her,' Gordon blurted. 'You saw what happened... It was an accident. You know it weren't my fault, don't you?' he pleaded.

Myrtle Best's head slowly lifted, and tears sprang from her accusing eyes as she screamed at Gordon, 'MURDERER! You've killed my daughter! MURDERER! You'll hang for this, and I'll make sure of it!'

'I didn't mean to do it... It was an accident... She fell. You all saw her fall and hit her head on the stove. I never pushed her or nothing. Please, Dickie, tell her it wasn't my fault. Tell her, Dickie. Tell her you saw Louisa fall over and bash her head.'

The desperation in Gordon's voice was clear for them all to hear.

'Tell her, Dickie. Go on. Louisa fell over and bashed her head on the stove. I didn't kill her, I didn't, Dickie.'

'It's all right, son. I saw what happened. Louisa fell and hit her head,' Dickie reassured him, though Gordon could see in Dickie's eyes that the man didn't believe his own words.

'You think I killed her, don't you?'

'No, son, I don't.'

Myrtle screamed again. 'You did! And you won't get away with it! Grace, fetch the police. Go, girl, run. Run and fetch the police.'

'No,' Dickie said firmly. 'No police.'

'I'll fetch them myself,' Myrtle argued, marching towards the door.

Dickie held out his arms and stopped her from passing. 'No police, Myrtle.'

'My daughter deserves justice, and I'll see him on the gallows!'

'Think very carefully before you do anything rash, Myrtle. If you go to the police, you'll still be in the same situation you are now – homeless and skint. On the other hand, keep your mouth shut and we'll continue as we always have.'

Gordon stared at Mrs Best hopefully.

There was a long pause before the woman finally answered. 'It doesn't feel right, but I don't seem to have a choice. I won't involve the police. Get out of my way.'

Gordon let out a sigh of relief, and Mrs Best darted out of the kitchen and up the stairs.

'What are we going to do?' Gordon muttered, looking at Dickie for an answer.

'We'll have to move her, hide her.'

Grace glared at her father. 'You mean dispose of her body! Oh, Papa, this is awful, and it's wrong. We can't do this. Grandma's right. We should fetch the police.'

Dickie's voice was unusually gentle. 'No, Grace. I want you to go upstairs to your room and you're not to come back down until the morning. Leave this to me and Gordon. All right?'

'You can't do this, Papa. Please. You can't do this to my mother. She at least deserves a proper funeral!'

Firmer now, Dickie ordered, 'Go to your room and don't question me, Grace. And never, ever mention this again. Is that clear?'

'But—'

'Do as you're told!' Dickie roared. 'And don't think that because you're my daughter, I won't come down on you like a ton of bricks if you dare to defy me! Go against me, Grace, and you'll find out what a nasty bastard I can be.'

Grace ran from the room.

Gordon was flabbergasted. He'd never heard Dickie talk to Grace like that. He was grateful that the man was backing him up.

'Get a shovel,' Dickie said. 'And dig a bloomin' big hole in the back garden.'

24

Grace didn't sleep. She lay in bed, listening. Her grandmother's sobs reached her ears.

'Oh, Louisa, Louisa, my dear daughter.'

Grace hadn't thought that her grandmother had any feelings of love; the woman always presented a hard façade, and seemed cold, yet her heart sounded as though it was breaking.

Strangely, Grace felt nothing. No tears fell, and she realised that she couldn't recall the last time she'd cried. Her mother was dead, surely she should feel some sense of loss? *It's the shock*, she thought. *I'm in shock.*

Over the sounds of her grandmother's sorrow, she heard a peculiar noise under her window. Climbing out of bed, she tiptoed across the room and pulled the curtain back just a smidgen to peer through a tiny gap in the curtains. Straining her eyes to focus through the darkness, she searched the back garden. And that's when she spotted Gordon. He was digging a hole under the oak tree where she'd played as a child on a swing her father had made. Her stomach flipped. That hole was obviously going to be her mother's final resting place.

Grace couldn't bear to look. The scene was far too

gruesome, and she tried to push away the image of her mother on the kitchen floor. Bile burned the back of her throat and vomit threatened to spew from her mouth. She swallowed hard, several times, and sat on the edge of her bed, gently rocking back and forth. The room was warm, yet Grace was shivering. Beads of sweat began to form across her forehead. *Gordon killed my mother*, she thought, as if it was only just sinking in, *and my father is covering it up and disposing of her body!*

Grace could feel her heart beating rapidly, and she struggled to pull air into her lungs. *My father isn't the man I thought he was. My dear, sweet mother is dead!*

She remembered how afraid her mother had been of him, and how he would humiliate her, even dragging her into Grace's room one night and calling her a slut. Why had her father treated her mother in such a despicable way? She wasn't a slut, far from it! Then Grace remembered the woman in the bakery shop and how she'd ranted about her father, the *spankings* Ernie was ordered to dish out to non-paying tenants and borrowers. She'd always dismissed the horrendous rumours about her father's brutality, but now they were flooding her mind. And shockingly, Grace realised that the man she loved so dearly, her hero, had feet of clay and she'd been blinkered. Blinded by love and adoration. Her grandmother was right. Dickie Newman was a thug. A brute. A man capable of burying his wife in the back garden with no remorse!

'I'm sorry, Mother,' she said quietly. 'I should have understood you better. I can't believe I'm never going to see you again. This isn't right! I love you, and I shouldn't allow them to do this to you!'

Her father's threat rang in her ears. *Go against me, Grace, and you'll find out what a nasty bastard I can be*. Fear slowly crept over her, shadowing her like a dark cloud, leaving her feeling cold and isolated. Grace didn't need to be threatened by the man. She'd already come to realise what a *nasty bastard* he could be, and he'd moulded Gordon to be just like him. Together, her father and Gordon were formidable, and Grace knew her life was never going to be the same again.

As the sun rose, Grace, although exhausted, forced herself out of bed. Downstairs, as she walked towards the kitchen, passing the drawing room, she glanced sideways and noticed that the large, Axminster floral rug was gone.

Shaking off gruesome imaginings of what could have happened to the rug, she stood outside the kitchen door, willing herself to step inside. *Come on, Grace, you're a Newman*, she reminded herself, though she no longer felt it was a name to be proud of. Even so, it was a name that evoked fear and was partnered with strength. Grace needed to find that strength within herself now.

Pushing open the door, she swallowed hard as she looked down at where her mother had taken her last breath. The floor had been scrubbed clean and there were no traces of blood. Even so, Grace stepped carefully around where her body had lain, and pain stabbed at her heart. She wished it had all been a nightmare. She wished she would hear her mother's footsteps coming down the stairs for breakfast.

Desperate for a hot drink, she pushed herself to warm some water on the stove. Peering at where her mother's head had whacked the enamelled top, Grace reminded herself that it wasn't the stove that had killed her mother – Gordon was responsible. If he hadn't elbowed her in the face, she'd never have fainted and hit her head. He claimed it had been an accident, but Grace had seen that his anger was out of control, and it had scared her.

Pouring herself a cup of tea, she plucked up the courage to look out of the window. She saw the disturbed ground under the oak tree, and knew that's where her mother's body was. Still, no tears came, though her raw grief felt almost suffocating. Her mother's grave was in a beautiful spot, shaded by the big oak and nestled near the rose garden. But it didn't make it right. 'Rest in peace, Mother,' she whispered, appalled that she couldn't say a proper goodbye. 'I hope you knew you were loved.'

Later that day, as Grace was about to close her shop, the door opened, and Anna came in. Grace could see from her puffy eyes that she'd been crying.

'I'm so sorry, Grace,' Anna said, sounding genuine. 'Gordon forced it out of me. I didn't want to tell him, but I had no choice. Please, say you forgive me?'

'I do. I know how *persuasive* Gordon can be.'

'I've not slept, Grace. I've been worried sick. What happened when Gordon got home?'

In her mind, Grace saw her mother's body on the kitchen floor and did her utmost to conceal her grief, repulsion and fear. 'They talked everything through, and it's all fine,' she lied.

'Really?'

'Yes. Obviously, there was a bit of a heated exchange, and my father told my grandma to leave, but then he calmed down and said she could stay. He must have taken pity on her because she's an old woman.'

'Blimey! Gawd, I'm so glad.'

'Yeah, me too.'

'Can we still be friends?'

Grace nodded. She needed a friend more than ever, especially now she knew she couldn't trust her father or Gordon.

When she arrived home that evening, the house was in silence and Grace was pleased her father and Gordon were out. She felt a draught blowing along the hallway and realised the kitchen back door was open. Walking into the room, and looking out of the window, she saw her grandmother standing over her mother's grave. The woman leaned over and placed a bunch of flowers on the dirt.

Grace approached but was unsure of what to say. Instead, she stood quietly beside the woman and stared down at the ground.

'I'm assuming this is where Louisa is?' Myrtle asked sharply.

'Yes, I believe so.'

'Your father made your mother's life a misery. I'm to blame. I should never have allowed her to marry him. Now, even in death, he hasn't given Louisa any respect or dignity. Look at what he's done, Grace! Why do you idolise him? He's evil, and I will have to spend the rest of my days in torment, knowing my daughter was murdered and her body hidden here where I am forced to confront her grave every day. It's sick, Grace, sick and evil!'

Grace agreed, but before she could say anything, they heard Gordon's voice behind them.

'What do you think you're doing?' he hissed, pushing between them. Grabbing the flowers that Myrtle had laid, he shook them in her face. 'Are you trying to get us found out? Flowers... bleedin' flowers. Yeah, I bet you'd love to see me swing for this, wouldn't you? Get indoors, and don't come out 'ere again!'

Grace took her grandmother's arm and gently led her into the kitchen. She could feel the woman trembling and saw her body tense when Gordon shoved the flowers into the rubbish bin.

Myrtle glared at him, and Grace could see the contempt and hatred she held for the man. He returned the look before clomping away.

Her grandmother sniffed, and whispered, 'You know, Grace, if your father was dead, you'd be a wealthy woman, and you could dismiss Gordon.'

Grace shot her a look, stunned.

'Just something to consider,' her grandmother added quietly.

25

Six months later
December 1934

As Grace came out of the picture house, she looped her arm through Anna's. Though she carried on her life as normal, her mother's fate was never far from her mind, and neither was the disillusionment she felt about her father. Though her mother had spent much time in her room, Grace still missed the moments they'd shared. The comedic film had been a good distraction.

'George Formby was so funny!' she said to Anna.

'Yes, I haven't giggled that much in ages.'

'Make the most of it,' Grace advised. 'You'll be a married woman soon.'

'I know, and I can't wait! I wish I could have married Gordon sooner, but I wanted my dad to be well enough to give me away.' Then, waving across the road, Anna called, 'John! John!' Smiling, she said to Grace, 'That's John Dander, my cousin. Let me introduce you, you'll like him.'

Grace looked over at the man crossing the road, and her blood ran cold. It was the same man whose mask had slipped when he'd been attacking her father, and the same man she'd witnessed her grandmother meeting on Clapham Common.

She should have been afraid, but anger had replaced her fear.

'Hello, Anna,' John beamed. 'Have you been to watch a film?'

'Yes, *Boots! Boots!* It was so funny. John, this is my best friend, Grace Newman.'

John gawped at Grace, clearly lost for words.

'I know who you are,' Grace said, her tone unfriendly.

The man gazed at her intensely, and Grace felt herself squirm under his long stare.

'I've, erm, I'm in a hurry, sorry, I can't stop,' John said, still holding Grace's glare.

As he dashed away, Anna turned to Grace. 'That was a bit odd. John's normally ever so friendly and chatty. How do you know him?'

Grace didn't want to upset her dear friend by telling her what she knew. Instead, she fibbed, 'I don't think I do know him. I must have made a mistake.'

'Well, I hope John will be on better form at my wedding.'

'He'll be at your wedding?' Grace blurted.

'Of course. He's my mum's sister's son. We were brought up together, practically as brother and sister.'

Christ, Grace thought, hoping her father wouldn't recognise him. Although Grace had come to despise Gordon, she thought the world of Anna and didn't want John Dander's death to ruin her friend's wedding day!

Myrtle peered out of the window to where her daughter was buried. The ground had settled now. There was nothing to mark Louisa's final resting place. 'I hope you're finding comfort in heaven with your father,' she whispered affectionately.

'She can't hear you and she won't talk back to you,' Gordon snickered.

Myrtle hadn't heard him come into the kitchen, and as she turned to him, a waft of whisky twitched her nostrils. He'd been drinking again, and when Gordon was drunk, he was nastier than usual.

'Excuse me,' Myrtle said curtly, avoiding eye contact as she side-stepped him.

Gordon blocked her way. 'Why, what ya done, you mad old bat?'

'Get out of my way,' she ordered.

'I wish it had been you that we'd put in the ground.'

Myrtle tried to conceal the fact that she felt intimidated. 'And I wish I'd gone to the police and watched you hang for murdering my daughter!'

'Yeah, well, you didn't, did ya! And if you know what's best for you, you'll keep your mouth shut. Unless you want to join your daughter?'

Myrtle sighed. 'I'm bored of your idle threats, Gordon. Just get out of my way!'

Gordon sniggered and moved aside, mocking, 'You're so stuck up, yet you're willing to live off the man who put your daughter in that grave. Hypocrite.'

Myrtle tried to keep her composure as she hurried along the hall and up the stairs to her bedroom. Gordon's words stabbed at her heart. She knew they were true, and not a day passed when she didn't regret allowing Dickie to cover up Louisa's death. *You'll be sorry one day*, she seethed, longing for their downfall.

26

Dickie drummed his fingers on the steering wheel as he sat outside the prison waiting for Pippa. She was being released early on the grounds of ill-health. He wasn't sure how he felt about seeing her, but he no longer held any animosity towards the woman. If anything, he felt a stirring of excitement and anticipation. Pippa was the only person he'd ever been himself with. He'd dropped his guard with her, and there had been a time when she'd got too close, but he'd pushed her away. Dickie regretted that now and could have kicked himself for never allowing himself to love her properly.

When he saw her, his heart dropped. Pippa looked frail and pale as she shuffled through the main gate, and Dickie gulped, stunned at how poorly she was. Jumping out of the car, he called her name and beckoned her over.

Pippa appeared nervous.

'I've come to drive you home,' he said softly. 'Hop in.'

'I don't know, Dickie …'

'It's all right, Pippa. Who do you think got you out of that shithole early, eh? When I heard about the cancer, I pulled a few strings. Come on, Pip, the past is the past. Let me take care of you.'

Pippa frowned as she climbed into the car beside Dickie. He could see she was in discomfort. 'I'll have the doctor take a look at you when we're home. Don't worry about a thing, Pippa, I'll see you're all right, whatever it costs.'

'Where's home?' she asked.

'I've sorted you a nice place, you'll see.'

She stared straight ahead, asking, 'Why are you doing this for me, Dickie?'

He couldn't answer. He knew he loved her, but the words stuck in his throat.

After a long silence, she spoke again. 'I'll always regret taking Grace, but I wasn't in my right mind.'

'I know.'

'How is she?'

'Grace? She's great. She's grown into a right beauty.'

'You never had any more children?'

'No. I took a lad in though, Gordon. His mother abandoned him, and he was homeless. It was years ago; he's like a son to me now.'

'You've done bad things, really bad, but I aways knew you were a soft touch and had a good heart, Dickie, despite what everyone said about you.'

'Yeah, well, you know me, Pip. I'm all heart.'

Pippa groaned and bent forward, clutching her stomach.

Dickie sped up, racing to get back to Battersea. 'Don't worry, Pip, the doc will make you feel better soon.'

'I hope so, Dickie. I hope so. Thanks for looking after me.'

'Why wouldn't you see me, Pip? It's been years.'

Pippa shrugged. 'I gave up on life, Dickie. I hated it in

there behind bars. I just wanted to die. And seeing you, it made me feel things that I wanted to forget. I missed you, though.'

'Yeah, well, you ain't banged up no more, so there's no reason to want to die.'

'It's too late, Dickie. I've spent years wishing that I was dead, and now I will be soon. But I don't want to die, Dickie, I don't.'

'Don't worry, you'll be all right. Let's get you home and seen by the doctor. You've always been a strong woman, Pip. You can fight this off, you'll see.'

Grace had met Anna outside Woolworths in Clapham Junction to do some Christmas shopping. Her father had given her a good sum of money to spend on gifts and treats, though Grace had been reluctant to accept it. She tried to behave normally around her father, but it wasn't easy, and she wasn't looking forward to spending Christmas Day with him. She didn't even want to buy any seasonal gifts for anyone, except for Anna.

'I thought I'd buy Gordon a smart lighter and get it engraved, what do you think?' Anna asked.

Grace couldn't care less. 'I'm sure he'd love that,' she replied, trying to sound enthusiastic.

'John popped round last night. He was asking about you. I told him he was naughty 'cos he's been seeing someone for a while, but I don't think he loves her. She's pushing for marriage, but John doesn't seem keen. I reckon he's sweet on you.'

Grace's head snapped round to look at her friend.

'He's a smashing fella, and he's got a heart of gold. Good looking an' all.'

'I'm really not interested,' Grace stated flatly.

'No, I don't suppose you would be. You must think he's not good enough for you, but he's got ambitions. John won't be lugging sacks of coal all his life, you know.'

'It's got nothing to do with his job, Anna. I'm not like that.'

'You are a bit,' Anna teased. 'You can be snobby sometimes.'

'Huh, what have I got to be snobby about?'

'You can't help it. I reckon your grandmother has rubbed off on you.'

'Tosh! I'm *nothing* like her!'

'If you say so. Then why aren't you interested in John?'

'I'm just not,' Grace replied.

'Well, I reckon he's interested in you. Anyway, let's get a move on. I've got lots to buy and not much time. My shift at the hospital starts soon.'

Grace wandered from shop to shop with Anna, oohing and ahhing at the appropriate times, but she couldn't find any festive joy. Loaded with Anna's shopping bags, she was relieved when it was time for Anna to go to work.

'Will you do me a really big favour, please?' Anna asked.

'It depends on what it is,' Grace smiled, knowing that she'd do almost anything for her dearest friend.

'Will you take this to Gordon for me?' Anna placed the bags on the ground and pulled out a wrapped package from one of them. 'No peeping inside.'

'Can't you give it to him yourself?'

'No. The truth is, we had a bit of a falling out the other day. I was mean to him, and I've not seen him since. This gift is my way of saying sorry. Will you take it to him, and tell him to meet me after work tonight?'

'You want me to take it to him now?'

'Yes, please. Pretty please.'

Grace sighed. She knew she wouldn't be welcomed on the streets where her father and Gordon would be collecting rents. And she had no desire to see either of them. 'All right,' she agreed, but only to make Anna happy.

Dickie sat in his car with Ernie, sucking on a fat cigar and enjoying the mellow aroma. When Ernie waved his hand in front of his face to rid the smoke, Dickie laughed.

'You've got no class, you,' he said.

'I dunno why you smoke them things, they bloody stink,' Ernie moaned. 'How's Pippa?'

'Not good. The doc reckons she's only got weeks to live.'

'Christ, she's young.'

'Yeah, it's a shame,' Dickie said, keeping his emotions in check. 'And, Ernie, not a word to anyone, all right?'

'Mum's the word,' Ernie said, tapping the side of his nose.

Dickie saw his daughter walking along the street and towards the car. 'What the bleedin' 'ell does she want?' he mumbled. He thought she looked out of place in this rundown part of Battersea, and he could see women sneering at her. His jaw tightened when men's heads turned to gawp. Dickie knew what carnal thoughts would be going through their minds.

Stepping outside the car, he asked, 'What are you doing here?'

'I'm doing a favour for Anna. She asked me to drop this off to Gordon,' Grace replied, lifting the package. 'Where is he?'

'He's in number eighty-nine. He'll be back soon.'

'I'll go and find him,' Grace said, strutting away.

'No, wait, Grace. Leave it here, I'll make sure Gordon gets it.'

'It's all right,' she called over her shoulder. 'See you later.'

Dickie cursed. He didn't want Grace walking into number eighty-nine and discovering what Gordon was up to. Throwing his cigar to the ground, he chased after her, shouting, 'Oi, Grace, wait.'

At that moment, young twin boys charged out of a house, running onto the pavement, their mother chasing them with a broom and yelling, 'Get back 'ere, you pair of buggers!'

One of the boys ran into Dickie, and the other tripped over his brother, falling to the ground. Dickie lost his footing too and stumbled over the boy on the ground, who was crying now.

Regaining his posture, Dickie glared at the mother. 'Keep your fuckin' sprogs under control!'

The mother, her apron mucky and worn, rushed over and hastily gathered her sons, saying anxiously, 'Sorry, Mr Newman. I'll give them a flippin' good hiding.'

Shit, Dickie thought, as he saw his daughter going into number eighty-nine, and ran to catch her.

Inside the dark and cold house, the downstairs room door opened, and Gordon emerged, his back to the hallway, tucking his shirt into his trousers. 'See you next week,' he purred at Sybil, who rented the room, and kissed her cheek. She stood semi-naked, holding the door and eyeing Gordon lustfully. But alarm flashed through her eyes when she saw Grace and Dickie standing in the hallway.

'What's going on?' Grace snapped.

Gordon spun and saw her, his mouth gaping, as Sybil slammed the door closed.

'Come on,' Dickie urged, trying to usher his daughter out of the house.

'It's not what you think,' Gordon said.

Dickie rolled his eyes. Gordon wouldn't be able to lie his way out of it. The scene with Sybil had spoken for itself, and it wouldn't need a genius to work it out.

Outside, trying to calm Grace, he explained, 'Look, darling, it's unfortunate that you saw what you saw, but this is business. Tenants offer all sorts when they can't pay the rent. It's no big deal.'

Grace threw him a disgusted look, and she glowered at Gordon accusingly. 'Does Anna know about this?'

Gordon's face hardened. 'You can't say anything. Dickie, tell her. Tell her to keep her mouth shut.'

'Why should I?' Grace spat. 'Anna's my friend. She has a right to know what sort of man she's marrying!'

Gordon stepped forward and, pulling back his lips and baring his teeth, he hissed, 'If you say a word to Anna, I swear, I'll cut your bleedin' tongue out!'

Dickie's anger flared and he grabbed Gordon by the throat with one hand. Jabbing his finger into Gordon's chest, he warned, 'Never, *never* make threats to my girl. Do you hear me?'

Gordon nodded and Dickie released his grip.

'Grace, get in the car. Gordon, go and calm down. That's an end to this. I don't want another word spoken about this again. That goes for you too, Grace. Nothing. Ever.'

The atmosphere in the car was taut as Dickie drove away. He could tell his daughter was seething, but he hoped she wouldn't tell Anna what she'd witnessed. But if she did, well, it was Gordon's lookout. After all, he'd warned Gordon to keep it in his trousers. If he lost Anna, then Gordon would only have himself to blame.

27

Grace was wracked with guilt but had managed to avoid seeing Anna for almost a week. Her shop was quiet, so when the door opened with a potential customer, Grace leapt to her feet. Her heart dropped when it was Anna who walked in.

'Hello, Grace. You weren't at the picture house last night. Is everything all right? Are you feeling unwell?'

Grace began to fiddle with some hats on display and kept her eyes averted from Anna's as she fibbed, saying, 'Sorry, yes, erm, I'm fine. I've just been busy, that's all.'

'Well, you missed a good film, but don't worry, John turned up, so I had some company. I'm sure he was hoping to see you. He looked sorely disappointed when he realised you weren't there. He told me he's called it off with the woman he was seeing. I never liked her. Anyway, I've got the day off. Shall we have lunch?'

'Oh, er, I'd love to, Anna, but I must get a stock check done.'

Anna walked around to stand in front of the display, where Grace was mindlessly moving one hat to another place and then back again. She could feel her friend's eyes on her.

'What's wrong?' Anna quizzed. 'I know you, Grace, and I know when you have something on your mind.'

Grace held her face in her hands and shook her head.

'Oh no, what is it?' Anna pressed.

'I want to tell you, I really do. But you're going to be so upset and I don't want to break your heart.'

'Please, Grace, just tell me.'

Grace knew she had to. 'Let me close the shop,' she said.

After locking the door, she invited Anna through to the back of the shop and poured her a cup of tea. Studying her friend's concerned face, she gulped hard. 'I'm so sorry, Anna, but what I'm going to tell you will be crushing... It's Gordon. He's accepting favours paid in kind from women who can't pay their rent. It's awful. I didn't want to tell you, but I can't stand by and watch you marry him.'

Anna looked down into her teacup, and asked, 'How do you know?'

'I caught him in the act, almost.'

'And you're sure?'

'Oh, yes, I'm sure. He threatened me and warned me not to tell you. But I had to, Anna. You're my best friend and I can't stand by and see you make the biggest mistake of your life. You deserve much better than Gordon.'

Anna placed her cup on a side table and pulled a handkerchief from her bag. Holding it to her nose, she sniffed, 'I love him, Grace. I love him with all my heart. How could he do this? He promised me, swore to me that he was content to wait until we were married. Now I understand why... because he's been getting his pleasure elsewhere!'

Grace knew she'd done the right thing in telling Anna, but it was painful for her to see her friend falling to pieces.

'I can't live without him, Grace. I love him so much,' Anna sobbed.

Grace held her friend and wished she could take away her heartache. 'It'll be all right,' she soothed. 'You deserve so much better than Gordon.'

Later that evening, Dickie reached across the sofa and held Pippa's hand. He was pleased to see that she'd perked up and was in less pain. The doctor had given her a Brompton Cocktail, a mixture of morphine and cocaine in a drink of gin mixed with honey, and it seemed to be working.

'I feel floaty,' Pippa said softly.

'That'll be the medicine.'

'Thank you for looking after me, Dickie. I've missed you.'

'I should never have let you walk out on me all those years ago.'

'I've always regretted that day. I was pregnant, you know.'

'You had our child?'

'No, Dickie. I wish I had, but I lost the baby.'

'I'm sorry, Pip. You've had a rough ride.'

'Never mind. We don't decide the cards that life deals us. My problems began when I fell in love with you. I've hated you, Dickie, but I've always loved you.'

Dickie moved closer and pulled Pippa into him, wrapping his arms around her thin body. 'I've always loved you too, Pip. What a bloody mess, eh, and what a waste of years.'

'You're here now,' she whispered. Then, lifting her eyes to gaze at him, she said, 'I don't want to die alone, Dickie. I'm scared. Promise me you'll be here.'

'Shush now, Pip. We don't need to be talking about death.'

'Please, Dickie, promise me.'

'Yes, Pip, I promise,' he assured her. And holding her a little tighter, he lied, 'But the doctor said that you've got ages yet.'

Dickie wished they could stay in that moment forever. The thought of losing her was almost unbearable. It felt like his insides were being ripped apart, and his stomach churned. He'd have moved heaven and earth to give Pippa more precious time, but it was rapidly running out.

Gordon kissed Anna goodnight, forcing a smile, but he was raging. Grace had told her about catching him with Sybil, and it had nearly blown their relationship. Somehow, and only by the skin of his teeth, Gordon had managed to talk Anna round. He'd told her it had been a mistake, a one off, and he'd never so much as look at another woman again. Surprisingly, she'd forgiven him, and the wedding was back on. No thanks to Grace!

Marching home through the frosty night, his anger simmered, festering away as malicious thoughts about Grace ran through his mind. He'd never liked her, though he'd always put on a good show. Now he hated her!

Arriving home, he noticed that Dickie's car wasn't outside. He guessed that Mrs Best was out, too. The snooty old witch was rarely home, always returning late and retiring straight to her bed, and out early most mornings. That suited Gordon. He didn't like the way she looked at him.

The lounge door stood ajar and an amber light from the fire glowed through. Gordon pushed it open and saw Grace sitting in front of the hearth, reading a book. When she glanced up and saw him, she rose to her feet, her eyes fixed ahead as she went to leave the room.

Gordon put his arm across the doorframe, blocking her way.

'You had to tell her. You couldn't keep your big mouth shut!' he seethed. 'But your plan to break up me and Anna has backfired.'

At last, Grace met his eyes, and he could see stunned disbelief in them.

'Yeah, that's right. Me and Anna are still getting married, and you ain't invited.'

'What lies did you tell her?'

'None of your business. But she ain't too trusting about you no more. I told her you're jealous and you want to split us up, because you want her all to yourself. Sad really, eh, but you're so lonely and pathetic, you ain't got any other friends. She believed me and felt sorry for you. I'd say she took pity on you.'

'You're disgusting and I won't allow Anna to marry you, over my dead body!'

Gordon grabbed Grace's face, his fingers and thumb digging deeply into her cheeks. 'Your dead body can be easily arranged,' he growled. Then, lifting his arm, he slapped her hard across her head.

As the blow took Grace off her feet and she landed heavily on the floor, Gordon heard Dickie's ferocious bark.

'Get your hands off her!'

Gordon backed away, terrified, as Dickie charged towards him.

'I'm sorry, Dickie, I lost my rag. She told Anna about Sybil. I didn't mean it, I was angry, that's all.'

He saw Dickie's eyes veiled in fury, and then the man's huge fist coming towards his face. He fell to his backside as blood drained from his burst lip. Dazed and looking up from the floor, he begged, 'Please, please, Dickie, don't hurt me.'

Dickie snarled down at him and shouted with venom, 'Get up and get out. You're nothing to me no more. Nothing! I don't want to set eyes on you ever again. No one hits my girl. Best you stay out of my way, boy, or I'll fuckin' kill you!'

Gordon scrambled to his feet, trying to keep his distance from Dickie. Then, running for the front door, his heart racing, he fled down the stairs and along the street. He'd got off with just a bloodied lip from Dickie, and he knew it could have been a lot worse. But the man he'd thought of as a father had now disowned him. It was Grace's fault. She'd ruined his life. *I hate her*, he thought. *I hate that bitch, Grace Newman!*

28

The following morning, Myrtle waited until she heard Dickie's car leave before going down the stairs. In the kitchen, she saw Grace and noticed some bruising on her face.

'What happened to you?' Myrtle asked.

'Gordon hit me.'

'He's a monster! You are not safe in this house, Grace. He killed your mother, and you will be next.'

'It's all right, Grandma. Papa disowned him, threw him out. We won't be seeing Gordon again.'

'Are you sure?' Myrtle asked hopefully.

'Yes.'

Myrtle felt quite lightheaded. It was such a relief to know that she'd never again have to look into the evil eyes of the man who had taken her daughter's life. She held onto the sink to steady herself and looked out of the window to where Louisa had been laid to rest. *Did you hear that, my dear child? One down, one to go*, she thought. Justice hadn't been served, but just knowing Gordon was gone brought Myrtle some satisfaction.

Grace came to stand beside her, and together they peered silently at the spot under the big oak tree.

'I wasn't a good mother,' Myrtle admitted. 'I made many mistakes. Louisa would have had a happier life if her father hadn't been killed in the Great War. Herbert, your grandfather, he was a good man, Grace. Kind and caring. The man wasn't a saint and had problems with gambling. But he loved your mother so dearly. He showed Louisa affection, something I always struggled to do.'

Myrtle flinched when she felt Grace's hand slip into hers, but she didn't pull away. 'I've failed as a grandmother, too,' she acknowledged, sighing. 'My exacting standards have always come before you.'

'I've always felt that I'm a disappointment to you, Grandma. I don't speak correctly, I can be boisterous, common… I suppose I take after Papa.'

'You do, dear, but I see much of your grandfather in you, too. You have his kind heart, as did your mother.'

'I miss her so much, Grandma. Why did she lock herself away in her bedroom for much of the time?'

'Your mother retreated from her insufferable life. She loved you, Grace, very much, and she wanted the best for you. Louisa was desperate for Dickie to love you, just as her father had loved her. But Dickie hadn't wanted a girl and had hoped for a son. He saw girls as weak. Louisa was weak and Dickie never showed her any respect. So, rightly or wrongly, your mother made you tough and strong, a girl who Dickie could love.'

'My mother wasn't weak. She showed her strength in raising me to be strong.'

'Yes, Grace, I suppose she did.'

'I'm not as strong as I pretend… I'm scared of Papa, and now I can understand your reasons for trying to have him killed.'

Myrtle was scared of the man too, though she'd never give Dickie the satisfaction of knowing that. 'Your father is abominable, but he would never hurt you. He adores you, Grace.'

'But I'm scared of what he's capable of.'

'Don't worry, dear. I'm here, and we shall look after each other.'

Grace gave her a quick hug. Myrtle wasn't accustomed to spontaneous displays of affection, especially from her granddaughter, but she liked it, though it felt rather uncomfortable. 'Haven't you got a boutique to open?'

'Yes, Grandma. Will you visit the shop one day?'

'I shall, tomorrow, though I've never been to Battersea,' she smiled. Her heart had softened towards her granddaughter, and she glanced towards the oak tree again. *Don't worry, Louisa. I shall take good care of Grace. And I'll love her, just as I should have done all these years past.*

John Dander heaved another sack of coal onto the rear of the cart. His back ached. For a man of twenty-five, he felt more like a sixty-year-old. Years of carrying the weight of the coal on his shoulders was making him old before his time. But John had plans. He wasn't going to be the coal man's lackey for much longer.

'All loaded,' he said to his boss, as he pulled himself up to sit at the front of the cart.

Mr Grimm flicked the horses' reins, saying, 'Walk on,' and the cart trundled slowly out of the coal yard.

John rubbed his sooty, gloved hands together. It was a fresh, chilly morning and Christmas was just around the corner. Then it would be the new year, and 1935 was going to bring him new beginnings. He was looking forward to being his own boss. *Dander's Deliveries.* He'd saved and scrimped to buy an old, broken truck, and he'd spent many long nights repairing it. Now his truck looked tidy and was mechanically sound, proudly displaying his company name. John was yet to break the news to Mr Grimm, though he believed the old man would wish him well. And John knew he would easily be replaced. Unemployment was rife in Britain. Not so much in London, but the North was suffering.

As the cart left the yard, he saw Anna running towards them, looking upset.

Mr Grimm stopped the horse and Anna peered up at John, distressed.

'John, you have to come quickly. It's Gordon. He's gone mad. I think he's going to hurt Grace!' she said, her voice high-pitched in panic.

John didn't give his job or Mr Grimm a second thought. Leaping down from the cart, he asked, 'Where is she?'

'In her shop, I should think. Oh, John, I'm so sorry, but I didn't know what to do. Mr Newman has thrown Gordon out and wants nothing to do with him. He was at my house this morning, ranting that he blames Grace. I'm worried, John. I've never seen Gordon like that before.'

'Go home, Anna. I'll see to it.'

'But—'

'Home, Anna,' John cut in. There was no time to argue. 'It'll be all right,' he assured her, before running off.

John knew where Grace's shop was located. He'd passed it

many times, yet hadn't had the courage to go in and ask her out, instead just getting a sneaky peek of her. She was stunning, and John doubted that a woman like Grace Newman would be interested in the likes of him, but he couldn't stop thinking about her. He'd never forgiven himself for being blackmailed into the robbery of her father. He owed it to Grace to protect her, regardless of his feelings for her.

Sprinting through the streets of Battersea, he finally came to her small boutique, and prayed he wasn't too late to protect her. He'd met Gordon a couple of times and hadn't liked the man. He wondered what his cousin saw in the bloke. *I'll kill him*, he thought. *If he's hurt Grace, I'll kill him.*

John wasn't a violent man and hadn't thrown a punch since leaving school. His heart pumped hard and fast. He knew who he was up against. Gordon was a hard man, one of the hardest men in Battersea, but John was ready to face him to safeguard Grace.

Grace was standing behind the cash register when the shop door was flung open with such force that it rattled. She looked up, startled, and gasped when she saw John Dander stomping in. The man was breathless and red-faced, his blond hair flopped forward.

Fear washed over her as she thought he'd come to rob her, just as he'd robbed her father. Grabbing the closest thing to hand, Grace's fingers curled tightly around a long hat pin, and she held it in front of her. 'Come one step closer and I'll have your eyes out,' she threatened.

'Where is he?' John asked, his eyes roaming the shop.

'Who?'

'Gordon. Is he here?'

'No. Why would Gordon be here?'

John turned to the door and closed it. 'Fetch the key,' he ordered.

'I'll do no such thing! Get out. Get out of my shop. You're not getting a penny from my till!'

John's head snapped around and he looked perplexed. 'Eh? Blimey, I'm not here to steal from you. Just bring me the blinkin' key, will you. Gordon's on the rampage.'

Grace's mind raced.

'The key ...' John pressed with urgency.

Fishing in her bag, her hands trembling, Grace found the key and hurried to John, who quickly locked the door.

'What makes you think that Gordon's coming here?' she asked.

'Anna told me. She was worried about you. She said Gordon was ranting and blames you for Mr Newman disowning him.'

Grace looked out of the window, anxiously scanning the street.

'You're safe now. He can't get in.'

Grace felt she should thank John, but this was the man who'd attacked her father. She wasn't sure she could trust him. What if this tale about Gordon was all an elaborate story to get her alone and rob her, or worse! 'I'd like you to leave now,' she said firmly.

'No, I don't think that's a good idea. I'll stay in case Gordon turns up.'

'I can deal with Gordon.'

'You didn't see Anna earlier. My cousin doesn't get that worked up without good cause.'

'Even so, I'd still like you to leave.'

John must have sensed her hostility, and asked, 'Why would you think that I'm here to steal from you?'

Grace was still holding the long hat pin and pointing it towards him. 'I know you were part of the gang who attacked my father,' she said boldly. 'And don't deny it. I saw your face and I saw you meeting my grandmother on Clapham Common.'

John's shoulders slumped and he exhaled loudly.

'You're lucky I haven't told my father or the police. Either do your worst or get out!'

'Please, Grace, let—'

'Miss Newman, to you,' she interrupted.

'Sorry, Miss Newman, please let me explain ...'

'There's nothing to explain. You left my father for dead and stole his money.'

'I didn't want to, I swear! And I had no idea that someone was carrying a knife. As for the money ... I gave my cut away because I felt so bad. Honestly, Miss Newman, I didn't want to do it.'

'Then why did you?' Grace asked. She didn't want to believe his lies, but he sounded convincing.

'Your grandmother didn't give me much choice. She said if I didn't carry out her wishes, she'd make sure I lost my job and swore that I'd never work again. She threatened to have me thrown into prison; said she'd get the police on me for stealing from her. I wouldn't do that, but who'd believe my word over hers?'

'How do you even know my grandmother?'

'I deliver coal to your house.'

Grace thought, her mind reeling.

John continued, 'If you saw me when your father was

being attacked, then you must know that I never put the boot in.'

'But you organised the gang to do it.'

'Yeah, I did, and I've regretted it ever since. I should have stood up to your grandmother, but I thought I had too much to lose.'

'Are they friends of yours?'

'Gawd, no! They're brothers, just people I loosely know from delivering the coal.'

Grace wasn't sure what to think of it all, and her thoughts returned to Gordon. 'Why are you putting yourself at risk to protect me from Gordon?'

John exhaled loudly again. Looking her straight in the eye, he said, 'Because I like you. I can't stop thinking about you.'

That wasn't the answer Grace was expecting. If things had been different, if he wasn't involved in attacking her father, she might have felt the same. There was no denying that her stomach fluttered when she looked at him, but Grace had attributed that to fear. Now though, she wasn't afraid of him anymore, yet her stomach was still fluttering and her blood rushing.

'I know I don't have a hope in hell of you feeling anything but hatred for me, but I won't let Gordon hurt you. He's gunning for you, and right now, all you've got is me. Will you trust me?'

Grace remembered the spiteful look in Gordon's eyes last night. She rubbed her cheek where his fingers had dug into her flesh. 'Yes, I trust you.'

'Good. Is there a back door?'

Grace shook her head. 'I don't want to run and hide from him.'

'Cor, you're a Newman for sure. But if you want to wait here like a sitting duck, then like I said, I'll stay with you.'

'Unlock the door,' Grace said defiantly.

'Are you sure about this? I'm not a fighting man, Miss Newman. There's a good chance that Gordon will overpower me.'

'You may not be a fighting man, but I'm a fighting woman. Unlock the door.'

29

The next day, as Grace locked up the shop, she saw John Dander approaching. His face was black with coal, as were his clothes. Yet he still looked attractive, and Grace felt her pulse quicken.

'Hello, Miss Newman. I wanted to make sure that you're all right?'

'Thank you. Yes, I'm fine.'

'Good.'

They stood gazing at each other for a few seconds, and then Grace said, 'I've just locked up, but you look as though you could do with a cup of tea. Would you like to come inside?'

John grinned. 'I'd love to, Miss Newman, but I wouldn't want to dirty your fancy hats. Look at the state of me, I'm covered in dust from the coal. But if your father isn't picking you up, then I'd be happy to walk you to the tram stop again, if that's all right with you? I wouldn't want to embarrass you, what with you looking all dolled up. If you don't mind me saying, you don't 'alf look a picture, Miss Newman.'

'Thank you. Please, walk with me, and call me Grace.'

As they strolled, Grace hoped her father wouldn't drive past and collect her. She was enjoying John's company and didn't want it to end. After spending the day together in the shop yesterday, they'd come to know each other quite well, and Grace had found herself opening up to him. She'd told him about how her mother had locked herself away for much of the time, yet how much she missed their daily chats, and how she was finding it difficult to express her grief, but she'd kept the secret about her death. And surprisingly, Grace had realised that she wanted to be closer to her grandmother.

Nearly at the tram stop, Grace was reluctant to say goodbye, and when his hand accidentally brushed hers, it felt as though an electric current had passed between them.

'I saw Anna last night,' he said. 'She's furious with Gordon.'

'But I think she'll still marry him. I know I've already said it, but thank you again for staying with me yesterday.'

'I would have stayed with you today an' all, if you'd allowed me to.'

'I know, and I'm grateful, but you can't be with me for every minute of every day. Anyway, I haven't seen or heard from Gordon, so I must assume he's calmed down.'

'Maybe. But be careful, Grace. He might just be biding his time. I still believe you should tell your father.'

'No, John, I can't. If I told my father, he'd kill Gordon. I don't want his blood on my hands, and Anna would never forgive me. She's my dearest friend. I won't lose my friendship with Anna for the sake of Gordon. And let's face it, if Anna forgives Gordon and is still determined to marry him, then she's going to need a friend too, more than ever.'

⋆

Gordon waited near the hospital for Anna's shift to finish. When he saw her, he smiled awkwardly.

She gave him a reproachful look and walked past.

'I'm sorry, Anna. I lost me head. I shouldn't have made such a scene at yours yesterday morning.'

'No, Gordon, you shouldn't have! You upset my mum, and it was a good job that my dad was at work.'

'It won't happen again, Anna, I promise.'

'Always promises with you. I won't sleep with other women, *I promise.* I won't rant and rave again, *I promise.* You scared me yesterday, Gordon. I thought you was going to do something really bad to Grace.'

'I was wound up and letting off steam. I didn't go to Grace's shop. Let's face it, if I had of done, Dickie would have made sure that I was a dead man walking now.'

'I know you didn't go to Grace's shop because I saw my cousin last night and he told me. But thanks to you, John lost a day's pay!'

'How has that got anything to do with me?'

'I was worried, Gordon, so I got my cousin to go to Grace's shop. He stayed with her all day in case you showed up.'

'And what was he gonna do, eh? Beat me up? John can't punch his way out of a paper bag.'

'That's not the point. He was doing the right thing and it cost him.'

'I'll pay him the wages he lost.'

'Make sure you do,' Anna snapped, and marched off.

'Don't walk away from me,' Gordon called. 'I'm an idiot. I've lost the man I thought of as my dad. I can't lose you an' all.'

Anna turned, her eyes filled with love, and Gordon smiled.

'Am I forgiven?' he asked.

'I suppose so. But you've got to learn to control your temper.'

Gordon placed his arm over her shoulder. 'I will, I promise.' He thought Anna was a pushover, and once again, he'd won her round and was back in her good books. 'Do you think your dad will let me kip on the sofa tonight?'

'Probably. But you're gonna have to find a job and a place to live. I won't marry you until you're working and can support me and our family.'

Gordon had a few shillings in his pocket, money he'd taken by force from a bloke outside the pub. He knew he needed to work, but he didn't like the thought of slogging all day on a factory line or as a builder's labourer for poor pay. Gordon only knew one way of earning money – violence. And he was good at it, shaped by Dickie Newman's influence. He'd just have to ensure he didn't step on the big man's toes.

Dickie could see that Pippa was going downhill rapidly. The doctor had said she had a few weeks left to live, but Dickie thought it would be days rather than weeks. She'd become weaker and her breathing sounded more laboured.

'It hurts,' she moaned.

Sitting beside her bed, Dickie reached for the medicine, and carefully lifted her head before offering the powerful concoction to her dry and cracked lips. She sipped the drink and tried to smile at him. Something in her eyes reminded him of his mother. She'd had that same look. It was an expression that spoke a thousand words without speaking, and Dickie understood, that just like his mother, Pippa didn't want to leave him but was at peace with her impending death. A wave of emotion caught him unawares, and he leaned over Pippa, pulling her almost weightless body close. Holding her in his arms, Dickie cried unashamedly.

'It'll be all right,' Pippa soothed.

Dickie cried harder. The unshed tears he'd held in on his mother's death poured out now, too.

'Don't leave me, Pip,' he sobbed. 'I love you. I bloody love you. I should have married you. I'm sorry, sweetheart, so sorry.'

'Yeah, you should have married me,' Pippa said faintly.

Laying her back down on the bed, Dickie wiped his eyes. 'Cor, I don't know where that came from. What a silly sod, eh.'

'I told you you're a softy really.'

'Yeah, I reckon you might be right,' he smiled, rolling his eyes. Pippa had seen every facet of his character, and he sometimes thought she knew him better than he knew himself.

'Does your wife know you're here?'

Dickie baulked. 'My wife is dead, Pip.'

'Oh. How did she die?'

'It's a long story.'

'Hmm, well, I don't have long, so best you make it quick.'

Dickie grabbed Pippa's hand and saw her eyes close as she slipped into sleep. 'Rest, my darling. I'll be here when you wake up. You and me, that's all that's important now.'

30

'Where's your father?' Myrtle asked.

'I've no idea,' Grace answered. 'He hasn't been home for four days.'

'One can only hope he's dead, but the devil looks after his own, so I'm sure he's fit and well somewhere.'

Grace had faced the truth about her father, yet she still loved him, and would never wish him dead. 'Please don't speak like that, Grandma.'

'I speak as I find, and I have no cause to say anything flattering about that man. But, out of respect for you, I shall refrain from mentioning my desire to see him dead.'

'Thank you. Though I must admit, the atmosphere at home has been far less tense in his absence, and it's been nice spending time with you.'

Myrtle smiled and poured a cup of tea for Grace. 'I try to stay out of your father's way, which is why I'm mostly out of the house. And knowing my daughter is buried just yards from me is most unsettling.'

'It used to upset me too, Grandma, but now I find comfort

in knowing she's so close. I often sit under the tree and talk to her. I miss her so much, it still hurts.'

'I miss her too, and my heart is filled with many regrets. The fact that Gordon and your father got away with what they did will always incense me. Your mother's grave is a constant reminder.'

'I wish I'd spent more time with her.'

'Don't start getting maudlin, Grace. Just think how pleased she would be to see us getting along so splendidly.'

Grace nodded. She felt a real fondness for her grandmother and found the woman's stories fascinating. Myrtle Best lived in a different world, one of wealth, pomp and ceremony. Gossip seemed to be rife in her grandmother's circle, but there was never any violence. The ladies were ladies indeed, and the men were gentlemen. Grace knew it was a place where she'd never fit in; she was too much like her father. But she didn't belong in his world, either.

Her grandmother's voice broke her thoughts.

'So, tell me. Have you considered marriage?'

Grace could feel her cheeks reddening as she thought of John Dander. 'No, Grandma, I haven't considered marriage.'

'I can see there's someone special, though. I'm right, aren't I?'

'Maybe.'

'Do tell.'

'There's nothing much to tell.'

'Come now, Grace. In my considerable years, I've seen many young ladies with that same expression on their faces. I'm sure I wore it too when I met your grandfather.'

Grace wanted to share her feelings about John with her

grandmother, but she wasn't sure how the woman would react. 'There is someone I like, but it's an impossible situation.'

'Oh, Grace, my dear girl, please don't tell me you're involved with a married man!'

'No! Of course not!'

'Then I'm sure that most *impossible* situations can be overcome. What is the problem?'

Grace drew in a long breath, before announcing bluntly, 'It's John Dander.'

Her grandmother's eyes widened.

'I know everything, Grandma. You were wrong to bully him into doing your dirty work, and he was wrong to organise the attack on Papa. But I can't help how I feel about him.'

Myrtle rose to her feet and smoothed down the front of her dress. 'I hope you understand my motives,' she said.

'Yes, Grandma, I do. I wanted to hate you for almost getting Papa killed, but I can see why you did it.'

'I just wanted your mother to be happy.'

'And you did it for yourself, too.'

'Yes, I did, Grace. I've carried so much bitterness in my heart for so long, it clouded my judgement. However, it may not be my place to say, but John Dander is not a suitable man for you.'

'I thought that's what you'd say. He's not who you think he is, Grandma. John is kind, caring and thoughtful.'

'But he's a coalman!'

'So?'

'So, Grace, he's simply too far below you.'

'Oh, Grandma, don't be such a snob. Look at who my father is. I'm the daughter of an aggressive, working-class man who beats up people for money. I don't think there's anyone below me, do you?'

'I need to lay down,' Myrtle said dramatically. 'It's your decision, Grace. I ruined your mother's life by forcing her to marry. I shan't interfere and ruin yours, too.'

Gordon had found a room to rent, though it wasn't of much higher standard than Dickie's properties. But it was cheap, and it was at least somewhere to lay his head at night.

Walking Anna home, it was clear she wasn't impressed with his living arrangements.

'You'll have to find somewhere better than that,' she said. 'I won't live there, Gordon. Once we're married, I want a proper home.'

'Yeah, yeah, I know. Stop nagging, woman. You're not my wife yet.'

'And I won't be, if you don't get us somewhere half decent to live.'

Anna's moaning irritated him, but he stayed quiet and tried to think of something to say to change the subject. 'How's work?' he asked.

'Work's work. I popped in to see Grace before my shift today. I was teasing her about John. It's obvious that they like each other.'

'Your cousin John?'

'Yeah. He's been sweet on her for a while, and she told me they went to the picture house together.'

Gordon's mind turned. He knew Dickie wouldn't approve of his precious daughter seeing John Dander. This information could give him leverage with Dickie. It might be just what he needed to worm his way back in with the man.

Anna continued, 'I'm meeting Grace tomorrow after work and we're going to exchange Christmas gifts. I hope she likes what I've got for her.'

'I don't want you seeing her,' Gordon snapped.

'I know you and Grace don't see eye to eye, Gordon, but she's my best friend.'

'She's a troublemaker, and have you forgotten how she tried to split us up?'

'It wasn't like that.'

'It was, Anna. I've told you before, Grace is jealous of you and me. She don't like me and she'll say anything she can to get between us. I don't want you to see her again.'

'That's not fair!'

'What, you think it's fair that my future wife puts her friend before me, eh?'

'Oh, Gordon, please …'

'It's true. It upsets me when you spend time with her. You're not being loyal to me, Anna. You should be thinking about how I feel.'

'There's no harm in me seeing Grace.'

'If you say so, but you clearly don't care about me, Anna. If you loved me as much as you say you do, then you'd cut Grace out of your life … for me.'

They walked in silence for a while, and then Gordon pushed further. 'I don't think I can marry a woman who ain't prepared to put her husband's feelings first.'

'What? Are you telling me I have to choose between you and Grace?'

'I'm saying that I don't like you seeing her; it upsets me. I ain't making you choose, but if you want to stay friends with her, then it might be best if we call off the wedding.'

'No, Gordon, I want to be your wife. If it means that much to you, then I won't see Grace again.'

Gordon inwardly smiled and thought of himself as a puppeteer and Anna as the puppet. He knew exactly what strings to pull to control her.

Pippa's slow, short breaths rattled as she struggled to pull air into her lungs. She hadn't opened her eyes or spoken all day, but Dickie knew she was still aware, because she'd squeezed his hand feebly when he'd told her he loved her.

The doctor removed his stethoscope from Pippa's chest and turned to Dickie, saying quietly, 'It's nearly time.'

Dickie hadn't wanted to hear those words. 'Get out!' he growled.

The doctor looked taken aback.

'Go on, get out!' he said, louder.

As the doctor quietly closed the bedroom door behind him, Dickie rushed to Pippa's bedside. Gently stroking her hair off her forehead, he leant over and lightly kissed her grey skin. Taking her hand, he said softly, 'I can't stand to see you suffering, Pip. It's all right, you can go now.'

Pippa drew in a breath and Dickie knew it would be her last. 'Be a good girl up there with them angels. Goodbye, sweetheart.'

Silent tears rolled down his cheeks. He'd been dreading this moment, but Pippa was gone. Dickie took solace in knowing she was no longer in pain, yet still he felt as though he was being stabbed in his chest, over and over again.

Pulling himself together and swallowing down the thick lump of grief in his throat, Dickie walked out of the room, nodded to the doctor and climbed into his car. As the engine turned, an unexplainable rage burned inside. He banged his hands several times on the steering wheel, struggling to stop himself from crying. 'NOOOOO!' he yelled and then gritted his teeth. 'No! No! Fuckin' no!'

31

The next day was bitterly cold. Grace met John after work, and they sat in the warmth of her shop, sharing a bag of sweets.

'My father would lose his head if he had any clue we were here together,' she said. 'I heard him come home last night. He was clomping around downstairs, so I stayed in my room.'

'I wish you didn't have to spend Christmas Day with him. My mum's invited you to our house.'

'That's kind of her, but I can't leave him all alone on Christmas Day of all days. It's his favourite day of the year. My grandmother won't be home; she'll be at her elite club having lunch with the *ladies.* I'd like to invite you to ours, but I worry that you'd end up getting stuffed instead of the bird.'

John laughed. 'Do you think your dad will ever accept me?'

Grace shrugged. She hoped so, but she doubted it.

'You know I'm falling for you, Grace.'

She nodded, beaming. 'Good, because it's the same for me.'

'Well, we can't keep hiding from your father forever. I'm going to have to brave it and introduce myself to him. But I think I'll wait until I've got Dander's Deliveries up and running. He might give me half a chance if he thinks I've got some gumption.'

'Leave Papa to me,' Grace said. 'Everyone has always thought I've got him wrapped around my little finger. If anyone can talk him round, it'll be me.'

'Can I kiss you?' John asked playfully.

'Yes, please,' Grace replied, and closed her eyes.

When she felt his lips on hers, she tingled all over like never before.

Pulling away, he peered into her eyes and said huskily, 'I love you, Grace Newman. I've never felt like this before. We haven't known each other long, and I don't want to scare you away, but you've blown my mind.'

'Shush, John. Stop talking. I love you, too. Kiss me again,' she replied breathlessly, and leaned in to feel his lips on hers once more.

Gordon knew Dickie would have finished work for the day, and he couldn't wait to tell him about John Dander.

As he walked around the corner of the impressive street in Clapham, he saw Dickie's car parked outside the house Gordon had once called home. He hoped to win good favour with Dickie, and that he'd soon be calling it home again.

His heart thumped hard against his chest as he knocked on the heavy door.

No one answered, but Gordon knew Dickie was inside, so he knocked again, harder.

When Dickie pulled the door open, he glared indignantly. 'You've got some bleedin' nerve,' he roared. 'Fuck off before I send you head first down them steps.'

'Wait, Dickie, please, hear me out... I've got something to tell you that you're gonna want to know about.'

'I ain't interested in anything you've got to say, so piss off!'

As Dickie went to slam the door closed, Gordon revealed, 'It's about Grace and some bloke she's seeing.'

Dickie opened the door wider again. 'Go on.'

'Can I come in, Dickie? It's flippin' freezing out here, mate.'

In his office, Dickie poured himself a large brandy, before demanding, 'Tell me what you know.'

Gordon fidgeted nervously, stepping from one foot to the other. 'I'm sorry about what I did, Dickie. I was out of order.'

'Tell me!' Dickie bellowed.

'Grace has been seeing the bloke who delivers coal here. John Dander. Turns out that he's Anna's cousin and Anna reckons the two of 'em are getting more than friendly. I knew you'd want to know, Dickie.'

Gordon watched as the enraged man paced the floor and knocked back a second and a third glass of brandy.

'I can sort him out, Dickie,' Gordon offered. 'I can make sure that John Dander never goes near Grace again. What do you think, eh, Dickie?'

'And what's in it for you? Hoping for my gratitude, are ya?'

Gordon should have known better than to think he could have fooled Dickie. The man had seen straight through him. He figured it was probably best to be honest. 'Yeah, Dickie. I messed up, but I want to put things right. I ain't being soppy or nothing, but you're like the dad I never had. So, yeah, I'm hoping that you'll give me another chance.'

'No one gets another chance when it comes to Grace, and you of all people should know that.'

'Right an' all, Dickie, but Grace is like a sister to me. Don't all families fall out now and then?'

'Let me make something very clear. We ain't family. Grace is my family, and she will always be my priority. You, Gordon, you ain't blood and you let me down. I raised you to protect Grace.'

'I know, and I will, I promise. I'd put my life on the line for her. I can't tell you how much I regret raising my hand to her, Dickie. It'll never happen again.'

'Get rid of John Dander and keep my name out of it. Grace can't ever know. I'll give you another chance, but if you ever touch a hair on my girl's head again, I'll fuckin' kill you.'

32

The following day, on Christmas Eve, Grace was expecting a busy day in the shop, with husbands purchasing last minute gifts for their wives. She glanced at the wrapped present under the counter that was meant for Anna, and wondered why her friend had been avoiding her. John seemed to think it had something to do with Gordon, and he'd questioned his cousin, but Anna had denied avoiding Grace and had told John she'd been busy.

The day passed quickly, and as Grace had hoped, there had been a continual flurry of men buying ladies' hats, scarves and gloves, which Grace had wrapped beautifully. Her cash register was full and her stocks low.

As she was about to close, later than usual, the door opened, and John came in.

'Hello, you,' she smiled, always pleased to see him.

John returned her smile, but Grace could see he wasn't happy. 'Is something wrong?' she asked.

'There's something I need to show you.'

'What?'

'Come with me, but brace yourself. You're going to get an awful shock, Grace.'

'I'm not sure that I want to.'

'And I wasn't sure if I should show you what I've seen, but you need to know. Something's got to change, Grace, and I think you're the only person who can change it.'

'John, what on earth are you talking about?'

'Just come with me. I'll tell you on the way.'

Grace was curious, though worried, too. Walking through Battersea with John, she asked him to explain.

'A gaunt-looking woman with a baby came into the coal yard this morning. She begged Mr Grimm for a bag of coal, said her kids were freezing. She sounded so desperate and asked for any scraps. Mr Grimm sent her on her way, but I had a quiet word with her and got her address. Once we'd finished our rounds, I paid Mr Grimm for a bag of the cheap stuff and took it to the woman's house.'

'Aw, John, that was kind of you.'

'Part of me wishes I hadn't. I can't unsee what I've seen, Grace.'

'What did you see?'

'Hell. I looked into the belly of hell.'

'And this is what you want to show me?' Grace asked, unsure.

'You'll understand soon enough.'

Grace trusted John, but she soon realised that they were close to some of her father's properties. 'Where exactly are we going?' she pressed.

John didn't answer, but a few minutes later, he stopped outside a tall house that looked derelict and unoccupied. 'Here,' he said. 'Downstairs.'

Grace looked at the moss-covered steps that led to a basement door and was surprised when John beckoned her down.

She stood beside him as he knocked on the door.

'It's me, Mrs May, John Dander, the coal man.'

Mrs May opened the door just a crack and peeked through suspiciously.

'This is my friend, Grace. Can we come in?'

The woman pulled the door open wider and the stench of damp and sewage hit Grace.

Inside, Mrs May led them through darkness into another dark room, the only light coming from the small fire in the hearth.

'Thanks for the coal, Mr Dander. It's keeping us warm a treat.'

Grace saw four small children in rags huddled around the fire, but the room was completely bare. No beds, chairs or tables. 'There's no furniture,' she whispered to John.

'Would you tell Grace what happened to your furniture please, Mrs May?'

'I had to burn some of it to keep me kids from freezing to death, and then my landlord took the rest. I got behind with the rent, so he took it to sell on. I begged him not to. He knew I had no money for coal. He didn't care and all my stuff was carted out, which left me with nothing to burn. My second youngest, Elsie, she got ill. The cold got her.'

'Oh, is Elsie feeling better?' Grace asked.

'No, she died.'

Grace gulped. 'I'm so sorry.'

John spoke again. 'Tell Grace what happens to your welfare money.'

'My landlord takes it. He gave me a loan to pay my rent,

but the money I owed kept going up and up 'cos he put so much interest on top. So now he comes round every week to collect my welfare. He said once I've paid him back, he's chucking us out. The only way I can keep a roof over me kids' heads is to take out another loan with him. But I can't afford to. How am I supposed to feed them?'

Grace looked at the hungry faces that Mrs May was pointing to.

'Go on, Mrs May, tell Grace everything that you told me,' John encouraged.

'That stench, that's a broken sewer pipe in the back yard that leeches into the house. Even the rats have moved out! The boarded windows ain't got no glass in. If we didn't have the fire going, we'd be sat in darkness 'cos I can't afford candles. And when it rains, water pours down these walls. They're thick with black mould and I'm sure it's giving my kids chest problems. This place ain't fit for an animal, but I'm stuck here. I can't pay for nowhere decent because the landlord takes all me money, and he reckons I'll be in debt to him for the next four years.'

John asked, 'And who's your landlord, Mrs May?'

Grace already knew the answer, so wasn't surprised when the woman answered, 'Mr Newman.'

She knew her father was an unscrupulous landlord, but she hadn't realised he was trapping vulnerable women and children into a cycle of debt and poverty. 'I've got to get out of here,' she mumbled, panicking. It felt as though the walls were closing in on her and she was desperate for fresh air.

Outside, Grace emptied her purse and told John to take the money to Mrs May. When he came back out, she shook her head angrily. 'How can my father treat people like this?'

'I'm sorry, Grace. I knew this would break your heart, but you had to see how dire these people's lives are, made worse by your father.'

'I had planned on talking to him about his business practices, but then what with one thing and another, it got pushed aside. But this, John, this is unacceptable. He can't do this to people. I'll try to make him change his ways.'

Gordon kept his distance as he followed John from the coal yard to Grace's shop and now to Mrs May's room. He wondered why the man had taken Grace to that shithole; it made no sense. Not that Gordon cared. He was waiting for the right moment to jump John and hoped to catch him unawares. He'd have to be careful. There couldn't be any witnesses. Gordon was willing to give the bloke a good kicking, but he didn't want to do time for it.

It was dark when John kissed Grace goodbye at the tram stop. He waited for her to embark, waved her off and then seemed to be heading towards home. Gordon smirked. He knew exactly where he could pounce – a rough piece of wasteland behind the pub that John would pass.

Walking faster to catch up with him, Gordon fingered the flick-knife in his pocket. He didn't plan on using it, but was carrying the blade as insurance. There wasn't a doubt in Gordon's mind that he could easily knock John to the ground, but on the off chance that John got a sly punch in, Gordon felt reassured knowing that he had the knife to hand.

The streets were unusually quiet, which suited Gordon. He imagined excited kids tucked up in their beds and waiting for a visit from Father Christmas. He'd never believed in the fat man with the red coat. When he'd been a child, Christmas hadn't been a time of celebration. He remembered his mother giving him an orange once, and another time, one of her fellas had slipped a shiny ha'penny into the pocket of his shorts. But other than that, Christmas had been another excuse for his mother to get drunk. He rarely thought about the woman who'd abandoned him, and when he did, it left a sour taste in his mouth.

Gordon flexed his cold hands. He was only a few feet behind John. He looked over his shoulder and all around. There was no one to witness what he was about to do. John was on the edge of the waste ground now. Gordon pulled a balaclava over his face and picked up his speed; he was now an arm's length behind the man.

'OI!' he shouted.

John turned, and before he could say or do anything, Gordon swung his fist forward and whacked him ferociously in the face. John's head snapped back but he remained on his feet. Gordon punched him again, the blow landing on the side of John's head, and then Gordon hooked him under the chin with a left-handed upper cut.

John lost his balance and fell backwards, lying helplessly on the frosty ground, but Gordon wasn't finished with him yet. He had to ensure that John got the message loud and clear. 'Stay away from Grace,' he cautioned, and kicked his booted foot into John's ribs. 'This is just a warning,' he said, kicking him again.

John cried out in agonised pain.

'Go near Grace again, and you'll be killed next time,' Gordon ground out, and booted him in the face.

John groaned and his head lolled to one side as he fell unconscious.

Quickly checking around him again, satisfied that the attack hadn't been seen, Gordon whipped off the balaclava and hunched his head into his shoulders before darting away. His work was done, and Christmas lunch around Dickie's table beckoned. It was more appealing than sitting in Anna's kitchen, under her dad's scrutinising eye.

33

Grace pulled back the bedroom curtains and looked out into the garden. The frost glistened in the early morning sun, sparkling like crushed diamonds on the ground. Her eyes fell on the spot under the oak tree. *Merry Christmas, Mother*, she thought sadly.

She heard a light tap on the door and turned to see her grandmother slipping into the room and closing the door quietly behind her. Myrtle rushed towards her, her face grave, and Grace's stomach knotted.

The old woman took hold of both of Grace's hands, whispering with urgency, 'You must get out of this house, Grace. Gordon is back. I heard him downstairs talking to Dickie, and they were laughing. It's not safe for you here. Please, Grace, leave.'

'Gordon, are you sure?'

'Yes! I'll never trust him, and I'm concerned for you.'

Grace pulled her hands away from her grandmother's vice-like grip and looked back out of the window, feeling let down. 'Well, I'm astonished that Papa has allowed Gordon back, but there's nothing to worry about, Grandma. Papa would never let Gordon hurt me.'

'I saw the bruises on your face. He's hurt you before and he will again. I haven't spoken out before now, but I've seen the way Gordon looks at you. He resents you, Grace. I'm sure he's jealous of you and always has been.'

'Do you think so?'

'Yes! And we both know what he's capable of. That's why you must listen to me and take notice. Get out. You have the shop, your own money. You can support yourself. Escape from Gordon and your father before it's too late.'

Grace peered at her mother's grave, her thoughts in disarray, and then Dickie's booming voice carried up the stairs.

'GRACE … GRACE … It's Christmas. Are you coming downstairs?'

'He always acts like a big kid on Christmas Day,' Grace said, rolling her eyes whilst lacking any Christmas joy.

'It's the one day of the year that he's in a good mood. Regardless of your father's seasonal spirit, I refuse to spend the day here, especially now that Gordon is back. I think you should get today out of the way, and then pack your bags.'

'I'll think about it,' Grace answered. She thought about Mrs May's untenable predicament. 'But before I do anything rash, I need to speak to Papa about something important, which means I must keep him in this good mood.'

'He won't like it when you move out.'

'No, Grandma, he won't!'

Dickie loved Christmas, though this year was tinged with sadness for him. Pippa's death had hit him hard, but he wouldn't allow anyone to see his pain. Instead, he knocked back a brandy and fixed a smile on his face.

'Are you sure no one saw you?' he asked Gordon quietly.

'Yeah, I'm sure. And I covered my face an' all. I gave him what for, Dickie. He'll stay out of Grace's life if he knows what's good for him.'

Patting Gordon on the back, Dickie reached into his pocket and pulled out a five-pound note. Shoving it into Gordon's hand, he said in his ear, 'A Christmas bonus. I'm feeling generous today.'

It felt good having Gordon back at home. He hadn't realised how much he'd missed the young man's company. He'd keep an eye on him though and watch him carefully. If Gordon dared to raise his voice or his hands to Grace, then Dickie would have no qualms about giving him the battering of a lifetime. He hoped it wouldn't come to that and didn't want to cut Gordon out of his life, but Grace would *always* come first.

When his daughter walked in, Dickie smiled warmly. Her beauty shone, brightening the room. He held his glass aloft, chanting, 'Merry Christmas, darling.'

Grace didn't look happy as she eyed Gordon, and Dickie wasn't surprised.

'We're gonna have a fresh start,' he explained. 'Gordon has moved back in.'

'So I see,' she replied tartly.

Gordon offered a wrapped box to Grace, saying shamefacedly, 'I'm sorry, Grace. I hope we can still be friends.'

Dickie saw his daughter looking at Gordon's swollen knuckles, and then giving him a hard stare, before turning her nose up at his offering. He'd assumed this would be

Grace's reaction. After all, the girl was a Newman and could be as tough as old boots when she wanted to be. He walked over, took the gift from Gordon, placed his arm over Grace's shoulder and asked nicely, 'Will you give him a second chance, darling, for me?'

Huffing, Grace snatched the gift and threw a disenchanted, sarcastic smile at Gordon.

'That's my girl,' Dickie said.

'Can I have a word, Papa, in private?'

'As long as you ain't gonna bend my ear about Gordon.'

'No.'

'All right,' he agreed. Then he told Gordon, 'Give us a minute.'

Once Gordon had left the room, Dickie poured himself another drink as Grace closed the door. 'Right, what's this all about?' he asked, noting that his daughter appeared uneasy.

'I've never been involved in your business, Papa, and you've kept me away from it. But I feel I must speak up on behalf of your tenants. The conditions they're living in are beyond awful, and the way you treat them is a disgrace.'

'Who are you, the spokesman for the tenants' union?' Dickie chuckled.

'This isn't a joking matter, Papa.'

'I know you mean well, darling, but you don't know the first thing about my business.'

'I know enough! I've seen the disgusting places some people call home, and I know you trap them into getting into debt with you. Children are dying, Papa! Kids are going hungry. Families are living in squalor. It's improper. You're not a poor man, surely you can do better.'

Dickie could feel his anger rising. He'd never been a

man who tolerated his decisions being questioned, and he refused to be made to feel responsible for other people's poverty. Trying to remain reasonable, he said calmly, 'I'm not a charity, Grace. Hard work got me to where I am today. There's nothing stopping anyone from improving their own lives. If they want to live like filthy beggars, then that's their look out, not mine.'

'But, Papa, I've seen it for myself first hand. You're forcing mothers to take out loans with you to pay their rent, then adding on exorbitant interest. It's impossible for them to ever get out of debt, and the living conditions, well, it turns my stomach. The properties are in a state of disrepair and, to be frank, they need demolishing! Most of your houses should have been on the plans for slum clearance, because that's what they are, Papa – slums!'

Dickie breathed in deeply. He didn't want to lose his temper with Grace, but it was simmering very close to the surface. 'You like this big house? And this nice part of town? Your boutique? Fancy clothes? The food in your belly? Who do you think pays for all of it, eh? Me, that's who. So don't dare to tell me how to run my business, Grace.'

'I'm not trying to tell you what to do, Papa. I just hoped you might make your properties more habitable, and be kinder to the families living in them. It would be the right thing to do.'

Again, Dickie breathed deeply. It was Christmas Day, and he was already struggling to put on a cheery face. 'All right, if it shuts you up, I'll tart up the houses a bit and be a bit *kinder.*' He had no intentions of either, but he hoped it would appease her.

Grace skipped over and planted a kiss on his cheek. 'Thank you, Papa, and merry Christmas.'

'There's something for you under the tree,' he said, looking forward to seeing her face light up. 'Go on, go and get it.'

When Grace opened the small package, she looked curiously at the set of keys. 'What are these for?' she asked.

'Those, my darling, are the keys for your second boutique. I've bought you a new shop in Chelsea. This is the start of a whole chain of your boutiques across London.'

Grace stared, speechless.

'Ain't you pleased?'

'Yes, Papa, thank you.'

'I've just had an idea. You could ask Anna if she'd like to manage the new shop. Keep it in the family, so to speak, and you'll need staff you can trust.'

'Er, yes, maybe.'

'Good. Don't give me my gift yet. I'll open mine after lunch. Talking of which, shouldn't you be getting on with cooking it?'

'Yeah, I will shortly. Maybe you'd like to peel the spuds?'

Dickie couldn't help roaring with laughter. 'That's women's work. I can't see me in an apron, can you?'

'No, probably not. But it's all getting too much for me, Papa, and you can't expect Grandma to do it. If I'm going to be running two shops, I won't have time for domestic duties.'

'Fair enough. Hire someone to do the cleaning and cooking.'

'Thank you. That's a weight off my mind.'

As Grace left the room, Gordon came back in and eyed Grace with suspicion.

'What was that all about?' he asked. 'It wasn't anything to do with John, was it?'

Dickie shook his head, his thoughts turning. He wondered how Grace was so informed about the business. And she hadn't seemed overly excited about the new shop he'd bought her. He'd felt a coldness from her, as if she were pulling away from him, and Dickie didn't like it. *She might think she's a grown woman, but she'll always be my little girl*, he thought, his injured heart about Pippa now swelling with love for his daughter. Grace was the light of his life. The only person who brought him joy. She was good, pure, and his creation. Nothing or no one was ever going to take her away from him.

34

As John awoke, he could feel a throbbing pain in his head and his body ached. Slowly opening his eyes, he squeezed them shut against the bright light.

'John ... John ... you're awake! It's me, Anna. John ...'

Forcing his heavy eyelids open again, his mouth felt so dry, he could barely swallow. 'Where am I?' he murmured.

'You're in the hospital. You've been badly beaten, but you're all right. You gave us quite a scare, though!'

'What happened?'

'Don't you remember?'

John closed his eyes again as flashbacks bombarded his mind. A bloke, his face covered ... the punches ... kicks ... the warning ...

'Who did this to you, John?'

Thinking hard, he hadn't recognised Gordon, but he'd known the man's voice when he'd made his threats. 'Gordon. It was Gordon.'

Anna gasped. 'Don't be daft, Gordon didn't do this. I think you're confused. Hang on, I'll fetch the doctor.'

John opened his weary eyes again. He was sore and guessed

he had at least a couple of broken ribs. He knew his face wouldn't be a pretty sight, either.

Anna came back along the ward and to his bedside. 'The doctor will come to see you soon,' she said.

'Can you get me some water, please?'

Anna poured him a glass from a jug on a table beside the bed, and helped him to lift his head and take a few sips.

'You've been unconscious since you were found. And it's lucky you were found when you were. The doctor said that had you been left on the ground for much longer, you would have frozen to death.'

'Who found me?'

'Some fella who'd come out of the pub at closing time, and had walked onto the waste ground to have a tinkle. He didn't see you at first and nearly peed on you! You were brought in here, but no one knew who you were. But when you weren't at home for Christmas dinner, your mum came round to our house, and I came straight here. That's when I found you. Your mum's here, she's just popped to the ladies. She's gonna be so happy to see you awake!'

'I've missed Christmas Day?'

'Yes, John. It's Boxing Day today.'

'Does Grace know?'

'No, I don't think so. Do you want me to tell her?'

John nodded. Gordon's threats wouldn't stop him from seeing Grace. 'Anna ... You've got to call it off with Gordon. He's dangerous. He did this to me and warned me to stay away from Grace.'

'No, John, why would Gordon do that? Like I said, I reckon you're confused. Rest, and I'm sure you'll get your memory back properly.'

John didn't need to rest to think clearly. He knew he had to make Anna believe him and convince her of the truth. She was making a big mistake marrying that man, and he felt sure it would end in disaster.

Grace answered the knocking on the front door and was surprised to see Anna standing there.

'Hello. Have you come to see me or Gordon?' she asked.

'I've come to see you. Gordon's here?'

'Yes. He's moved back in. Didn't you know?'

'No, I didn't, but that explains a lot. He was at my house yesterday evening, and when I questioned where he'd been all day because he'd missed Christmas dinner, he said he'd drunk too much the night before and had slept through most of the day. The lying toe rag.'

'You'd better come in,' Grace suggested, feeling uncomfortable.

'Actually, Grace, I've got some bad news. It's John. He's all right, but he's been in the hospital after getting beaten up. He was being discharged when I left, so he'll be home by now. But he wanted me to let you know.'

'Oh, good Lord! Who attacked him?'

'I, erm, I'm not sure. You should talk to John. I've got to go back to the hospital, my shift starts in half an hour.'

'Thanks for letting me know, Anna. Can we meet soon?'

'Er, yeah, sure,' Anna answered vaguely, as she hurried away.

Grace had the feeling that Anna was being cagey, and she couldn't understand why her friend seemed to be dodging spending time with her. But none of that mattered now. Grace had to see John. Throwing on her coat, she hurried out of the house and made her way to Battersea.

*

Mrs Dander answered the door and ushered Grace in. 'Come in, love, John will be pleased to see you. He's upstairs in bed. I'll bring you a cup of tea.'

John's mother had the same blue eyes and blonde hair as her son. A homely woman, she always made Grace feel welcome.

When she walked into John's bedroom, a shocked gasp caught in her throat. She barely recognised the man in the bed. His cheek was twice the size it should be, and with a swollen lip and two black eyes, he looked a pitiful sight.

'Goodness, John, you look awful. How are you feeling?'

'Better for seeing you,' he said, and smiled, though Grace could see it stung his lip.

'Are you badly injured?'

'Cracked ribs, but nothing that won't mend.'

'What happened?'

'Gordon jumped me.'

'Gordon?' Grace parroted, her blood running cold.

'Yeah, and he warned me to stay away from you.'

'Why? Why would he do that?'

'I don't know, Grace. Maybe he wants you for himself?'

'No, that's absurd. He doesn't even like me.'

'Perhaps he thinks I'm not good enough for you? Whatever his reasons, Anna won't listen. She reckons I'm confused. She won't have it that Gordon did this.'

Grace's mind whirled. She recalled Gordon's swollen knuckles. And it was too much of a coincidence that Gordon had moved back in the day after John had been attacked. 'My father is behind it,' she mumbled, horrified. 'Gordon's got his feet back under the table at home and I wondered how he'd done it. Can't you see, John, my father orchestrated this. He must have!'

'I dunno, Grace. How does your father even know about us?'

'Anna. Anna's told Gordon about us, and that's why she's been avoiding me. She feels guilty.'

'Yeah, you could be right.'

'I know I am. What did Gordon say to you about me?'

'That he'd kill me if I don't stay away from you.'

Grace's hand flew to her mouth. 'Oh, no, John. What are we going to do?' she babbled.

'I won't be intimidated, Grace.'

'But it's not safe for you to be with me.'

'I don't care.'

'I do! You know what my father is like. The next time you're beaten up will be so much worse. It's too risky.'

'You're worth it,' John assured her, trying to smile again.

'No. No, I can't see you hurt because of me.'

'I'm not gonna let you walk away from me, Grace.'

She didn't want to lose John, and sat quietly, thinking. 'I'll speak to Papa. He listened to me about the state of his properties and promised to fix them up. I'll make him listen to me about you, too.'

'We've got nothing to lose, so I suppose it's worth a try.'

'Yes, but for now, let's keep things quiet. We can meet in secret, and don't tell Anna anything!'

Grace was fuming, but hid her anger from John. Gordon couldn't be allowed to get away with what he'd done, albeit under her father's instruction. The man had murdered her mother, and now he had threatened to do the same to John. Her eyes narrowed as she considered how to bring him down, and the perfect plan struck her. She couldn't tell John because she knew he'd try to talk her out of it. *I'm coming for you, Gordon*, she thought. *You should have known better than to upset me – I'm a Newman, and I can play dirty, just like my father.*

35

Two days had passed, and Grace was pretending that everything at home was fine and dandy. Her grandmother was relentless, keeping on at her, trying to persuade her to pack her things and move out, but Grace couldn't yet. She had to ruin Gordon's life first.

Grace had arranged for the young girl who collected the laundry to introduce her to her older sister. She often saw the poor girl traipsing around Clapham, pushing a bulky pram overloaded with laundry. Whenever she bumped into her, Grace would give her a few coins, and she tipped her generously on laundry days, too. Right on time, she heard a knock on the front door.

'Hello, Miss Newman. This is Maud Scarrow, me sister who can cook and clean, the one I was telling you about.'

'It's nice to meet you, Maud, come in.'

After leading them into the kitchen, Grace poured them a cup of tea and found that she instantly liked Maud. The young woman was polite and had a kind smile. She was pretty, with thick, chestnut hair pinned off her face and tumbling down her back. A sprinkling of freckles across her small nose, and with the colour of her eyes almost matching her hair, Maud Scarrow was a striking beauty. She hoped Gordon would keep his hands off her, but Grace wouldn't have to worry about that for much longer. He'd be gone soon, she was going to make sure of that!

'Thank you for the opportunity, Miss Newman. I'm hard working and can turn out a good meal an' all, especially pies.'

'That's reassuring to know. My cooking skills don't extend to pastry making. The job will be six days a week, from nine in the morning until five in the evening. Cleaning, shopping and cooking. If you're happy with the hours and the wage, can you start tomorrow?'

Maud glanced around the kitchen, her eyes falling on the pile of unwashed plates, cups and saucers. 'I can start now, if you like?'

Grace grinned. 'Yes, that would be great, thank you. Let me show you around and where to find everything.'

Maud had walked down this street in Clapham many times and had always wondered what the grand houses looked like inside. She hadn't imagined that the ceilings would be so high, and this house even had newly laid wall-to-wall carpet in the lounge. Maud had never seen anything quite like it, and she'd never drunk out of such fine bone china. It was her job to get the house spick and span, but she was already worrying about breaking the expensive crockery and smart ornaments.

Miss Newman had showed her from room to room. She'd stifled an amazed gasp when she'd seen the bathroom. It was very different to what Maud was accustomed to – a table, which had a lift-off top to reveal the bath, and a privy in the back garden.

She discreetly eyed Miss Newman's elegant dress. She could see the woman wasn't made for domestic duties, and that became even more apparent when Maud saw the cobwebs lurking in the corners.

Miss Newman clapped her hands together, saying, 'Right, that's just about everything covered. Any questions?'

'No, Miss Newman, thank you. You just leave everything to me. I'll soon have this place looking ship-shape and your larder stocked. If you don't mind, I'll get on now.'

'Oh, fine. Great. Thank you. I'm popping out for a few hours. Are you sure you'll be all right?'

'Yes, Miss Newman. I've got plenty to do to keep me busy.'

Miss Newman rolled her eyes. 'Yes, you have. I've let the housework slip. You're going to be a godsend to me. I'll see you later.'

Maud smiled, and when the front door closed behind Miss Newman, her smile changed to a scowl. *Yes, Miss Newman. No, Miss Newman*, she mimicked in her head. She'd put on a good show, yet she'd wanted to scratch the woman's eyes out! Grace Newman had everything. A fine home, nice clothes, her posh boutique. The woman could have had any man she wanted, yet she had stolen John Dander. He'd belonged to Maud, and they should have been getting married. Instead, she'd been left with a broken heart, humiliated, and with a baby growing in her womb.

36

John groaned with frustration. 'Talking to you is like banging me head against a brick wall,' he spat at Anna. 'Why would I lie to you? You're my cousin, Anna, more like a sister. I love you and I don't want to see you get hurt. Gordon did this to me, and I'm scared for you. Please, don't marry that man.'

'I asked Gordon, and he said he had nothing to do with it. I'm sorry, John, but I believe him.'

'Fine. You go ahead and marry him. But you'll live to regret it.'

Anna scraped her seat back and stood abruptly. 'If that's how you feel, then I don't think you should come to the wedding.'

'Don't you worry, I've got no intentions of watching you make the biggest mistake of your life! I'd sooner pull me own teeth out than see you marry him!'

Anna stormed out and John heard the front door slam behind her. Minutes later, his mother came into the bedroom.

'I've warmed you some milk and added a good spoonful of sugar,' she said, placing the cup beside him.

'Thanks, Mum.'

'Do you want anything to eat? I've got a nice rice pudding in the oven.'

'No, thanks, I'm still stuffed from breakfast. If you keep feeding me like this, I reckon my trousers will need letting out at the waist.'

'You need to build your strength up.'

John was desperate to get out of bed and back to work, but he knew he was in no fit state yet, and had resigned himself to allowing his mother to fuss around him.

She sat on the edge of his bed, and probed, 'Why did Anna storm out of here earlier? She looked right cheesed off.'

'I dunno,' John fibbed. He didn't want to tell his mum that Gordon had attacked him and warned him off seeing Grace. He knew she'd worry, and he thought she already had enough on her plate without him adding to it. He just wished Anna would believe him!

'You must have said something to annoy her,' his mother pushed.

'I think she was just peeved about having to cover some extra shifts at work.'

'I've not seen Anna in a mood like that before, and I know when you're lying to me, John. It's written all over your face.'

'Honestly, Mum, there's nothing to tell.'

'If you say so,' she said, and tutted. 'Is Miss High and Mighty Fancy Drawers calling in to see you today?'

'If you mean Grace, then yes, I expect so.'

'I don't know what you see in her, John. She thinks she's a cut above the rest of us, but she's nothing special.'

'You don't know her, Mum. Grace ain't a snob and you shouldn't judge her on how she dresses and carries herself. I thought you liked her. You act as if you do.'

'I don't dislike her; I just don't think she's right for you. It's your choice, son. But I still think you should have stuck with Maud. She came round again last night to ask about you. I told her you still weren't up for visitors, but I hate lying to her. I'm telling you, John, that woman is holding a torch for you. After the way you treated her, gawd knows why she still loves you.'

John felt bad for ending his relationship with Maud so abruptly. He hadn't liked seeing her cry, and when she'd yanked on his arm and begged him to stay, it had almost split his heart in two. But Grace Newman had walked into his life, and she'd eclipsed everything. 'I hope Maud finds a good husband,' he said sincerely.

'The poor girl thought she'd found a good husband in you! I wish you hadn't led her on, John. Mrs Scarrow collared me in the butcher's last week. Cor, she gave me a right bloomin' earful, going on about your broken promises to Maud and the money they'd saved for the wedding. I didn't know where to put my face, I was so embarrassed.'

'Sorry, Mum, I didn't mean to put you in an awkward position, and I didn't mean to hurt Maud.'

His mother sighed. 'I know, love. What's done is done, so I suppose I should try and like Miss Fancy Drawers.'

'Grace, Mum, her name is Grace Newman. It's too soon yet, but one day, I hope she'll be Mrs John Dander.'

Anna turned the corner and saw Gordon waiting for her.

'Well? Is he still saying I did it?' Gordon asked.

'Yeah,' Anna sighed. 'He's insistent.'

'You don't believe him, do you?'

'I don't want to believe him, Gordon, but why did you

lie to me about that night? You said you was drunk, and you spent the next day in bed, which is why you missed Christmas lunch. But then I discover that you were with Dickie Newman that day.'

'I'm sorry, Anna, I didn't want to hurt your feelings. I said I was ill 'cos of too much booze because I thought that if I told you I was spending Christmas Day with Dickie, then you'd think I wanted to be with him more than you. And that ain't true. But you know how much it meant for me to be back in good favour with Dickie. I reckon if I'd turned down his invitation to Christmas dinner, then I wouldn't have got another chance. I wanted to be with you though, Anna, and I'm sorry that I didn't tell you the truth.'

'No more lies, Gordon. I mean it.'

'Cross my heart.'

'So, if you weren't drunk the night John was attacked, what was you doing?'

'Bloody hell, Anna! You believe him, don't ya? You think I beat up John!'

'No, that's not what I'm saying. I just asked what you were doing that night.'

Gordon stormed on ahead, shaking his head.

'Gordon, wait,' Anna called, and caught up with him.

'This is the last time I'm gonna say it, Anna. I. Didn't. Beat. Up. John. If you want to believe him over me, then go and marry your cousin instead!'

'That's just stupid!'

Gordon spun and faced Anna, anger flashing through his eyes. 'So, I'm a liar and I'm stupid, eh? Wow, you're showing your true colours now. It's nice to see what you really think of me.'

'No, Gordon, that's not what I meant.'

'Ain't it? Are you sure about that? See, the thing is, Anna – I love you. If you tell me that black is white, then I'll believe you. But you won't give me that same respect back. You'd rather believe your cousin over me. Think about it, Anna … Why would I want to hurt anyone in your family? Your family are gonna be my family, too … Or maybe not. I ain't prepared to marry into a family who thinks I'm capable of doing something like that to John.'

'I do believe you, Gordon, and I'll make John see that he's got it all wrong.'

Gordon inwardly smiled. 'You better had, or I can't marry you.'

'What if John won't drop it?'

'If John wants to stick to his bullshit story, then you'll have to walk away from him. You can't allow that sort of talk about your husband, can you?'

'No, I suppose not,' Anna replied sadly.

'It'll be his loss, Anna. But don't worry, you'll always have me.'

They walked quietly for a while, and then Gordon asked, 'Has John seen any more of Grace? He's a brave bloke if he has. I mean, from what you've told me, John is lucky to be alive.'

'He saw her on Boxing Day and told her it would be the last time. John's not a coward, but he ain't stupid, either. Who do you think did it, Gordon? Who would want John to stay away from Grace?'

'I dunno. Maybe some bloke who fancies her. It could have been that woman you told me about, the one who John was going to marry before Grace came along. Perhaps she organised someone to do it. Her dad? A brother? I ain't got a clue, Anna, but I'm bloody relieved that you've stopped pointing the finger at me at last.'

Gordon was pleased when they arrived at the hospital. Quickly kissing Anna goodbye, he couldn't wait to see Dickie to tell him the good news. Their plan had worked, and Grace was no longer seeing John Dander.

Grace sat holding John's hand and gazing into his eyes. 'I couldn't wait to get out of the house and see you,' she whispered. 'Have you told your mum to keep quiet about my visits?'

'Yeah, and she wanted to know why, so I told her that we're keeping me and you a secret until you've spoken to your father about us.'

'Did Anna ask if you'd seen me?'

'I told her that I hadn't seen you since Boxing Day and I wouldn't be seeing you again.'

'Good. I'm sure she'll feed that information back to Gordon.'

'We had a bit of a falling out. I'm no longer invited to the wedding.'

'I shan't be going either. Oh, John, I wish she would see sense, but she seems to be completely under Gordon's spell. I don't know why she loves him so much, do you?'

'Gawd knows! I knew a bloke like him once. He was horrible, a right nasty piece of work, but he could charm the birds from the trees and had women eating out of his hand. I wondered how he did it, and why women fell for him. Then I noticed how he twisted their minds and sort of controlled them, got them to think like him.'

'You mean he manipulated them?'

'Yeah, that's the word I'm looking for. I reckon Gordon has manipulated Anna.'

Grace agreed. 'Poor Anna,' she said.

Spurred on by thoughts of her friend being manipulated by Gordon, Grace was even more determined to ruin his life. It was time to put her plan into action!

37

The following morning, Grace looked around the house, pleased with Maud's work. The place was gleaming. Everything looked fresh and it smelled good, too. Maud had clearly laboured hard, and the woman just got on with it, without any bother. In fact, Grace barely noticed she was in the house.

Sitting at the kitchen table, her mind turned. So, it had transpired that Gordon was manipulative. *Well*, thought Grace, *it's time for me to be manipulative, too!*

She heard her father's footsteps coming down the stairs and knew that Gordon would be coming up from the basement soon. Grabbing the opportunity to catch her father alone, Grace hurried to the bottom of the stairs with a steaming cup of coffee.

'Good morning, Papa,' she greeted him, offering him the drink.

'Good morning, sweetheart. You're chirpy today.'

'I am. It's New Year's Eve tomorrow and I'm looking forward to starting 1935 with not one, but two boutiques!'

'Ah, it's nice to see you excited.'

'I am, Papa, thank you. And I was thinking, I've got so

much to be grateful to you for, I'd like to throw you a very special dinner tomorrow, to see in the New Year with you.'

'Well, I did have plans to attend a party with the chief constable and a top crown court judge, but I'd much rather spend the evening with my girl.'

'Thanks, Papa. And I was thinking, now that me and Gordon have put that *incident* behind us, perhaps Gordon could stay at home with me tomorrow and help me prepare the special evening. It would be good for us to spend some time together. What do you think?'

'I think that's a smashing idea, but don't let Gordon in the kitchen. I want to eat something edible,' Dickie chuckled.

Great, thought Grace. Everything was panning out perfectly!

Grace had brightened Dickie's day, and he hummed a tune as he climbed into his car.

'You're in a good mood,' Gordon observed, as he got in.

'I am. Grace is organising a special New Year's Eve dinner tomorrow, and you're to stay home and give her a hand.'

Gordon's head shot round to look at Dickie, and he could see that the young man looked mortified. 'Don't worry, I've told her to keep you out of the kitchen. You won't have to do any cooking.'

'Thank Gawd for that. What am I supposed to help her with?'

'I dunno,' Dickie shrugged. 'She's got plans. Just go along with her.'

'I was gonna see in the new year with Anna ... if that's all right with you?'

'If that's what you want.'

'Not really, but I don't want her nagging me.'

'Invite her to ours. She's friends with Grace, so I'm sure Grace won't mind.'

'They're not as friendly as they used to be. I don't think they've seen each other in a while. And to be honest, Dickie, that suits me. Anna keeps banging on about me giving John a bashing. I don't want her bending Grace's ear about it.'

Dickie's mood instantly darkened. 'Why is Anna saying that? I thought you said no one saw you?'

Gordon was quick to answer. 'They didn't, Dickie. No one saw me and me face was covered, but I think John must have recognised my voice.'

'Shit!'

'It's all right. I've been denying it and I'm sure I've convinced Anna.'

'What about John? I can't have him accusing you and it getting back to me. Grace must never know.'

'They ain't seeing each other no more. John took notice of my warning.'

Dickie sighed with relief, and Gordon continued, 'But if you want to make sure John doesn't talk, I could shut him up for good.'

'No. I don't think that's necessary. Just keep your ear to the ground, and I want to be informed of anything and everything. Got it?'

'Yes, Dickie, course. Stop here,' he said. 'This is Mrs May's house, the one I saw Dander take Grace to. It must have been Mrs May who complained to Grace.'

Pulling up outside Mrs May's rented property, Dickie sat in the car. He couldn't stand the stench in the basement room and sent Gordon in to fetch the woman. When she followed Gordon to the car, Dickie stepped out.

Mrs May appeared anxious as she fiddled fretfully with the hem of her filthy apron. 'I'm not late with my payments, Mr Newman, am I?' she asked.

'No, you're not. But your payments have just gone up by ten percent.'

'No, Mr Newman, please, you can't do that! I can't afford to pay no more!'

'You should have thought about that before you went spurting your mouth off. I would have expected you to be grateful to have a roof over your head, but instead of gratitude, you've been moaning about my generous loan to you and about your living conditions. You're lucky I loaned you the money to pay the rent. No one else would have given you a loan, would they?'

'No, Mr Newman, but—'

'Shut it! Ten percent more, and it ain't open for debate. If you can't pay it, you'll be on the streets, but you'll still owe me, and believe you me, Mrs May, I'll find you. Wherever you are, I'll track you down and you'll pay back every fuckin' penny you owe me. The choice is yours, so what's it to be, eh?'

'I'll pay the extra. I don't know where I'll find the money, but I'll pay you.'

Dickie climbed back in the car with his promise to Grace ringing in his ears. *Sod 'em*, he thought. These people didn't deserve his sympathy. He owed them nothing. It was down to them to better themselves. He'd made good of his own life, and no one had helped him or given him free handouts. It had been hard work! As far as he was concerned, Mrs May and the rest of them were lazy defeatists, with no ambition – just the same as his father had been. Bitter memories infiltrated his mind. He tried to push them away, but he saw images of his father throwing booze down his neck. Beating his mother. Lazing all day in a drunken stupor, instead of working to put food on the table. His mother, crying, hopeless, making a watery soup with scrap vegetable peelings. Hunger gnawing his stomach. Bare feet, cold chilling his bones.

'You all right?' Gordon asked.

Dickie gripped the steering wheel until his knuckles were white, forcing his terrible childhood memories away. 'Yeah, I'm all right. I'm better than all right. In fact, I'm bleedin' wonderful!'

Gordon grinned, and it struck Dickie that he'd had an unfortunate start to life, too. 'Do you ever think about your mum?' he asked.

After a thoughtful pause, Gordon replied, 'Sometimes. I wonder where she is, what she's doing.'

'She didn't do right by you, son.'

'I know. We were piss poor, like Mrs May, I suppose. But Mrs May ain't abandoned her kids. I don't think me mum ever wanted me.'

'Never mind, eh. You're better off without her.'

'Yeah, Dickie, I am, thanks to you. You and Grace are all the family I need.'

Dickie had formed a sincere fondness for Gordon. 'I've said it before, you're like the son I never had, and it's time I put my money where my mouth is, so I'm gonna change my will. You'll be taken care of when I die.'

38

Grace hadn't slept well, her head bombarded with thoughts of today's plan to rid her life of Gordon. She could feel her heart racing and a knot of anxiety tightened in her stomach. She had to time everything perfectly.

Downstairs, she handed her father his coat and hat, and instructed him, 'You're not to work late today. I want you home at exactly five o'clock. Not a minute early or a minute late.'

'Yeah, yeah, I know.'

'I mean it, Papa. Promise me you'll be home on time, or you'll spoil my surprise for you.'

'I promise, darling. I said so, didn't I?'

'Thank you, Papa.'

'Don't work Gordon too hard,' Dickie chuckled, as he descended the steps and waved goodbye.

Grace bit on her bottom lip. She had much to do before she ruined Gordon's life. Calling down the stairs to him, he emerged in his pyjamas.

'I'm making the most of a day off,' he yawned.

'You haven't got a day off. I've a list as long as my arm for you to get on with. Come on, get dressed. There's no peace for the wicked.'

Myrtle walked gracefully down the stairs and stood beside Grace.

'I don't know how you can bring yourself to speak to him,' she said scornfully.

Grace flicked her head towards the kitchen and held her finger to her lips, murmuring, 'Shush.'

In the kitchen, she quietly closed the door and lowered her voice to no more than a whisper. 'I need you to stay out all day, preferably all night, too.'

'Why?'

'I haven't got time to explain, but please, Grandma, will you stay away?'

'You're up to something, and I fear you are putting yourself in harm's way.'

'Don't worry, Grandma, I know what I'm doing. If all goes well, we shall see the end of Gordon today.'

Myrtle shook her head. 'I don't like the sound of this.'

'Please, Grandma, trust me. I'm my father's daughter. I know what I'm doing, and I know how to look after myself. We both want to see the back of Gordon and I'm going to make sure his life is ruined. I just need you to do as I ask.'

Grace was grateful when her grandmother reluctantly agreed.

The door was flung open, and Gordon asked, 'Where's this list then? What's the big surprise?'

Myrtle threw him a disdainful look and hastily left the kitchen.

'Here,' Grace answered, pulling some scribbled notes from

her pocket. 'And as for the big surprise, well, read the list,' she explained, forcing a smile.

Gordon's eyes scanned the notes. 'Pick up cake and champagne … Pick up wireless radio. A wireless radio?'

'Yes. I thought it would be nice to ring in the new year with a wireless broadcast. It's very modern, you know.'

'If you say so. What's this about a piano?'

'I've hired one. I need you to clear some space for it in the lounge.'

'Have you hired someone to play it an' all? None of us have got musical bones.'

'That's another part of my big surprise. I've been having lessons and I'm going to play 'Auld Lang Syne', so I hope you know the words.'

'Cor blimey, Grace, you really are going to town with this!'

'I want everything to be perfect! The piano will be arriving at midday, so you'll need to be back with the cake, champagne and wireless by then. All clear?'

'Yes, sir,' Gordon answered, clicking his heels together and saluting.

Once Gordon had left the room to run the errands, Grace dashed up the stairs to her bedroom and gazed in the mirror. 'Your face won't look so pretty tomorrow,' she said to her reflection. 'But it will be worth it to bring Gordon to his knees.'

Maud blew out her breath slowly, sighing with relief when she heard Miss Newman trotting up the stairs. Hiding in the pantry cupboard, she pushed open the door, glad to see that the kitchen was empty. Her mind raced. She'd heard everything!

Hurrying out of the kitchen, Maud just caught a glimpse of Gordon as he closed the front door behind him. She chased after him, catching him at the bottom of the steps.

'I need a word with you,' she said, placing a staying hand on his arm.

'Make it quick, I'm a busy man,' Gordon replied, and gave her a mischievous wink.

Maud checked over her shoulder and looked up at the windows to ensure that Miss Newman wasn't looking. 'You need to watch your back with Miss Newman. I heard her telling Mrs Best that she was going to ruin your life today.'

'She what?'

'She's up to something. They want to see the back of you.'

Gordon's jaw tightened, and he slowly nodded. 'Why are you telling me? What's in it for you?'

'Nothing … I … I, erm … I don't like underhand work, that's all.'

'And the rest,' Gordon pressed.

'All right. I don't like Miss Newman – but don't tell her.'

'Don't worry, Maud, I don't like her, either.'

Maud hurried back inside as a wave of nausea washed over her. She'd been vomiting most mornings, a cruel reminder of the baby she was carrying. Running to the bathroom, she pushed the door closed just in time to hang her head over the toilet and empty the contents of her stomach.

To her dismay, she heard Miss Newman's voice outside the door, and realised she hadn't closed it properly.

'Are you all right in there?' the woman asked.

'Yes, I'm fine, thank you,' Maud answered, standing upright. She went to the sink and ran the cold tap, splashing the water over her pale face.

When she came out of the bathroom, her heart dropped at the sight of Miss Newman waiting for her, looking concerned, though Maud was sure she was feigning it.

'I heard you being sick. Are you sure you're all right?'

'Yes, I feel better now, thank you, Miss Newman.'

'Are you sure? Only, I thought I heard you being ill yesterday, too.'

'Must have been something I ate,' Maud lied.

She noticed Miss Newman's eyes fall to look at her stomach, so she quickly pulled her cardigan around herself to hide the slight swelling.

'Maud, are you in the family way?'

'That's none of your business!' Maud blurted, and instantly regretted her reaction when she saw the woman's stunned expression. 'I'm sorry, Miss Newman. I didn't mean to speak to you like that.'

'No, you're right, it's none of my business. But I hope you're not. We know the consequences of having a child without a husband. It won't be easy for you.'

Maud hung her head, biting her tongue. She would have had a husband if he hadn't been stolen from her. Trying to sound demure, she asked, 'You won't tell no one, will you?'

'No, Maud, of course I won't. But what are you going to do?'

Maud shrugged. She wanted John back, but she knew she'd lost him to Miss Newman forever. Without a husband, she'd be ostracised, especially by her mother. She'd be all alone in the world, jobless, penniless and homeless. She'd thought her only option would be giving up the child for adoption, and that had been her plan. The idea of handing her baby over had broken her heart, so when her little sister had mentioned the cleaning job in this grand house, Maud had seen an opportunity that was too good to miss. In the few days she'd been there, she'd stolen several pieces of Miss Newman's expensive jewellery, and some from Mrs Best, too. Secretly stashing away her hoard, Maud hoped to thieve enough to set her and her child up for some time to come. *They've all got plenty*, she thought. They had so much, Miss Newman and Mrs Best hadn't even noticed anything was missing!

'Go home, Maud. Rest.'

'I need this job, Miss Newman. Please don't sack me.'

'You're not sacked,' Miss Newman smiled. 'I'll see you tomorrow, if you're feeling better, and we'll talk more then.'

Maud nodded and scurried away, grateful to be away from Miss Newman's busybody questions and condescending manner. She couldn't abide the woman, and hoped she'd scuppered whatever plans Miss Newman had for Gordon's downfall. She'd seen the sideways glances he'd given her with lust in his eyes. It had crossed her mind that if she lured Gordon to bed, told him that the child in her belly was his, maybe she could trap him into marrying her. But she'd have to act quickly. She'd missed three monthlies and soon, she wouldn't be able to hide her expanding stomach.

Fingering the stolen pearl earrings in her pocket, she smirked. If Gordon wouldn't marry her and give her bastard child a name, at least she'd have money to support herself.

39

Later that day, Gordon was seething and watching Grace's every move as he jumped to do her bidding. So, she was planning to see him off. Well, he was one step ahead of her now, and forewarned was forearmed. He'd gone along with her ruse, and had picked up the champagne, the cake, and the wireless radio. But he couldn't fathom what she was going to do next that was going to ruin his life.

The minutes and the hours slowly ticked by. Grace appeared jolly, laughing, joking and excited for the celebrations later. He hadn't spotted even the tiniest of cracks in her merry performance, and he began to question if Maud had been wrong, or maybe she'd fed him lies.

'Papa will be home soon,' Grace chirped. And then the tone of her voice changed. 'You must detest me, Gordon. I'm sure you're jealous of me. After all, I'm a Newman and that's something you'll *never* be.'

So here it was. Her perfect demeanour had finally broken. Gordon was lounging in an armchair, and smirked, gloating, 'No, I'll never have your name, but I'll have some of your inheritance. Dickie's writing me into his will. How do you like that, eh?'

'I wouldn't count on that.'

'It's true. He told me yesterday. I bet that makes your piss boil,' he chortled.

'I don't care about his money, and I care even less for you. I know it was you who attacked John, and I'm going to do everything in my power to make sure Anna sees you for who you really are. She won't marry you. Anna's not that stupid.'

Gordon refused to rise to Grace's provocation. Acting nonchalant, he said, 'Do what you have to do, Grace. Whether Anna marries me or not, I'm still gonna be a wealthy bloke one day, and there's plenty more fish in the sea.'

'You're disgusting,' Grace hissed, walking towards him. 'A child from the gutter. A bastard. Your own mother abandoned you, and gawd knows who your father is. From what I've heard about your mother, your father could have been any bloke who paid for her services.'

'Yeah, probably. It's a good job Dickie took pity on me.'

Gordon could see that his complacency was riling Grace. She was pushing for a reaction, and he wasn't going to give her the satisfaction of responding to her in the way she wanted.

She continued to push. 'Pity ... that's a good word. You're pitiful. A scrounger. Living off a man who uses you to keep his own hands clean. That's all you are to my father, just someone he can order around. He only ever wanted you to do his dirty work.'

'Leave off, Grace. Dickie's always saying I'm like the son he never had.'

'Huh, and you believe that? Christ, you're even more

ridiculous than I gave you credit for. Tell me then, if you're like the son he never had, why didn't he send you to school and give you an education? Why are you on a wage and living in our basement? He hasn't set you up in your own business like he has for me with my boutiques. And if you're so much of a son to him, when we were younger, why did he punish you for calling him Papa? You're no more of a son to him than any young man who works for him. You're nothing but a paid thug.'

Grace's words were getting to Gordon, stinging like a slap around the face. But he tried to stay calm. 'If I'm not like a son to him, then why is he putting me in his will?'

Grace laughed. 'He'll probably leave you a token gesture. Maybe his car or a derelict house. You won't see any more than that. Think about it, Gordon. I'm his princess. Do you really believe that he'd take what's rightfully mine and give it to you? No chance, and you're delusional if you think otherwise.'

Gordon jumped to his feet, anger coursing through him. Deep down, he knew Grace was right. 'Let's see it, then. What are you gonna do to ruin me?'

'I don't know what you're talking about.'

'You want to see the back of me. Oh yeah, that's right, I know about your plan. Come on, then. Do your worst,' he shouted.

Grace stepped closer and pushed her face towards him, their noses almost touching. 'You're not family. You'll never be my father's family. You're nothing but his lackey, someone he's trained to fight. If my father had had a son, that boy would have been lavished with the best of everything, and not dragged up around the murky world of the Newman business. Are you getting it now, Gordon? You've been used.' Jabbing her finger into his temple, she mocked, 'Is it going into that thick skull?'

Gordon whacked her hand away, rage burning his chest. Had Dickie been using him for all these years?

'Truth hurts, doesn't it?' she leered smugly.

He wanted to slap that look off her face, but he knew that's what she wanted.

'Go on,' Grace encouraged. 'Hit me. I can see it in your eyes, Gordon. Violence, anger, manipulation ... they're the only emotions you know. Do it. Hit me.'

Gordon gritted his teeth. He had to use all his strength to refrain from punching Grace hard in the mouth. 'I ain't playing your game,' he spat, and went to sidestep around her.

Grace jumped in front of him. 'Call yourself a man? Are you going to let me get away with belittling you? Pathetic.'

Breathing deeply, he gently urged her to one side. As he began to walk away, Gordon heard a terrific thud and then Grace cried out. He spun to see her on the floor and holding her cheek.

'You hit me!' she screamed.

Gordon stood speechless. She'd obviously inflicted the injury on herself. 'Get up,' he said, panicking. 'You know I never laid a finger on you. Get up!'

Grace looked at the clock on the mantel and smiled maliciously, a wicked glint in her eyes. Reaching to a small side table beside her, she grabbed a porcelain vase. Gordon couldn't believe his eyes as he watched her smash the vase over her head. She looked dazed as a trickle of blood seeped from the wound and down her neck.

At that moment, he heard Dickie coming through the

front door, and Gordon knew his life was over. 'Please, Grace, I'm begging you. Don't do this!'

'No, Gordon, no!' she shrieked. 'Please don't hit me again!'

Gordon stepped back as Dickie flew into the room. The man took just seconds to evaluate the scene – his daughter bleeding on the floor, the smashed vase scattered around her. He pounded towards Gordon, his face twisted with fury.

Gordon went to bolt, running from the room, but Dickie was quick, and he felt the man's heavy fist land a blow on the back of his head. The force knocked Gordon forward and off his feet. Landing face down and spread-eagled on the floor, he rolled over to face the man who appeared to have every intention of killing him.

'I didn't touch her, Dickie, I swear. She did it to herself!'

There were no words. Just agonising punch after punch after punch. Gordon was grateful when the world began to fade away. At last, it was over.

40

Grace's head was still sore as she ran a brush through her hair. It had been a week since her father had pulverised Gordon, beating him almost to death. Grace was pleased her plan had worked. Retribution had been exacted for her mother's death, and for what Gordon had inflicted on John. She didn't feel even a hint of guilt, though when her father had been laying into Gordon, Grace had been unable to watch and had turned her face away.

Where's my brooch? she wondered, searching her jewellery box. The silver lizard decorated with crushed diamonds was a favourite of hers, though she hadn't worn it for some time. *And where are my pearl earrings?* She was looking forward to seeing John and wanted to look her best.

Grace quickly realised that several pieces were missing. She knew she hadn't misplaced them, and a dreadful thought crossed her mind.

Marching down the stairs, she found Maud in the drawing room, polishing the silver. 'Stop that,' she ordered, 'I need to have a word with you.'

Maud didn't look nervous, and Grace hoped the woman was innocent.

'I'm missing several items of jewellery. I know they've been stolen, so I must conclude that you have taken them. Do you have anything to say for yourself?'

Maud glared bitterly.

'I want the items returned. At once.'

Throwing her cleaning cloth to the floor and whipping off her apron, Maud stormed across the room. 'I ain't pinched your jewellery, and I ain't gonna stand for being accused of it. You can do your own bleedin' skivvying, I quit!'

Grace blocked the woman's way. 'Return everything that you have stolen from this house, or you'll be sorry.'

'Are you threatening me? What ya gonna do? Have the living daylights beaten out of me like you did Gordon? *Papa's* favourite, eh? Yeah, I know all about you, Miss Newman. Gordon didn't hit you. You did it to yourself. You made sure your scheming worked.'

Grace's lips pursed as her mind turned. Gordon had known she'd set out to ruin him, he'd said as much, and it suddenly dawned on her that Maud must have warned him. 'You're so ungrateful,' she spat. 'I've allowed you to remain in my employment, even though I know you're with child and without a husband. Anyone else would have sacked you on the spot, but I was willing to help you. And this is how you repay my kindness! Not only did you go behind my back to Gordon, but you've stolen from me, too. You're despicable, Maud, and I'm so disappointed in you. Return my items, immediately.'

There was nothing in Maud's stance or face that showed any remorse. She glanced down at the floor, shaking her head, and when she looked back up, Grace could see unshed tears in her angry eyes.

'I'm despicable … me … what about you?' Maud blurted heatedly. 'You've got everything,' she said, with a sweep of her hand. 'Everything! Including my man!'

Grace had no idea what the woman was talking about, and stood looking at her with confusion.

Tears began to fall from Maud's eyes and her hand rested on her stomach. 'John Dander is the father of this baby. He was going to marry me until you came along. So, yes, I stole a few pieces of jewellery from you, but that's nothing compared to what you stole from me!'

The room began to spin as Grace absorbed Maud's words. She grabbed the back of a chair to steady herself.

'I took the jewellery to sell, to make a life for me and my baby.'

Grace swallowed hard. 'Does John know about the child?' she asked.

'Yeah, he knows, but he's denying it's his. It can't be anyone else's. I'm not that sort of woman! John was going to be my husband. We had plans to get wed. I'd never have laid with him otherwise, and I've never laid with another man.'

Gathering her thoughts, Grace breathed in deeply. 'Wait here,' she instructed, 'I need a glass of water.'

In the kitchen, as Grace held a glass under the tap, she noticed her hand was shaking, and hurrying back to the drawing room, she questioned Maud further. 'Why did you take the job here?'

Maud shrugged. 'I dunno, Miss Newman. It was stupid really. I suppose I wanted to hurt the woman who'd buggered everything up for me. But then you was nice to me. I ain't a thief, not normally, but I can't give this baby up for adoption and without John, well, I ain't got no way of supporting us, so I helped meself to your stuff. I ain't sorry for what I did. I'm only sorry that I've been found out.'

Grace pulled out a chair and sat down, inviting Maud to do the same. 'As Stan Laurel would say, *here's another nice mess you've gotten me into.*'

Maud half-smiled. 'It's me in the mess, Miss Newman, not you.'

'Oh, Maud, what are we to do?' Grace said, and then added decisively, 'Get back to work. Return my things tomorrow, and leave everything else to me.'

Mrs Dander plumped up John's pillows, saying jollily, 'Back to work for you tomorrow.'

'Yeah, and I can't wait, Mum. Tomorrow will be the start of Dander's Deliveries. I hope I can make a good go of it.'

'I'm sure you will. You've never been afraid of hard work. Fancy you being your own boss! Who'd have thought it. I'm proud of you, John.'

'Thanks, Mum. I want to earn a small fortune so I can ease your burden, too.'

'Don't worry about me, love, I muddle on through.'

'I've seen you struggling to pay the bills since dad had the stroke. I'm gonna do everything I can to help.'

'You're a good boy, John.' Then, hearing a knock on the front door, she rolled her eyes, saying, 'That'll be Miss Fancy Drawers again.'

John chuckled. *Miss Fancy Drawers.* He wondered what Grace would think of the name his mother had given her.

Minutes later, when Grace walked in, John could see by

her serious face that something was wrong. 'What is it?' he asked, troubled.

Grace didn't sit in the seat beside his bed. Instead, she walked to the window and looked out onto the street. 'Maud Scarrow is working for me.'

John cringed. 'Oh,' he said.

'*Oh*. That's all you've got to say for yourself, *oh*.' She quickly turned to face him with accusing eyes. 'She's carrying your child, John!'

John shifted uncomfortably. 'We don't know that it's mine.'

'Of course it is, and you know full well you got her in the family way! How could you, John? How could you leave her in that condition?'

John's eyes fell. 'I don't love her, Grace. I love you.'

'You loved her well enough when you put a child in her!'

'That was a mistake. We only did it once and it shouldn't have happened.'

'But it did happen, John, and Maud's having a baby. Whether you love her or not, you must do the right thing and marry her.'

'What? No, Grace, I can't! What about us?'

'You think I'd be with you, knowing that another woman is walking around carrying your child? No, John, I don't think so. You must marry Maud; there's no other option.'

John could feel his heart racing. 'I don't want to marry Maud. It's you I want. Please, Grace, don't push me away.'

Grace pulled open the bedroom door and John thought she was going to walk away. Instead, she called, 'Mrs Dander … Mrs Dander … Would you mind coming up here, please?'

John, his eyes wide, pleaded, 'No, Grace … For Gawd's sake, don't get my mum involved.'

Mrs Dander was breathless by the time she reached the top of the stairs. 'What's all this fuss about?' she demanded.

Grace looked at John, but he couldn't bring himself to speak.

'Well?' Mrs Dander asked. 'Would one of you like to explain what's going on?'

Clearing her throat, Grace answered, 'John has got Maud in the family way. I've told him he must marry her.'

Mrs Dander's mouth hung wide open. After a moment of stunned silence, she burst out with, 'Goodness gracious!' Then, wagging her finger at her son, she said sternly, 'Don't be thinking of shirking your responsibilities. You're to marry Maud, no question.'

'Doesn't anyone care about what I want?'

'No, John. If Maud's having a baby, then it doesn't matter what you want. She needs a husband.'

'But I'm in love with Grace!'

John saw his mother look at Grace, waiting for her to say something.

'Your mother's right, John. Marry Maud. I won't be seeing you again.'

As Grace left the room, John wanted to call out to her, but he knew he'd lost her forever.

'I'm going to be a grandma!' his mother trilled. 'I shall have to speak to Mrs Scarrow. We need to organise this wedding pretty bloomin' sharpish!'

John lay his head on the pillow and closed his eyes as his mother's excited voice washed over him. The love of his life had just walked away, and he was going to be lumbered with a wife and child. He liked Maud, but he didn't love her. No one could ever hold a candle to Grace Newman.

*

Grace felt engulfed in sadness as she walked away from John's house, yet still tears failed to fall. A thick smog blanketed the city, leaving the streets in a dull gloom that seemed to correspond with her mood. John had been her first love, and though they'd only spent weeks together, she'd imagined becoming his wife one day. *I'll never give anyone my heart again so easily*, she thought, realising she hadn't really known John at all. She'd never have believed he could have been capable of treating Maud so thoughtlessly if she hadn't seen it with her own eyes. She never wanted to set eyes on him again, and she'd have to find a new cleaner, too.

Wandering aimlessly, Grace found herself peering through the window of her shop. Inside, she locked the door and tucked herself behind the counter. The hat boutique was her refuge. It was somewhere she felt safe, and it was hers, the only thing she had to feel proud of.

Loneliness crept over her. Grace couldn't talk to her father about losing John, especially as she suspected he was behind John being attacked. And she doubted that her grandmother would offer any sympathy. Though they were closer than they'd ever been, Myrtle Best had strongly disapproved of her relationship with John. Anna would be the only person to understand, and Grace desperately wanted to see her dear friend and pour out her heart. But Grace knew from John that Gordon was licking his wounds at Anna's house and had been sleeping on her parents' sofa.

There was no one else, and Grace had never felt so isolated.

41

Three months later
April 1935

Business in Grace's shop was booming and, since the new year, she'd thrown herself into her work. She'd even taken out adverts in the local newspaper and had held successful fashion shows. It had been her only focus and a healthy distraction from the crippling loneliness that left her heart aching. Her second boutique was yet to open. Grace had stocked the shelves and everything was in place, but she required a manager, and today she was looking forward to holding several interviews in the hope of finding a suitable candidate.

'Stop fidgeting, Grace, and sit up straight,' Myrtle admonished. 'You should be radiating an air of authority, but you look nervous.'

'I am nervous, Grandma. I've never interviewed anyone before. I took Maud on and replaced her with Mrs Conners, but I didn't interview either of them, not properly.'

'That is precisely the reason I insisted on being here today. You are neither old nor wise enough to be a good judge of character. I, on the other hand, am very good at seeing through people. The position you are offering is one of high importance and the person to fill it must be trustworthy.'

'I quite agree, Grandma. Thank you for being here. But please don't scare anyone away.'

'My dear, if the candidates fear my abrupt tone, then they are inadequately equipped to deal with customers who may frequent your Chelsea boutique. Trust me, I know how uppity the ladies of that area can be.'

Grace smiled, knowing that her grandmother herself was often patronising towards shop staff.

The door opened and a mature woman walked in. On first impressions, Grace thought she looked smart, and her greying hair was tidy. But the woman had a matronly look about her and a stern face. Grace instinctively felt she wasn't the right person for the job.

After a swift interview, the second candidate arrived, and Grace's hopes lifted. She looked to be about the same age as Grace, and her attire suggested that she was fashion conscious, too. Glancing at her grandmother, Grace could see Myrtle looking down her nose and could tell she wasn't impressed. The interview flowed well, and Grace found her nerves fading and her confidence growing. As it turned out, her grandmother's initial disapproval of the second candidate had been soundly founded.

Third time lucky, Grace thought, smiling at a tall lady who entered the shop with gusto.

'Good afternoon, it's a pleasure to meet you. I'm Miss Elizabeth Parnell and I'm here to accept the offer of the managerial position of the hat boutique in Chelsea.'

Grace's eyebrows raised. She liked Miss Parnell's forthrightness, though she felt sure her grandmother would find the woman too forward. 'Good afternoon. I'm Grace Newman and this is my grandmother, Mrs Best. I haven't offered you the position yet,' Grace stated.

'I know, but you will.'

'You sound very sure.'

'I am, Miss Newman. I have a wealth of experience in high-end retail, excellent references, a positive attitude and a warm personality. I'm clean, hard-working and trustworthy. I'd be an asset to your business, so I can't see any reason why you wouldn't offer me the position.'

Miss Parnell pushed her references across the counter, which Grace picked up and cast her eyes over. 'Indeed, you do have excellent references, from Arding and Hobbs and Selfridges. Why did you leave your last position in Selfridges?'

Before Miss Parnell could respond, Myrtle chipped in, sounding haughty when she commented, 'Selfridges may be, as you say, *high-end*, but the store is owned by a vulgar, gaudy American. I met Mrs Selfridge in 1917. An accomplished woman by all accounts, but following her untimely death from the Spanish flu, Mr Selfridge's dalliance with the Dolly Sisters only added to my contempt of Americans. Did you meet him during your time working at the store?'

'Yes, Mrs Best, I met Mr Selfridge on many occasions, though only in passing. I'm sure you'll agree that as a previous employee of the store, it wouldn't be correct for me to pass comment on my superiors.'

'Quite right,' Myrtle said.

Grace steered the interview back, asking, 'So why did you leave?'

'A clash of personality with the head of the fashion department. Our ideas differed greatly. I'm strong-willed, Miss Newman, and I have an excellent eye for fashion and displays.

I am better suited to a position of authority where my talents will excel and won't be undermined.'

After further questioning, Grace gleaned that Miss Parnell was single, lived with her mother, intended on cycling to work and would require a printed brooch to pin on her dress, clearly stating MANAGER.

'Would you mind giving us a minute?' Grace asked politely.

Miss Parnell rose to her feet. 'I'll be outside.'

'I like her, Grandma. What do you think?'

'Hmm . . . yes, I believe she will do.'

'Great. I'll call her back in and offer her the position.'

'But you have four more women to interview.'

'I'll put a sign on the door saying that the position has been filled.'

'Fine. I shall leave you to become better acquainted with your staff. Remember, Grace, Miss Parnell is working for you. Do not treat her as a friend.'

Once Myrtle had left the shop, Grace offered Miss Parnell a cup of tea, which she gratefully accepted. The woman was several inches taller than Grace and seemed far more sophisticated than her. With auburn hair neatly waved, sapphire-blue eyes and long, dark eyelashes, Miss Parnell had the ingredients to be a beauty. But her thin lips and long, pointed nose gave her face a harshness.

'May I start work tomorrow?' Miss Parnell asked.

'Yes. I shall meet you outside at nine.'

'I realise that this must be quite daunting for you, Miss Newman. You'll be leaving your shop in my hands and putting a lot of faith in me. I want to assure you that I won't let you down and I'm grateful for the opportunity.'

The more time Grace spent getting to know Miss Parnell,

the more she liked the young and intriguing woman, though her grandmother's words rolled through Grace's mind. *Do not treat her as a friend*. But more than ever, Grace needed a friend, and company of her own age. Hoping she didn't sound desperate and lonely, she asked, 'Do you have plans for this evening, Miss Parnell? I wondered if you'd like to come to the picture house with me?'

Miss Parnell grinned, and replied, 'I'd like that very much, and please call me Betty.'

Grace was thrilled. She missed Anna and she sometimes thought about John, but Betty was a breath of fresh air, and Grace was looking forward to laughing again.

Gordon threw the newspaper angrily to the floor beside the sofa. He didn't know why he bothered to look at the thing. He could only read a few very basic words and struggled with them. It didn't help that since Dickie had battered him, he'd lost the sight in his left eye.

Bitterness gnawed at him every waking second of the day. He hadn't deserved what Dickie had dished out to him, and Grace had got away with destroying his life. He'd make her pay one day. For now, though, he'd have to bide his time.

It was a welcome relief from boredom when he heard Anna arrive home from work.

She walked in, smiling, and kissed his cheek, then asked, 'Have you missed your wife?'

'Yeah, I have. I'm gasping. Put the kettle on,' he slurred.

Anna shook her head. 'I've just done a ten-hour shift. What have you been doing? Sitting on your arse again all day? You should be making me a cuppa!'

Gordon jumped to his feet and lunged at Anna. Pointing

his finger in her face, his words slurred, he shouted, 'Who do you think you are, talking to me like that! You're my wife and you'll do as you're bloody well told! Now get in that kitchen and make me a cup of tea.'

Anna didn't flinch. 'You're half blind and you can't talk properly no more, but there's no reason why you can't look for work, Gordon. I'm fed up with living here with my mum and dad. I want us to have our own place. When you're a proper husband bringing home a wage, I'll happily make you a cup of tea. Until then, you can make your own tea, and while you're at it, I'll have a cuppa too and a cheese sandwich.'

Rage boiled through Gordon's veins, and he swiped the back of his hand across Anna's face. 'Watch your bleedin' mouth, woman!' he spat, as her cheek flamed red. 'Don't ever back-chat me again and do as you're told.'

Anna fled the room.

Gordon shouted after her, 'You'd better be making me a cuppa.'

It wasn't the first time he'd had to use force to put his wife back in her place. She tended to get above her station now and then, giving him lip or answering him back. But Gordon had found that a swift slap would remind her of who the boss was.

When she came back into the room with a cup of tea, and sat in the armchair, he could see that her face still looked red. He thought maybe he'd hit her a bit too hard. After all, he didn't want Anna's dad confronting him. Not that Gordon was worried about the man. He knew he could easily put his father-in-law on his backside, but they needed the man's hospitality, or they'd find themselves living somewhere unsuitable that Anna's wage alone could afford.

'You need to put some cold water on your face,' Gordon advised, calmer. 'I don't like raising my hand to you, Anna, but you've got to learn that it ain't right to talk back to your husband. And remember what I told you – what goes on between a man and his wife is private business. Don't talk about it to anyone, all right?'

'Yes, Gordon, and I'm sorry.'

Gordon could hear his slurred words. He sounded drunk even though he hadn't touched a drop of alcohol. No one in their right mind would offer him employment. The only way Gordon could earn money was by taking it from others with violence. The thought of fighting made his blood run cold. Since he'd been on the receiving end of Dickie's harrowing punishment, Gordon had been left with an unexplainable fear. Yes, he could give Anna a slap now and then if she asked for it, and yes, he fantasised about throttling the life out of Grace, but coming face to face with another man, fists flying, lips bursting, noses breaking, eye sockets swelling – he shuddered at the thought.

Anna's soft voice broke into his thoughts. 'I know I shouldn't have gone on at you about finding work, and I'm sorry, but I'm desperate for us to have our own home because ... because I think I'm going to have a baby.'

Gordon's fears, his negative thoughts, his bitterness and dark mood instantly faded away as his heart swelled with joy. 'Are you sure?' he asked, trying to hide his excitement.

'Yes, I think so. It's very early days, but I reckon it happened on our wedding night last month.'

Leaping from the sofa, he pulled Anna to her feet and

threw his arms around her. Lifting her off the floor, he spun around, holding her tight. After planting a big kiss on her lips, he looked into her eyes. 'You've made me the happiest man in Battersea. Blimey, Anna, I can't believe it! I'm gonna be a father!'

He'd get his revenge on Grace one day, but thoughts of her were pushed to the back of his mind as his head filled with images of him playing football with his son or buying ice-cream for his daughter. 'I'm gonna be a great dad,' he gushed. 'I don't know how a father is supposed to be 'cos I never had one, but I know I ain't gonna be like Dickie Newman. You're bloody lovely, Anna, you really are. I'm gonna have a family. My own, real family.'

42

A week later, as Grace ate her breakfast that had been tastily prepared by Mrs Conners, she looked across the table to her father. The man smiled warmly at her, and she returned the gesture, but she still found it difficult to be in his company. *How am I ever going to forgive you, Papa?* she mused, thinking about how he'd arranged for Gordon to hurt John so badly. And it wasn't the only inexcusable thing that played on Grace's mind. There was her mother buried in the back garden, and the intolerable conditions of her father's tenants. Grace couldn't be sure, but she didn't believe him when he said he'd made improvements to his properties, or that he was any kinder to the people who were forced to live in them.

'Are you happy with Miss Parnell's work?' her father asked.

'Yes, Papa, Betty is amazing. I'm supposed to be her boss, but she's taught me a thing or two. I'm meeting her today in my shop. We're going to start planning our window displays for the King's Jubilee celebrations next month. I've ordered some terrific hats that Betty believes will sell like hot cakes.'

'Betty, eh? Sounds a bit too familiar,' he said, raising an eyebrow.

'We've become good friends.'

'Well, I hope you don't have to give her the sack. Being friends might make that uncomfortable for you.'

'I can't see any reason why that would ever happen. Betty's doing such a smashing job, and I know I can trust her with the finances.'

Her father's voice lowered, and he said seriously, 'Never trust anyone in business, Grace, especially with your money.'

'You trust Ernie, don't you?'

'To some degree, but I check every penny. Anyway, Ernie knows better than to try and get one over on me. He respects me. You just make sure that Betty respects you. Perhaps you should remind her that you're a Newman.'

'Yes, I will, Papa, thank you.' *Unlikely*, she thought. Grace didn't want Betty to think of her as uncouth, which was a word often associated with the name Dickie Newman.

'Right, talking of Ernie, I'd better get to work. See you later.'

'Will you be late this evening?' Grace asked.

'I dunno, maybe. Eat without me. These new thirty-mile an hour speed limits on the roads slow me down,' he grumbled.

Half an hour later, Grace was making her way to her shop. She smiled, enjoying the spring sun on her face, and was excited to be meeting Betty again. As she hopped off the tram, she noticed a woman in the crowd, dressed tattily, her hair hanging in greasy strands around her dirty face. The woman moved through the commuters with cupped hands, begging for any spare change. Most people pushed past her, ignored her or glared at her contemptuously. But Grace recognised the pitiful woman.

'Mrs May,' she said. 'How are you? Oh, I'm sorry, that

was a daft question. Here, I have some money,' she offered, rummaging in her bag for her purse.

'Don't speak to me,' the woman snapped. 'Go away!'

'Please, Mrs May, I'd like to help you,' Grace protested gently.

'*Help me*, huh! The last time I spoke to you and that fella you was wiv, it cost me dear! I ain't speaking to you or no one again. Bugger off!'

Grace, perplexed, asked, 'I beg your pardon, but what do you mean?'

'When I showed you and that coalman how me and mine lived, it got back to my landlord, and he put my rent and loan payments up as a punishment for opening me gob. I can't afford to talk to you again, so do me a favour and leave me be.'

Grace's heart plummeted. 'I'm so sorry, Mrs May. Take this money and I'll leave you in peace,' she insisted, and pushed her purse into the woman's hand.

'I can't take your purse. The coppers will think I've pinched it!'

'Take it and put it in your pocket, Mrs May.'

Grace felt heavily burdened as she watched Mrs May scuttle away. *The poor woman*, she thought, realising that not only was it her fault that the woman's life had become harder, but also that her suspicions had been confirmed – her father had been feeding her lies. His properties remained neglected, and he obviously hadn't been showing any kindness to the likes of Mrs May. If anything, he'd become more of a bullying tyrant!

Seeing Betty waiting outside the shop didn't lighten Grace's mood.

'Good morning. Why the glum face?' Betty enquired.

'I'd rather not discuss it,' Grace replied curtly.

'Well, Grace, I'm sorry, but I can't work with you all day if you're going to be foul-tempered. You've got a face on you that would sour milk. Either share your problem with me, or put on a smile and pretend that everything's all right.'

'Put the kettle on then, but when I tell you about my father, I hope it won't change your opinion of me.'

'Oh, Grace, you can be so naïve sometimes,' Betty said, rubbing her long-fingered hand on Grace's arm. 'I'm a Battersea girl, of course I know all about Dickie Newman. Christ, who doesn't, your father's notorious. But you, Grace, the landlord's daughter, you're nothing like him.'

Grace blew out a sigh of relief. She'd avoided talking about her father to Betty, believing the woman wouldn't want to be friends with Dickie Newman's daughter. Betty seemed to be too refined for the Newman world. She had an elegance about her, a grace and style that didn't quite fit into Battersea.

'We can't help who we're born to,' Betty reassured her. 'I've worked hard on my image, and on how I talk, but my dad was an entertainer who ended up doing time for armed robbery and is living at His Majesty's pleasure in Wandsworth Prison. My mum's a cleaner, nothing wrong with that, but honestly, Grace, you've never heard anything as bad as the language that comes out of her mouth! That's why I haven't invited you round to mine. Cor, what a pair, we're as bad as each other.'

'And there was me thinking you were a bit classy,' Grace laughed.

'I am, dahhhling,' Betty giggled. 'I must admit, I was unsure about working for a Newman, but when I first saw you, I thought to myself, I'm going to like that woman, and I wasn't wrong. And your grandmother, she's a card!'

'Oh, don't get me started on her,' Grace said with a roll of her eyes. 'She's a good woman whose family were wealthy, and there's some aristocratic lineage somewhere, but my grandfather gambled away all their money. She's not had it easy, and living with my father has been difficult for her, but she maintains *appearances* and is exceptionally good at it.'

'I love her, Grace! Do you think she'd give me lessons on how to talk like her?'

Grace burst out laughing. 'Probably. She's quick to pick me up on my speech. I know it grates on her that I don't talk with a plum in my mouth.'

'Maybe we could have lessons together?'

'That would be fun.'

'Do you mind me asking you something personal, Grace?'

'No, go on.'

'Do you have any friends? Only you never mention anyone.'

Grace sighed, and answered honestly, 'No, Betty, I don't have any friends. I went to a private school, so my friends aren't from around here. I did have a friend, Anna. We didn't fall out or anything, but we drifted apart and now she's married to a man I can't stand. Gordon hates me and the feeling is mutual.'

'I know Anna! We went to school together and she lives around the corner from me. I've met her husband, and I got the feeling he didn't want Anna to talk to me. It was as though he wanted to keep her all to himself, which I thought was very odd.'

Grace hoped that Gordon was treating Anna well, and asked, 'How is she?'

'I'm not sure. I've bumped into her a couple of times, only briefly, but she doesn't seem herself. She says she's fine, but she seems out of sorts. Quiet, on edge, do you know what I mean?'

'I can imagine. I wish she'd never married Gordon. I tried to talk her out of it. Do you think you could persuade her to visit the shop? I'd love to see her.'

'I'll knock on her door on my way home later.'

'Thanks, Betty. Now, tell me about the wonderful ideas you have for the King's Jubilee window displays.'

Dickie sat waiting patiently in his car for Ernie to return. And when Ernie opened the car door, his beaming face told Dickie all he needed to know.

'I paid the lad, like you said. He's watching Grace from morning 'til night and he reckons she ain't seen no one except for Miss Parnell.'

'Good. Did you emphasise that Grace mustn't notice him, and if she does, he's not to mention my name?'

'Yes, Boss. He knows to keep you out of it, and he knows that if he messes this up, he'll be seeing my fists.'

Dickie relaxed in the knowledge that Grace wasn't liaising with any men. Now that he didn't have Gordon to report on any news of her, he was relying on a thirteen-year-old boy to watch his daughter. The boy had been bought easily with a shiny new bicycle and a few pennies a week. He hadn't minded spending the money on the bicycle as it had been for Dickie's benefit – it enabled the lad to follow the tram.

'I want you to do some digging, Ernie. Find out what you can about Elizabeth Parnell.'

'Yes, Boss, will do.'

'Right, I'll see you tomorrow. I'm off for a meeting with the Old Bill.'

'That gaffer bloke again?'

'Yeah. They don't come much higher than him in the force, and if there's anything to unearth about Betty Parnell, then he'll be the one to dig it up.'

'Right you are. You can't be too careful, Boss.'

No, you can't, thought Dickie. He'd do everything in his power to protect Grace. She was the only good thing he had in his life, and he loved her beyond words. He loved her so much, that he couldn't even consider a man taking her away from him. It was never going to happen. No man would ever be good enough for his daughter!

43

'I feel so ugly,' Maud moaned, arching her back and rubbing her hugely rounded belly. 'Look at me, John, I'm so fat and my ankles are swollen to twice the size.'

'You're not fat, Maud, you're carrying our child,' John reassured her.

'Do you think you'll still fancy me after the baby's born?'

'Of course I will.'

'But I'll never be as pretty as Grace Newman.'

John stood up from the kitchen table, walked to the sink where Maud was cleaning the breakfast plates, wrapped his arms around her, and whispered in her ear, 'You're my wife, Maud. Forget about Grace.'

'Can you forget about her?'

'I have,' John lied. 'She's in the past. It's me, you and this little one,' he said, placing a hand on her stomach.

Maud's eyes lit up, and she smiled delightedly, asking, 'Did you feel that? The baby kicked.'

'Oh, yeah, I felt it! Blimey, Maud, I reckon you've got a Jack Bowers in there!'

'No, John, I don't think so. This ain't a little footballer. I think she's a ballerina.'

John chuckled, saying, 'Gawd help us both if we're going to have a tiny Maud on our hands.'

Maud slapped his arm playfully, and then asked seriously, 'You do love me, don't you, John?'

'Yes, Maud, I do,' he replied with as much sincerity as he could muster. 'I've told you time and time again how much I love you.'

'I know, but I can't help thinking that you'd rather be with Grace.'

'I'm not having this conversation again,' he said impatiently, and kissed his wife's forehead. 'I've got to go to work. I'll see you tonight.'

I'm a rotten husband, he chastised himself. Maud was the size of the barrage balloons he'd seen in the skies as a young boy during the Great War, and she moaned that her back ached. He felt he should be more patient with her, but Maud's constant need for reassurance seemed to be getting worse the bigger she got. He was glad to be out of the house and in the van.

Dander's Deliveries had become busier far quicker than John had anticipated, which had been a great relief for him. Now, with the added pressure of a wife to support, and soon a child, he needed every penny he could earn. Keeping busy also gave him a good excuse to leave home early and not return until late. Guilt panged, but he couldn't help his feelings for Grace and the aversion towards his wife.

As he drove his van along Falcon Road, he slowed down to look in the window of Grace's hat boutique. The merest glimpse of her would set his heart racing. He knew it was wrong to be longing to hold Grace in his arms, but he couldn't stop thinking about her. Maud seemed to sense his feelings for Grace. He didn't mean to push his wife away, and though he tried to love her, she wasn't Grace.

Grace had seen John's van drive past, and though her stomach had flipped, she'd tried not to allow thoughts of him to cram her mind. He was a married man now, and Maud would be giving birth soon. There could never be any future with John, and Grace knew she had to overcome the feelings she still held for him.

With a feather duster in hand, she gently flicked the hats displayed in the window. Betty's suggestions and her talented knack for displays had proven to be successful. The Silver Jubilee of King George V was weeks away, yet the stylish hats that Betty had selected for sale were already flying out of the shop. As Grace dusted and considered ordering more hats, she spotted a lad across the street, the same young boy she'd seen several times. There was something about him that looked out of place. The boy was a scruff, with unkempt hair that needed a good cut, and his short trousers were a size too small. Grace studied the youngster and realised what it was that didn't seem right – the shiny, new bicycle. *I suspect he's pinched it*, she thought. It seemed strange that she kept seeing him lately. He was always hanging around the shop, and she was sure that when she'd looked out of the tram window the other day, it had been the same lad racing along the street beside the tram in Clapham.

Thoughts about the young boy disappeared when a customer entered the shop. Grace spent half an hour with the woman, helping her to select the perfect hat for her daughter's wedding. And then another woman came in, excited to try on one of the hats from the window display. A busy morning followed, and Grace was glad of a break during a lull in customers. She made herself a cup of strong coffee, and as she rested her legs and sat behind the counter, she saw the young lad peering through the window.

Jumping to her feet, Grace dashed to the door and yanked it open, but the boy was gone. He'd seen her coming and had raced off on his bicycle. *What are you up to?* she wondered, and hoped he wasn't planning to rob her. She reckoned he couldn't be any older than twelve, and she didn't like the idea of confronting a child. *I'll be keeping my eye out for you*, she thought suspiciously.

'Good luck today. You look very smart in your woollen suit,' Anna beamed, handing Gordon a small tin. 'I've packed you a fish paste sandwich and a hardboiled egg. You're a working man; you'll need to keep your strength up.'

'Thanks. This is gonna be the first honest day's work I've ever done.'

'I'm proud of you. You're going to be a good father to this baby, and with two wages coming in, we'll have our own place soon.'

'Maybe, but you won't be able to work for much longer, and I ain't gonna earn much cleaning windows.'

'It's a start, Gordon. We'll manage. And you're lucky to have landed yourself a job. I've seen blokes sleeping rough; too many of them are desperate for work.'

'Yeah, it ain't a nice sight. A lot of them have come down from the North to look for work. I hear it's bad up there and jobs are few and far between.'

Gordon limped to work, hoping he could cope with the physical demands of cleaning windows. Neville Boon, who owned the window cleaning round, had offered Gordon the job on a trial basis and, due to Gordon's ailments, he'd said Gordon would only have to clean the windows on the lower floors. The fella was an acquaintance from the pub where Gordon used to drink, and they'd bumped into each other yesterday. Neville had mentioned expanding his business, and Gordon had persuaded the man to take him on. After some reluctance, Neville had agreed, but only because Gordon had said he'd work for half pay.

'Hello, mate,' Gordon greeted him.

'Morning. Sling your lunch on the cart and we'll get cracking,' Neville answered. He was a few years older than Gordon, a stout man, and though he wore a flat cap, Gordon knew Neville was bald beneath his hat.

The two-wheeled wooden cart, laden with ladders, buckets, chamois leathers and scrims, was heavier than Gordon had expected. As he pulled it along the street, he asked, 'How far to our first job?'

'Three miles,' Neville answered.

They walked the distance in silence. Neville had never been a man of many words and Gordon knew little about him. The quiet time gave Gordon space to think. He'd be working a sixty-hour week for a pittance, but this job offered him the perfect opportunity to scout for richer pickings. He'd be peering through the windows of the wealthier folk of Battersea, noting their valuables and surveying their homes for easy access.

Gordon had a family to support, and he had big dreams for his child. No son or daughter of his was ever going to know the gnawing ache of hunger or the stinging pain of cold. His child would be raised with a mother's love and a father who could provide for his family. A window cleaner by day, Gordon planned on being a thief by night.

44

Later that day, business in the shop had been fruitful, which pleased Grace, but her heart dropped at the thought of going home. Her grandmother was away on an extended spring trip through Europe with an elderly widow, Mrs Hawkett, and the woman's young lady companion. Mrs Hawkett had funded the vacation. Her family had lived in India and had owned a large tea plantation, and Mr Hawkett, when he'd been alive, had worked on the London Stock Exchange. According to Grace's grandmother, Mrs Hawkett had become most upset when the Great Depression had hit America and reached across to Britain. She'd said that Mr Hawkett would have been devastated with the crash in share prices, and the family would have lost much of their wealth. Fortunately, Mr Hawkett had been an excellent investor and had withdrawn their stocks and shares before his death, re-investing the money in new industries such as rayon and ferrous metals. Myrtle had spoken very animatedly about Mrs Hawkett, and Grace hoped the pair were enjoying themselves. But with her grandmother away for three months, that only left her father at home, and Grace didn't like to be in his company, though, so far, she'd managed to conceal her animosity from him.

Hopping off the tram at her stop in Clapham, the sun was beginning to set, and clouds covered the rising moon. She wished it was summer and the days longer. If there had still been any natural light, Grace would have taken a stroll across the common. Anything rather than going home. Instead, with a chill in the evening air, Grace braced herself to be in her father's company.

Crossing the road, Grace had a feeling she was being watched. Glancing over her shoulder, she once again spotted the lad on the shiny bicycle. He was quite a way behind her, and seemed to be holding back, but she knew he was following her. Turning on her heel, she hurried towards him. The boy looked alarmed and quickly rode away.

'Hey,' Grace called. 'Wait, I want to talk to you.'

He looked back briefly as he cycled away.

'Wait! You're not in any trouble. Just talk to me.'

Again, the boy looked behind him and, as he did, his bicycle appeared to clip something on the pavement, and the front wheel wobbled. Losing his balance, the bicycle leaned to the left, and the boy crashed to the ground with his bike beside him.

Grace ran, hoping to reach him before he found his feet and scurried away again.

'Are you all right?' she asked, breathless.

He looked embarrassed and Grace saw a trickle of blood running down his shin from a sore-looking graze on his knee.

The boy nodded and threw his leg over the crossbar of his bike, finding the pedal with his foot.

Grace stood in front of him and grabbed the handlebars.

'You're not going anywhere until you explain to me why you're following me.'

'I ain't.'

'Yes, you are. I've seen you outside my shop. In fact, everywhere I look, there you are. What are you up to?'

'I ain't up to nothing,' the boy protested. 'Let go of me bike.'

'No, I won't. If you don't tell me the reason why you're following me, I shall drag you and your bicycle to the police station, and you can explain to them where you got this from.'

'I didn't nick it.'

'The police will think you did.'

'They can think what they like. I didn't and they can't prove that I did!'

'It would make your life much easier if you would simply tell me why you're constantly hanging around me.'

The boy hung his head.

'Right, have it your way. I'm taking you to the police station.'

'No, I won't go, and you can't make me.'

'You can run off, I won't chase after you, but I'm not letting go of this bicycle.'

'Please, miss, let me go with me bike. I'll get in an awful lot of trouble if you don't.'

'Trouble with whom?'

'I can't say, miss, I ain't allowed.'

'Why aren't you allowed?'

'It's the rules. If I tell you anything or lose me bike, I'll end up with me face being rearranged.'

Grace was confused and more than intrigued. 'Are you too scared to talk to me?' she probed.

The boy nodded.

She thought for a moment. If anyone was scared, it was normally because her father had threatened them. 'Do you know who I am and who my father is?'

'No, miss, I ain't got a clue.'

'So why are you scared to talk to me?'

'I can't say, miss. Please, you've got to let me take my bike,' he pleaded.

'Talk to me, and I can promise you won't have your face rearranged. I'll make sure no one hurts you, but you must tell me why you're following me.'

'You can't protect me. I have to keep me mouth shut, and I mustn't lose my bike.'

'I've given you your options and I've told you I can protect you. You either talk to me, or this bicycle is going to the police station. So, young man, why are you following me?'

'How are you gonna stop me getting bashed up?'

'Never you mind... Oh, look, there's a policeman up at the end of the road. I think I'll call him over.'

'No! Don't! Please don't... I'll talk to you, but you've got to promise I won't get hurt.'

'Promise.'

'I'm being paid to watch you. I've got to report back if I see you with any fellas.'

'Report to whom?' she asked, already knowing it would be her father.

'To Ernie. You won't tell him, will ya? You won't say I told you?'

The panic in the boy's voice upset Grace. 'No, I won't say anything. You carry on following me, and I'll pretend I've never seen you.'

Grace released the handlebars, and the boy raced away, leaving her standing dumbfounded. Her father had stooped low. He'd already had John warned off. Was that his plan for any man she met? Did he want to keep her a maiden all her life? Would she become a spinster, trapped at home with him, under his control and watchful eye? Grace was fuming with the man, but she couldn't confront him and put the young boy at risk. And she couldn't play *Papa's little girl* anymore either.

Gordon ached. It had been a long first day of hard graft and he was pleased it was finally over. Anna would have a hot meal waiting for him, and he couldn't wait to crawl into bed, especially as he was going to be sneaking out again in the small hours. A few hours' sleep, and then he planned on raiding a house he'd cleaned the windows of earlier. The occupants were away, returning tomorrow. The house was empty tonight, and Gordon had spied several items of value through the windows. He'd also noticed that the small lock on the rear window was broken. He could easily lift the pane of glass and slip inside the property, and he'd be out of sight from the road. It was perfect!

'Same time tomorrow,' Neville said, as Gordon parked the hand-drawn cart.

'Yeah, mate, see you tomorrow.'

Eager to get home, Gordon cursed his limp for slowing him down. Then, rounding a corner, and stepping off the pavement, he was blinded by dazzling headlights coming towards him. Leaping backwards, out of the way of the oncoming vehicle, he shouted at the small truck as it passed, 'Oi, slow down and watch it, will ya!'

That's when he noticed the sign on the side. *Dander's Deliveries.* He'd heard through Anna's mother that John's new business had taken off well, and Gordon had been jealous. Now, seeing the truck, and noting the sign, another thought struck him – he could get his revenge on Grace Newman and keep his name out of it. A wry smile crept across his face as he thought, *I can kill two birds with one stone.*

45

A few days later, on the way to her boutique, Grace had come to a decision. Stopping outside a newsagent, she scanned the handwritten adverts displayed in the shop window, hoping to find accommodation. Both of her shops were turning a healthy profit, which meant she could support herself on her income. Grace could no longer bear to be under the same roof as her father. Sitting across the table from him, making small talk, faking a smile, it had become torturous, and she was struggling to bite her tongue to stop from spilling her true feelings. The adverts offered nothing, and as she turned to walk away, she spotted the boy following her. He was yet another reminder of why she needed to get away from her father.

As Grace unlocked the door of her shop, she glanced behind when she heard a vehicle pulling up to the kerb. Her pulse began to race. It was the Dander's Deliveries truck, and she felt the old familiar feeling of butterflies in her stomach. John had always had that effect on her.

He climbed out of the truck, looking as handsome as ever,

his blond hair gleaming in the morning sun and his blue eyes piercing as they met hers.

'Good morning, Grace,' he said, somewhat uncomfortably. 'I, erm, I saw you and thought I'd pull over to say hello.'

Grace swallowed hard, before replying, 'Hello.'

'How are you?' he asked.

'Very well, thank you. And you, is your new business going well?'

'Yeah, really well, thanks.'

He held her gaze and Grace could feel herself melting into his eyes. *Stop it!* she said inwardly, and reminded herself of the reason why she and John had split up. 'How's Maud?' she asked with a hint of sarcasm.

'Big and grumpy.'

Pushing open the door, Grace went to walk inside, saying, 'I have a lot to do today, I must get on. It was nice to see you, John.'

'Wait, Grace ... Maybe we could meet later? A cup of tea and a bun in the café on York Road?'

Grace was tempted, but fighting her feelings, she answered, 'No, John, I don't think that's a good idea.'

'Please, Grace,' he asked desperately. 'I miss you. I can't stop thinking about you. I know I messed up and we can't go back to what we were, but just a cuppa as friends. That's all I'm asking for.'

Sighing heavily, and against her better judgement, she nodded. 'All right, but nothing more than friends. I'll see you at lunch time.'

Her legs felt shaky, and she was lightheaded as she closed the door behind her and leaned against it, breathing in a deep breath and slowly pushing the air out through her lips. 'What have I done?' she asked out loud. 'You stupid, stupid woman!'

The hours ticked by slowly as Grace watched the time. She knew it had been a reckless mistake to agree to meet John, and she was going to rectify it. She'd tell him they couldn't be friends, as it wasn't fair on Maud, and they could never meet again. Yet still her stomach was somersaulting at the thought of seeing him soon.

It was almost lunchtime. Grace checked her reflection in the mirror. 'It doesn't matter what you look like,' she told herself. 'You're to say goodbye, and tell him that this must stop!'

Ten minutes later, on York Road, she saw John's truck parked near the café and that he was sitting at a table in the window. *This will be your final goodbye*, she thought. *Be firm*.

Inside the café, John scraped back his seat and gestured her to the table. 'I wasn't sure you'd come,' he smiled.

'I've only come to say goodbye, John. This isn't right. You're married to Maud and she's having your child. We shouldn't meet like this.'

'There's no harm, Grace. We're only friends.'

'We both know there's more to it than that.'

John sat down, looking deflated. 'You're right. But you're here now, so you may as well have a cuppa.'

Grace was about to decline his offer, but before she could, the café door burst open and Maud's screeching voice filled the room.

'How could you, John?' Maud cried loudly. 'With *her*! I knew it . . . I flamin' well knew it!' Then, waddling towards Grace, she screamed in her face, 'Leave my man alone! He's *my* husband, and this is his child. You might dress fancy, but you're nothing but a tart, Grace Newman!'

The customers in the café fell silent and Grace could feel all eyes on her.

Maud continued shouting, 'Find your own man, 'cos you ain't having mine!'

Grace hadn't seen it coming, but she felt a sting on her cheek when Maud slapped her.

'That's it, Maud, give her what for,' an older woman urged.

Grace assumed she was Maud's mother, Mrs Scarrow.

The woman looked down her nose derisively at Grace. 'My Maud's right. You're nothing but a fancy tart with the morals of an alley cat. You can find someone else to do your laundry. I ain't cleaning your sheets no more. Gawd only knows who's been laying on 'em! Disgusting.'

'Stay away from my husband!' Maud added. Then, glaring at John, she ordered, 'You. Home. Now.'

Grace lowered her eyes. The shame burned more than the slap to her face did. She wished the earth would open and swallow her, and she knew it would be a waste of breath to try to explain to Maud that she was telling John that they'd never see each other again. Fleeing the café, Grace kept her eyes averted, too ashamed to look at Maud, Mrs Scarrow, John or any of the customers. Hurrying along the street, cringing at what had just occurred, she couldn't wait to be back in the sanctuary of her boutique.

John marched out of the café with Maud, his mother-in-law in his wake. On the pavement outside, he spun and shouted defensively, 'You've got it all wrong, Maud! There was no bloomin' need to make a scene like that! There ain't nothing going on with me and Grace.'

Maud didn't reply. Instead, she leaned over, holding her stomach with one hand whilst steadying herself with the other on a wall.

'You all right, love?' her mother asked.

Maud cried out in pain. 'The baby! Oh, Mum, I think the baby's coming!'

'It can't be, you're much too early.'

'It's coming! Oh, blimey, what do I do? Stop it, please, Mum, stop it from coming!'

Maud's mother turned to John with panicked eyes. 'Help me get her in the truck,' she demanded. 'We'll have to get her to the Bolingbroke hospital; it's the nearest one.'

John's eyes were wide with fear. Maud wasn't due to give birth for at least another two months.

Mrs Scarrow raised her voice. 'John! Don't just stand there, help me!'

Placing his shoulder under Maud's arm, John almost dragged her to his truck and heaved her inside as she groaned loudly in pain.

Maud's mother squeezed in too, telling John, 'Hurry up, drive as fast as you can. There ain't no time to hang about.'

John gripped the steering wheel and put his foot down hard, racing through the streets with Maud's cries piercing his ears.

'It can't come yet,' Maud sobbed in between her howls of agony. 'Oh, God, please keep my baby safe … I'm begging you, don't let her die. Please don't let her die …'

Finally reaching the hospital, John carried Maud inside, running, shouting, 'We need help here!'

Medical staff quickly assessed the situation, and John was instructed to place Maud on a bed with wheels, before she was rushed away with her mother following. He stood in the stark corridor, panting, and running his hand through his hair as he watched his wife being taken away.

'You can wait here, sir,' a kindly nurse offered, coaxing him to a seat.

'Will… will she be all right?' John asked anxiously.

'The doctor will know more soon.'

It seemed an endless wait. He could hear his wife screaming in pain, and then moments of quiet. He was desperate for news of his wife and child. The sound of Maud's screams became more frequent. He knew that it meant the baby would be born soon. His leg jigged and he bit on his nails. *They've got to be all right*, he thought, *they've got to be!*

After a long and tense wait, the faint sound of an infant's wail reached John's ears. As relief flooded through him, he fought to hold back tears.

The door opened and Maud's mother beckoned him over. 'You'd better come and meet your daughter,' she said, still glaring at him angrily.

John rushed past her, and saw Maud sitting in a bed, resting on pillows behind her and with a small bundle in her arms. He couldn't take his eyes off his wife; she'd never looked so beautiful. Her hair was wet with sweat and her face glowed red, but her eyes shone with love.

'The doctor reckons I got my timings wrong. She's five pounds, John, she's gonna be all right. Do you want to hold her?'

John nodded, overwhelmed, and carefully took the baby. He'd never seen another human who looked so tiny, and his heart instantly filled with love. Finally finding his voice, he said softly, 'She's beautiful. You're amazing, Maud, look what you've done.'

'She looks like you,' Maud whispered.

'I hope not,' John scoffed. 'I hope she grows up to look just like her beautiful mum.'

Gazing down adoringly at his daughter, John was suddenly aware of a flurry of activity around Maud's bed.

'What's happening?' Maud's mother asked, alarmed. 'What's wrong with my girl?'

John saw that Maud had lost consciousness. Her face had drained of colour, and she didn't appear to be breathing. 'Is she all right? Will someone answer me! What's wrong with my wife?'

A nurse eased him away from the bed. 'The doctor's doing everything he can,' she soothed. 'Let me take the baby. You should wait outside.'

John couldn't think clearly. His heart was pounding with fear as he watched the doctor working on Maud. Handing his daughter to the nurse, she ushered him towards the door. He was vaguely aware of Maud's mother whimpering in the corner of the room as he went outside. Pacing the corridor worriedly, he waited for news.

Ten minutes later, when the door opened, Maud's mother walked out determinedly, her face ashen and streaked with tears. Lifting her hand, she struck John around the face.

'It's your fault my daughter's dead!' she hissed. 'Her heart gave up. You broke it when she caught you with that hussy today!'

John's mind whirred. *Dead? Maud can't be dead!* But then

the doctor came out, and John could tell by the man's grave expression that it was true.

'I'm very sorry, Mr Dander. We did everything we could, but your wife has passed away.'

John thought his legs were going to give way, and he staggered to the seat where he'd been waiting for Maud to give birth. She was gone. It didn't seem real. His daughter didn't have a mother. 'What am I going to do?' he mumbled. 'I'm sorry, Maud. I'm really sorry. But I'll make sure our girl has the best life, and I'll tell her how much you would have loved her, and what a smashing mum you would have been. Christ, Maud, I'm so bloody sorry!'

46

It was pouring with rain the next day. The skies were dark, and thunder rumbled over Battersea. Gordon's clothes were soaked through, and his feet squelched in wet socks.

'Might as well knock off early today. Blinkin' Blighty weather,' Neville moaned.

Gordon was grateful. He couldn't wait to be sitting in front of the coal fire in the warmth of home. The only fly in the ointment would be Anna's mother. The woman would be at home too, and she didn't shut up. It seemed she liked to fill any silence with words. It didn't matter what the subject was, she just chatted on and on, driving Gordon up the wall. He couldn't wait to find his own place with Anna, and he hoped it would be soon, especially now he'd found a reliable fence to pass on his stolen valuables. Already, his finances were on the up.

Reaching home, he was surprised to find Mrs Dander leaving and looking miserable.

'Nice weather for ducks,' he joked, as he passed her at the front door. 'I ain't complaining, a bit of rain never killed no one.'

Anna was standing in the hallway, and she threw him a warning look.

'What?' he asked.

'It's Maud,' Anna whispered. 'She passed away yesterday.'

'Bloody 'ell, sorry, I didn't know.'

Anna's mother looked disapprovingly at the puddle beginning to form on her floor from his dripping wet clothes.

'Go and get changed,' Anna advised. 'I'll make you a hot drink.'

Minutes later, Anna came into their bedroom and placed a steaming cup of coffee on the dressing table. 'Maud had the baby yesterday, a girl, but her heart packed up and she died shortly after.'

'That's a shocker!'

'Yeah, it's awful. My aunt said that John is inconsolable, and Maud's mum, Mrs Scarrow, she's got the baby and won't let John see her. My mum said John should go to the police; I mean he's the father, he's got rights. But John wants to give Maud's mum some time. After all, she's only just lost her daughter.' Then, looking down at her stomach, Anna said sadly, 'Oh, Gordon, I'm beside meself with worry.'

He sat next to Anna on the edge of the bed and took her warm hand in his. 'Don't worry, the same thing won't happen to you. You're gonna be here for our kid.'

'But what if I ain't, Gordon? No one would have thought Maud would die. What if I die, too? Who'd look after my baby?'

Wrapping his arms around her, Gordon pulled her close. 'You won't die, Anna. You can't. Me and this kid need you too much. You're strong, you'll be all right.'

'I should visit John. He needs his family around him at a time like this.'

'I reckon he'll need space. I mean, if it was me, if I'd just lost you, the last thing I'd want would be to see anyone. I'd want to be by meself, and I think John would an' all.'

'Really? Do you really think so?'

'I do, Anna,' Gordon lied.

Anna's mother called up the stairs. 'Anna … Betty's at the door.'

As Anna went to rise to her feet, Gordon urged her to stay sitting. 'I'll go. You must rest. You've had a nasty shock. Stay here, put your feet up. I'll tell Betty to call round another time.'

'I'm fine, Gordon, and I'd like to see Betty.'

'I know what's best for you, Anna, and I'm telling you to rest. Christ, look at what's just happened to Maud! Is that what you want, eh? Stop being selfish and think about our baby. Now, do as you're told and have a lie down.'

Anna nodded, and Gordon helped lift her legs onto the bed.

'Good girl,' he smiled, before going downstairs.

Betty Parnell was standing inside, looking her usual haughty self. The woman's skirt was wet, but her hat and hair were immaculate.

Gordon sidled up to her. She was almost as tall as him and he could see from the look in her eyes that she didn't like him. Gordon wasn't bothered. He didn't think much of her, either. 'Anna's having a lie down. She needs her rest,' he said.

'Fine. I'll call back tomorrow.'

'I wouldn't bother. She'll be resting then, too.'

'Do you have a problem with me seeing Anna?' Betty asked, forthright.

'No, why would I?'

'I don't know, Gordon, but you seem to be keeping me away from her.'

'Perhaps Anna doesn't like you. Have you thought of that, eh?'

Anna's mother appeared from the kitchen. 'Isn't Anna coming down?' she asked Gordon.

'No, she's resting.'

Looking at Betty, the woman explained, 'We've had a family bereavement, dear. My sister's son lost his wife yesterday in tragic circumstances. Poor Maud had just given birth when she passed away. Now John will have a daughter to raise with no mother. It's so sad.'

'Oh, I'm terribly sorry,' Betty said. 'Please accept my condolences.'

Gordon closed the door behind Betty, pleased that he'd kept his wife from spending time with her. Betty was too outspoken, and he didn't want Anna to be friends with her. It wouldn't do for Anna to emulate Betty's ways or believe that it was acceptable for a woman to voice her opinions. And he didn't want his wife cosying up with John again, either. He resented how close John and Anna had been. After all, Anna was *his* wife, and he should be the only man in her life. Oddly, Gordon felt a tinge of sympathy for John's unexpected predicament, and he hoped with all his heart that he wouldn't find himself in the same boat.

Whilst all the shops in Battersea were long closed for the day, Grace stayed late in her boutique. The weather outside was atrocious, and she didn't expect any customers, but she couldn't face going home yet. With the local newspaper spread open across the counter, Grace surveyed the classifieds, circling any advertisements that looked hopeful. Many of the properties available for rent were too expensive. A few offered rooms, but Grace knew the area and thought they were better suited to men. 'There must be something, somewhere,' she sighed, and chewed on the end of her pencil.

Lifting her eyes from the newspaper, Grace looked across the boutique and through the window. Once again, she saw the boy. He looked wet and cold, and Grace felt sorry for him. 'You poor lad, you can't go home until I do.'

After pulling on her coat and gloves, and adjusting her hat, she grabbed her bag and umbrella, turned off the lights, and stepped outside into the rain. Pushing her brolly up, a gust of wind caught it as she tried to lock the door.

'Bloody Nora,' Grace cursed, as she dropped the shop keys on the wet pavement and tried to keep hold of her umbrella that had turned inside out.

'Here, let me help you,' a voice said. The man bent down and picked up the keys, handing them to Grace.

'Thank you,' she said, studying his face. There was something familiar about him.

'Would you like me to lock the door?' he offered.

'Yes, thanks,' she agreed, and placed the keys in his hand. She noticed his cane and could just see tufts of light brown hair under his trilby hat. Something at the back of her mind made her think she knew the kind gentleman.

'There you go, all safe and secure,' he smiled.

'Do I know you?' Grace asked.

'I shouldn't think so.'

'I do, I'm sure we've met before.'

'No, I haven't been in Battersea for years.'

'Thank you for your help. Look at us, we're both drenched now. I'm Miss Newman, and this is my boutique.'

The man's eyebrows shot up. 'Grace? Grace Newman?' he blurted.

'Yes. See, I knew we'd met before, I just can't place where.'

'Clapham Common, feeding the ducks. You used to come into my grocery store as well, you and your mum.'

Grace wracked her brain, searching for the memory, and then it came flooding back. 'Mr Pope!' she exclaimed, beaming.

'Yep, Jack Pope, at your service. I must say, young Grace, you've grown into a stunning young woman,' he grinned. 'Tell me, how is your mother?'

Grace gulped, and answered, 'My mother passed away.'

'Oh no, I'm so sorry to hear that,' he said. Then, rubbing his forehead with his finger and thumb, he added, 'I thought very highly of your mother. She was a wonderful woman, wonderful. I hope she didn't suffer?'

'Erm, no, not really, I suppose not, but my mother had been poorly. Her mind wasn't right, Mr Pope, she suffered with some sort of depression that took over her life.'

'That's most upsetting to hear. Louisa was a vibrant lady, so full of life. What caused her breakdown?' he probed.

Grace shrugged. She'd never understood her mother's struggles, and no one had been able to explain her mother's reason for locking herself away for much of the time. Gordon had hinted at something once, but it hadn't made any sense. He'd said that Dickie was a killer and had murdered Louisa's friend, but when questioned, he'd retracted his statement and denied any knowledge of anything.

'Did … erm … did your mother ever talk about me?'

'No,' Grace answered. 'Why would she? Mr Pope, is there something you're not telling me?'

'I'm sorry, it's nice to see you, but we're both getting soaked, and I need to get going. Good evening, young Grace.'

'Oh no you don't! You're not getting off the hook that easily. If you know something about my mother and why she took to her bed, then you need to tell me. Please, Mr Pope, I demand to know the truth!'

Jack Pope shook his head. 'It's not safe for me to be back in Battersea, and talking to you is putting me in serious danger. I'm sorry, Grace, but I must go.'

'No, Mr Pope, please don't run away … It's my father, isn't it? You're scared of my father.'

Jack nodded. 'Yes, Grace, I'm terrified of the man. I shouldn't have come back, but it's my niece's wedding and she wants me to give her away. I couldn't say no, but being in London is bad for my health. I'm a coward, and I'm sorry that I ran away to Scotland and left your mother behind.'

Grace shoved the keys back into his hand. 'Open the door,' she ordered. 'We're going inside and you're going to tell me everything.'

Hours later, Grace hammered on Betty's front door.

Betty opened the door, looking dazed as she tied a belt around her dressing gown. 'Grace, are you all right? What are you doing here at this time of night?'

'I'm sorry, Betty, I didn't know where else I could go. I can't go home.'

'Come in, you look wet and cold.'

As Grace stepped over the threshold, she saw Mrs Parnell

on the stairs. The woman was tall like her daughter, but much broader, and her expression showed annoyance.

'What the flippin' 'ell is going on down here? Who's bashing me door down?'

'Sorry, Mum, it's only Grace. Go back to bed.'

As Mrs Parnell climbed back up the stairs, she grumbled, 'Bloody Newmans. They think they can do what they want, when they want. It's a diabolical liberty, that's what it is, a diabolical liberty.'

'Sorry about her,' Betty whispered. 'Go through to the kitchen, I'll be back in a tick.'

Grace turned on the light, and sat at the small kitchen table, drumming her cold fingers as she tried to make sense of what Jack Pope had told her.

Betty soon came in and closed the door, before handing Grace a towel. 'Dry yourself off and tell me what this is all about. I'll make us a cup of cocoa.'

Grace removed her hat and rubbed her hair with the towel as she spoke. 'I can't believe what I've just heard,' she sighed. 'It's my father, Betty, he's a monster! I can't go home. Please, can I stay here tonight? I'll find somewhere tomorrow.'

'You can stay here for as long as you like, but you'll have to put up with my mum.'

'Thank you, I'm ever so grateful, and that's a weight off my mind.'

'What's happened? You said your father's a monster.'

Grace sighed deeply again. 'Where do I start? Oh, Betty, it's all so awful! I'm too ashamed to even talk about it.'

Betty poured warmed milk into cups, spooned in cocoa powder and sugar, and placed them on the table. Sitting beside her friend, she put her hand over Grace's. 'You don't have to feel ashamed with me, Grace. You're not responsible for anything that your father has done.'

'I know, but I should have done something about it a long time before now.'

'What's he done?'

Grace began to explain. 'The way he treats his tenants is just the tip of the iceberg. He had John beaten and warned off me, and now he's paying a boy to follow me and report back on my movements and who I'm speaking to. And I've just bumped into someone who was friends with my mother. Actually, they were more than friends. They loved each other. My mother had a terrible life with my father, and she found comfort with a gentle man, a storekeeper. But my father burned down the man's shop with him inside. Fortunately, he escaped and fled the area. But it all makes sense now! That was the cause of my mother's sadness. And to top it all… I can't believe I'm going say this out loud, it sounds crazy… he buried my mother in our back garden!'

Betty sat speechless, her jaw hanging wide.

'Now you can understand why I can't go home.'

'Did he kill your mother?'

'No, not directly, but he destroyed her spirit, and he covered up her death for Gordon's benefit.'

'Gordon killed her?'

'Yes. What am I going to do, Betty?' Grace asked despairingly.

Betty was quiet for a moment, and then replied, 'You must go the police, Grace.'

'I can't. The police are as bad as my father. He pays for their silence and support.'

'You need some time to gather your thoughts. We'll work

this out together, Grace. I'll get you a nightie. You'll have to bunk in with me, I'm afraid, but at least you're safe here and away from your father. You can stay for as long as you need.'

'Thanks, Betty, but I can't stay here after tonight. That boy, the one who's watching me, he'll tell my father where I am. I'll find somewhere to live tomorrow, and you're right, I need some time to think. I must do something about my father, he can't get away with it all. I don't know what I'm going to do, but I'm going to act!'

47

Dickie had waited up all night, but Grace hadn't come home, and she hadn't opened her shop this morning. He had the Old Bill looking for her, and now he'd tracked down his little spy. Leaping out of his car with Ernie following, Dickie grabbed Tim by the scruff of his grubby shirt. 'Where is she?' he growled.

'She's stayed at a house not far from 'ere,' Tim answered, trembling. 'I was coming to tell you, honest I was.'

'Whose house?'

'I dunno. I can show you where it is. It's on Edna Street.'

Ernie piped up, 'That's Parnell's house.'

Dickie released his grip on the boy, relieved to know where his daughter was, and grateful that she was safe and unharmed. 'Has she seen anyone?'

'No, sir,' Tim replied, shaking his head. 'Only some bloke about the same age as you. He had a cane. She opened the shop for him, and they were in there for ages, but then he came out with a hat box, so I reckon he was a customer.'

'Good lad. Get back to Edna Street and do what I pay you to do,' he ordered the boy.

Back behind the steering wheel of his car, Dickie lit a big cigar. 'That girl will turn my hair grey,' he grumbled to Ernie. 'I can't have her staying out all night and not telling me. We'll be having words later.'

Sleep had evaded Grace. There hadn't been much room in the bed with Betty, though even if there had been, her mind wouldn't have let her rest. She'd been thinking about the wrongs her father had done, and when she wasn't thinking about him, sadness for John had filled her heart. It had come as a horrific shock to hear about Maud's death. When Betty had told her, Grace desperately regretted meeting John in the café, and wished she could have turned back time. She wondered how he was coping with fatherhood, especially without Maud by his side. And then her mind would return to harrowing thoughts about her father.

Approaching midday, and now in Clapham, Grace was pleased when she saw her father's car wasn't parked outside the house. Sneaking inside, she pulled out a suitcase from a large cupboard under the stairs and lugged it to her bedroom. Before she began packing her clothes, she sat at her dressing table, took a writing pad from a drawer, and penned a quick note to her grandmother. She explained that she'd moved out, and was temporarily staying with Betty, whilst she looked for somewhere to rent.

She'd leave the note in her grandmother's room, though it would be several weeks until Myrtle returned from her European trip. Grace knew her grandmother would be happy that Grace had finally left home.

Looking through her wardrobe, she realised she had far too many clothes, and rummaged for what she needed, folding the items and placing them neatly in her case. She glanced towards the window overlooking the extensive gardens. She wasn't upset about turning her back on her family home, but it didn't feel right to be leaving her mother behind.

As she clicked the locks on the case closed, Grace caught her breath when she heard a noise from downstairs. Padding quietly out of her bedroom, she leaned over the banisters and peered down to the hallway below. She saw her father's coat and hat on a peg and her heart sank. He was home, so now it would be impossible to leave unless she could sneak out of the door, though she thought it was a spineless way to escape.

Tip-toeing back into her bedroom, Grace collected her suitcase and the note to her grandmother. Myrtle had locked her bedroom door, so Grace pushed the folded piece of paper underneath. Then she crept towards the stairs. Her heart was hammering so loudly that she thought her father might hear it! Thankfully, sounds from his vinyl records floated up the stairs, and Grace pictured him sitting in his office with a brandy glass in his hand, smoking a cigar whilst listening to his music. Edging slowly down the stairs, she prayed she wouldn't step on a creaky floorboard!

Finally reaching the front door, Grace began to believe she'd get away undiscovered, but her body went rigid when she heard her father's dreaded voice.

'Grace ... Where are you going?'

Closing her eyes, her mind spinning, she turned to look at the man she'd once adored, who now left her disgusted. 'Hello, Papa. I didn't want to disturb you. I'm going away for a few days.'

'Was you going to tell me?'

'Like I said, I didn't want to disturb you. I was going to leave you a note.'

'So, where is the note?'

'I forgot about it. Sorry, Papa, it's just that I'm so excited!'

'Where is it you're going? And who with?'

'A short trip to Bedfordshire with Betty. Luton to be exact. It's a working trip, to visit the milliners. You know Luton is famous for hat-making.'

'That's a big case for a short trip.'

'You know me, Papa, I don't travel lightly.'

'And where were you last night?'

'I, erm, I stayed with Betty. We were making plans for the trip until late, and the weather was dreadful, so I stayed over. Sorry, I hope I didn't worry you?'

'You did. Don't do that again, Grace. I was worried sick and had the Old Bill looking for you. In future, you must inform me of your whereabouts.'

'Yes, of course, sorry, Papa. Anyway, I've got to dash, or we'll miss our train.'

Dickie's eyes narrowed, and Grace had the feeling he didn't believe her tale.

'Are you meeting Betty at the station?'

'Yes.'

'I'll drive you.'

'Thanks, Papa, but there's no need.'

'That case looks heavy. I can't have my girl hauling it on and off trams. It's no bother for me to drop you off. And on the way, you can give me the details of where you'll be staying and when I can expect you home.'

Grace could feel herself panicking and her pulse racing. 'Really, Papa, I can manage.'

'I can't pretend that I'm happy about you travelling out of London, so I'd still like to know where you'll be staying. I'll give the premises a call to make sure they look after you properly.'

'Please don't, Papa, that would be embarrassing.'

'Either that or you won't be going anywhere, my girl.'

Grace wracked her brains. She supposed she could give him a made-up name and address of a hotel. He wouldn't be able to call immediately. It would give her time to get away. 'All right,' she said, sighing. 'We'll be staying at the Regal on Luton High Road for two nights.'

'Do you have their telephone number?'

'No, Papa, I don't.'

'Then we shall make a stop at a telephone box on the way to the station, and the operator can put me through. The Regal on Luton High Road, you say?'

Grace nodded, feeling sick to the pit of her stomach. She knew her lies were going to be exposed. She'd dug herself a big hole and she had no idea how she was going to get out of it.

Dickie wasn't a stupid man. He hadn't got where he had through gullibility and ignorance. One of the things he prided himself on was his ability to see through bullshit. And as much as he hated to admit it, he sensed that Grace was feeding him a string of lies. Why? He wasn't sure, but he intended to get to the bottom of it.

After pulling on his coat, Dickie went to pick up Grace's case, but she was quick to protest.

'It's fine, I can carry it, thanks, Papa.'

Dickie's suspicions deepened. Grace never did anything for

herself if he was around to do it for her. 'Don't be daft,' he insisted, and grabbed it from her.

When he felt the weight of the case, he knew Grace hadn't packed for only a couple of days. Slamming the door closed, he turned to look at his daughter and could see she was anxious.

'What's really going on?' he asked, his voice low. Dickie wouldn't allow his daughter to make a fool of him, and his anger flared. Throwing the suitcase past Grace and along the hallway, it landed with a thud and broke open, spilling a lot of Grace's wardrobe across the floor.

Dickie looked at Grace for an explanation.

She pushed her chin out defiantly, and after a sharp intake of breath, she announced, 'I'm moving out.'

He tried to hide how incensed he felt, and told her calmly, 'No, Grace, you're not. You're staying right here where you belong.'

'I'm not a little girl anymore, Papa. If I choose to leave home, you can't stop me.'

'Is that right?' he smirked. 'All grown up, are ya? A woman of means?'

'Yes, I am. I can pay my own way.'

'I think you're forgetting something, Grace … Your boutiques belong to me. I own the freeholds on both properties, and if I choose, I can close both those shops.'

Grace glared at him with consternation. 'You wouldn't do that, would you? I've worked so hard to make the business profitable, and Betty would be out of a job … Please, Papa, it's not fair!'

'Life ain't fair, Grace, and I've never been a fair man. Pick your clothes up off the floor, take them back upstairs and put them away in your wardrobe, 'cos you ain't going nowhere, my girl.'

Grace stamped her foot, just like she'd done many times as a toddler. 'You can't do this to me!'

'I can, Grace, and I am. As of now, your boutiques are no longer trading. I'll give you a small allowance, you won't go without, but it won't be enough to pay rent anywhere. Oh, and another thing… If I find out you've stayed at Betty Parnell's house again, I'll burn the fuckin' place down. Got it?'

'What, like you burned down Jack Pope's shop? I know *everything* about you, Papa, and I hate you!'

Grace's voice had become a screech, and Dickie was pleased when she stamped up the stairs and out of earshot. She was having a tantrum, which he supposed was understandable. Calling up to her, he boomed, 'I'm doing you a favour, and one day you'll thank me for it. You can have all you want, Grace, and you don't have to work for it. You're a fortunate girl, very fortunate. It wouldn't hurt for you to show a bit of gratitude to your father.'

Grace's answer was to slam her bedroom door shut so hard that Dickie thought the plaster might fall off the walls. The girl had a temper, but she was a Newman, and he expected nothing less. He was sure she'd calm down eventually and he hoped she'd see the benefits of being a lady of leisure. All that mattered to Dickie was that Grace was home, and would be remaining at home for the foreseeable future. That way, he could keep a close eye on his daughter and ensure she was out of harm's way.

48

'You should get back to work,' John's mum encouraged. 'It'll do you good and will help to take your mind off things. It'll be better than moping around the house all day.'

John knew his mother meant well, and he thought she was probably right, but he lacked any motivation to get Dander's Deliveries back on the road. 'What's the point?' he asked glumly. 'I haven't got a wife to support.'

'You still have a daughter, John.'

'Have I? I haven't seen her since she was born. Maud's mum won't let me near her. I don't even know if she's been given a name!'

'This isn't on, and I've had enough of it! We've been considerate to Mrs Scarrow's feelings, but enough is enough. I'm going round there, and I'll rip the baby from her arms if I have to, but one way or another, your daughter is coming home!'

'No, Mum, I'll go.'

'You've been round there every day since Maud passed, and you've come back empty-handed. Bugger politeness! Mrs

Scarrow is going to get a piece of my mind, and I won't be leaving without my granddaughter!'

There was no point in John attempting to stop his mother. The woman could be like a dog with a bone when she wanted to be, and he could see she was more determined than ever. 'I'll come with you.'

'I'd rather you didn't, son. This could get nasty, and I don't want you involved.'

'What do mean?' John asked, concerned.

'I mean I'll do whatever it takes to bring your daughter home. Stay here, I won't be long.'

John sat in the kitchen, twiddling his thumbs as he waited for his mother to return. He had no doubt she'd have a baby in her arms. A myriad of thoughts cascaded through his mind. How could he continue with Dander's Deliveries and care for his daughter at the same time? And how were formula bottles made? Was it easy to change a nappy? He dreaded the idea of washing them! Would his daughter sleep through the night or keep the whole household awake with her cries? She'd require bathing and dressing; that felt daunting! Unanswerable questions tumbled through his mind, over and over, until his head began to thump.

He hadn't noticed the time pass, and as he walked to the sink to get a glass of water, his mother popped her head around the door, beaming with happiness.

'Your daughter would like a cuddle,' she smiled.

John grinned, overjoyed. 'You got her! Thanks, Mum, I can't believe it!'

'I told you I would. Mrs Scarrow knew she didn't have a leg to stand on. I've agreed that Maggie can go back to her in a couple of days, and we're going to discuss sharing the load of caring for her, so that you can go to work. Here you are then, take her.'

John couldn't wait to scoop his daughter from his mother's arms, but he felt nervous. Holding such a tiny baby didn't come naturally, though the moment he gazed down at her, his fears dissipated. 'She's beautiful, Mum,' he whispered. The image he'd had imprinted on his memory of the child he'd held in the hospital was different to how she looked now. 'I can't believe how much she's changed in such a short time.'

'Yeah, babies do that. Her eyes will change colour, too. They're blue now, but they might turn brown or green.'

'Hello, Maggie. I'm your daddy,' he said softly.

'You can change her name, if you like? She hasn't been registered yet.'

'I like Maggie, and I reckon Maud would have approved.'

Maggie became restless and started crying. 'What's wrong with her, Mum?' John asked, slightly panicked.

'Nothing, love. She'll need changing or feeding, that's all. There's a bag by the door with her bottles and formula. Mrs Scarrow was good enough to give me a few nappies an' all. Give me Maggie and fetch the bag. We'll soon have her in a good routine, but you'll need to get back to work, John. Maggie's going to need a pram and all sorts.'

As John handed his daughter to his mother, he was filled with pride and a renewed drive to make Dander's Deliveries a success. He had to. His daughter was relying on him.

'I've got the flu, Anna. I felt rough yesterday and told Neville that if I got any worse, then I'd take the day off.'

'Well, I hope you're not going to be too ill to go to work

for long. You don't get paid for being off sick, and we need every penny for our savings.'

'For Christ's sake, woman, give your mouth a bleedin' rest, will ya! Can't a man get a moment's peace from your incessant nagging, even when I'm sick!'

Anna sat on the edge of their bed and tutted as she slipped her feet into her shoes. 'You don't look that ill to me,' she snapped.

Gordon would have jumped out of the bed and given her a backhander if she wasn't carrying his child. His wife was getting too lippy again and needed putting in her place. Sitting upright, he reached across to her and grabbed her arm, pinching his fingers into her flesh. 'Just because I ain't moaning about how ropey I feel, doesn't mean I ain't ill. I tell you what, Anna, you're getting right on my wick, and I've had just about enough of you,' he ground out. 'Best you show me a bit more respect.'

Anna tried to yank her arm free, but Gordon dug his fingers in deeper. 'You're always trying to make me look small. What's the matter, Anna, don't you think I'm good enough for you? Sometimes you make me think that you regret marrying me. I love you, but I wonder if you love me. If you did, you wouldn't talk to me in the way you do.'

'Let go of my arm,' Anna spat.

'I'm right, ain't I?'

'You're hurting me, Gordon. Let go.'

Gordon was taken aback by his wife's response. Normally Anna would gush, saying how much she loved him and how sorry she was for making him feel that way. But this time, her face was hard. As he released her arm, Anna rose to her feet and walked out of the room. She didn't even glance back at him. Gordon had never seen Anna behave this way, and he worried he was losing control of her.

'Anna … Anna …' he shouted.

He was reassured when the door opened and she asked, 'What do you want?'

'Any chance of a cuppa before you go to work?' he asked. 'And a kiss?'

Anna walked towards the bed, though she didn't look happy. As she leaned over to give him a light peck, Gordon grabbed her and pulled her down on top of him. Holding her close, he murmured huskily, 'I love it when you're angry with me. You're so sexy, Anna.'

At last, she smiled, and he slipped his hand up her blouse. Pregnancy had swelled Anna's breasts, and as he rubbed her erect nipples, she pulled his hand away.

'We can't, Gordon. It wouldn't feel right, not with a baby in me.'

'Don't be silly. It won't hurt the baby.'

'I thought you were feeling poorly.'

'I was, but I feel loads better now,' he said, feeling his groin stirring. As he rolled her over onto her back, and ran his hand up her thigh, Gordon murmured in her ear, 'I'll always look after you and our kid. Now show me how much you love me.'

After their passionate lovemaking, Anna had rushed to her job at the hospital, moaning that she was going to be late. Gordon threw on his clothes and thoughts of Grace's demise filled his head. This might be his one chance, and Gordon was ready to take it.

Pulling his flat cap low, he shoved his hands into his trouser pockets and made his way to John's house. He was hoping that the fella was in the throes of grief and hadn't taken his truck out, so he was pleased when he saw Dander's Deliveries parked outside.

Gordon glanced up and down the street. There were too many people around. Housewives chalking their front steps, women in aprons gathered for a gossip, curtain twitchers, watching all the comings and goings. He'd guessed that daylight robbery of John's truck would be impossible without raising the alarm, so he continued with the next step of his sketchily thought-out plan. Knocking on John's door, he braced himself for a frosty greeting.

'Hello, mate,' he smiled, when John answered the door.

'What do you want?' the man asked, in an unfriendly manner.

'We're cousins by marriage and I thought that, given what's happened with Maud, it was time we buried the hatchet. I'm offering you a handshake, and my sincere condolences.'

Gordon held his hand out to John but was hastily rebuked.

'I don't want your handshake or your condolences.'

Gordon tried again. 'Can we make an effort, for Anna's sake?'

John shook his head, his face grim. 'Anna made her choice when she married you. Clear off, me and you will never be mates and you're not my cousin.'

The door closed in his face, leaving Gordon fuming. He'd been sure that John would accept the olive branch but had been proved wrong. Now his plan was scuppered. He'd have to rethink it. Come what may, Gordon would find a way to exact his revenge on Grace, though for today, she'd still be breathing the same air as him.

49

The morning sun streaming through the window woke Grace from a fretful sleep. Throwing her legs over the edge of the bed, a new day brought a new determination. Grace was going to make her father listen and hoped to change his mind.

Pulling on her dressing gown, she hurried down the stairs to catch him before he left for work.

Mrs Conners stood in the frame of the kitchen doorway. 'Good morning, Miss Newman. Scrambled eggs for breakfast?'

'No, nothing for me, thank you,' Grace replied. Her stomach was too knotted to consider eating food.

As expected, she found her father sitting at the dining room table mulling over the morning newspaper.

'I hope you've calmed down and seen reason,' he said, and sipped on a cup of coffee.

Grace pulled out a seat at the opposite end of the table and poured herself a cup before sitting down. 'We need to talk, Papa,' she said, forcing any aggression from her voice.

'If it's about the boutiques or you moving out, then I don't think there's much to add.'

'Don't you think you're being unreasonable?'

'No, Grace, I don't. Like I said, one day you'll thank me. You live in a grand house with staff, so you don't have to lift a finger, and now you don't have to work, either. You've got it made, my girl. Some might think I'm spoiling you, but I only want the best for you.'

Grace studied her father's face, astounded to see that he truly believed his words. There wasn't any malice in his eyes; he really did think he was doing what was right for her. Although Grace was deeply upset, she kept her tone level, knowing the only way she could win this battle was to play him at his own game. 'You're so good to me, Papa, and I'm grateful. But I enjoy working in my boutiques. I'd go mad with boredom if you took them away from me. Please reconsider, it would mean the world to me.'

Dickie folded the newspaper and placed it on the table beside his breakfast plate, and then smiled across at Grace. But his smile didn't reach his eyes, and Grace had a sinking feeling.

'You're good, Grace, but you've learned from the best – me. I'm the world's greatest schemer, and I know a scam when I see one. There's only one reason why you want your shops to stay open, and that's so you'll have money of your own, and then you'll up and leave me. I'm sorry, Grace, but it ain't happening.'

'Why, Papa? I don't understand. Why are you being so mean?'

Dickie drew in a long breath. He sounded exasperated, but Grace wasn't going to give in without an explanation.

'Please, Papa. It's not fair on Betty, either. She relies on my boutique to help her mother pay the rent.'

'I've always told you that I'm not a charity. If Betty is as smart as you're always telling me, then she'll easily find herself another job.'

'At least she's allowed to! What about me? How will I fill my days? You say you want the best for me, but you're ruining my life!'

'I haven't got time for this, Grace, and your whining is doing my head in. It's an ugly world out there, and I'm doing everything I can to protect you from it. I'm your father and it's my job to keep you safe. So forget any childish notions you might have about running away, 'cos I've got people watching the house and you. If you're bored, find a hobby. Do art classes or music lessons, I dunno, I'm sure you'll find something to occupy your time, but that's an end to this now. I'm going to work, I'll see you tonight.'

As he went to leave the room, Grace asked, 'Am I permitted to have friends visit me?'

'You're not a bloody prisoner, Grace. You can come and go as you please, and invite whoever you want round. I'm sorry if you can't see the benefits of it right now, but you won't be working anywhere. Not in your shops or for anyone else. I forbid it, and just remember, I'll know your every move.'

Grace stared down at the table. Their discussion hadn't gone as she'd hoped. He'd said she wasn't a prisoner, but she felt like one. The situation felt more hopeless than ever, and Grace was desperate to get away from him. But how? It seemed impossible, and she thought she might be trapped in the house with her father forever.

At around midday, Mrs Conners informed Grace that she had a visitor. Grace ran down the stairs from her bedroom, hoping to find Betty, and flew into her arms when she saw her friend.

'I've been so worried about you,' Betty whispered. 'I went

to the shop, but the window has been painted over. What's going on?'

'Come outside to the garden. I don't want Mrs Conners hearing anything, because I wouldn't be surprised if my father is paying her to spy on me.'

Sitting on a bench in the mild sun, Grace noticed Betty's eyes flitting around the garden.

'She's under the oak tree,' Grace said, flicking her head towards her mother's unmarked grave.

'Sorry,' Betty cringed. 'Was I that obvious?'

'Yeah, but I would have been the same if the shoe was on the other foot.'

'Are you all right?'

Grace shook her head. 'No, not really. I'm sorry, Betty, but my father has closed the boutiques. You're out of a job.'

'Oh, don't worry about that,' Betty reassured her. 'I'm very employable. I won't have a problem finding work. But why has he done that? And how? I thought you owned the shops.'

'Hmm, so did I. It didn't occur to me that the buildings belong to my father. I never really gave it any thought. Anyway, he's taken the boutiques away from me to stop my income, which means I won't be able to afford to move out. He's got me trapped.'

'Well, I don't think he's thought it through very well. What's to stop you finding employment elsewhere? We could look together; it would be such fun! We'll look up town, in Liberty or Fenwick or something equally as posh.'

The idea appealed to Grace and her voice dripped with disappointment when she answered, 'I can't. Papa has forbidden me to work, and he has people watching me.'

'You've got to be kidding me?'

'No, Betty, I wish I was. I can't stand being stuck here with him, but I don't know what I can do.'

They sat quietly wrapped in their own thoughts for a while, and then Betty said, 'You'll have to go to the police, Grace. It's the only way you'll ever escape him, and he should be doing time for what he's done. He could keep my dad company,' she chuckled.

'I've told you, the police won't help. He's always bragging about how he's corrupted the top coppers in London.'

'If you say so, but no matter how much he's paying them, the Old Bill can't turn a blind eye to … you know …' Betty said, nodding towards the ground under the oak tree.

Grace suspected Betty had made a good point. 'Even if the police would arrest my father for his part in burying my mother over there, how would I get to the police station and tell them? I'm being watched. My father would know, and I dread to think of the consequences.'

'Can you sew?' Betty asked.

'No, why?'

'I've got a stonker of an idea! It'll work, I know it will!'

'Tell me, I'm dying to know.'

'Well …' Betty said, grinning. 'I shall have to drag out my sewing machine. Lucky for you, I'm a dab hand at dress-making, not like little rich girl here, who's probably never had to sew a garment in her life.'

Betty playfully elbowed Grace in the ribs.

'I don't even know how to thread a needle,' Grace admitted.

'Never mind. Let's go to your room. We're going to select an outfit and I'm going to make an exact replica.'

'Why? I don't understand.'

'I shall wait in the underground toilets on Bog Island, you

know where I mean, just across the road from Arding and Hobbs, and I'll be wearing an outfit that looks the same as yours. You go down to the toilet, I'll have a bag down there ready. There'll be a change of clothes and even a wig. You'll leave in a disguise and go straight to the police station, I'll come out of the toilets looking like you, and it's me who will be followed.'

Grace gasped. 'That's genius! Do you really think we can pull it off?'

'I don't see why not.'

'You're several inches taller than me and much slimmer.'

'That's easily remedied. I'll ask my friend to help. Gerty is about the same size as you and I'm sure she'll pull it off.'

'I don't want to put anyone at risk. If my father were to find out…'

'He won't, how could he? The only people who'll be in trouble are the ones following you, because they'll be following the wrong person.'

Grace clapped her hands together, quietly squealing, 'You're so clever, Betty! But if Gerty is about my size, then we could just swap clothes. If I can get to the police station unnoticed, I hope the police act on the information I give them. It feels wrong to be sending my father to prison, but if I don't, he'll ruin so many more lives.'

50

6th May 1935

Gordon woke late on Monday morning, stretching his arms and yawning as his eyes fell on Anna. She was sitting at the dressing table, brushing her hair, already dressed in her best clothes and smiling.

Looking at Gordon through the reflection in the mirror, she greeted him, 'Good morning, sleepy-head.'

'What's the time?' he asked.

'Time you were out of bed and getting your good clobber on. Aren't you excited?'

'No, I can't say I am. I don't know why we're celebrating King George V being on the throne for twenty-five years, but I'm not complaining about the bank holiday.'

'It's going to be a big street party today, maybe not as big as the one on Orville Road, but Mum took her tablecloths this morning. She said it's all looking smashing. The trestle tables are up, there's red, white and blue bunting everywhere and she said she saw a couple of people wheeling pianos along the road. Mum's making some iced buns and I'm going to prepare a plate of sandwiches. Mrs Stanford next door has made a few bowls of Jubilee chicken. Everyone's pooling their food, it's going to be wonderful, and I'm looking forward to trying the chicken. Oh, Gordon, I can't wait!'

Gordon sniffed. He didn't like the idea of Anna fraternising with all and sundry at the street party, but today's Silver Jubilee celebrations were going to be the perfect distraction for him to carry out his plan. Pretending to be interested, he asked, 'What's Jubilee chicken?'

'Chicken in mayonnaise and curry powder.'

'Sounds bleedin' awful. I'll tell you what though, Anna, it's a shame the baby ain't due for a while. They're giving out silver commemorative cups to all the kids born today.'

'I've a long way to go yet. Come on, Gordon, can you get up and dressed, please? Me and mum need you to help us take some stuff out.'

'Can't your dad help?'

'He's already there and has been putting up the decorations. There's a big white sheet hanging up, I don't know who painted it, but it's ever so nice and it congratulates the King and Queen.'

Gordon rolled his eyes. 'A lot of fuss over nothing. There are millions of blokes up North out of work, starving, living rough. I don't suppose they're celebrating. Poor buggers. Do you know the government inspects their houses before they can get any welfare help? It's bloody humiliating for them.'

'Since when have you cared about the unemployed?'

'I'm just saying, all this Jubilee fuss is a joke, that's all.'

'Please don't ruin today for me, Gordon,' Anna asked, pouting.

'I won't. Bring me up a cup of tea and I'll get dressed.'

Gordon wasn't the least bit excited about the first ever

celebrated Silver Jubilee, but he was excited to be finally dishing out his just deserts to Grace. And best of all, he knew that hurting Grace would hurt Dickie, too!

It had felt like an eternity, but today, at last, Grace was going to escape her father's clutches and get justice for her mother's untimely and brutal death. She wasn't concerned about the cunning scheme that Betty had meticulously thought through. But she was worried that the police wouldn't act on the information she was going to give them. If her father wasn't arrested and charged, then Grace would be trapped with him forever, and that reality was too horrendous to consider.

Over the breakfast table, she didn't allow her nerves to show. 'Betty will be here soon. We're looking forward to the parties today,' she said brightly.

'Where are you going?'

'We're not sure yet. Betty thinks we should have a wander around Battersea and join in every party we find.'

'Just so long as you behave yourself and get home here by nine.'

'Ten?' Grace pushed. 'Please, Papa, it's such a special day.'

'All right, ten, but don't be late. Do you and Betty want me to drop you off?'

'That would be great, thanks, Papa. Betty can leave her bicycle here and I can ride it back to her tomorrow.'

'You? On a bike?' Dickie scoffed.

'Yes, why not?'

'Have you ever ridden a bicycle, Grace?'

'No, but it can't be that difficult. Everyone rides them. I see hundreds of people going to work in the factories on their bicycles, and if children can ride them, then I'm sure I can.'

'I'll drop her bicycle off to her tomorrow, save you an injury.'

Grace stood up from the table and twirled. 'Do you like my outfit for today?' she asked, swishing her red skirt.

'Very fetching. And the colours are appropriate.'

'I thought so too, Papa. Red skirt, white blouse and blue jacket. I'm sure King George would approve.'

A while later, at eleven o' clock, Grace heard knocking on the front door and knew it would be Betty. Her heart skipped a beat. Today was so important, and now it was beginning to feel real.

'Come in,' Grace greeted her. 'Papa's going to drive us to Battersea, and he'll drop your bicycle back to you tomorrow morning.'

Betty's eyes widened. 'That's kind of him,' she said, sounding unsure.

Dickie came out from his office. 'Are you ready to leave, ladies?'

'Yes. Today is going to be the best day,' Grace exclaimed.

In the car, she could see that Betty was feeling uneasy.

'Grace tells me you're working back at Arding and Hobbs,' Dickie said, addressing Betty.

'Yes, Mr Newman, I am. Though there wasn't a position available in fashion, so I'm working in the housewares department, but I hope to be in fashion soon.'

'You can drop us here, Papa, on Lavender Hill. We can walk and it's such a bright morning.'

As Dickie pulled up to the kerb, they climbed out of the car and Grace was sure that her father didn't suspect anything. She looked around, wondering if she was being followed, and saw the young boy on his bike. *He won't be much of a challenge*, she thought.

Dickie drove away and Betty looped her arm through Grace's.

'It's all in place,' Betty said. 'Gerty will be in the toilets at midday. You're to exchange clothes with her, and don't forget to wear the wig. How are you feeling?'

'I'm not worried about this part, but I'm not convinced the police will take me seriously.'

'What will you do if they don't arrest your father?'

'I've no idea, Betty. I haven't thought that far ahead. One step at a time.'

The shops on Lavender Hill were closed, but there was plenty of activity around. Many children were in fancy dress and there was a delightful buzz in the air. It seemed that all of Battersea was in the party spirit.

'Is anyone spying on us?' Betty asked.

'I think so. The young boy on the bicycle is paid by my father, and I've noticed a fella on the other side of the road. Stop at the next shop window and pretend to have a look. We'll check for his reflection and see what he does.'

Grace oohed and ahhed at the window display, and she saw the man on the other side of the road stop and light a cigarette. 'Yes, he's following me, too,' she said quietly to Betty.

'That's fine. He'll be following Gerty soon.'

Ambling slowly down the hill towards Clapham Junction, Grace tried to act relaxed. 'Is it nearly time?'

'Yes. Let's hurry. At least the lad and that man won't be able to follow us into the ladies' toilets.'

They passed a large group of Girl Guides, smartly dressed in their uniforms and carrying large Union Jacks. Cheers and laughter sounded from many of the street parties, and merriment abounded, though not for Grace. Her heart pounded as she crossed the street to a central island with a small dome in the middle. Two young girls were climbing on the dome and sliding off, probably waiting for their mother to return from the Victorian under-street public toilets.

Grace descended the stairs to the ladies', noticing the clean white tiled walls. Betty followed. Down below the street, Betty went to a sink and washed her hands.

'Where's Gerty?' Grace asked.

'I'm here,' a voice said.

Grace saw a young woman emerge from a cubicle, carrying a cheap cloth bag.

'Here,' said Gerty, handing her the bag. 'Go in there and get changed, then throw your clothes over the top to the toilet next door, and I'll throw mine to you.'

'As quick as you can,' Betty urged.

Grace garbled a quick thank you to Gerty. She'd never met the woman and couldn't believe that a stranger would do this for her. Five minutes later, Grace came out of the toilet and looked in the mirror. Gerty came out soon after.

'We're definitely going to pull this off!' Betty beamed. 'Come on, Gerty. I'm going to call you Grace from now on. Let's go and party, *Grace*.'

'Good luck,' Grace called quietly, as the women walked away. She glanced again at her reflection. The blonde wig didn't suit her, and the clothes were a little tight, and far scruffier than Grace would normally wear. They'd even exchanged shoes, and Grace found that Gerty's pinched. But none of that mattered now.

She counted to twenty and climbed the stairs back up to

the street. Arding and Hobbs department store loomed tall, shadowing the smaller buildings around it. Grace covertly searched the streets, her eyes probing the small crowds. She couldn't see the boy and his bicycle, or the man who'd been close on their heels. Betty's plan had worked! Her father's spies were now following Betty and Gerty.

Grace hurried and headed for the police station. This could be her one and only chance to bring her father down. She didn't want to see him caged behind bars, but he deserved to be in prison. Battersea would be a better place without him, and her mother could finally rest in peace.

51

John walked by his mother's side as she pushed Maggie in a pram.

'See this, Maggie. You're watching history being made,' he said to his daughter.

'You daft bugger,' his mother smiled, 'she can't understand a word you're saying, and she won't remember any of this.'

'I know. I wish her mum was here to see it. Maud loved a party.'

'She did, and I reckon she's here, John, and would be proud to see Maggie's pram decorated with the flags. You did a lovely job.'

Rows of excited children sat at tables laden with goodies and there were even some vases of freshly cut flowers. His mother and the residents of their street had worked hard to organise the street party, and as his mother looked around, John saw her eyes fill with tears.

'What's wrong?' he asked.

'Nothing. I'm knackered, but it's been worth it to see the smiles on the kiddies' faces. Folk on our street haven't got much, John, but look how happy everyone is.'

'You did well, Mum. I'm going to get myself a beer. Do you want a glass of sherry?'

'Yeah, a large one,' she said, and winked.

John greeted his neighbours as he made his way through the throng of people. Mrs Sands was wearing a large, cardboard crown, and Mrs Willow had sewn flags to her apron. A sprinkling of light rain began to fall, but it wasn't dampening the spirits of the merrymakers. Mr Gately poured John a glass of beer directly from a wooden keg. 'Long live the King,' he cheered, raising his glass aloft, and the men and women around him chorused, 'Long live the King.' Someone had a battery wireless and had tuned into a station playing lively jazz music. John watched with pleasure as Mr and Mrs Bamber jumped down from a garden wall and began dancing. He thought of Maud, of holding her in his arms and swaying to the beat of the tune. Maud had enjoyed dancing and singing. She'd had a zest for life that he hoped Maggie would have, too. Thoughts of his departed wife were always punctuated with thoughts of Grace. He realised he had no idea if she liked to sing and dance. They'd been to the picture house quite a few times, and had shared many pots of tea, but they hadn't known each other for long. John wished he could escape from his thoughts of her. The images of Grace that flashed through his mind always left him feeling guilty. He should never have met her behind Maud's back. He didn't believe that his disloyalty had caused Maud's death. The doctor had explained that her heart had been weak. But he felt awful knowing that Maud had died feeling betrayed instead of loved. He'd never rid himself of the guilt and deep remorse.

⋆

Gordon had managed to slip away from Anna. With the chaos of the street party in full swing, and the drinks flowing, it had been easy to lose himself in the crowd. In a rush, he headed towards John's house, which was just a few streets away.

As he'd expected, the street where John lived was throwing their own party, and the Dander's Deliveries truck had been moved out of the way. Gordon had to find it and avoid being seen by John or his mother.

Darting around a corner, on a quiet and narrow street, Gordon saw the truck. Now he had to get the keys, which he thought would be straightforward. After all, everyone was busy enjoying themselves and most houses were empty.

He leapt over the wall into John's back yard. It was a small, paved area with an outbuilding that housed the toilet. He peered through the kitchen window before trying the handle on the back door. It opened, which wasn't a surprise. Most folk left their doors unlocked. Gordon never would. He'd never give a thief an open invitation, but thanks to people's trust, he'd easily stolen valuable items from several homes.

It felt strange walking through the silence of John's house. He was an intruder, which wasn't a comfortable feeling. It hadn't bothered him when he'd been inside the homes of Neville's customers on the window cleaning round. It was different being here though, in the house of someone he knew. He was grateful that John's father had made it to the party outside. The man wasn't good on his legs since the stroke.

Gordon rummaged in the kitchen drawers, searched the table tops, looked in the sideboard, but he couldn't find the keys for John's truck. Dashing up the stairs, he hoped to find them in the man's bedroom. And there they were, sitting on a cupboard beside the bed. Snatching up the keys, he ran to the back door, through the yard, over the wall and to the truck.

Sitting behind the steering wheel, it suddenly occurred to him that he had no idea where Grace was. Cursing to himself, he realised he'd put so much thought into stealing the truck that he'd forgotten to consider where to find Grace. When the idea had first popped into his head of how to get his revenge on her, she'd been working in her boutique, and he'd known exactly where to find her. For reasons unknown to him, the shop had closed. Stupidly, Gordon now was clueless about her whereabouts, and he could have kicked himself! One thing he was sure of, she'd be out with Betty Parnell, and probably locally, so that would be as good a place as any to look for her.

Turning the key to start the engine, Gordon sucked in a deep breath. He'd never driven a vehicle before, though he'd watched Dickie doing it many times. There was talk about a mandatory driving test being introduced next month, but it wasn't compulsory yet.

The engine revved, and Gordon found the correct gear before setting off. The ride was bumpy at first and he stalled the truck a few times, but he soon picked up the knack of driving, growing in confidence as he skilfully navigated corners.

Along York Road, it wasn't long before he was close to where Betty Parnell lived. With one eye on the road, he kept another peeled for Grace. Frustration burned inside as he realised that finding her would be like finding a needle in a haystack, though Gordon was determined and wouldn't give up at the first hurdle. After all, he'd been clever enough to steal John's truck unnoticed. He hoped that luck was on his side.

'Where are you?' he muttered angrily. 'Come on, woman, show yourself.'

Many streets were inaccessible, filled with revellers and even some small parades. He circled around again, coming back onto the main road. *She could be anywhere*, he thought, *and might not even be out with Betty in Battersea.* Over half an hour passed, and Gordon noticed the fuel gauge needle had dropped. 'Come on,' he shouted, banging the steering wheel with the flat of his hand. 'Where the fuckin' 'ell are you, Grace!'

Furious, Gordon knew he'd have to return the truck soon, before it ran out of fuel and before anyone noticed it was missing. On the verge of giving up on his quest to find Grace, he pulled over. He was wasting his time searching for her. Battersea was a big place, and she may have stayed in Clapham or gone up town to visit Buckingham Palace. He knew that huge crowds would have gathered to get a rare glimpse of King George and Queen Mary. It wasn't his cup of tea, he couldn't give two hoots about the monarchy, but he could imagine Grace standing in the crowds, thinking she was bloody royalty, too!

Gordon's fists clenched, and he snarled. 'Bitch!' he spat, though he was more angry with himself. *You're a dumb idiot*, he thought, staring ahead through the windscreen. As he was about to pull out from the kerb, two women caught his eye. He could hardly believe what he was seeing, but it was definitely Betty Parnell. The woman stood inches taller than most women, she was easy to spot in a crowd. And lo and behold, Grace bleedin' Newman was walking beside her.

'Hah! Thank you, Lord,' Gordon grinned. 'Gotcha!'

He pressed hard on the accelerator pedal, the smell of rubber tyres burning on the tarmac as the truck screeched forward.

Grace and Betty stepped off the pavement, crossing the main road towards Battersea High Street. Gordon aimed the truck directly at them. His arms rigid, his eyes wide, he kept his foot pressed firmly down on the accelerator as the engine roared and the truck gained speed.

Just feet away from them, Betty was closest to him, and she turned her head. For the briefest of seconds, their eyes met, and he saw her terrified expression. Her mouth opened and Betty screamed, though Gordon couldn't hear her horror over the sound of the engine. At the moment of impact, he braced himself, closing his eyes as he went to mow down the women. He expected a terrific thud, maybe their bodies would bounce over the top of the truck, but there was nothing. Opening his eyes, he hit the brakes hard and, glancing sideways, he saw Betty and Grace on the ground, both dazed and scrambling to get back on to their feet. People were beginning to bunch around them. Fingers were pointing towards the truck, and three men began running towards him.

Gordon revved the engine again and sped away from the scene, angry and sorely disappointed. Betty must have pushed Grace clear of the truck. His chance to destroy her had been foiled.

There was only one compensation – John Dander would be blamed for the attempted hit-and-run. The man's name was clearly displayed on the truck. A scorned lover, lost in grief, John had motive. Gordon hoped Betty hadn't recognised him, and if she had, he'd simply deny it. He'd been with

Anna at the time of the crime. His wife would give him a solid alibi. No one could prove he'd been driving the truck. He'd got away with murder before when he'd accidentally killed Louisa Newman, and there was no reason to think he wouldn't get away with this.

But it wasn't over yet. He'd get rid of Grace one way or another. And next time, he wouldn't fail.

52

A bright, bare lightbulb hung low over a desk, illuminating the otherwise windowless room. Grace sat with her hands on her lap beneath the desk, trying to keep from fidgeting nervously. She glanced at the uniformed officer standing in the corner of the small room near the closed door. His eyes were fixed ahead and his face stony. She wondered if he knew her father and was one of the coppers who would, for a small fee, turn a blind eye to Dickie's activities.

The door opened and two plain-clothed detectives returned. Sitting opposite her, the younger of the two took a cigarette from a packet and offered her one.

'No, thank you,' Grace declined.

As he struck a match and lit his cigarette, the older detective opened his small notebook and glanced at his scribblings.

'So, Miss Newman, we just need to go over this one more time.'

'I've told you everything there is to tell. Are you going to arrest my father and Gordon Moss or not?'

The detectives exchanged a glance, but Grace couldn't read their thoughts.

'As it happens, Miss Newman, we're looking for them and they'll be brought in for questioning, but we can't charge them without evidence.'

'The evidence is in my back garden!'

'Yes, yes, we know, and there are officers ready to search the area. I'd like to know why you haven't come forward sooner?'

'I was too afraid. I'd seen what they'd done to my mother, so I feared for my life. Do you know my father? Have you got any idea what the man is capable of?'

The older detective coughed and shifted in his seat. 'Yes, Miss Newman, I know your father. If, as you say, you've been living in fear for your life, why have you spoken out now?'

'I haven't wanted to be responsible for putting my father behind bars, and it's taken me a while to come to terms with it. But I realise that they shouldn't be allowed to get away with what they've done. Please, Detective, you must see how difficult it is for me to do this.'

Grace sucked in a long breath of musty air. The room smelt damp, and of old paper. Boxes of files sat on floor-to-ceiling wooden shelves behind her.

'We can't keep you here, Miss Newman, but I strongly suggest that, for your own protection, you remain in the police station for now. It's not the most comfortable of places, but Constable Innings will fetch you a cup of tea.'

Grace nodded. She didn't want to be at home whilst the police dug up her mother's grave, and she was grateful that her grandmother wasn't around to witness it. 'I'll stay until my father has been charged and locked away in a police cell.'

*

Dickie heard loud banging on the front door and went to the window to look outside. He wasn't expecting anyone, and was surprised to see two police cars in the street. When he opened the door, two plain-clothed detectives stepped forward, flanked by four uniformed officers.

'What do you want?' he growled.

'We don't want any trouble, Newman. We'd like you to accompany us to the police station for questioning.'

'What about?'

'Your wife, Louisa Newman.'

'My wife? She walked out years ago. If she's got herself in trouble with you lot, then it's nothing to do with me.'

'I'm sure we can clear this up quickly, if you'd come with us.'

'No, I won't. Either arrest me or piss off!'

The detective looked at his colleague, who gave a short nod, and then said, 'As you wish. You're nicked, Newman.' Stepping aside, he ordered a constable, 'Cuff him.'

Dickie laughed. 'You're making a big mistake.'

'Well, we'll see about that when we dig up your back garden.'

'Your Chief Inspector will have something to say about this. We're good friends, so you ladies can kiss goodbye to your jobs.'

The younger detective smirked. 'Right you are, so that'll be Chief Inspector Crawford? Yeah, I can't say I'm surprised you know him. Crawford is under investigation for accepting bribes, but I'm sure you know all about that shady side of his work. So when we dig up your wife, you needn't think you'll be getting off with just a caution.'

The older detective added, 'And I'll be making sure that you won't be standing in front of Judge Hewitson, 'cos we all know he's as bent as Crawford.'

Dickie's top lip curled, and he snarled, 'Whatever you think you're gonna find, you can't pin nothing on me.'

'Is that right? We'll see about that.'

Being led away in handcuffs was an undignified experience for Dickie. He'd always thought of himself as above the law. As the police car drove off with Dickie in the back, a demoralising heaviness weighed on him. It wouldn't take the police long to find Louisa, and once they did, Dickie knew his life as he knew it would be changed forever. His mind turned. How did the Old Bill know? Someone must have told them, but who? His first thought was Gordon, but he didn't believe even Gordon would be that foolish. After all, if Gordon snitched, he'd be implicating himself in murder. It couldn't be Myrtle, as she wasn't in the country, and Grace would never have put him in this situation.

Dickie couldn't envisage how he was ever going to be a free man again, especially without Chief Inspector Crawford's protection. Only one thought gave him any peace of mind – Grace would be financially secure. He could rely on Ernie and continue to run his business from behind bars, even keep an eye on Grace, too. And though he'd miss her terribly, she would visit him. His daughter was the only light at the end of a very dark tunnel.

After returning John's truck to where he'd found it, and slipping the keys back into the house, Gordon minced along the street, acting casually as he mingled with the party revellers.

'Where have you been?' Anna asked. 'I've been looking everywhere for you.'

'I had a bit of a dicky tummy. I've been sat on the privy for ages.'

'Oh no, are you feeling better?'

'Yeah, I think so. I could do with a drink. Get us a beer.'

Anna jumped to do his bidding, and Gordon looked around, smiling, pretending to be enjoying himself. He'd failed miserably in his mission to damage or even end Grace's life, but at least he wouldn't be held responsible for the *accident*. He pictured John's face when the police questioned him about Dander's Deliveries, the reckless driving and possibly the attempted murder of two women. Gordon didn't particularly wish John any harm; the bloke was just incidental damage. He didn't really understand what the term meant, but he'd heard Dickie use it often. Yes, John was incidental damage, and though Gordon's plan had failed, he was feeling smug, and thought the use of the Dander's Deliveries truck had been a stroke of genius. So when he saw several coppers milling through the crowds, and when one pointed directly at him, Gordon didn't panic.

Anna came to stand beside him, holding a tankard of beer. 'What's going on?' she asked quietly, sounding alarmed.

Gordon shrugged. 'No idea, but I ain't done nothing wrong, so there's no need to worry.'

'Are you sure, Gordon?'

'Yeah, I'm sure.'

As the coppers surrounded him, two fellas without uniforms pushed through. Gordon assumed they were detectives, and with his chin jutting forward, he looked them up and down jeeringly. Then he glanced around at the police in uniforms, and said, 'Only the kids are supposed to have come to the party wearing fancy dress costumes.'

Po-faced, one of the detectives asked, 'Gordon Moss?'

'I might be. But then again, I might not be. You're a

detective, you work it out.' His cocky manner concealed the fact that Gordon was beginning to feel anxious. He'd been sure he'd got away with today's incident, but there were a lot of police around him, more than he would have expected to turn up to question him about a road accident.

The music and laughter had stopped, replaced by nosey whispers and quiet gasps.

Anna reached out her hand and slipped it into his. He could hear her soft whimpers, and though he couldn't look at her, Gordon knew she was crying. He squeezed her hand, hoping to reassure her.

'Gordon Moss, I'm arresting you for the murder of Louise Newman.'

Gordon felt his insides churn. This was the last thing he'd expected. 'Leave off,' he argued. 'You can't do this ... my missus is pregnant ... you're upsetting her. I ain't murdered no one, this is a set-up!'

As a uniformed policeman tried to place handcuffs on him, Anna refused to let go of his hand.

'Get off him!' she shouted. 'He hasn't killed anyone! You can't take him!'

Another policeman gently but firmly pulled her away, and Anna ran into her mother's arms, sobbing.

As Gordon was dragged away and led to a police car, he looked behind and met Anna's eyes. 'I'm sorry ... they've got it wrong. I'll see you soon, I promise.'

'I wouldn't count on it,' the detective said, 'the only thing you'll be seeing are the gallows.'

53

When the door opened, Grace stood from her seat expectantly. 'Did you find my mother?' she asked the detective.

'Yes, Miss Newman. The remains of a body were located in the garden.'

'Have you arrested my father and Gordon?'

'They're both in police custody. You're free to leave. We'll want to speak to you again, and probably take another statement from you.'

'Fine. I'll do whatever is necessary to keep my father locked up. He won't be released, will he?'

'No, Miss Newman. Mr Newman and Mr Moss will be held on remand until the case comes to court.'

'That's good to know.'

'Constable Innings will show you out.'

Grace kept her head down as she followed the policeman through the station. It was a stark place, and though there were now a few women officers working in the force, Grace didn't see any. At the end of a long and dimly lit corridor, she was about to walk around a corner when she heard Gordon's unmistakable voice.

'I didn't do it, I tell ya, I'm not a murderer!'

Grace felt her body go rigid and her stomach tighten. His words were slurred; she assumed he must be drunk. Looking back, she saw two policemen hauling Gordon towards the area she'd seen marked as cells. He was thrashing his head, pulling against the policemen, spittle coming from his mouth as he protested his innocence. When his wild eyes fell on Grace, he became instantly still.

'You!' he spat. 'I should have known it was you!'

Grace stood statue-like. She'd never seen such hatred in anyone's eyes. Fear crept through her. If Gordon was found innocent or was released from custody, she knew her life would be in danger.

As the police dragged him away, his shouts echoed through the corridors.

'I'll get you for this, Grace Newman! You're dead … Do you hear me? You're fuckin' dead!'

Police Constable Innings beckoned. 'This way,' he urged.

Grace was trembling, and her legs had turned to jelly. The quiet policeman, who'd barely spoken more than a couple of words, must have noticed her fearful state.

'Don't worry about him, Miss Newman. He won't be seeing the light of day for a long time to come, if ever.'

'Thank you.'

'My shift is about to finish. Can I get you a cup of tea in the café up the road? I'd like to walk you home and make sure you're all right.'

Grace peered at the constable, unsure of what to say. She didn't know if he was being kind or if there was more to his motives. 'I don't mean to offend, and I hope I haven't got the wrong end of the stick. Thank you for your offer, but

I'm not in the right frame of mind to consider a cup of tea with a man.'

PC Innings's face reddened. 'God, what was I thinking? Please accept my apologies, Miss Newman, that was thoughtless of me.'

Grace hadn't noticed before now, but she thought PC Innings had a kind face, and his mannerisms were gentle. He was attractive, with light-brown hair and almost-green eyes, though he looked very flustered.

'Actually, there's no need to apologise. You've distracted me and now I feel much calmer. I think I could do with a good cup of tea. The stuff you drink in this place is like dishwater. But won't the café be closed?'

'The only day Mr Elkins closes his café is on Christmas Day. It's a bit of a greasy spoon, but he does serve up a good cuppa.'

A short while later, sitting in the café under the watchful eye of Mr Elkins, Grace ordered her second cup of tea. She found PC Innings's company charming and told him about how she'd escaped her father's spies.

'That's a stroke of genius. Your friend Betty should be working for the Special Branch of our police force,' he chuckled.

'And talking of Betty, I really should update her. She'll be desperate for news.'

'May I walk with you?'

'Yes, PC Innings, you may.'

'Please, call me Norman. And if you'll accept an invitation to a dance on Saturday evening, may I call you Grace?'

'You can call me Grace.'

'Does that mean you'll accept my invitation?'

'I will, Norman, thank you. I must warn you; I've never

been to a dance. I hope you have sturdy boots, because I fear I might be trampling on your feet.'

It took some time to walk to Betty's house, though Grace didn't mind. She was enjoying getting to know Norman better, and the streets were filled with folk in high spirits, creating a gay atmosphere. She felt relaxed and carefree, no longer under her father's oppressive rule.

'This is Betty's house,' she said, sad to be saying goodbye to Norman. 'Thank you for walking with me.'

'It was a pleasure. I'll call for you at six on Saturday, and I'll be wearing my police issue boots,' Norman replied jokingly.

'I don't think I can face going home yet. It's too upsetting to think of my mother's grave being empty. I'll stay here with Betty for a while. Call for me here.'

'Would Betty care to join us? I can bring a friend with me, so she wouldn't feel like a spare part.'

'That's a smashing idea. I'm sure Betty will agree. See you on Saturday.'

After saying goodbye, Grace took a moment to collect her thoughts. Her head was in turmoil. Her father behind bars at her hands, her mother's body in the morgue, Gordon's threats, and Norman, who seemed to be the perfect gentleman and through all the horridness, he'd made her laugh.

Grace knocked on the door, eager to tell Betty everything. When Betty pulled the front door open, Grace's eyes almost popped out on stalks.

'We had a bit of an accident,' Betty explained. 'Come in.'

'What on earth happened?' Grace asked, as she followed her friend to the kitchen.

'Sit down, do you want a cuppa?'

'No, thanks, I've had so much tea, I feel like an urn. What

happened to you, Betty? That's a nasty graze on your cheek and you've got a lump on your forehead the size of an egg!'

Betty pulled out a chair and sat adjacent to Grace, shaking her head. 'Just tell me one thing,' she said. 'Has Gordon been arrested?'

'Yes.'

'Good. That lunatic needs locking away. He tried to kill me, Grace, me and Gerty, but he must have thought Gerty was you.'

'What? How?'

'He tried to knock us down. I've heard that your life flashes before your eyes before you die, but I never believed it until today. Gordon drove straight for us. He wanted to run the truck over us. I heard the engine and looked round. I don't know how, but I managed to push Gerty out the way and we both took a tumble. He wasn't going to stop, Grace. A second later and I swear I'd be dead, and Gerty, too.'

'Blimey! We must go to the police.'

'Yes, I will, and there are several witnesses who are willing to talk to the police about what they saw, but I wanted to hear from you first. The thing is, Grace … Gordon was driving John's truck. You can't miss Dander's Deliveries written on the side. And I know it was Gordon because I looked him straight in the face.'

'He must have stolen it.'

'I think so.'

Mrs Parnell bustled into the kitchen and threw Grace a filthy look. Filling the kettle and putting it on the stove to boil, she turned and glared at Grace.

'I told Betty I wouldn't say anything to you, but I can't keep it in. Look at my Betty … Look at the flamin' state of her face. She can't go to work looking like that! My daughter could have been killed today, thanks to you! She never had problems like this 'til you came along. You're a Newman and you're trouble. Bad things happen around you and I don't want my daughter dragged into it. I'd like you to leave.'

'No, Mum,' Betty argued. 'None of what's happened is Grace's fault!'

'Of course it's her fault. I warned you, didn't I? When you took that job in the hat shop, I said to you that it would come with strife. That's what happens when you work for a Newman.'

Grace felt uncomfortable and pushed her seat back. As she went to stand, Betty's head snapped round to look at her.

'Stay where you are, Grace. You don't have to leave.'

Mrs Parnell disagreed. 'Yes, she bloody well does. This is my house, and I'll say who's welcome in it.'

'Your house?' Betty said sardonically. 'It's me who pays the rent, Mum. And who are you to judge people? My dad is in prison for armed robbery. You're quick to slate the Newmans, but our family isn't any better!'

'You were never involved, Betty. Now look at you, you're neck deep in trouble.'

'I'm not, Mum. Grace's dad and Gordon have been arrested, and me and Gerty will go to the police today and tell them about Gordon trying to kill us. He'll be going down for ages, and that's an end to it all. Grace can get on with her life, and no one in Battersea will ever have to worry about Mr Newman again.'

'Hmm, well, I still ain't happy about *her* being here.'

'Grace is my friend and if she wants to stay, then she's more than welcome, so you can like it or lump it.'

Mrs Parnell huffed as she left the kitchen.

'I'm sorry, Grace. Take no notice of her,' Betty said.

'I'd love to stay, Betty. I can't face going home, but I don't want you and your mum to fall out over it.'

'We won't. Mum moans about everything. She'll get over it.'

'I don't know about you, but I'm worn out. It's been such a stressful day, but I've got something a bit more light-hearted to tell you about.'

'Oh, go on, I'm listening.'

'Well, we're going to a dance on Saturday.'

'Are we?'

'Yes, with Norman and a friend of his. Norman is a copper I met at the station today. He's ever so nice, Betty,' Grace swooned. 'And he invited us out and said he'd bring a friend.'

'I hope you told him to make sure his friend is tall. I shan't be dancing with any fellas who I have to look down at,' Betty chuckled.

'You're not *that* tall. And if you're worried, then wear flat shoes. You've got nothing to be concerned about, but me, well, I can't dance. I think I'm going to show myself up.'

Betty smiled and rose to her feet, instructing, 'Stand up. Come on, stand up. We can't have you looking silly. I'll show you how to dance.'

As Betty twirled her around the kitchen, Grace stood on her friend's foot several times, and they both giggled, but thoughts of her father were never far away. She laughed, they joked, they ate a plate of chips, and Grace tried her best to dismiss the image of him behind bars. For all his faults and everything he'd put her through, she still loved him. He was her father, and though he'd made her life difficult, she knew he'd only had her best interests in his heart. *I'm sorry, Papa, and I hope you're all right*, she thought, the burden of guilt hanging over her like a dark cloud.

54

Two days after the King's Jubilee celebrations, John arrived home from his delivery round to find two men sitting in the front room with his mother.

His mother appeared upset, and jumped from the armchair when he walked in.

'Oh, John, I'm so glad you're home. These detectives are here to speak to you.'

John looked at the two men on the sofa and wondered what they wanted.

'John Dander?' the older man asked.

'Yes.'

'I'm Detective Maxted, and I'd like to ask you a few questions about your whereabouts on Monday, the sixth of May.'

'I was here, outside mostly. There was a street party.'

'And did you take your truck anywhere that day?'

'No. I parked it up around the corner and out of the way. Erm, what's this about?'

'Your truck has been reported to have been involved in a very serious incident, Mr Dander.'

'My truck? What incident? I don't understand. I didn't use my truck on Monday.'

'Did you notice it missing?'

'No... but I could have sworn I'd left the tank half full, yet it was almost empty on Tuesday morning. Will you please explain to me what is going on?'

'We believe your truck was stolen, but that's as much as I'm at liberty to say at this moment. We'll talk again shortly. Good day.'

His mother saw the detectives out, leaving John flummoxed. He thought back to Monday and couldn't think of anything suspicious that he'd seen.

'What do you suppose that was all about?' his mother asked.

'Your guess is as good as mine, but if someone took my truck, they must have been in the house, too. The keys were in my room.'

His mother gasped. 'That's a horrible thought! I don't like the idea of a stranger in our house. What if we'd been home? We might have got hurt. Lock the back door, John. This goes to show that you can't be too careful.'

As John locked the back door, he heard a knock on the front and then Anna's voice, talking to his mother.

In the front room, Anna was on the sofa holding her face in her hands and sobbing.

'What's wrong?' John asked, looking to his mother for an explanation.

'Gordon's been arrested,' she answered quietly. 'For murder.'

John hurried to sit beside Anna and placed his arm around her shoulders. 'I'm sorry, Anna, that's terrible for you.'

'Oh, John!' she cried. 'He's been accused of killing Grace's mum and burying her in their back garden. Gordon swears blind he didn't do it. It's Grace. She hates him. She went to the police and got her father and Gordon arrested.'

John quickly tried to digest what Anna had told him, but he couldn't get his head around it.

'What am I going to do? He's innocent, John, I know he is! Gordon could swing for this!'

'Do you really believe he's innocent?' John asked.

'Of course I do! I wouldn't expect you to think he's innocent. You've always thought the worst of him and held a thing for Grace, but I swear, John, she's done this out of spite.'

John didn't think so. He knew Grace wouldn't fabricate a tale of her mother's murder. It had to be true, and poor Anna was blinded by love again.

'I'm … I'm in the family way. Oh, John, my baby's going to grow up without a father.'

'It'll be all right, Anna. If Gordon's innocent like you say, the courts won't convict him if he's not guilty. You sit tight. It might take a while, but Gordon won't be hung for a murder he didn't commit.'

'Do you really think so, John?'

'Yeah, I do,' he lied. If Grace had said Gordon had murdered her mother, then John knew that the man must be as guilty as sin. 'Don't worry, Anna,' he added, 'you've got us. We'll help you. Me and Mum will look after you.'

Gordon was dragged from his cell and taken to a room for questioning again. Only this time, the detectives weren't concerned about the murder of Louisa Newman. They wanted to know about him stealing John's truck and attempting to run over Betty and a woman called Gerty.

Gordon was confused at first. He'd been sure the woman he'd seen with Betty was Grace, but the police were saying differently. She'd dressed the same as Grace, and there weren't many women in Battersea who could afford the expensive clobber that Grace wore. Maybe he'd been mistaken, but either way, he'd never confess to the crime.

Detective Maxted pushed an open packet of cigarettes across the desk towards him, saying, 'Help yourself, Moss.'

'You reckon you're clever,' Gordon smirked. 'You think if you're nice to me, I'll own up to a crime I ain't done.'

'Just admit that you stole Dander's truck on Monday and attempted to run down two women on the junction of Falcon Road and York Road. There are several witnesses, Moss, you won't get away with it. Look, you're already looking at a long stretch or the gallows for the murder of Louise Newman, it's a capital crime. So you may as well save us all some time and bother and admit to what you did.'

'I didn't kill her! And you can't pin this on me neither. Who said I stole Dander's truck, eh? Grace Newman? She's got it in for me!'

'No, Moss, Miss Newman didn't report this incident.'

The younger detective, Gordon couldn't remember his name, slammed his hands down hard on the desk. 'You're as thick as pig's shit, Moss. We've got you bang to rights.'

'Help us, and we'll help you,' Detective Maxted encouraged.

'I ain't got nothing more to say to you. Charge me. I'll have my day in court, and you'll see me get a not guilty. You're gonna look like a right pair of chumps. I want to go back to my cell now.'

*

Dickie had found that even from the remand wing of prison, money bought favours, and the prison officers were more unscrupulous than the criminals they were guarding. The promise of a few pounds had secured him an out-of-hours visit with Ernie. Sitting in the small room opposite Ernie with a guard standing at the door, Dickie was raging.

'Are you sure you got your facts right?' he asked.

'Yes, Boss. Gordon stole Dander's truck and tried to kill Betty Parnell and some other woman with it. Gordon thought the other woman was Grace. It was her he was after.'

'The bastard! I'll fuckin' kill him, Ernie.'

'I reckon the hangman might kill him first.'

'I can get to him. A word in the right ear, and Gordon won't know what's hit him. I'll make his life hell. He'll be glad to get to the gallows by the time I've finished with him. No one hurts my girl, no one!'

'I ain't being funny, Boss, but knowing what you know about Grace putting you in here, how are you all right with it?'

'Grace will have her reasons for getting me in trouble with the law, and when she visits, I'll get to the bottom of it. But in my eyes, Ernie, that girl can't do no wrong.'

Ernie rubbed his bristly chin, looking dubious.

'I want you to put some money in an envelope, mark it to Grace and shove it through Betty's door.'

Ernie's eyebrows lifted.

'Do it!' Dickie barked. 'And don't fuckin' question my orders again!'

'Yes, Boss, sorry, Boss.'

'And give our little friend a bonus. He's shown himself to

be loyal and has given you good information. I want to keep him on side. I've always said that money talks.'

'Right you are, Boss.'

'And while you're at it, I want a couple of blokes given a good hiding. Make sure it's done publicly. Let it be seen and make it known that it's from me. I don't want people thinking they can get away with shit just 'cos I'm in here. They need to see that I'm still running things.'

'Who do you want me to beat up?'

'I dunno. Use your head, Ernie. Someone who owes me money.'

'Will do, Boss.'

'Good man. I'm gonna see about getting Gordon's head kicked in, so you can bugger off now, and next time you come, bring me more cigars.'

'Will do, Boss. Look after yourself.'

Dickie was led back to his cell, manic with anger. If he could have got his hands on Gordon, he would have ripped the bloke's head off. How dare he attempt to harm Grace!

Gordon wasn't being held in the same prison as him, but Dickie had already worked out the system. He knew how to get to Gordon, and he was going to make sure he paid for what he'd done.

55

Grace looked in the mirror, pleased with her reflection.

'You look smashing,' Betty said. 'But look at the state of me, I'm sweating buckets!'

'I don't know why you're so nervous. I'm sure Norman's friend will be lovely. It's funny seeing you like this, you're normally so confident.'

'I've never had a date with a man, Grace. It's terrifying! What should I talk about? Will he try to kiss me? Should I let him kiss me? What if he doesn't like me?'

Grace laughed. 'Oh, Betty, you are funny. Try and relax. Trust me, there's nothing terrifying about going out on a date. And no kissing! You may allow a light peck on the cheek and that's it, nothing more.'

'Do you think I'm ridiculous?'

'No, not at all.'

'Sometimes I feel ridiculous. A lot of women my age are married and starting families, and here's me, never even been kissed. I'm so relieved Gordon didn't kill me that day. I'd hate to die untouched and intact.'

'I've been kissed, and it's wonderful, but I won't be doing

anything more than that until I'm married. Look what happened to Maud, God rest her soul. She nearly got caught out and would have had a bastard child. As it is, people already talk about me. I wouldn't want to give them more gossip or ruin my reputation.'

'Quite right, Grace. I agree. But I do worry that I'll never be married.'

'You've got nothing to worry about, Betty. I've seen the attention you get from men. In fact, if you're not married by Christmas next year, I'll eat my hat!'

'Talking of hats, which of mine do you want to wear?'

'The white one, I think. Thank you for letting me borrow your clothes. I really must go home and collect some of my belongings, but the idea of going into that house fills me with dread.'

'It's a good job I'm accomplished on the sewing machine, otherwise that dress would be down to the floor. You're welcome to wear any of my clothes and I'll happily adjust them for you, but why don't you give me your keys and I'll go to your house and fetch your things?'

As Grace agreed and expressed her gratitude, they heard a knock on the front door.

Betty's eyes widened. 'That will be Norman and his friend.'

'Yes, I should think so. Take a deep breath and don't forget to smile. Come on, let's have some much-deserved fun!'

Grace had been thrilled when Norman had moved her dexterously around the dance floor, and at the end of the night, when she'd lifted her face to him, passions had stirred when he'd kissed her goodnight. The evening had been magical, and Grace was eager to see him again, so when he suggested meeting on Sunday morning for a stroll through Battersea Park, she'd been quick to accept his invitation.

Unfortunately, Betty hadn't been enamoured with Norman's friend. The man had been an inch or two shorter than her, which had made Betty feel uncomfortable. Still, she'd enjoyed the dance and had shown off the skills she'd learned from her father. Her father had danced on some of London's stages, but when his work as an entertainer had dried up, desperate, he'd turned to armed robbery to support his family and had been arrested on his first job. Betty said he was a better dancer than a robber.

The stroll through the park had been enjoyable, and Grace found she was fast becoming fond of Norman. He was so easy to talk to, a good listener, and he made her laugh. They'd spent three hours together, but the time had flown by. Norman had said he was expected at his mother's house for Sunday lunch, and though he'd rather have spent the time with her, he couldn't disappoint his mother. Grace understood, and they had made arrangements to meet again on Tuesday evening; it couldn't come soon enough!

Now, on Monday morning, Betty had gone to work, and Mrs Parnell had left for one of her cleaning jobs. The house was empty, and Grace was bored, though she knew she should be out looking for employment. It wasn't going to be an easy task. Grace was willing to do most things, but she worried that her Newman name would put employers off from offering her a position. Still, she had to try. Without her father to support her, Grace was out of money.

After expertly positioning another of Betty's hats on her head, Grace went to the front door, determined to find a job. As she was about to leave, she saw an envelope had been pushed through the letterbox, and when she picked it up from the floor, she was surprised to see it was addressed to her. Carefully peeling it open, her eyes bulged when she found the envelope was stuffed with three five-pound notes. She pulled the money out and looked inside the envelope again, but there was no letter. 'It must be from my father,' she muttered, recognising the style of envelopes he always used, and she assumed Ernie had delivered it. Grace didn't want her father's ill-gotten gains, but she needed the money. She couldn't keep relying on Betty's generosity. Another thought crossed her mind – the bills for the house in Clapham. Would her father make arrangements or was she now responsible? There was so much to think about!

With the cash secured in her bag, Grace stepped outside to a bright and warm day. She'd decided that Clapham Junction was a good place to look for work as it was packed with shops, and shop experience was all she had to offer.

Stepping around a corner, she came face to face with Anna, almost bumping into her. With Anna living so close to Betty, she'd thought there was a likely chance that they'd run into each other.

'Good morning,' Grace greeted her, feeling awkward.

'You've got some nerve to speak to me after what you've done!'

'I'm sorry you feel that way, Anna, but I did the right thing. Gordon killed my mother. There's no denying it; I witnessed the whole thing. And he tried to kill me too, only it was Betty and Gerty who took the brunt of his attack.'

'You're a liar!' Anna spat. 'You've always had it in for him. What is it, Grace? Are you jealous because he took some of your father's attention away from you?'

'Don't be absurd, Anna. You know I'm not jealous of Gordon. The man is a murderer and he's where he belongs.'

'So you say, but when you went to the police, did you give *me* so much as a second thought? No, I don't suppose you did. Well, thank you very much. I'm having his child! My baby won't know its father because of you! I don't know how I'll cope with no money! I hope you're proud of yourself.'

Anna marched off in tears, leaving Grace reeling. *Poor Anna*, she thought. But the woman's predicament didn't change the fact that Gordon deserved to be in prison. Grace felt justified in what she'd done and had no regrets, but her heart ached for Anna.

Gordon was struggling with the confines of Brixton Prison. The cells were cold and damp, he'd not been issued a blanket, and the prison hadn't been fitted with electricity. The wardens were rude at best, and violent at worst. Gordon was treated as a man convicted, yet he'd pleaded his innocence. Until his trial day, he thought he'd be shown the respect of *innocent until proven guilty*. That attitude didn't apply in Brixton.

It would be sloshing-out time soon, a task that turned his stomach. He hated emptying his ablutions bucket and couldn't stand the stench. But it was more than the foul stink that worried him. He'd seen a couple of local faces; blokes he'd thumped and extracted money from on Dickie's orders. When they'd seen him incarcerated, they'd glared at him maliciously. Sitting on the edge of his hard bed with the thinnest of mattresses, Gordon listened as metal mugs were clanged against the prison bars, the noise almost deafening. But it didn't drown out the chants of the prisoners, and Gordon clearly heard his name.

You're a goner, Moss.

I'll get you, Gordon.

Watch your back, Moss, you bastard.

Gordon dreaded stepping out of his small cell, but he knew he'd have no choice.

Standing outside his door, two floors up and on a long platform that ran in a rectangular shape around the inner building, Gordon, with his bucket in hand, kept his eyes fixed ahead. Turning left, and in line with the other prisoners, he made his way to the stairs, where prisoners from the floors below joined the line. His heart thudded. He knew he wasn't safe and if anyone attempted to jump him, he believed the guards would probably allow it to happen.

He felt a shove in his back, like a punch, and lurched forward, almost pushing into the prisoner in front of him.

'Oi!' Gordon ground out, looking over his shoulder to the man behind him.

The man shrugged.

The guards shouted their orders.

'QUIET!'

'Keep in line.'

'Get a move on.'

Gordon's back ached where he'd been punched. And then he felt a wet sensation trickling down his skin. Reaching his arm around, he felt the area and then, looking at his hand, panicked when he saw blood.

'You've stabbed me,' he said, stunned, to the man behind. 'You've fuckin' stabbed me!'

A gaoler's deep voice echoed through the prison. 'Shut it up there!'

Gordon began to feel weak and light-headed. He saw he

was dripping a trail of blood. 'Help me,' he shouted, 'I've been stabbed! Help me, I'm dying!'

'QUIET!'

Falling to his knees, he dropped the bucket, and the stinking contents sloshed out.

'Please, help me,' he called weakly.

Gordon's strength was waning, and as he fell to his side and rolled onto his back, he looked up and saw leering faces hovering over him.

'Don't let me die,' he begged, though he knew his pleas would be ignored.

A guard's voice again. 'Get out the way.'

Gordon's eyelids felt heavy and as he closed his eyes, he could feel himself drifting into a peaceful abyss as men spoke around him.

'You're too late, Guv, he's dead.'

'He's been shanked.'

'Who did it?'

'Never saw a thing, Guv.'

'He's died in his own shit.'

'Get him up, we can't leave him there, he's making a mess. I want him moved to the hospital wing.'

'If you say so, Guv. Waste of time if you ask me, he'd be better off in the morgue.'

Gordon was vaguely aware of being carried roughly, but he felt no pain, just a strange sense of serenity. Then the image of Anna came into his mind, and he remembered she was having his child. Fear coursed through his veins. *I can't die*, he thought, willing himself to survive. *I'm gonna be a dad*. But as the blood drained from Gordon's body, his world turned dark.

56

The prison governor had granted Dickie almost unlimited visits. It had come at a cost, and though it was useful to see his solicitor and Ernie, the only person Dickie really wanted a visit from was Grace.

Sitting opposite Ernie, he said, 'Gordon's dead.'

'Shit! What happened?'

'I arranged for him to get a good hiding, but it went further than that. I wasn't happy that his time was over so quickly. I wanted him to suffer for trying to kill Grace. Did you drop the money in to her?'

'Yes, Boss.'

'I need you to bring her here. She ain't visited yet and it's time she did.'

'Will do, Boss, but what do I do if she won't come?'

'She will, but you might have to persuade her. Any more updates from our *friend*?'

'Yeah ... Grace is still staying with Betty and she's looking for a job. That's about it.'

'All right. Give him another payment and tell him to stay on the job. I want to know Grace's every movement. I ain't there to look out for her, so I need him. Don't fuck it up, Ernie.'

'Yes, Boss.'

'Have you been keeping proper records of the rents and loans like I showed you?'

'Yeah, every penny.'

'Good. You're to drop the books to my solicitor's office every fortnight. He's agreed to take on some accountancy work for me. Humperton will check them over. It ain't that I don't trust you, Ernie, 'cos I do. But you're not gifted with brains, are you?'

Ernie chuckled, a deep belly laugh. 'No, Boss. I'm all brawn.'

Dickie relaxed back in the hard, wooden seat, and lit a big, fat cigar. Stretching out his legs, he blew smoke in the air, thinking it wasn't so bad in prison. He was fed and watered and his backhanders paid for good quality food, not the slop the other prisoners were served. His bed was comfortable enough and he could still dish out his orders, make money and smoke his cigars. But he missed his daughter.

'Bring Grace to see me, Ernie. I need a visit from my girl.'

John held Anna as she sobbed. It hurt to see his cousin's heart breaking, though he wasn't sorry to learn about Gordon's death.

'Come on, Anna, try and pull yourself together. Think about that little one in your belly.'

'I am thinking about my baby, John. That's why I'm so upset. Gordon was convinced we'd have a son. My boy will never know his father. It's not fair and this has happened because of Grace!'

John baulked. He couldn't understand why Anna failed to see the truth about Gordon. 'You can't keep blaming Grace. From what I've heard, there's evidence to prove Gordon buried Mrs Newman in the back garden. He used his braces to tie her legs together.'

'Dickie Newman could have used Gordon's braces. Can't you see, John, they've ganged up against Gordon.'

'If you believe that, then why did Grace turn her father in? Face facts, Anna. Gordon was guilty. He attacked me and left me for dead, and he stole my van and tried to run over Betty. The bloke was bad through and through.'

'I loved him, and he loved me. I can't accept he did those things. Could he really have attacked you, knowing how much I love you?'

'Yes, Anna, he did. I know you don't want to hear it, but it's the truth.' John was pleased to finally hear some doubt in Anna's voice. 'I've known you my whole life and I've never lied to you. Ask yourself, how well did you *really* know Gordon? Me, Grace, Betty, Gerty, the police, we can't all be wrong.'

'Oh, God, John, was I married to a murderer?'

'Sorry, Anna, but the simple answer is yes.'

Anna began to sob again, and John pulled a handkerchief from his trouser pocket. 'Here,' he said, handing it to her. 'It's clean. Dry your eyes and blow your nose.'

Anna's eyes were swollen, but wide with fear. 'What if my baby turns out like his father? Am I growing something hideous?'

'Your baby will be beautiful and will grow up to be a kind, generous person, just like you. Gordon's gone. He'll never have any influence over your baby, and you'll raise a smashing kid.'

Anna sniffed. 'I hope you're right, John. Your Maggie and my baby will grow up together, just like me and you did. They're going to be the best of friends. I don't know what I'd do without you.'

'You'll be like a mum to my Maggie, and I'll be a father figure to your baby. They won't miss out on anything, Anna, we'll make sure of it.'

John didn't believe that Anna's baby would be anything like Gordon, though a shudder ran through his body. Gordon was dead; it was time for the family to pull together and move on. He hoped the tide had turned and some good fortune was coming their way, especially after all the tragedy they'd been through of late.

Grace tore through the homewares department of Arding and Hobbs store, looking for Betty. She found her friend advising a customer on crystal-cut glasses and had to wait patiently. Once the sale was secured, Grace rushed over.

'I'm bursting to tell you something,' Grace announced.

'I can see,' Betty chuckled.

'I've been offered a job!'

'Oh, Grace, that's great, congratulations. Where will you be working?'

'In the ironmonger's shop, you know the one, on St John's Hill. It's not ideal, but it's a start. I can't wait to tell Norman; he's going to be so pleased for me. I might be able to persuade him to take me out tonight to celebrate.'

'He'll be at work now. You're not going to look for him, are you?'

'Yes. I really want to share my news with him.'

'Be careful, Grace. You know he'll be on the beat around where your father's properties are. I'm not sure that it's safe for you around there, not with your father in prison.'

'I'll be fine. You've got a customer. I'll see you later.'

Grace was pleased the hovering dark clouds were holding back from letting go of the water they held. She didn't have an umbrella with her and wanted to look her best when she found Norman. Just the thought of him made her feel tingly inside. She wished she could see more of him, but understood he did an important job, which was demanding and came with long hours.

Hurrying through Battersea, Grace was breathless by the time she reached the slummier area of town. Standing on a corner, wondering which way to turn, she glanced along both streets looking for Norman's distinctive uniform. There was no sign of him, which meant she'd have to risk looking for him closer to the area that her father pretty much owned.

Spits of rain began to fall and she hoped to find him soon. Turning onto the street where she knew she wasn't welcome, she saw her father's car and her racing heart fell. Ernie had been driving it since her father's arrest and he was the last person Grace wanted to see. As she was about to spin on her heel and walk away, her eyes fell on Norman, and she saw he was talking with Ernie. Grace's jaw dropped as she watched Ernie slip Norman an envelope. She knew those envelopes. They were the ones her father always used to hand out his bribes, and the same as the one that had been pushed through Betty's door.

Her arms swinging, her lips pursed, Grace marched towards

them. When they saw her coming, Ernie puffed out his chest and Norman looked sheepish.

'I should have known!' she blurted, looking from one man to another. 'My father's bought you and is paying you to snoop on me!'

'It's not what you think, Grace,' Norman replied.

'Isn't it? Go on then, explain.'

'I, erm, I've been doing some work for your father, but it doesn't involve you.'

Grace gave Norman a hard stare and he looked down to the ground, which told her all she needed to know.

'You must think I'm stupid, Norman. Maybe I am; after all, I trusted you. What an idiot I've been.'

'You haven't, Grace. You can trust me. I think a lot of you. Please, give me a chance.'

'No. No chances. You all seem to forget that I'm a Newman too, which means I'm no one's fool. I never want to set eyes on you again!'

Grace just caught Ernie's words when he mumbled under his breath, 'Dickie ain't gonna be happy about this.'

Her eyes shot to him, and she snapped, 'You can report back to him that I'm not happy about it, either!'

She held out her hand to Norman. 'Give me that envelope,' she demanded.

Norman looked at her, perplexed.

'Give it to me,' she hissed. 'You haven't earned the money because you've been caught out. Give me my father's cash.'

Norman looked to Ernie.

'She's got a fair point,' Ernie said. 'And Grace is second in command of the Newman business.'

'No way. This is my money and it's not my problem.'

'Give her the envelope,' Ernie growled, 'or it will be your problem.'

'I need this money,' Norman protested, sounding panicked. 'I'm counting on it. You can't take it.'

'Do you want me to *make* you hand it over?' Ernie threatened.

'Please, mate, you don't understand... Me wife and kids are depending on me... I'm in debt with the bank and I could lose my house. You can't take this money from me.'

'Wife and kids?' Grace parroted. 'You're married? This is going from bad to worse!'

Feeling humiliated, Grace snatched the envelope from Norman's hand. 'Go,' she ordered. 'As Ernie said, I'm second in command of my father's business. Get out of my sight before I set Ernie on you.'

For a moment, Norman looked as though he was going to say something, but instead he turned and walked away, scowling.

Grace looked at Ernie with disgust. 'You can tell my father that I've had enough. If he wants to know what I'm doing, just flippin' ask me! No more spies. No more set ups. It stops now.'

'You can tell him yourself. He wants to see you.'

'No, that's not going to happen.'

'He told me I've got to persuade you, but words ain't my strong point. I only know how to persuade people by using me fists, and I ain't gonna do that to you. Do me a favour and let me take you to see him. He'll only keep on and on until you do.'

'I don't want to see him, ever!'

'Please, Grace. He's your dad. Just give him a few minutes of your time.'

'Why should I, Ernie?'

'Because he loves ya.'

Grace loved him, too. She hated the things he'd done and would never forgive him, but she couldn't help but feel a daughter's love for a father. 'All right. I'll see him. You can pick me up from Betty's tomorrow morning. And, Ernie, despite what you claim, you *are* good at persuading people with your words.'

57

Early the next morning, sitting at the kitchen table, Betty cocked her head to one side and looked at Grace compassionately. 'Are you sure you're all right?' she asked.

Grace sipped on a cup of hot tea before answering. 'I think so. My head's in a bit of a spin, and I didn't sleep well last night.'

'I know. You were very restless, but that's not surprising considering what you're doing today.'

'I don't know what to expect. I put my father behind bars. He must hate me.'

'If that's the case, why has he given you money?'

'Guilt? Only my father knows how his mind works. I'm still reeling about Norman, too. I liked him, but what hurts the most is this feeling I have of being made to feel so bloody stupid!'

'I can't believe it, Grace. You're not stupid. He had me fooled too, he seemed so genuine. To think he was working for your father, and getting close to you was all a ruse, it's shocking. And married with children, too!'

'It makes sense now. Norman said he couldn't see me as

much as he'd like because of the long hours he had to put in for his job. And Sunday lunch at his mother's. Rubbish! He was with his wife. I don't think I'll ever trust another man again.'

'Are you sure you don't want me to come with you?'

'No, Betty, I'll be fine, thank you. Anyway, you need to go to work.'

'But I could pretend to be sick.'

'No, honestly, I'll be all right.'

An hour later, Grace sat silently beside Ernie as he drove her to Wandsworth Prison.

A small crowd had gathered outside the daunting building. 'What's that all about?' she asked.

'They'll be looking to see if there's any notices of executions. They've got a hanging shed in the prison. Your father said one of the other prisoners told him that when they hang someone, the sound of the drop can be heard through the building. Bleedin' ghoulish, if you ask me.'

Grace recoiled, dreading entering the prison. The entrance faced Wandsworth Common on the other side of the road, a place of two stark contrasts.

Parking the car, Ernie asked, 'Are you ready?'

Grace nodded. She wasn't, but she pretended to be feeling brave. It wasn't going to be easy to face her father. She'd betrayed him in the worst way possible, and though she still believed she'd done the right thing, it didn't stop her from feeling guilty.

Dickie's morning hadn't been great. He'd heard about the flogging stand, a wooden contraption where inmates who'd assaulted wardens would have their arms hoisted above their heads and tied to the stand, and then a severe whipping would be administered. Dickie thought it sounded like something out of the dark ages, and he didn't think it was right. It wasn't unusual for a prison guard to give a prisoner a beating, or throw harsh words, and if the prisoner retaliated, the flogging stand would be his punishment. The balance of fairness was definitely tilted towards the prison staff.

After hearing about the flogging stand, Dickie had been summoned to the Governor's office. The short, rotund, balding man had demanded more money from Dickie in return for keeping his life sweet. Dickie didn't like being blackmailed and had resented agreeing, but he'd been left with no choice.

Being led from the Governor's office and back to the cells, another warden approached and spoke to Dickie's guard.

'Newman's got visitors.'

Dickie noticed the man had said visitors in plural, and his bad mood instantly lifted.

'It'll be my daughter,' he said proudly.

When Dickie was taken into the visiting area, he felt choked up at seeing Grace sitting there. She looked a radiant beauty, out of place within the confines of the grim prison walls. As he walked towards her, he couldn't decide if she was scared, angry or sad. But she didn't seem pleased to see him.

'Hello, my darling,' he beamed. 'It's good to see you.'

'I thought you'd be furious with me,' she said bluntly.

Dickie chortled. 'Well, I ain't happy about you putting me away, and I'd like to know why. It knocked me sideways when I found out it was you who went to the Old Bill. I never expected that of you, Grace, but I'm sure you've got your reasons. So come on then, let's hear them.'

He could see the look of defiance in her eyes and admired

her courage. There wasn't another person living who'd have the guts to stand up to him. Although he didn't like or agree with what she'd done, he was proud of her.

'I went to the police because it was the right thing to do,' she said, her tone lacking emotion.

'Would you care to elaborate on that?'

'Where do I start? Jack Pope, the way you treated my mother, then allowing Gordon to get away with murder, burying my mother in our back garden, your bullying tactics with your tenants and total disregard for anyone, having John Dander beaten half to death, having me followed . . . You made me feel like a prisoner and now you know what it feels like! And that's only the things I know about. I'm sure there's much more.'

Dickie huffed. 'That's quite a list. When you say it like that, I suppose it doesn't look good on my part. But everything I did, Grace, I did for you.'

'Huh? For *me*? No, Papa, you did it for yourself.'

Dickie leaned closer, looking Grace straight in the eyes. 'You're my girl, Grace, but how I conduct my business and what went on between your mother and me has got nothing to do with you. Yeah, hands up, I admit I made sure that Dander was warned off you, and I've had people keeping an eye on you, but that was for your own good. My worst fault is being overprotective with you. But can you blame me, eh? I know what fellas are like. It's my job to look after you.'

'You're not sorry, are you? You're not apologetic for any of it!'

'No, Grace, I ain't, and why should I be? I'm only sorry you can't see it from my point of view. That's the problem . . . You're stubborn. You're too much like me.'

'I'm *nothing* like you,' she scoffed. 'Yes, I'm tough, I'm resilient and I won't take crap from no one, but that's where the similarity ends. You don't care about destroying lives to get what you want. You don't have a conscience. You say you love me, but I'm not even sure you know what love is.'

'I do love you, Grace, with all me heart. You're my world, darling. I ain't gonna be banged up in here forever, and when I get out, we can put all of this behind us and make a fresh start. You and me, eh? Against the world.'

Grace's eyes widened and she looked disturbed. 'I want nothing more to do with you! I'll always love you because you're the man who gave life to me, but I don't like you and I can't put this behind me.'

'Grace, darling, you don't mean that. You're angry, and just like me, you lash out when you're angry. I get it. But once you've calmed down, you'll see that you've always been the centre of my world. Me and you, we need each other.'

Grace shook her head. 'I don't need you, Papa,' she said, her tone more serene. 'I need you to pay for what you've done. My mother needs justice.'

'Why do you keep bringing your mother into this? I didn't kill her, and the bloke who did is dead now.'

'You killed her. You killed her on the day that you burned down Mr Pope's shop. She was never the same after that. You took away the only bit of happiness she'd ever had. She was my mother, and I loved her, and I can't forgive you for destroying her.'

'Your mother was *my* wife, Grace. She should never have betrayed me with Pope. *She* was in the wrong, not me.'

Closing her eyes, looking exasperated, Grace said, 'You

never take responsibility for your wrongdoings, Papa. It's never your fault.'

'I'll put my hands up when I'm wrong, but you've got everything all mixed up in that young head of yours. I swear, Grace, once you're thinking straight, you'll see I'm not as bad as all that.'

'Don't patronise me, Papa. We can keep talking and going over the same things, but it doesn't change anything.' Then, scraping her seat back and standing abruptly, she added, 'You'll never change, Papa. Part of me feels bad for putting you in here, but it's what you deserve and I'm not sorry. I'm leaving now. Don't attempt to contact me. I never want to see you again.'

As she walked away, Dickie leapt to his feet. 'Grace!' he called desperately. 'Grace ...'

Ernie followed her, mumbling something about he'd be back next week, but Dickie wasn't listening. His eyes were fixed on Grace as she walked out, and his world came crashing down around him. He'd never felt so devastated, and tears leaked down his reddened face.

The warden tried to take him back to his cell, but Dickie wanted to chase after his daughter. He ran to the locked gate, gripped the bars, frantically rattling the metal as if he were deranged. 'Grace!' he screamed. 'Grace!'

Two wardens grabbed his shoulders and took an arm each. Dickie yanked himself free, lashing out and shrieking. An alarm bell sounded, and several more guards piled into the room. Dickie charged towards them, his head down, swinging his arms. He bit into flesh; a guard yelled in pain. Punching and kicking, he headbutted someone, as batons pounded his body.

'Come on then,' he screeched, flailing furiously. 'Come and get me. Kill me ... Fuckin' kill me ... Do it ... Kill me,' he cried, sinking to his knees.

Defeated, his body broken, a couple of guards picked him up, and dragged him to an isolation cell. The door was opened, and he was unceremoniously thrown inside, landing in a twisted heap.

As the door slammed shut, Dickie flinched. 'You should have killed me,' he mumbled, 'You should have put me out of me misery.'

58

Three weeks later

On Sunday afternoon, John and Anna meandered through Battersea Park.

'Here you are,' John said, letting go of the pram handle. 'You push Maggie for a while. It'll be good practice for you.'

Anna smiled. 'I thought you'd never ask.'

'It's nice to see that pretty smile again.'

'I felt the baby kick this morning. How can I not be happy? What about you, John? Are you happy?'

John thought hard before answering. 'Maggie makes me smile every day,' he said, gazing lovingly into her pram.

'That's not what I asked.'

'Dander's Deliveries is doing well.'

'You still haven't answered the question.'

'I don't know, Anna. Life's treating me well at the moment, but something is missing.'

'Maud?'

'No. Well, yeah, it upsets me that Maggie won't know her mum, but it's not that. I can't put my finger on it.'

'Grace?'

'Maybe. Have you seen her since your run-in a few weeks ago?'

'No. I feel I should apologise to her, but I'm too embarrassed to knock on her door.'

'Is she still staying at Betty's?' John asked.

'Yes, I think so.'

'Then you've got no excuse. It's only round the corner. We'll knock on our way home.'

Anna nodded, and John realised he was excited at the prospect of seeing Grace. Yet the excitement was doused with guilt. 'Maybe you should knock without me,' he suggested.

'I couldn't, John. Please come with me. I'm sure Grace will be polite to you. You never know, she might even be pleased to see you.'

John wanted to see her. He really did. But he couldn't help feeling it was disloyal to Maud's memory. He'd already let his late wife down when she'd been alive.

'Please, John,' Anna asked in her sweetest voice.

'All right. But let's head there now before I change my mind.'

On the approach to Betty's house, John could feel his pulse racing at the thought of seeing Grace and berated himself.

Standing beside Anna, he knocked on the door.

'I hope she doesn't slam it shut in my face,' Anna whispered through the side of her mouth.

When Betty pulled the door open, she looked surprised. 'Oh, hello.'

'Hello, Betty. Is Grace home?'

'Yes. Just a minute.'

She left the door only slightly ajar. John could hear urgent whispers and strained his ears, but he couldn't hear what was being said. The door opened wider again and Grace stood there, looking splendid.

He discreetly nudged Anna but she was speechless.

'Hello, Grace,' John said. 'Sorry to disturb you, but Anna has something she'd like to say to you.'

Grace looked at Anna, her face hard.

'Go on,' John encouraged his cousin.

Anna cleared her throat. 'I'm so sorry, Grace. I should never have believed a word that came out of Gordon's mouth. I hope you can forgive me for the awful things I said to you.'

Grace's body relaxed and her face softened. 'You don't need to apologise, Anna. Would you like to come in? Betty's just put the kettle on.'

'Can we?' Anna asked John.

He nodded and then flicked his head to the pram behind him. 'Maggie's asleep. She'll be all right in her pram out here.'

Grace stretched her neck to look past him and at the pram. 'May I have a peek at her?'

'Yes. She's a beauty and looks just like Maud.'

She stepped past him and leaned over the pram, tucking her hair behind her ears and cooing, 'Oh, she really is a pretty little dot.'

Inside, Betty joined them around the kitchen table. 'My mum has made some ginger biscuits,' she said, placing a plate down. 'Help yourselves, but at your own risk. I warn you; you might break your teeth.'

'I really am sorry,' Anna reiterated. 'I can't believe I was so adamant about Gordon's innocence. I've been so stupid.'

Grace placed a cup of tea in front of Anna and rested a hand on her shoulder. 'You haven't been stupid. I know what makes my father tick. He likes to have power, to control, and he's good at what he does. Gordon was just like him. It took me years to see my father for what he really is, so I know how Gordon managed to fool you. Don't feel bad, Anna.'

Betty sat at the table, saying, 'And I don't want to sound cruel, but Gordon wasn't the sharpest knife in the block. Did he really think he'd get away with stealing John's truck and doing what he did? It was obvious to me that John would be able to account for his movements that day and the finger wouldn't point at him. Gordon didn't even try to hide his face. He was the stupid one, Anna, not you.'

John tried not to stare at Grace, but he couldn't pull his eyes away, and she kept giving him sideways glances. There was clearly still a strong attraction between them. Once again, that overwhelming feeling of guilt swamped him.

'I agree, Betty,' Grace said. 'Gordon wasn't very bright. He never had any schooling and was moulded by my father.'

Anna's eyes welled with tears. 'I wish I'd listened to you and John and never married him.'

'Don't cry,' Betty soothed. 'Here, have a biscuit,' she said, picking one from the plate and handing it to Anna.

Anna smiled slightly and tried to bite into the biscuit. 'Blimey, I'd need a hammer and chisel to get through this!'

'Dunk it in your tea, it might soften it,' Betty suggested with a giggle.

There was a knock on the door and John noticed Grace cringe.

Betty stood up, saying, 'I'll get it.'

'Are you all right?' John asked Grace.

'Yes, I'm fine, but that will be Ernie with another letter from my father.'

'Yes, it is,' Betty said, coming back into the kitchen.

Chucking the letter in the rubbish bin, she added, 'I told Ernie to tell your dad he's wasting his time.'

'Aren't you going to read it?' Anna asked.

Grace looked sad when she answered, 'No. I don't want anything to do with my father.'

Betty explained, 'Grace visited him in prison and told him she never wanted to see him again. Since then, she's been bombarded with letters from him.'

'Going to the police was a brave thing to do, Grace.'

'I don't think it was brave. I think it was a necessity. Anyway, that's all in the past now. Let's look forward. Have you thought of any names for the baby?'

'No, not yet, and I'm open to suggestions. I'd like a film star name, like Marlene for a girl, or Clark for a boy.'

'That reminds me, I should check on Maggie,' John said. 'I'll leave you ladies to catch up. It's been nice seeing you, Grace.'

'Yes, and you,' she said, holding his gaze.

Outside, John blew out a long breath of air. His head was a mess of conflicting thoughts. Seeing Grace had brought back the feelings he'd had for her and the lust. *Pack it in*, he told himself. Regardless of how he felt, he knew Grace wouldn't be interested in rekindling their relationship, especially now he had a child. He doubted there'd be many women who'd want to get involved with him. 'Never mind,' he said, looking down at Maggie. 'You're the special lady in my life now.'

'I've had a smashing afternoon,' Grace beamed. 'It's been so lovely to see you, Anna.'

'Yes, me too. I still can't believe you're working in an

ironmonger's shop. I bet they've never had such a glamorous assistant selling nails and candles.'

'I quite enjoy it, and don't laugh.'

'See you again soon,' Anna said, waving goodbye. 'And the next time you see me, I might be wearing a smock. I'm really starting to show now.'

'It suits you, Anna.'

Back in the kitchen, Grace glanced at the rubbish bin.

Betty must have noticed, and asked, 'I can fish the letter out of the bin, if you like?'

'No,' Grace replied, adamant. 'I don't want to waver, but sometimes it's difficult to stay firm. It's too easy to forget about all the terrible things he did and only remember the happy times.'

'The mind is good at playing tricks. Grace, no one will think any less of you if you want a relationship with your dad.'

'I don't. And I think it's time I went home. I've loved being here, but you need your bed back to yourself, and my grandmother will be returning from Europe soon.'

'You don't have to leave if you don't want to.'

'Thanks, Betty, but I'm ready. I'll pack my things. Strike while the iron's hot.'

'You're leaving today?'

'Yes. It's quite a walk but a lovely day. I'll be home before sunset.'

'You can't walk all the way to Clapham with a heavy suitcase. Ask John to drive you there. I'm sure he wouldn't mind.'

'That's not a bad idea,' Grace said, glad that they could be friends after all that had happened.

An hour later, her suitcase full, Grace left it near the front door and walked around to John's house.

Mrs Dander didn't look pleased to see her on the doorstep, and Grace heard the woman call to John, 'Miss High and Mighty Fancy Drawers is outside.'

John came to the door looking flushed.

'Fancy drawers?' Grace grinned.

'You heard that? Sorry, Grace.'

'I'm sure I've been called worse. Erm, John, I've got a favour to ask... would you mind running me and my suitcase to Clapham, please?'

'Sure, I'll grab my keys and tell my mum to keep an eye on Maggie.'

Grace found the truck to be a bumpier ride than she'd expected, though John was driving very slowly. 'Doesn't this go any faster?' she asked.

'Yes, but I wanted to take my time with you.'

'Are you flirting with me, John Dander?'

'Would it be acceptable if I was, Grace Newman?'

No, it wasn't. She felt it was very inappropriate and a betrayal to Maud's memory. John's friendship was valued. He wasn't a bad man, but he'd made a mistake in how he'd treated Maud – denying that Maggie was his, leaving the woman when she'd needed him most. And he'd kept everything about Maud from her. Grace had felt deceived and let down and hadn't liked him very much at the time. But as Anna's cousin and a friend, Grace was willing to put the past behind them.

'Your silence suggests I should behave like a gentleman,' John said.

'I think that would be best,' she answered firmly. 'John, when we get to my house, will you come in with me, please?'

'Of course I will. Are you uncomfortable about going home?'

'Yes,' she admitted. 'It's the garden. I don't know how I'm going to feel when I see it.'

When they pulled up outside, Grace gazed at the impressive building. 'It's a big house for just me and my grandmother,' she sighed. 'I don't know what the future holds. Now that I've cut off ties with my father, he may arrange for the house to be sold. And even if he doesn't, my salary won't maintain a property of this stature. There's so much to think about.'

Inside, the familiarity of home was warming, but Grace hovered outside the kitchen. 'Will you go in please, John, and look out of the window? Tell me what you can see under the oak tree.'

Grace waited.

'Erm … there's not much to tell, Grace.'

'Isn't there a big hole and a pile of dirt?'

'No. I can see where the police have dug, but only because there's no grass on that patch.'

Grace walked into the kitchen slowly, holding her breath. Standing beside John at the sink, she lifted her eyes and was pleasantly surprised to see the police had left the garden in a good condition. 'It's not as bad as I was expecting. Thanks, John.'

'Do you want me to stay for a while?'

'I think I'd rather settle back in by myself.'

Once she'd seen John out, she wandered upstairs, firmly closing the door to her father's bedroom. There had been a time not long ago when Grace had despised her grandmother for arranging the assault on her father, but now Grace could understand the woman's motives and realised how much guts it must have taken. Passing her grandmother's room, she recognised how much she missed her and was looking forward to Myrtle returning. Her grandmother was the only family Grace had now, and she couldn't wait to see her.

Day in, day out, Dickie waited to hear from Grace. And as the days passed into weeks, he became more and more despondent. He'd even considered attempting escape, just to see Grace, but had soon realised that it would be impossible. Thoughts of his daughter consumed his mind, and the pain of her rejection ate away at him, gnawing through his veins, stabbing his insides. He couldn't understand what mistakes he'd made that would make her hate him as she did. He'd explained to her, everything he'd done, he'd done it for her. Why couldn't she see that?

Ernie had visited again and had told him that Grace wasn't reading his letters. The message was, *tell him he's wasting his time.* The words had been like an axe through his heart.

The four walls of his cell felt as though they were closing in on him, suffocating him, squeezing his chest. Throwing his head back, he roared, 'What's the point? What's the fuckin' point?'

A stark realisation hit him – he couldn't face another day of carrying so much agony. He'd always been a strong, tough man, but this felt like nothing he'd ever known, and it was crippling. So, when Dickie came to his decision, a sense of relief replaced his despair. He was happy with his choice. There would be no turning back, but it felt right. He'd seen many inmates in a state of oblivion due to the drugs they'd injected into their veins. Dickie would do the same. He'd block out his pain with cocaine and opiates. But first, he'd instruct his solicitor to sign over his business to Grace, and he'd write her one last letter. He knew that once the drugs were flowing through his blood and into his brain, he'd be incapable of writing to his beautiful daughter. From what he'd seen of some of his fellow inmates, they couldn't even lift their heads, let alone lift a hand to paper and write a letter. Dickie had never before entertained the notion of taking drugs. He remembered the concoction he'd fed Pippa during her final days. The woman had been left in a dreamy state. And he'd heard an inmate describe the effects of opiates, saying that it felt like being wrapped in cotton wool. Dickie could carry on living in misery or he could comfort himself with drugs, and his choice had been made.

Sitting at a small table, with unshed tears in his eyes, Dickie began to pen his last letter to Grace. *Goodbye, my darling girl.*

He still hoped she would visit him one day or at least write back to him.

59

Grace was pleased to be home after a long day on her feet in the ironmonger's. It hadn't taken her long to discover why Mr McCall had employed her. The man was lecherous, always inappropriately brushing up against her, and leering at her, too. An older man of nearly sixty, Mr McCall made Grace's skin crawl. She'd been looking for work elsewhere, but until a job became available, she'd have to remain in Mr McCall's employ and continue to fight off his unwanted attention.

Sitting with her stockinged feet up on the sofa, Grace sipped on a cup of hot soup from a tin. It was all she could be bothered to prepare for herself, and she was looking forward to a long soak in the bath, followed by her comfortable bed. So she was irritated when she heard a knock on the front door.

'Who can that be? Disturbing my peace and quiet,' she moaned, going to the door.

Pulling it open, Grace found a smartly dressed man on her doorstep. His expensive suit and flashy car on the kerb suggested he wasn't a salesman.

'Can I help you?' she asked.

'Miss Newman, I assume?'

'You assume correctly.'

'Miss Newman, good evening. I am Mr Humperton, your father's solicitor. I apologise for intruding, but please, may I come in?'

'No, Mr Humperton, you may not. I've made it more than clear to my father that I don't want anything to do with him. If you don't mind, I'm busy. Good evening to you.'

Mr Humperton reached out his arm and placed his hand on the door to prevent Grace from closing it.

'Please, Miss Newman, I must speak to you. I'm afraid I have bad news.'

Grace recognised the look in the man's dark eyes – it was sympathy. Her heart began to pound, and she asked, 'Is my father dead?'

'Please, let's go inside to discuss this.'

Grace stepped aside, allowing Mr Humperton in, and led him into the drawing room. 'Is he?' she pushed.

The man nodded sadly. 'Yes, Miss Newman. I regret to inform you that your father passed away this morning.'

'How?' she asked numbly.

'He, erm ... it was a drugs overdose.'

Grace drew in a sharp intake of breath. 'Drugs?'

Again, the man nodded. 'It seems that Mr Newman had developed quite a habit and very rapidly.'

It didn't seem possible to Grace. Her father was strong, the strongest man she'd ever known. She couldn't imagine that he'd ever take drugs. 'Are you sure? Could he have been murdered?'

'There were no suspicious circumstances, and Mr Newman left you this ...' He held his briefcase aloft, indicating that he'd like to place it on the writing bureau, and asked, 'Do you mind?'

Grace shook her head.

Mr Humperton put the smart case down and clicked open the locks before pulling out an envelope. 'It's a letter to you, from your father,' he said softly, holding it towards her.

'I don't want to read it,' Grace said, and turned her back.

'Would you like me to read it to you?'

'No.'

'I'll, erm, I will leave it here, on the bureau. There is the matter of his estate. As his next of kin and only living relative, and as per Mr Newman's wishes in his final will and testament, you will be inheriting the entirety of the properties, business and monies. Probate will be straightforward, and I would be willing to represent you, if that is agreeable?'

Grace kept her back to the man and nodded again. Her brain seemed to be frozen. She couldn't think clearly or feel anything.

'Is there anyone who could be with you now? I have my car outside; I could drive you.'

The only person Grace wanted was her grandmother. Turning to look at the solicitor, she replied, 'No, thank you. I'll see you out.'

Mr Humperton appeared awkward on the doorstep. 'I'll be in touch, Miss Newman.'

Grace closed the door, her thoughts in a jumble. Why had her father turned to drugs, and how had he managed to take such a high dose that it had killed him? Was it her fault because she'd placed him in that hellish prison? He was dead… dead… though she hadn't wanted to see him again, she'd believed he'd always be there.

In a mechanical fashion, Grace wandered into her father's office. She stared at the large oil painting of him hanging on the wall behind his oversized desk. The artist had captured his image perfectly, and his eyes looked alive. Gazing into them, she saw the love he'd held for her, and for the first time in as long as she could recall, tears welled and slipped down her cheeks.

'Oh, Papa,' she cried. 'I'm so sorry ... I love you, Papa. Please forgive me,' she wailed.

Dropping to her knees, Grace held her face in her hands as she sobbed for the man she'd both adored and detested. Her cries filled the large room as remorse and grief broke her heart. She thought of her mother too, wishing she could feel the woman's arms embracing her, speaking softly in her ear, soothing her and reassuring her that everything would be all right. The pain was physical, causing her throat to constrict and her chest to ache. 'Oh, Mother, I need you now more than ever. And Papa ... Come back, Papa, please come back,' she bawled. Guilt drenched her. She'd said she'd never wanted to see him again, and now she never would.

As John pulled up outside home, he saw Betty and Anna racing towards him.

'Hello, ladies,' he greeted them cheerily, but his face fell when he saw their dismayed expressions. 'What's wrong?' he asked.

Anna answered solemnly. 'Grace's father's dead. Haven't you heard? Everyone in Battersea is talking about it.'

'Dead? How?'

'We don't know,' Betty replied. 'But have you seen Grace today?'

'No.'

'I'm worried about her, John,' Anna said. 'She's all alone in that big house.'

'She'll be all right. Grace didn't like the man and had him imprisoned. She wanted nothing more to do with him. Be careful what you wish for, eh.'

Betty shook her head, her lips set in a grim line. 'He was her father, John! It wasn't easy for her to go the police, and though she didn't approve of his actions, she still loved him. She shouldn't be alone. We're all she's got, and she'll need us.'

John realised he'd sounded callous, and the women were right. He didn't like to think of Grace upset and with no one to offer her any comfort. 'Climb in,' he said gravely, opening the door of his truck.

John didn't speak on the journey to Clapham, not that he could have got a word in edgeways between Betty and Anna. The women chatted constantly, voicing concerns for their friend, and speculating about what might have happened to Mr Newman.

When they pulled up outside Grace's home, the place was in darkness.

'Maybe she's not here,' Anna said.

Betty knocked on the door, and when Grace didn't answer, she knocked again louder. 'Grace,' she shouted through the letterbox. 'It's us, Betty, Anna and John. Please let us in. We're worried about you.'

'She's coming,' Betty said, 'I can see her.'

When Grace opened the door, John's heart went out to her. He could see she'd been crying, and she looked so lost.

'Oh, sweetheart,' Betty said, pulling her friend into her arms and holding her close.

'I'll put the kettle on,' Anna said, passing the embracing friends on the step.

John looked at Betty and Grace, wishing Grace was in his arms instead of Betty's.

Betty pulled back, saying gently, 'Let's go inside. I've brought clean hankies and a big bar of chocolate.'

John followed them in, amazed again at the grandeur of the house. He thought Grace seemed so small under the high ceilings.

In the kitchen, Anna had poured hot water into a teapot, and instructed everyone to sit down.

Grace's eyes swept around the table to each of her friends, and she sniffed, clearly fighting to hold back tears as she announced, 'He injected a lethal dose of opiates.'

'Deliberately?' John asked.

'I don't think so. No one will ever really know the truth, but I can't imagine that my father would have taken his own life. I think he was using drugs to escape from the hell of his confinement and accidentally took too much.'

'That's tragic,' Anna said.

'I feel responsible. If I hadn't gone to the police, he'd still be alive,' Grace cried.

Betty handed Grace a handkerchief, saying, 'You can't think like that, Grace. You have never been responsible for your father's actions, so you're certainly not responsible for his death. It was your father's choice to take the drugs.'

'But he chose to inject himself because of what I'd done.'

'No, Grace, you haven't done anything wrong. You did the correct thing, and you know you did. It's because you're upset that you're not thinking straight. You've had an awful shock, but once you've calmed down, you'll see that none of this is your fault.'

'Betty's right, Grace,' Anna said. 'Please don't blame yourself.'

Grace blew her nose into the handkerchief. 'I can't believe you're all here. Thank you.'

'We're your friends, you daft mare,' Betty smiled. 'I'll stay with you tonight and Anna can let our bosses know we won't be in work tomorrow.'

'There's no need,' Grace protested.

'Yes, there is,' Anna said firmly. 'You shouldn't be alone right now.'

'I was going to send a telegram to my grandmother and ask her to come home.'

John spoke. 'I'll pop back tomorrow and drive you and Betty to the post office.'

'Thanks, but there's one not far from here.'

'I'll pop round anyway, and I'll bring fresh milk. That bottle looks like it's on the turn.'

He was glad to help in any way he could. Grace's heart was shattered, and John would have done anything he could to help her piece it back together.

60

When Myrtle had received Grace's distressing telegram, it had taken her over a week to travel back to England. It had been frustrating as she'd wanted to be by Grace's side, but it had also given her time to think. The girl would be inheriting a substantial estate, and Myrtle believed her granddaughter was far too young and inexperienced to manage the complexities of finances. She'd have to offer a guiding hand to Grace and advise on the girl's decisions. Myrtle knew she wouldn't be best placed to give comfort to her. She'd never been good at displays of affection and didn't tolerate tears and hysteria well. But she could help in other ways, which she felt were more practical and important.

Walking into the house that had never felt like home, she instructed the taxi-cab driver to place her bags inside and at the foot of the stairs. Pulling off her gloves, fingertips first, she called Grace's name.

The girl came bounding down the stairs, and Myrtle had to refrain from telling her to walk like a lady.

'Grandma, thank goodness you're home!' Grace exclaimed,

running towards her and throwing her arms around her. 'Thank you for cutting short your trip.'

Myrtle, her body somewhat rigid, peeled Grace's arms off. 'I'm sorry I wasn't back sooner. It was a dreadful crossing over the Channel, and I was forced to accept a second-class carriage on the train to London; not an experience I would ever wish to repeat.'

'I'm just so glad you're back.'

Myrtle looked around the ostentatious hallway, and then, sweeping her arm around, she stated, 'You must sell this house, Grace. I assume you are the sole inheritor?'

Grace appeared perplexed. 'Yes, I am. There's paperwork to conclude before I can do anything. Mr Humperton, my father's solicitor, is helping with it. But sell this house ... I hadn't considered anything like that yet.'

'I've never liked this vulgar property, and it holds too many memories that I'd rather forget. The sooner it is sold, the better for us both.'

'Maybe. Would you like tea, Grandma? You must be parched after your journey.'

'No, Grace, I'd rather we sit down and discuss your future.'

'I'd be grateful for your help, but I don't know the extent of my father's estate yet.'

'Then we must find out. Call the solicitor and demand that he attends immediately with all the relevant paperwork.'

'Really?'

'Yes, Grace, immediately. Go on, off you pop to the telephone box. Why your father never had a telephone installed here is beyond me.'

Myrtle waited in the drawing room and concluded that she'd been correct in assuming her granddaughter would require her assistance with the financial matters. The girl hadn't put any thought into it at all!

Grace soon returned, pink-faced from hurrying. 'Mr Humperton will be here shortly.'

'Good. Now tea will be acceptable, thank you.'

Myrtle was keen to cast her eyes over Mr Humperton. Grace had mentioned that he'd been her father's solicitor, which had made Myrtle's hackles rise. She wasn't convinced she could trust a man who'd worked for Dickie. She had no doubt Grace trusted the man implicitly. Her granddaughter wasn't yet wise enough to question people's motives. But if Mr Humperton thought that he could pull the wool over Myrtle's eyes, then the man was going to be sorely disappointed.

When Mr Humperton had finished listing the assets that Grace would inherit, she was astounded and felt quite overwhelmed. 'How will I manage it all?' she muttered, thinking out loud.

'You will need help, Grace, people you can trust,' her grandmother answered.

'If I may be so presumptuous to offer my services, Miss Newman. I'm competent with accounting and I know local planning laws.'

Her grandmother looked astonished and not in a good way. 'To be frank, Mr Humperton, you must have heard me say that my granddaughter will need people she can *trust*, trust being the operative word. You worked for Mr Newman, which suggests you are neither trustworthy nor honest. One must question the ethics of anyone in Mr Newman's service. Do you have any scruples?'

Mr Humperton shuffled some papers. 'If we are talking

frankly, Mrs Best, then I will be honest. I had reservations about engaging with Mr Newman, but as a junior partner in the firm, I wasn't given a choice. I found Mr Newman to be, how can I say this, erm, devious. My ethics are unquestionable, and I made it clear to Mr Newman that I would only work inside the law.'

'I see. Well, perhaps we will consider your offer.'

Grace admired her grandmother. Like Betty, the woman was confident and forthright. And she appreciated her help with her father's estate. She felt that Mr Humperton had handled her grandmother rather well, and she liked the man. He was gawky in his mannerisms, with an ungainly walk, but she sensed he had compassion, and with dark hair and eyes, a tidy moustache and strong jawline, he looked very smart. But Grace thought he appeared too young to be a solicitor.

Mr Humperton continued. 'I feel I must inform you of the behaviour of your father's associate, Ernie. He has been collecting rents and loan repayments, and I believe he is embezzling the money. We must finalise probate rapidly, and fortunately, the senior partners have good contacts in the Court of Probate. I can assure you of my undivided attention.'

'Thank you, Mr Humperton,' Grace said. 'And in the meantime, I will deal with Ernie.'

Grace had no idea how to deal with Ernie. Without her father controlling everything with intimidation and violence, she knew there would be many people who would take advantage. She'd hoped for better from Ernie. He'd worked for her father for as long as she could remember, but she wasn't shocked to learn that he was helping himself to money. Ernie was going to be a challenge, and probably the first problem of many more to come. But with her grandmother bolstering her up, Grace felt strong and ready to face the tasks ahead. It would at least take her mind off the crippling guilt of her father's death that tormented her mind. *I refuse to cry again*, she told herself. *You're a Newman and it's time to act like one!*

'May I ask, Miss Newman, and please forgive me for intruding on your grief, but have you read the letter from your father that I delivered to you?'

'No, not yet.'

Her grandmother's head flicked from Mr Humperton to Grace, as she asked, 'Letter? What letter?'

'Father left a *goodbye* letter for me.'

'A suicide note?' Myrtle asked.

Mr Humperton cleared his throat. 'No, I don't believe it was meant as a suicide note, Mrs Best. Mr Newman had already instructed me to transfer his assets into Miss Newman's name. If he had intended to commit suicide, then there would have been no need for his instruction to begin the transfer, as his estate was already bequeathed to Miss Newman in his last will and testament.'

'Then why would he have written a goodbye letter to my granddaughter?'

'He told me he had accepted Miss Newman's decision to reject him, and that he'd found a way to make living in confinement more bearable, but he wanted to say a few last things to his daughter that would help her with the business.'

'Where is it?' Myrtle asked.

'In his office on his desk,' Grace replied.

'Fetch it to me.'

'I don't want to know what he wrote, Grandma. I'm not ready to hear it yet.'

'Fine, but I would still like to see it.'

Grace collected the envelope and handed it to her grandmother, saying quietly, 'Please don't tell me what my father wrote.'

Myrtle slowly read the letter and then, stuffing it back inside the envelope, she said, 'As I thought. There are many unsavoury words I could use to describe your father, but he cannot be faulted on his business acumen and judgement of people. Your father has expressed his concerns about Ernie and has left instructions on how the man should be dealt with.'

Grace's back straightened. 'What does he suggest?'

'Your father had taken out an insurance policy. There is an address you must visit and explain that you are there to make an insurance claim.'

'I don't understand,' Grace muttered.

Mr Humperton cleared his throat again. 'May I see the letter, Mrs Best?'

Myrtle passed him the letter, and once he'd read it, he said, 'I think I understand, Miss Newman. Your father paid a substantial amount of money to Benny Denner. In fact, I was asked to facilitate the transaction. The insurance policy your father is referring to is protection, supplied by Mr Denner, paid for by Mr Newman.'

'No … I'm not going down this route. Mr Denner is probably some sort of thug, just like Ernie. I'm not going to run the business in the same way my father did. There won't be aggression and brutality used.'

'Grace, my dear granddaughter, you have much to learn. Do you have an alternative solution for the problem with Ernie?'

'No, not yet,' Grace admitted.

'Then you must fight fire with fire. Violence is the only language Ernie understands, and I'm sure Mr Denner will speak it loudly and clearly.'

'But this isn't what I want, Grandma!'

'And rightly so. Once Ernie has been dealt with, you can run the business how you see fit.'

'I agree with Mrs Best,' Mr Humperton said.

Grace sighed deeply. 'All right. I'll contact Mr Denner, but after the problem with Ernie is resolved, I'll do things *my* way from then on.'

61

On Sunday afternoon, John had driven Betty and Anna to Grace's house. Grace had invited them for a meal, but when they'd arrived, smoke had been billowing from the kitchen. Anna had taken over the cooking and had managed to salvage a joint of pork. Sitting around the dining table, enjoying the lunch prepared by Anna, Grace seemed in good spirits, but John wondered if she was masking her sadness. She'd been consumed with guilt over her father's death, and John knew better than anyone how much of a burden guilt was. It was his guilt that prevented him from ever having a future with Grace as anything more than good friends. He knew he couldn't hold Grace in his arms and love her passionately without thinking about how he'd betrayed Maud. But John was comfortable with friendship instead. Anyway, Grace had made it clear there could never be anything more.

'Are you going back to work tomorrow?' Betty asked.

'No, I don't think I will. Mr McCall is a dirty old man, and my grandmother said she has enough money to see us through until the inheritance is finalised.'

'You're gonna have a lot on your plate,' John said. 'Your father owns a load of houses.'

'Yes, but the first thing I have to do is sort out Ernie. He's been going around collecting the rents and pocketing it for himself.'

'Cheeky bleeder!' Betty exclaimed. 'What will you do? Go to the police?'

'No, the police won't do anything. I'm going to meet a fella called Benny Denner. My father paid him to protect me if I needed it.'

John placed his knife and fork on his plate, saying worriedly, 'Blimey, Grace, I don't like the sound of this.'

'It's not ideal. I don't want to conduct business in the same way as my father did, but Ernie needs stopping in his tracks.'

'I'll come with you to see this Denner bloke,' John offered.

'Thanks, but I don't want to drag anyone else into this.'

'I'm coming with you. You're not going alone, and don't bother trying to argue with me.'

'Oooh,' Betty smiled. 'Look at John getting all masterful. But seriously, have you given much consideration to what you're going to do with everything? I know you've never been happy with the condition of your father's properties.'

'Actually, I have, and that's the reason for inviting you all around today. I'm so excited to share my plans with you!'

'Go on then,' Anna encouraged. 'I'm excited for you!'

'Firstly, I intend to put this monstrosity of a house on the market. It must be worth a good bob or two. I'll use the funds to upgrade the terrible state of the rental properties.'

'Where will you and your grandmother live?' John asked.

'My grandmother wishes to be on the other side of the Thames, closer to her friends and her club. She's already got her eye on a swanky apartment in Kensington that's available to rent. I'm not sure where I'll live yet, but as you know, I will have quite a few houses to choose from.'

Betty sounded doubtful when she said, 'I think you might need more money than what you'll raise from the sale of this house to bring all the other properties up to a reasonable living standard.'

'Yes, I thought so too, so I'm going to sell the shop in Chelsea. And the other one, the shop on Falcon Road … I'm signing it over to you, Betty. It's still stocked, and you can take the remaining stock from the Chelsea shop, too.'

'I'd be more than happy to manage the Battersea boutique, thanks, Grace.'

'No, Betty, you won't be the manager … you'll be the owner. It's yours. The building and everything. You can sell it if you don't want to run a boutique there, it's up to you what you do with it.'

John was blown away by Grace's generosity, and Betty clearly was, too.

'I don't know what to say,' Betty uttered, her eyes filling with tears.

'Don't say anything. And I've got something for you too, Anna. I've learned that my father owned a very nice property, one of the villas near the park. He had his secrets, and I've heard that he housed his lover there. From what I can gather, she died, and the house has been empty since. It's yours. You can rent it out, sell it or live in it. But it will be the security you need for you and the baby.'

'You can't do that!' Anna exclaimed. 'You can't give away a house!'

'I can and I have. My solicitor is drawing up the paperwork.

Please just accept it. We've been friends for many years, Anna. I know Gordon came between us, but that's all in the past. If things had worked out differently with my father and Gordon, then you and I would have almost been sisters-in-law. We're not quite family, but I was raised with Gordon as my brother, which makes your unborn child my niece or nephew, sort of.'

'Oh my God, Grace, you're mad but I love you! Thank you ... thank you so much!'

John was pleased for Anna. He knew it would put her mind at rest. His cousin had been fretting about the expense of a child, especially as she'd have to give up her job at the hospital soon.

Grace then looked at John, and he squirmed in his seat. He hoped she wasn't going to give him something. He was a proud man and would find it difficult to receive a gift, especially as he hadn't known Grace for very long and he'd treated her badly.

'I've wracked my brains about you, John. I know you well enough to realise you'd struggle with the notion of accepting anything from me. I thought about offering you a job, for my benefit as much as yours. I need people around me who I can trust. But I know you wouldn't want to give up Dander's Deliveries, it's a growing and thriving business. So ... and please don't be annoyed with me ... I'm going to offer your mum and dad a house. It's a nice house, with a bedroom downstairs, which I thought would be ideal for your dad with his mobility issues since the stroke. And there are three bedrooms upstairs, which means Maggie would have her own room, too. You can't say no, because I'm not offering it to you. Like I said, I'll speak to your mum about it.'

John rolled his eyes. He had to admit, they were short of

space in the small two-up, two-down they rented now. And his father often slept on the sofa because he struggled to get up and down the stairs. But accepting a house from Grace didn't sit right with him.

'I know what you're thinking,' Grace said, 'but please allow me to do this. It's for my benefit as much as yours.'

'How is it for your benefit?' he questioned.

Grace looked down at the table, and speaking quietly, she explained, 'I've always felt terrible about what happened with me and Maud in the café on the day she passed away. I can't change any of that, but I can help to make a better future for her daughter. Please, John, allow me to ease my conscience a little. Anyway, it's your mum's decision to make, not yours. I hope she isn't too proud to accept a house from Miss High and Mighty Fancy Drawers.'

'*Fancy Drawers?*' Betty repeated.

'Yes,' Grace said with a giggle. 'That's what Mrs Dander calls me.'

'Ha, I love it! That's what we'll all call you from now on.'

Anna looked across at John, her face serious. 'Please, John. Think about your family, about Maggie. Don't allow your pride to stand in the way of what's best for them.'

John interlocked his fingers, and bent them back, clicking his knuckles. 'I'll pay you a fair rent for the house,' he said to Grace.

'It won't be my house, John; your mother will own it.'

'Listen to me, Dander,' Betty ordered. 'This is something that Grace wants to do for us because we're her friends. If the boot was on the other foot, we'd want to do the same. Don't be a fool, man, and get that sulky look off your face.

You've just been set up for your future, we all have, thanks to Grace. Don't bloody ruin it.'

'Well said, Betty,' Anna cheered. 'She's right, John. You're being very surly, and don't you go thinking you'll be able to persuade your mum to decline Miss Fancy Drawers' offer, because I'll be speaking to her, too. Let's raise a glass ... To Miss Fancy Drawers, our dear friend.'

John felt a bit picked on and knew it would be pointless to try to argue with the three women around the table. Betty spoke as she found and wasn't afraid to say her piece, Anna was back to her old self and stronger than she'd ever been before, and Grace, well, Grace was incredible. He didn't want to hurt her feelings. Giving away the properties to her nearest and dearest obviously meant a lot to her and he could see how much pleasure it brought. And, he reasoned, she still owned so many more!

'All right, I give in,' he said, smiling at last. 'To Miss Fancy Drawers,' he chanted. 'Thank you, Grace.'

The following morning, Grace felt tense as she waited for John to pick her up. She didn't know what to expect from Benny Denner, and nerves were making her stomach twist.

When she heard an engine outside, she looked through the window expecting to see John's truck, and was surprised to find Mr Humperton pulling up.

'Mr Humperton,' she greeted him on the step. 'Good morning. I wasn't expecting to see you today. Please, come in, though I'm on my way out shortly.'

'Good morning, Miss Newman. I shan't keep you long. I have news.'

'Please, come through,' Grace said, beckoning him into the lounge. 'Take a seat. Would you like tea or coffee?'

'No, thank you. I, erm, I hope you don't mind, but I took the liberty of visiting Benny Denner. I was already acquainted with the man from when I arranged the insurance for Mr Newman. I, erm, I found Denner to be an unsavoury character. That being the case, I took it upon myself to put in the insurance claim, so to speak. I didn't think Denner's environment was a suitable place for you to be, Miss Newman.'

'Oh. Thank you. I was on my way there this morning, but you've saved me a job that I wasn't looking forward to. What was the outcome of your visit to Mr Denner?'

'I have the man's assurance that Ernie will cease to be a problem. Denner seems to think that a word in Ernie's ear from him will be enough to, as he said, *scare the shit out of him*. However, if Ernie persists with stealing the rental income, Denner will, and again, I quote, *cut his*, actually, I won't quote what he said. Suffice to say it will be dealt with.'

'That's a relief. I'm grateful, Mr Humperton.'

'I hope you'll consider using my services in the future, Miss Newman. As I previously stated, I'd be happy to work for you.'

'I'm going to need help, Mr Humperton, so I would like to come to some sort of arrangement with you.'

John called out, 'Hello ...'

'In here,' Grace called back.

He came into the room, with his flat cap in his hand, dressed in a shabby pair of loose-fitting trousers, a collarless shirt that had once been white but had now greyed, a sleeveless hand-knitted pullover and a pair of boots. He looked so different from Mr Humperton, who wore a tailored suit, a bow tie and a smart fedora.

'The front door was open,' he said, eyeing Mr Humperton suspiciously.

'John, this is Mr Humperton, my solicitor.'

John extended his arm and shook the man's hand. 'Pleased to meet you, Mr Humperton. John Dander.'

'Likewise, Mr Dander.'

'John, Mr Humperton has already been to see Benny Denner. There's no need for us to go now. Ernie will be warned.'

'Great … Well, if there's nothing else, I'll get off. I've got a busy day today.'

'No, and thanks, John. Are you sure you won't stay for a cuppa?'

'No, thanks, Grace. But I'll see you soon.'

Once John had left, Mr Humperton asked, 'Are you and Mr Dander, erm, involved with each other?'

'That's a rather personal question,' Grace blurted, taken aback. 'No, we're not. John and I are just good friends.'

Mr Humperton removed his hat and ran the brim through his fingers, appearing anxious. 'I wondered, erm, I hope you don't think this is inappropriate, but I wondered if you might join me for supper this evening?'

'Oh,' Grace said, stunned. She liked Mr Humperton, but he didn't give her the same butterflies that John or Norman had once done. She knew she'd never get back together with John. He was a dear and cherished friend, but Grace couldn't forgive how he'd kept the situation with Maud a secret from her, and she'd been so hurt when she'd discovered that Maud was carrying his child.

'I'm sorry, I've overstepped the mark,' Mr Humperton said, looking embarrassed. 'I shouldn't have asked, please forgive me.'

Grace smiled. She found the man's awkwardness endearing. 'I'll forgive you over supper this evening,' she said. 'But I must make it quite clear that I'm not looking for a relationship. Friends, yes, but nothing more.'

Mr Humperton grinned, looking thrilled. 'Wonderful. Terrific. *Friends* works well for me, Miss Newman. I'll, erm, I'll pick you up at seven?'

'Yes, seven is perfect.'

As Mr Humperton climbed into his car, Grace saw a taxicab pull up and her grandmother elegantly stepped out.

'Was that the solicitor?' Myrtle asked.

'Yes. He's sorted the problem with Ernie and he asked me to join him for supper this evening.'

'Tell me you didn't accept his invitation! One should never mix business with pleasure, my dear.'

'Too late. I said yes, but before you jump down my throat, I've made it clear that we can only be friends.'

'I hope that isn't a decision you will come to regret. Like I said, he is a business associate, not a friend.'

'I don't think I'll regret it, Grandma. Mr Humperton is a very nice man and he's already shown he cares about me. He went to see Benny Denner. Do you realise how much courage that must have taken? We can both guess what sort of man Mr Denner is, but Mr Humperton did it for me, to protect me. That's the sort of friend I like.'

'His bravery is commendable, though I would never have thought he would be to your liking. He is very different from your other friends. Dander is a thug, regardless of what you say, Anna was married to Gordon so that says all there is to say, and Betty's father is in prison. You do surprise me sometimes, Grace.'

Grace threw her arms around her grandmother and felt the woman's body tense. She smiled, thinking that maybe, one day, her grandmother might relax and enjoy a cuddle, but until she did, Grace would persist.

Releasing the woman, Grace beamed. 'It's a fresh start, Grandma. A new life. I have the best friends, and they aren't quite as you describe them. I've been fortunate enough to have been able to help them. I have you, whom I love dearly, and I'll have more than enough money to have choices in life. As for Mr Humperton, well, he's different, but different in a good way. I like him, Grandma, and I'm looking forward to enjoying his friendship and company. But it will never be anything more than that. I remember promising my mother that I would only marry for true love, and that I'd be financially independent. It's a promise I intend to keep.'

'Good. And, well, one does need friends, and one can never have too many.'

'Mr Humperton has ever such a funny name, don't you think?' she chuckled.

'In my opinion, any name is better than Newman.'

Grace agreed. Newman wasn't a name to be proud of. Her father had created a reputation around it – feared by some, despised by others. 'I'm going to change things, Grandma. I'm going to make Newman a name that people will admire for the right reasons.'

Myrtle placed her hand on Grace's arm and smiled warmly. 'I know you will, Grace. You are kind, and have a good heart like your grandfather, and you're a dreamer, too. Always have big dreams. It's your time to spread your wings and fly high.'

'I can't drag people out of poverty, but I can help to improve their lives by offering them decent homes.'

'I know you will be fair and generous. I'm terribly proud of you. Grace, the landlord's daughter, and now the landlord herself.'

Acknowledgments

I'd like to say a big thank you to my readers – thank you for continuing to embrace the Kitty Neale books, and thank you for supporting me on my journey, especially through the grief of losing my mum.

A BIG shout out to all the lovely people on my Kitty Neale Facebook page. It's a great pleasure to interact with you, and the photos you send of my books in the supermarkets are always such a joy to see! I'd also like to let you know how much I appreciate the posts you share, and for the recommendations of my books that you give to your friends and family. Thank you xxx

Thank you to my gorgeous editor, Rhea. I feel so blessed to work with such a very special lady. And to the team at Orion Publishing who work hard behind the scenes to bring my stories into the world, and always with beautiful front covers!

I'd also like to thank Annie Aldington, the narrator of my books. She brings my characters to life in such a vivid way, delivering the audio story perfectly. Annie is most definitely the voice of Kitty Neale, and what an amazing job she does!

Thank you also to my agent, Judith Murdoch, who is always there for me.

Credits

Orion Fiction would like to thank everyone at Orion who worked on the publication of *Fall from Grace*.

Agent
Judith Murdoch

Editor
Rhea Kurien

Copyeditor
Alice Fewery

Proofreader
Lucy Brem

Design
Charlotte Abrams Simpson
Nick Shah
Deborah Francois
Helen Ewing

Editorial Management
Sanah Ahmed
Jane Hughes
Charlie Panayiotou
Lucy Bilton
Patrice Nelson

Audio
Paul Stark
Louise Richardson
Georgina Cutler-Ross

Finance
Nick Gibson
Jasdip Nandra
Sue Baker
Tom Costello

Photo Shoots & Image Research
Natalie Dawkins

Sales
Dave Murphy
Victoria Laws
Sammy Luton
Group Sales teams across Digital, Field, International and Non-Trade

Inventory
Jo Jacobs
Dan Stevens

Production
Ruth Sharvell
Katie Horrocks

Operations
Group Sales Operations team

Contracts
Rachel Monte
Ellie Bowker
Tabitha Gresty

Rights
Rebecca Folland
Tara Hiatt
Ben Fowler
Maddie Stephens
Ruth Blakemore
Marie Henckel